Coached to Death

Coached to Death

VICTORIA LAURIE

KENSINGTON BOOKS
www.kensingtonbooks.com

KENSINGTON BOOKS are published by

Kensington Publishing Corp.
119 West 40th Street
New York, NY 10018

All Kensington titles, imprints, and distributed lines are available at special quantity discounts for bulk purchases for sales promotion, premiums, fund-raising, educational, or institutional use. Special book excerpts or customized printings can also be created to fit specific needs. For details, write or phone the office of the Kensington Special Sales Manager: Attn. Special Sales Department. Kensington Publishing Corp, 119 West 40th Street, New York, NY 10018. Phone: 1-800-221-2647.

Library of Congress Card Catalogue Number: 2019944836

Kensington and the K logo Reg. U.S. Pat. & TM Off.

ISBN-13: 978-1-4967-2033-7
ISBN-10: 1-4967-2033-4
First Kensington Hardcover Edition: November 2019

ISBN-13: 978-1-4967-2037-5 (ebook)
ISBN-10: 1-4967-2037-7 (ebook)

10 9 8 7 6 5 4 3 2 1

Printed in the United States of America

For my sister, Sandy. Thank you for Cat.
Love you and her to the moon and back.

Acknowledgments

I'm not gonna lie. When I set out to write a spinoff series featuring Cat and Gilley, I was really worried that it'd be a long, slow slog through the quagmire of characters who sometimes had their moments, but weren't especially "gifted" with any extra talent other than the ability to engage in some witty repartee. In fact, it's safe to say that I was a tiny bit terrified that they'd be all talk and no substance.

But then about a third of the way through this novel, I realized that I was having an absolute *blast*, and that Gilley and Cat were actually the *perfect* characters to immerse in a good old-fashioned mystery because they each carry just enough brash impulsiveness, lack of common sense, and an alarming inability to sense the danger around them as to find themselves perpetually in trouble.

And now after having just completed the second book, I keep wondering what took me so long to break these two out into their own series, because Cat and Gilley are *hilarious* together, and they can really tell a great, thrilling, suspense-filled story without any extra props, gifts, or flashy stuff.

Who knew?

Anyhoo, to that end, I would like very much to thank my publisher Kensington Books for their unfailing faith in me as a storyteller. At a time when most publishing houses are shrinking their lists, Kensington found the courage to add at least one more, (me!) to their roster, and as such, my faith in humanity is restored. ☺

I would also specifically like to thank my editor, John Scognamiglio for his encouragement, feedback, edits, and wisdom. I'd wanted to work with John for years, and I'm so thrilled to be partnered on this particular series with him. Finally, both the timing and the project feel right!

Thanks as well to Monika Roe, the incredible artist and illustrator who's managed to strike the absolute *perfect* balance between my Ghost Hunter Mysteries covers and the Psychic Eye Mysteries covers to form a new, unique look for all of the Cat and Gilley adventures to come.

Jim McCarthy, my agent of nearly two decades now. (Ugh, we're old!) Thank you for giving me Gilley. I've loved him nearly as much as I've loved you all of these years. Oh, and of course, thank you also for all that agency stuff you do. Totes appreciate that!

Sandy Upham, my sister, my confidant, my muse, my friend. Thank you for Cat. I know it's been hard having a sister who *literally* has a notebook dedicated to all of your most embarrassing stories, but you bear it well . . . and you keep having interesting and embarrassing stories to tell, so I see it as a win/win. ☺

Leanne Sorrento, my BFF, the Candice to my Abby . . . love you to pieces, girl!

Katie Coppedge, thank you for helping to keep the V.L. machine going strong, and also for one of the *best* and *truest* friendships I've ever had. Love you, dollface.

Terry Gilman, Nicole Grey, Shannon Anderson, John and Matt McDougall, Sally Woods, Anne Kimbol, Juliet Blackwell, Cindy Elavsky, Drue Rowean, Suzanne Parsons, Nora and Bob Brosseau; thank you for your continued love and support. You guys are the BEST and I heart you fierce!

Coached to
Death

Chapter 1

"You can do this," I said firmly. My reflection eyed me doubtfully. Fluffing my blond hair before adding another spritz of hair spray, I faced my concerned expression in the mirror one more time, squared my shoulders, and said, "You can. Your sister gives advice all the time, and look at how successful she is!"

My reflection rolled her eyes. She knew that, while my sister was a world-renowned psychic who was so good that she had a four-month waiting list *and* was often recruited by the FBI to help solve their toughest cases, I was most definitely *not* my sister. I didn't have an intuitive bone in my body.

But I did have a few decades of keen business experience on my résumé, and a very large marketing firm that I'd built from the ground up and had recently sold for just over fifty million. *That* had to be worth some street cred when it came to handing out life advice.

Still, it was one thing to run a fast-paced business, and another to help a soccer mom find her inner purpose beyond being a glorified caterer, childcare provider, and chauffeur.

While my reflection and I silently exchanged frustrated looks, my cell rang. I answered it immediately. "I need you," I said, perhaps a weensy bit desperately.

"I'm on my way," Gilley sang.

I lifted my wrist to eye my watch and frowned in annoyance. "It's almost ten. You're late."

"I had to stop and get some doughnuts. You wouldn't want your first client to walk in and not have access to doughnuts, would you?"

I pinched the bridge of my nose. A headache was certainly destined to make its way onto the morning's agenda. "Gilley," I said, using the same voice I saved for those times when my sons were being difficult. "Erma's e-mail clearly stated that she's been using food to help her cope with all the negativity in her life."

"Oh," Gil said. "Sorry. I'll get rid of them."

I glanced at my reflection again. She cocked a skeptical eyebrow. She knew that "get rid of" was code for "swallow them whole like a python."

"You really need to pace yourself," I told him after a few seconds of silence.

"Wha?" Gilley said, his voice muffled by a mouthful of doughnut. "I'm not going to waste them, Cat."

I sighed and glanced again at my watch. It was five minutes to ten. My client, Erma Kirkland, would be here any minute. "Please, just hurry, okay?"

Gilley muffled a reply, which I couldn't make sense of. The python had perhaps moved on to its second doughnut. Ending the call, I came out of the small restroom located in my newly decorated office suite to nervously stare one more time at the ambience I'd created.

My work space is located in the heart of East Hampton's downtown. The building itself is nearly two hundred years old. Hunting for an appropriate location, I stumbled upon this lucky find and was delighted by the fact that the exterior still had such strong old-world charm. When I inquired about the building itself, I was additionally delighted to find that it was up for sale. I bought it even before I'd secured the lot for my new home. In fact, the old building was the first thing I'd purchased after the ink dried on my divorce papers.

It may have been a little impulsive, actually, but can you blame me? My husband of twenty-one years announced the day *after* I received the wire from the sale of my marketing firm that *he* wasn't happy with our relationship. It turns out he was *much* happier with the bartender from the country club, where he's the resident pro. She's a perky brunette named Lisa. He's clearly having a midlife crisis, and they're now living together in Connecticut in a house he purchased with his share of our divorce settlement—roughly half my earnings from the sale of my business.

Bastard.

Ah, well, at least he didn't get the thing he'd wanted even more than my money—full custody of our boys. Matt and Mike, my twin fourteen-year-old sons . . . such smart, gorgeous, mischievous young men. They're in boarding school just three hours away, and I miss them terribly, but it's what they wanted as things between me and their father escalated through the divorce courts. I can't say that I blame them for wanting to be away from both of us. The drama was a little much for teen boys to handle.

I'm hoping the year at boarding school will allow the dust to settle and they'll be eager to come live with me again. Fingers crossed on that, because right now I'm all alone in an enormous, nearly complete home (which my sister has dubbed Chez Cat), and it feels empty and sad. That's probably why I spend most of my time at the guest house (Chez Kitty), where Gilley has essentially moved in while his husband, Michel, gallivants all over the globe, photographing the world's most beautiful models. Still, their marriage seems strong, even though I know Gilley is heartsick about Michel being in such demand and away from home most of the time.

He and I formed our own little lonely-hearts club, and to keep ourselves from getting too depressed over the past seven months, we threw ourselves into the project of bringing this old office building up to code and up to snuff.

Nine charming suites occupy the space, three per floor. When I initially purchased the building, each suite had a tenant, except for my office here on the ground floor and one on the third floor, left of the stairs. I'd renovated and decorated that one first, but for some reason I hadn't yet been able to rent it out. Plenty of people had come to take a look at it in the past few weeks, but no one had leased it just yet.

Still, there was a podiatrist who'd shown some promising interest in it earlier in the week, and I was hopeful he'd come back with a check in hand, ready to sign.

Nervously, I moved around my own suite, fluffing the pillows on the love seat and trimming an odd thread from the throw rug. Surveying the large suite one final time, I sighed contentedly. I loved this space.

I'd used soothing tones of creamy cocoa on the walls of my office, balancing that with bright white trim and a smoky brown hardwood for the flooring. The love seat, where my clients would sit, was vanilla cream leather, soft as butter to the touch. My own chair was a high-back wing chair with a small side table pre-set with pen and paper, ready for taking notes. I'd also set a similar notebook with pen on a small side table next to the love seat for my first client, Erma, just in case she forgot to bring her own.

I tried to picture the scene of the two of us, sitting together. She would be a pretty but nervous woman, lacking confidence and direction. She'd fiddle with her pearls as she told me about herself. And I'd listen to her story and learn what was holding her back, and then I'd lend her some insightful advice—some gentle coaching to steer her in the right direction. And through this process of my trademark Listen, Learn, Lend technique, Erma would gradually evolve, like an awkward duckling, into a confident swan.

I imagined her back on that love seat after a few months, fresher, prettier, more styled, and confident. She'd be Erma Kirkland 2.0, and she'd rave about her new life and tell everyone how working with me had helped her. Her friends would come to me, and I'd fix them, then their friends would line up, and soon I'd have a blog, a waiting list, and a massive following. There'd be a book—aptly titled *Listen, Learn, Lend*, and a morning-talk-show book tour, where I'd turn on the charm, and then some producer somewhere would step out of the shadows and suggest a show of my own. I'd be the queen of advice for lost women everywhere.

I'd be the new Oprah, and Gilley would be my Gail.

I sighed happily, imagining myself on the cover of *Time*, and was pulled abruptly out of my thoughts by the jangle of the front door opening. Gilley sashayed in, smiling broadly, his lips still wearing a dusting of powdered sugar. "Cat," he said, pausing mid-sashay to look me up and down. "You. Look. Radiant!"

I blushed in spite of myself. I'd taken considerable care with my appearance this morning. Not wanting to appear too businesslike or otherwise intimidating in one of my usual Hermès suits, I'd opted instead for a pair of suede brown dress slacks, a bulky cream sweater that hung off one exposed shoulder, and spikey Stuart Weitzman ankle boots. I'd topped off the ensemble with some chunky gold jewelry. "Thank you," I said, running a recently manicured finger under my bangs to move them out of my eyes. "But you're still late."

Gilley waved his hand casually before shutting the door and setting down his messenger bag. "I still made it here before your client. Technically, that's a win."

"How about next time we avoid getting technical, and you just show up early?"

Gilley regarded me with half-lidded eyes. "For years, M.J. lectured me on the importance of punctuality, and . . ."

M.J. was M.J. Holliday, Gilley's former partner in crime. The pair went *way* back, to elementary school in Georgia. They'd grown up more like siblings than classmates, and the best friends had even attended college together in Boston, eventually beginning their own ghostbusting business which took on a whole life of its own when it blossomed into a hit cable TV show and then a movie called *Ghoul Getters*. M.J. was married now to Heath Whitefeather, who, like her, was a fellow spiritual medium. The pair were mostly retired from that life now, and were currently settled down in New Mexico, raising a family.

"And? And what?" I asked, when Gilley refused to finish his thought.

Gilley waved his hand nonchalantly. "*And* you can see how well that worked out."

I sighed. "Point taken. Still, can I at least convince you to sit down at your desk before Erma gets here?"

Gilley curtsied before bouncing over to his desk to pull out the chair and sit down in one graceful move. Opening up his laptop, he pretended to type furiously while smiling at me.

As I was rolling my eyes, the front door opened again, and a giant walked into our office.

The woman was at least six feet tall, with flaming red, curly hair, small squinty eyes, and large manly hands. Dressed in layers of black, she was a dramatic creature. And sweaty. And so nervous her hands were shaking. "*Hi!*" she boomed.

Gilley and I both winced at the volume of the greeting. "Hello," Gil said softly, as if encouraging her to use her inside voice. Getting up, he walked around the desk to extend his hand to her. "Welcome to Cat's Coaching Corner. I'm Gilley."

"I'm Erma!"

Gil and I both winced again, but he managed to cover it by pushing that big smile onto his lips. Erma looked at him and his outstretched hand as if she wasn't quite sure what to do with it, but then she seemed to remember herself and engulfed his hand in her palm. I watched him grit his teeth, likely from the force of the handshake. "It's great to meet you!" she said, pumping his poor arm like a gambler on a hot streak at a slot machine. And then, all of a sudden, she stopped pumping and pulled him toward her with a jerk. Inhaling deeply, she said, "Holy cow, you smell like doughnuts!"

Gilley's eyes widened, and he looked at me in alarm, but I had no idea what to do. Before I could even say a word, Erma tugged Gilley forward even more—practically into her chest—as she said, "*Are* there doughnuts?"

"Uh," Gilley said, staring up at Erma, who was about six inches taller than him. "No. No doughnuts. Sorry."

Erma scrunched up her face into an impressively disappointed frown, but in the next instant, the frown was gone, replaced by that beaming smile again as she wrapped Gilley into a big bear hug. "Aw, it's okay," she said, inhaling deeply again after she let out a satisfied sigh. "Man! It's like breathing in heaven."

Gilley squeaked when Erma squeezed him tightly one last time before releasing him. She then turned to regard me, and I couldn't help the small step back I took as her slightly wild eyes lit on me. "You must be Cat!"

"Yes," I said, my mind racing with possible escape routes. This woman was so much more than I was prepared to deal with. When Erma looked ready to charge and sweep me up in a big hug too, I reacted by turning my back slightly to her before making a large sweeping motion with one arm. "Won't you please join me in the seating area, Erma? We'll get right to your session."

Erma seemed a little unsure what to do, as if she were caught between attempting to still come at me for a hug and following my directive and proceeding to the sofa. Meanwhile, Gilley slinked away from her, clutching his hand, as though it was painful, all the way back to his desk. At last, Erma followed my instructions, lowering her arms and trotting forward like an obedient Saint Bernard.

As we entered the seating area, I motioned her over to the love seat and sat down in the big wing chair. I had a whole speech prepared to get us started. Something inspiring. Something motivational. Something she'd likely pull quotes from and post to her Facebook page.

"I can't believe I actually get to meet you!" she giggled before I'd had a chance to even open my mouth. "You're like the most famous person I've ever met!"

The statement caught me a little off guard. "I am?"

"Well, yeah! I mean, I saw you speak at that Empowering Women seminar thingy? Ohmigod, you were, like, incredible! And then I saw you speak at the Women in Charge seminar, and then again at the Women Can Have It All conference, and all three times you were so . . ." Erma waved her hands in frantic circles in front of me. "So, you know . . . *amazing!*"

I blinked again. "You were at all three conferences?"

"Oh, yeah. Those three and, like, twenty others. I go to all of 'em. Can't get enough of that girl-empowerment stuff. Not that any of it's helped. My life right now is definitely circling the drain, but, you know . . . gotta keep fakin' it till you're makin' it, am I right?" Erma held up one large, meaty palm in an invitation for a high five, and I felt myself recoil slightly. One good high five from the woman across from me and I'd probably go flying, ass over teakettle.

Sitting firmly in my chair, I compromised by raising my hand slightly to give her an air high five. She didn't seem to notice my lack of enthusiasm because she slapped at the air too. "Yeah!" she shouted. "Girl power! Unh!"

My wide-eyed, somewhat panicked gaze flickered to Gilley. His back was to us, but I could see him hunched over and shuddering with laughter. The little hobgoblin.

"So," I said to her, trying to get us back on track. "Talk to me about what's not going well with your life, Erma?"

She snorted out a chuckle. "It'd be faster to tell you what *is* going right with my life."

"Okay," I said. "That's a good place to start. Tell me about that."

"Well, I'm sitting here with the *famous* Catherine Cooper-Masters!" she said, her smile so wide it hurt to look at her. "Or is it Catherine Cooper now? I heard you got divorced."

I cringed inwardly. It was hard to be reminded of that still painfully fresh experience. "It's just Cooper now," I told her. "But you can simply call me Cat."

"Oh, that's so cool!"

I smiled nervously. Good Lord, what'd I gotten myself into?

"Cat," she said, taking it for a test run. "Cat, Cat, Cat, Cat, Cat!" she added, taking several loops around the track.

"Yes," I said. "But let's focus on you, Erma. I was really looking for something more specific that had to do with just you. What's going right in your life?"

"Um, well, I guess my car hasn't been repossessed yet. I'm ninety days past due on my payment, so I think that's *super* positive!"

Out of the corner of my eye, I saw Gilley stand up abruptly. "Erma?" he said.

She swiveled in her seat.

"Yeah?"

"Do you own a green Chevrolet?"

"Yeah, why?"

"There's a man with a tow truck breaking into it."

Erma flew up off the couch faster than anyone of that size should've been able to. Dashing out the door, we heard her shout, "No! Not today! Any day but today!"

I was slower to react, but I quickly joined Gilley at the window. "Oh. My. God," I whispered.

"Where did you *find* her?" Gil asked me as we watched Erma flap her arms wildly at a man almost her match in size who was clearly repossessing her car right in front of my office.

"She was the first person to answer my ad."

"Didn't you do a little background check on her first? You know, check her social media profile to make sure she wasn't someone like . . ." Gil paused to wave a hand at the window. "That."

"No," I said crossly. "I'm a life coach. I'm supposed to help people in crisis, not stalk them on Facebook to see if they're only slightly in crisis."

"Honey," Gil said seriously, "there're people in crisis, and then there're people in the circus, and you got the later."

I stared out the window at Erma as she began to flap her arms up and down and hop about like an angry chicken. "Craaaaap."

"What should we do?" Gil asked as we watched Erma's dance escalate when she threw herself onto the hood of the tow truck in a desperate attempt to stop the man from taking her car.

"Hand me my purse," I said.

Gil reached under his desk to retrieve my purse and offer it to me. I took it outside and waved to the driver, who was currently yelling at Erma to get off his truck or he'd call the police.

"Yoo hoo!" I sang.

Both the repo man and Erma stopped their yelling and turned to regard me silently. I fished inside my purse and retrieved my checkbook. "How much?" I asked as I stepped up to them.

"How much what?" the man asked.

"How much does she owe? Including your towing fee, of course."

"I get three fifty to tow the car and not answer questions about how much anybody owes," he said to me.

"Ah," I said as Erma wiped at her cheeks and eyed me with desperation. "Well, what if I give you three hundred and fifty dollars not to tow the car?"

The tow-truck driver wiped his hands on a bandana he re-trieved from a back pocket. Leaning against his truck, he said, "That's not how this works, lady. The bank gives me three fifty for this car, plus thirty other cars to repo a month. If I take your money and don't bring this hunk of junk in, then I risk losing that business, and unless you've got a hundred grand to give me, which is what I'll lose if I take your money, then I ain't gonna do that. Now, I'm sorry, but I gotta take the car. There's no gettin' around it."

Erma let out a loud sob and buried her face in her hands.

I pressed my lips together in frustration. Then I peered around the tow truck to take in Erma's car, which had definitely seen better days. "Erma?"

"Y-y-yeah?" she said between tearful sobs.

"How much do you owe on this car? Total."

Lifting her chin to reveal splotches of red all over her pale face, Erma said, "I don't know. A little over two thousand, maybe?" She then looked at the car herself and added, "I know it's not much, Ms. Cooper, but it's the only asset I've got."

"How did you get so behind on the payments?" I asked as gently as I could.

"Well, I don't make a lot of money at my job, and you're pretty expensive, so I made a few monthly sacrifices in order to come here and get your advice."

I bit my lip again. I knew it wasn't my fault that Erma appeared to be such a mess both socially and financially, but it was still tough to hear that I was the reason she'd been skipping her car payments. Just then the tow-truck driver finished hooking Erma's car to his vehicle, and before getting into his rig, he said to her, "If you want your car back, you'll need to talk to your bank. They'll let you know how to get it out of the yard. And if you don't come up with the cash to pay all the fees and catch up with your payments, they'll sell it at auction after thirty days."

Gilley joined us just as the driver pulled away with Erma's car. When he turned left at the light at the end of the block, my new client sat down on the curb, buried her face in her hands again, and sobbed in earnest.

Gil eyed her with pity, but I was already formulating a plan. "Gilley," I said softly.

"Yeah?"

Shoving a twenty at him, I said, "I need you to go to the nearest doughnut shop and bring back some goodies for Erma. Then I need you to head to the house and retrieve the Audi from the garage. Bring it back here as fast as you can." I owned several cars. The Audi had been a favorite of my ex-husband's, so I'd made sure to take it in the divorce.

"Why am I retrieving the Audi?" Gil asked.

"I'm going to loan it to Erma."

Gilley raised his eyebrows, but he didn't otherwise question me. Loaning out one of my cars to a relative stranger wasn't the smartest thing I could do, for sure, but this woman needed help, and at the moment, it was a means to an end until we could get the rest of it sorted out.

Gilley left, and I took Erma gently by the arm, leading her back inside, where she flopped down on the love seat and continued to weep into her hands. "I needed that car," she said at last.

I offered her a box of tissues and some water, which she took, and then I sat down across from her. "Hey," I said to get her attention when she simply stared forlornly at the floor.

"I'm sorry," she said, lifting her eyes to mine. "Now you know why I needed your help. I'm a disaster!"

"Yes," I said bluntly. "You are definitely a disaster." That won me a startled look. "But you know the good thing about disasters? They're very effective at wiping the slate clean. Once we clear away the debris, Erma, we can rebuild your life into something that will work for the long haul."

Her lower lip trembled. "But how can I do that without transportation? There's no way I can come up with the money to get my car back if I can't get to work and earn the money. And I need it to get to work."

"What about the train?" I asked.

Erma's frown deepened, and she went back to staring at the floor. "I used to take it in to work, but with all the stops I'd have to get up at five to get to the train by six to get to work on time, and I just can't seem to get myself together in the mornings in time to make it into work before eight. My boss threatened to fire me if I was late even one more time."

"Well, then, it's settled. I'll be loaning you my car for now, and I'm going to loan you the money to pay off your car and get it out of the yard. You may pay me back over the course of the next several months with whatever payments you can afford."

Erma's wide eyes blinked several times. "You . . . you're . . . gonna loan me your car? And help me get mine back?"

"Yes. I have a very comfortable spare car that I'm going to allow you to borrow. And I'm not going to take any more of your money for our sessions together, Erma. You can't afford me."

A look of panic replaced the incredulity on her face. "But I need you, Ms. Cooper! I need a life coach!"

I smiled reassuringly. "I agree. Which is why I'm going to coach you pro bono."

Erma began to weep again in earnest. "It's too much," she sniveled. "I feel like I can't accept because it's just too much."

"It's not, Erma. It's not. And you *will* accept my offer to help you. That's the first step to getting your life back on track. You've got to recognize when it's okay to both ask for and accept help."

"I'm not so good at that."

I sat back in my chair, knowing I had the perfect advice to give this woman for our first session together. "The only way to be good at something is to have lots of practice at it. So, on that front, between now and our next session, I want you to ask ten people for help."

Her eyes bugged. "*Ten?*"

"Yes. Ten. And not a person less."

Erma bit her lower lip. "Okay. I guess I can do that."

"No, no," I said, wagging my finger. "You don't guess. You *will*. You *will* ask ten people for help. It doesn't have to be for something big—heck, you can ask a stranger to hold the door for you, and that'll count as one, but you should ask at least a few people for some kind of meaningful help in some way over the course of the next week."

Erma nodded, and her eyes finally reflected more determination. "Got it. Ask for help. Okay, I'll do it!"

"That's the spirit!"

Twenty minutes later, Gilley pulled up in my Audi A3, and after scarfing down a doughnut, Erma was happily on her way. As we watched her drive off, Gilley bumped my shoulder with his. "That was a nice thing you did," he said.

"Thanks," I replied, allowing a satisfied smile to rest on my lips. It felt good to help people. I liked this feeling even more than I liked closing a major marketing campaign, which until today had been my absolute favorite thing—professionally speaking.

"Should we go to lunch?" Gil asked after Erma had turned the corner.

I eyed my watch. "I can't today. I've got that luncheon to attend at Heather Holland's."

Gilley made a face. "Oh, ugh, is that today?"

I mirrored his expression. "Yes."

He put a hand on my arm. "My condolences."

"Thank you."

"Why are you going, again? That woman hates you."

It was true. I'd moved to the Hamptons just six months earlier, choosing to live in Chez Kitty—the guest house—until the main house was complete. From the moment the moving van had appeared to cart a few essentials into the guest house, my neighbor, Heather Holland, had made it very clear that I was persona non grata by calling the police about the expired tag on the moving van and filing complaint after complaint with the East Hampton Town Board all through the construction process of my new home. "Oh, I know she hates me," I said. "And I'm positive that she's hoping I don't show up, which is *exactly* why I have to attend. If I don't go, she can claim that I've snubbed her invite and the opportunity to bury the hatchet."

"Huh," Gil said, pondering that. "How are you so sure that's what she's up to?"

I bounced my eyebrows. "I'm sure because after nearly twenty years of running my own marketing firm in a highly competitive field populated mostly by women, I'm now fluent in bitch."

Gilley laughed. "I almost feel sorry for Heather."

"Don't," I told him. "She started this feud, and I've tolerated it only because standing up to her before the house was finished would've worked against me—especially with her considerable influence over the town's planning department."

Gilley scrunched up his nose. "How many inspections did you have to go through again?"

I shook my head in disgust. "Seven," I said. "The nitpicky things they found to write up and delay my certificate of occupancy were ridiculous, and I'm certain that Heather was behind all of it. Her or one of her cronies," I added, referring to one of the dozen women from the town who'd aligned themselves with Heather against me. Most of them would likely be in attendance at her luncheon, the better to either provoke me or talk about me behind my back if I didn't show up.

"Are you sure you don't want me to go with you?" Gilley asked again. "You're gonna be swimming in shark-infested waters over there."

"I can handle myself—not to worry, my friend."

The truth, however, was that I would've loved to have taken Gilley with me, but I was afraid that he'd bristle when either Heather or one of the other women insulted me—which I totally expected to happen—and that would then turn into a thing, and I'd never make friends in this town.

"Well, how about a coffee and a scone right now to help bolster your courage?" Gil said hopefully.

I touched his cheek. Gilley was such a dear. Always looking after my empty stomach. "I can't, lovey. I've got a little business to attend to, and then I'll have to scoot home to change."

"Business?"

"Yes. Someone's coming to look at the upstairs office space. He should be here in a few minutes."

"Will it take long?" Gil asked.

"Maybe a half hour or so. Why?"

"Would you mind if I borrowed your car for a little shopping spree? I'm putting together a care package to send to Michel, just to let him know how much I miss him."

"That's sweet," I said, feeling a tiny pang in my heart. Gilley and Michel adored each other, and they were always doing little thoughtful things for one another just to keep the spark alive. In the first few years of our marriage, Tommy—my ex-husband—and I had done similar little thoughtful things for each other, but in the two years before we finally called it quits, we hadn't even exchanged gifts at Christmas. Odd how I hadn't really missed having a romantic relationship with Tommy until well after we were divorced.

"Of course you can take the car," I said, handing Gilley my keys. "Just be back here no later than eleven-fifteen, okay?"

"Pinkie swear," Gil said as he all but dashed away.

I sighed and moved over to the entrance of the staircase leading to the other office suites. After making my way to the top floor, I came up short when I spotted the figure of a man at the end of the hallway, standing in front of the available office suite. "Oh," I said, to him, "I didn't realize you'd already arrived."

The figure turned, and I found my breath catching. He was an absolutely gorgeous man. Tall and broad-shouldered, he carried himself with obvious confidence, and there was a slight tilt to his chin as he regarded me. The rest of his face was somewhat square, but compelling in a roguishly handsome way. He was fair-skinned and light-eyed, with dark blond hair. His features weren't necessarily classically handsome, but there was something about the whole package that drew me in.

"Hello," he said. "Are you Catherine?"

I detected a Slavic accent as he addressed me, something that I should've expected given the name he'd left in his e-mail. "Yes," I said, resisting the urge to fan myself as I walked to him. "And you must be Mr. Grinkov."

Extending his hand to shake mine, he said, "Please, call me Maks."

I placed my palm in his, and he, in turn, placed his other palm on top of our joined hands and held on for an extended moment, as if he enjoyed the feeling of our skins touching. It was a subtle but intimate and delicious moment that caused a small shiver of pleasure to tickle my backbone. (Okay, and maybe also my hoo-ha.) "It's lovely to meet you, Catherine."

My free hand moved to cover my heart. "The pleasure is mine."

For another moment, we simply stood there, looking at each other. I felt caught up in the stare of his beautiful hazel eyes. I didn't want to blink or turn away. Ever.

At last, however, the moment began to turn awkward, and Maks let go of my hand. "Shall we have a look at the space?" he asked.

I pulled at my sweater. Why was it so hot in this hallway? "Yes!" I said, too quickly and definitely too loudly. "This way, Mr. Grinkov."

"Maks," he reminded.

I stepped in front of him, and the chemistry between us buzzed a degree hotter. *Good God, Cat!* I thought. *Get ahold of yourself!*

Doing my best not to fumble the keys, I led us through the doorway, then stepped to the side to allow him to inspect the office. Maks walked to the center of the room and surveyed the area, like a lion coming into a new territory.

"Hmm," he said as he moved again to tour the suite. Stepping up to one of three large windows, he peered out at the street below. "Nice view," he said after turning to look at me.

I felt another wave of heat touch my cheeks. "You're a bit of a flirt, Maks."

He smiled mischievously. "I'm more than a bit, Catherine."

"Yes," I said grinning. "I can see that. What business are you in?"

"Oh, I dabble in a few things, like imports and exports and other investments," he said.

"Stocks and bonds?"

"Real estate."

"Really? Me too. I mean, obviously," I added, with a roll of my eyes and a wave of my hand toward the room we were in.

Maks nodded. "C.C. Management," he said, indicating the LLC I'd formed when I bought the building. I'd listed it on the ad for the office suite, and I liked that he'd remembered it.

"Yes," I said. "That's me."

Maks continued to walk around and survey the office, opening a closet door and peering inside before he asked, "Do you own other commercial real estate in the area?"

"No," I confessed. "Just the one property. And I only bought this place because it spoke to me."

Maks paused his inspection to cock his head curiously at me. "What did it say?"

I laughed nervously. Why did I feel like everything that came out of my mouth was something silly? "Well, it didn't actually speak words, but I discovered this place when I was searching for my own office to rent, and when I pulled up to this old building and saw how neglected it'd been and that all it needed was someone with a little vision and a lot of TLC, I couldn't resist purchasing it outright. Real estate around here comes at a premium, but because this building required extensive capital to bring it back to its full glory, many other investors had passed up the chance to own it."

Maks stood in the center of the room and nodded, tapping his chin thoughtfully. "I thought it looked freshly renovated. You've done an excellent job."

I dipped my chin gratefully at the compliment. I liked this man, and I really wanted him as a tenant. "So, what do you think of the space?"

Maks didn't answer me right away. Instead, he turned and walked purposefully toward the window again, peering out at the view. "Yes," he said at last.

I blinked. "Yes?" I hadn't realized I'd asked a yes/no question. Laughing a bit, I said, "Yes, you like it, and yes, you want to rent it?"

"Yes."

His simple but straightforward reply was a bit startling. I was used to being told by prospective renters that they'd have to think about it. "Great," I said, unable to keep the surprise out of my voice.

"Is there a rental application to fill out?" Maks asked, turning back to me.

"Absolutely. Ha, of course there is." Fumbling around in my bag to retrieve a copy of the rental application, I handed it to him. "If you could fill out the front and back of both pages, and drop it in the mail slot of the door for suite 1A downstairs, that'd be great."

Maks took the papers, his gaze steady as he seemed to study me. "I'll get this to you by tomorrow."

I nodded and pressed my lips together lest I appear too eager. "Perfect," I said, then turned toward the door. He was flustering me, and I wasn't sure what to do other than try to extricate myself. Opening the door again, I stood just inside the doorjamb, with what I hoped was a friendly but professional smile.

Maks tucked the rental application into the inner pocket of his blazer and also moved to leave, but then he hesitated when he was about to cross the threshold. "Catherine," he said softly.

"Yes?" I said, equally softly. We were inches from each other, and I could smell his aftershave. It wasn't a scent I recognized, but, Lord, did it smell divine. And for a moment, all of my attention was focused on the small hollow at the base of Maks's throat.

Silent seconds passed, and I realized he hadn't said anything. Lifting my gaze, I saw that he appeared to be searching for the words he wanted to speak. "Would you like to have lunch with me?"

I stared in slight confusion at him for a few beats; sure, we'd just been flirting, but I certainly hadn't expected for him to ask me out so quickly after meeting me. "Um . . . ," I said, struggling with a reply.

Maks shook his head ruefully. "I'm sorry. That was too forward. I know we just met, but you're a beautiful woman whose company I find charming, and you aren't wearing a wedding band, so I'd hoped you weren't attached."

"I . . . um . . . no," I stammered.

"Yes, of course," he said, already moving past me. "I understand. Please forgive my boldness and forget I ever mentioned it."

"No!" I said, realizing he thought I was turning him down. Maks looked back over his shoulder, and I stepped toward him. "I mean, I'm not attached, and lunch would be . . . delightful."

Maks smiled. It was like the rest of him—spectacular. His whole face lit up, and I couldn't help but smile too. "Are you free now?" he asked.

"Yes," I said, then abruptly remembered the luncheon at Heather's. "Oh, I mean, no. Not today. I have a . . ." I didn't quite know how to phrase it. "I have a thing."

"Ah," he said. "I have those all the time."

I chuckled. "You're quite the charmer too, aren't you?"

Maks cocked one eyebrow and leveled his gaze at me. "I haven't even begun to charm you, Ms. . . . what is your last name?"

I laughed again. "It's Cooper," I told him.

An odd look played across Maks's face. "Cooper is a very common last name in this country, correct?"

"It is," I said. "But I'm afraid our line of Coopers is going to die out with my sister and me. There were no boys born to pass on the name. My twin sons have my ex-husband's surname. Abby—my sister, still goes by Cooper even though she's married, but she's adamant about not having kids."

Another look passed over Maks's face, and it was so strange, but I swore he looked truly surprised for a moment. Maybe even shocked. "You have a sister named Abby?"

"Yes. Her given name is Abigail, but she goes by Abby." I didn't know why I was offering up so much information, but I couldn't seem to stop. "She's my younger sister by three years. She and her husband, Dutch, live in Texas."

Maks's eyes widened again, and he gave his head a slight shake. He seemed to study me intently again, and then he mumbled something under his breath that sounded a lot like "What're the odds?"

"Excuse me?" I said.

"Nothing," he said, dialing up the wattage on that fantastic smile. "When are you free, then?"

"I'm free tomorrow," I said, turning briefly to lock the office door. Truth be told, I wasn't sure if I was free or not, but I was willing to reschedule anything I might have planned for the chance to sit across from this gorgeous, interesting man and break bread.

"I can't do lunch tomorrow, but I could do dinner. Would that be acceptable?"

"It would," I said, feeling my cheeks heat up again.

"Perfect," Maks said as we strolled toward the stairs. "Would seven o'clock fit into your plans?"

"It would," I said as we started down.

"Excellent," he replied. Reaching inside his blazer, he produced a card and tapped the phone number on it. "Text me your address tomorrow, and I'll pick you up."

We reached the landing, and Maks extended his arm in front of me to open the door to the outside. "I'll be ready," I told him.

"Excellent," he repeated. "And say hi to your sister for me."

With that rather cryptic sentence, Maks turned and walked away, leaving me to wonder if he was simply poking a little fun at me for the overshare or if, by some crazy coincidence, he actually knew my sister.

Chapter 2

When I entered my suite again, Gilley was nowhere in sight, and as he'd taken my car, I had to figure out a way to get home, do a quick change, and get over to Heather's. Luckily, just as I was considering ordering an Uber, Gilley pulled up to the office and dashed in to deliver my keys. "Sorry, sorry, sorry!" he said when he came through the door. "I was at White's Apothecary, and you know how I loves me some scented candles . . ."

"*I have a date!*" I shouted.

I must've startled Gil, because he jumped a little. "Wait, what?"

"I have a date!" I repeated, lowering the volume.

Gil looked over his shoulder toward the door, then back at me. "I've only been gone a half hour. How could that happen?"

I picked up an envelope from the desk and fanned myself. "It happened," I said. "And he's spectacular."

Gilley hopped up onto his desk and crossed his legs. "Tell me *everything!*"

I'd been sitting down and stood up to make a sweeping motion. "In the car. I've got to get home and change for Heather's luncheon."

Gil scowled. "That again. Why do you have to go home and change? That outfit is fabulous."

"Heather's invite said that it was a black and white attire themed luncheon."

"A what now?" Gil said, his brow creasing. "What the heck is that about?"

I rolled my eyes. "I have no idea, but I'm not arguing. I'm wearing my black Chanel suit with a white shell."

"I love that suit on you," Gilley said. "Why didn't you wear it this morning?"

"It's far too severe for a first meeting with a new client. I usually only wear it to high-level business meetings. And funerals."

Gil offered me a crooked smile. "Then it'll be *perfect* for Heather's get-together."

"Exactly."

"Ugh, I still wish you didn't have to go. Especially now that you have a date. We need to go shopping for a new outfit for this hottie Mctacular."

Grabbing my purse and ushering Gilley to the door, I said, "I have to attend. If I don't, I'll be forever snubbed in this town. We can go outfit shopping afterward."

Gilley replied, but I was momentarily distracted by the pinging of my cell phone. "Hang on," I told him while I studied the screen. "Heather's asking me if I'm still coming. Again. Really, that woman is so annoying." Pausing in my rush out the door, I tapped out a quick reply and said, "There. Now she knows I'll definitely attend. Let's—" Before I could even finish my sentence my phone pinged again with an incoming text. I sighed loudly and lifted it to look at the screen. "You've *got* to be kidding me."

"What is it?" Gilley asked.

I showed him the phone and watched his forehead crinkle as he read the text and the attached photo of a recipe. "Heather wants you to bring punch? Enough to serve eighteen people? And she's insisting you follow this recipe to the letter? Is she *kidding?*"

I glanced again at my watch. "And she's letting me know just thirty minutes before the luncheon!"

"Why doesn't she get her own damn punch?" Gilley said, nearly as indignant as I was.

"The grocery store is in the opposite direction from here! It'll take me half an hour just to get there and get back home!" I said, working myself into a good panic. I didn't know what to do. I'd barely have enough time to get home and change, let alone shop for and make up a batch of punch for eighteen people. And how was I supposed to get it from my house to hers? Yes, she was my neighbor, but I'd have to load it into the car, not spill a drop, then lug it into her house like some lackey from the catering company. "If I'm late, she'll hold it against me. If I show up without punch, she'll hold it against me."

Gilley placed a hand on my shoulder. "Hey," he said. "I got you, boo."

I stood there shaking my head at him. I couldn't imagine how he could help me. "How?"

"First, let's get you home. Give me the keys, I'm a faster driver."

I handed him the keys. "Then what?"

"Lucky you, I went shopping yesterday, and I've got fresh apples at Chez Kitty. And I'm pretty sure I've got cloves, cinnamon, and apple cider in the pantry, which leaves only Sprite, cranberry juice, and OJ to complete the recipe, and I'm positive I can get those at that little convenience store a block from here. We can stop really quick to grab that, then race home, . . . which reminds me, do you have a punch bowl big enough to serve eighteen people at Chez Cat?"

"I do," I said. I'd unpacked my formal crystal just a week ago.

"Perfect," he said. "We can whip this punch up in no time!"

"How are we going to get it to Heather's, though?" I asked.

"I'll wrap the whole bowl in that press-and-seal wrap. It works wonders. You'll see, we'll be good."

I felt some of the tension in my shoulders loosen. "If I haven't told you lately, Gilley Gillespie, I love you."

"Aww," he said, opening the car door for me and waiting for me to scoot into the passenger seat. "That's sweet, but we have no time for sweet. Now, get in and strap yourself down. We're on a deadline!"

Exactly twenty-eight minutes later, we were leaving my driveway. Gilley had sliced the apples while I mixed together the other ingredients for the punch, and then we'd wrapped the bowl very carefully in plastic wrap, and even when we tipped it, no liquid spilled out. Gilley walked with the heavy punch bowl to the car and got in, holding the bowl in his lap.

We'd agreed that he would hold the punch all the way to Heather's and help me to the front entrance with the Waterford crystal punch bowl. "You're a lifesaver," I told him, as we wound our way out of the drive and over to Heather's.

Gilley dipped his chin humbly. "Happy to help."

Once we arrived, we got out of the car, and I stared up at Heather's domicile. Although Heather was my neighbor, I'd only ever really glimpsed her house from the back side, and that was a good way off given the size of our respective lots.

Up close and personal, Heather's house was quite a sight. Ornately grand, with charcoal-colored slate sides, severe angles, dark wood trim, and lavish stonework, it stood like a grumpy guard of the open ocean just beyond. Surrounding the behemoth mansion were ornate gardens, teaming with colorful mums and perfectly sculpted topiary. To our left was a sizable parking area where well over a dozen luxury vehicles were already parked, indicating we were hardly the first to arrive.

"My, my," Gilley said, his voice dripping with sarcasm. "How delightfully understated."

"Mmm hmm, just like the owner," I agreed, my mouth twisting in distaste. This was going to be a long afternoon.

Carrying the punch bowl, Gilley followed me to the front door. Before I could raise my hand to depress the doorbell, however, it opened to reveal a severe-looking woman with jet-black hair, a pale complexion, and horribly overgrown eyebrows. As we stepped up to her, a clearly displeased frown formed on her thin lips, and she said, "Yes?"

I was a tiny bit thrown by the question and the absolute absence of a polite greeting for one of the luncheon guests. But then, Heather had a reputation for being a hateful beast to people; so why would her staff be any different? Pushing a forced smile onto my lips, I said, "Hello, I'm Catherine Cooper. I'm here for the luncheon."

The woman's steely eyes roved to Gilley. Lifting the punch bowl up slightly, he said, "Simply delivering the punch. I'm not staying for the party."

"Take it to the back," Heather's housekeeper said, pointing to a walkway that headed off to the left. "I'll let you in there."

Gil and I had both turned to look in the direction she was pointing, and when we turned to face her again, we were both shocked that she'd already stepped back and was closing the door in our faces.

"Wait!" I tried, but it was too late. The woman had already firmly shut the door.

"Well, that was just rude," Gilley said, shifting the weight of the heavy bowl.

"And infuriating," I said, raising my hand to knock on the door.

"Cat, don't," Gil said softly. "We can walk to the back and avoid making a scene after you've just arrived, which is probably exactly what Heather is hoping for. I bet she put her housekeeper up to that."

I retracted my hand, but my temper was still quietly flaring. It seemed that Heather meant to bait me from the second I set foot

Victoria Laurie

on her property. Gilley was right, though; it wouldn't do me a bit of good to make a scene. "Fine," I said through clenched teeth. "Let's get this over with."

I led Gilley down the path, which was longer than it appeared, and wound my way toward the back of the house. As we turned the corner, I realized two things; first, Heather's view of the ocean was somewhat marred by her own guest house, which was quite large in its own right. Second, the other thing obstructing what should've been a simply spectacular view of the ocean, given the mansion's prime location, was my own home, which blocked much of her view from the pool and the large patio area on the left.

I hadn't realized until just that moment that some of the animosity Heather held for me might've had more to do with the building of my home in a spot that obstructed her view than for me personally. Still, I hardly felt sorry for her. I'd acquired the property fair and square, although the lot had come into my hands by a rather timely bit of good fortune.

Not long after my divorce was finalized, I was having lunch with a business acquaintance, and the conversation drifted to what I wanted to do next. When I mentioned—almost as a joke—that I should probably move to the Hamptons, he happened to mention that he knew of a man who owned a sizable lot in East Hampton that he was getting ready to put on the market.

I'd met with the owner of the lot—an elderly gentleman named Nigel—a day later, and I'd been struck by how charming and delightful he was. He'd flirted shamelessly with me, and I might've been guilty of flirting shamelessly, but harmlessly, back, and we'd struck a deal over lunch, sealing it at the title office just two weeks later.

At the time, I'd thought I'd come out much the winner, because Nigel had sold me the property for an amount that was significantly less than what he could've gotten on the open market, and my ego had allowed me to believe that it was because he was a sweet elderly man who'd also been sweet on me, but after meeting Heather, I'd had to reevaluate that notion, and I'd often wondered if Nigel and Heather had had a contentious relationship too. Nigel had let on when I inquired that the lot had been in his family for nearly seventy years, and when I asked him why he'd never built on it, he'd waved his hand casually and said that he had a perfectly lovely home just two miles away, and while his wasn't an oceanfront view, he'd never felt that developing the lot was quite worth the trouble.

On that I had to disagree with him, because even after all that Heather Holland and the East Hampton planning board had put me through, I loved my beautiful new home.

"Cat?" I heard Gilley say.

I jumped a little. "Yes, Gil?"

"You okay? You've been standing there, staring at your house for a long time."

"Sorry," I told him, moving forward down the walk again. "I just love my home, and in spite of all the trouble, I'm happy I built it and moved here."

"Me too," Gilley said, with a grin.

We reached the back door, and my knock was answered by the same severe woman who'd greeted us at the front entrance. She didn't speak to us; she merely opened the door, then turned away to walk back inside.

"Well, that was doubly rude," Gil said. Even he was starting to get angry at the way we were being treated.

I sighed. This was going to be a long afternoon. Turning to him, I held out my hands and said, "Give me the punch bowl, and take the car, Gilley. Go have a lovely afternoon. Do some shopping or take in a movie, and I'll call you when the luncheon is over, and you can come pick me up."

Gilley carefully set the punch bowl into my outstretched arms and kissed my cheek. "Tootles, sugar. Good luck, and remember, you're a successful, beautiful woman in a killer suit, and Heather Holland can go suck eggs."

I chuckled as Gilley turned away. He always knew just what to say.

Moving through the open door, I found myself in a large kitchen filled with men and women in black pants, white shirts, and black blazers bustling about and picking up carefully pre-pared trays of food and drink. "Where should I set this?" I asked the grouchy housekeeper.

She pointed to the kitchen island. I moved carefully to the designated spot and set down the punch bowl. I was about to turn away from it and leave it for the catering staff to deal with when the housekeeper said, "Wait!"

"What?" I asked.

She produced a large butcher knife, and I took a step back, but then realized she was only going to use it to slice through the plastic wrap. After cutting into the wrap and pulling it off the punch bowl, the woman dipped a spoon into my concoction and held it to her lips. "Did you follow the recipe?"

"Yes," I said, unable to hide the annoyance in my voice.

"Exactly as it was written?" she pressed.

I took a deep breath and stared hard at this woman. Who did she think she was? "Yes," I said sharply. "Why? Is there a problem?"

The woman bent forward and sipped at the juice. She then smacked her lips a few times before setting down the spoon. "I will give it a pass," she said, then had the *nerve* to point to the swinging door of the kitchen and add, "You may take it out to the guests."

Narrowing my eyes, I said, "Oh, *may* I? That's *fantastic.*"

The grumpy housekeeper narrowed her own eyes but didn't comment further.

A small growl of annoyance escaped my lips, but I again re-minded myself that I shouldn't be taking the bait on anything that Heather wanted to serve up to me and, instead, reached again for the punch bowl, lifting it up and carrying it very slowly and very carefully through the swinging door and out into the main gathering for the luncheon.

As the door behind me began to shut, I heard the housekeeper call out to me, "Put it on the side table next to the ice sculpture."

Stepping into the large room, which was alive with chatter, I realized two things immediately. One: by the looks of the half-consumed cocktails in many of the women's hands, I was at least a half hour late. Two: every woman holding a cocktail was also wearing some sort of jewel-toned colored ensemble.

"Over there," said a voice behind me when I paused to take in the room.

I recognized it as the housekeeper's, and my gaze followed her finger as it pointed to a spot on the bar where about two dozen crystal punch glasses were arranged.

Still thrown by my first two impressions of the room, I hastened to the bar but continued to hold the bowl in my arms without setting it down. My mind was starting to put two and two together, and my cheeks got hot when I confirmed my suspicions by glancing around the room again, verifying that all of the guests attending the luncheon were dressed in bright vivid colors, while all of the help—that is, all staff currently carrying trays and catering to the guests—were clad in black and white.

Just like me.

I could feel my cheeks heat with embarrassment, fury, and panic. Heather had set me up perfectly, and I'd fallen for it.

Looking around while I considered a fight-or-flight plan, my gaze landed on a woman with lovely features and very long, straight blond hair dressed in a smart indigo-blue dress that almost hid a baby bump and matching suede flats. She smiled warmly and approached me. "Hello," she said while I simply stood there, frozen in indecision.

"Good afternoon," I managed.

She pointed to the burden in my arms. "Is that punch?"

"Yes."

"Does it have alcohol in it?"

"Um . . . no," I said, my mind working furiously back through the recipe. "It's just apple cider, Sprite, orange juice, and cranberry cocktail. With some cloves and cinnamon thrown in."

Her smile widened, and she added a laugh. "Sounds delicious. Can I have some?"

"Yes . . . yes, of course," I stammered, quickly setting the punch bowl down to the relief of my aching my arms. Meanwhile the woman started to chat me up.

"Heather almost never has anything but sparkling water and alcohol at these things," she began. Patting her baby bump, she said, "Obviously I'm avoiding alcohol, but sparkling water just gives me gas."

I nodded stiffly while I ladled some of the punch into a crystal punch glass and handed it to her. "Thanks," she said. After taking a sip, she added, "Oh, that's heaven." Then she pointed at me. "I love your uniform, by the way. All these other helpers look like they shop at the thrift store, but your suit looks so professional."

I wanted to sink into the floor. I opened my mouth to let her know that my "uniform" was actually Chanel, but at that moment, three other women appeared in front of us, and one of them pointed toward the bar. "We'd like some punch, please."

Not knowing what else to do, I ladled each of them a glass and handed them over. Thinking I could still salvage some dignity, I pushed a friendly smile to my face and said, "I'm Catherine Cooper."

"Good for you, honey," one of them said.

My smile faltered. "I'm from next door," I said, trying to clarify.

"Oh, are you Anastasia's girl?" another woman asked while she gave me the up-down.

"N-no . . . I—"

"Ana's help is always so well dressed," she continued, cutting me off and further insulting me by speaking to her friends as if I wasn't standing right in front of her. Turning back to me, she said, "When you go back, tell Ana we hope she feels better soon. Such a shame she couldn't make it today."

With a tisk, she and the three others left, but the pregnant woman still stood there and considered me curiously. "Hmm," she said. "I don't remember you from Ana's Labor Day barbecue. Were you working that day?"

A bubble of emotions began to ride up from my stomach. I was embarrassed, and furious, and didn't quite trust my voice, so I took a moment to swallow hard before saying, "I'm not on anyone's staff. I'm Catherine Cooper. Heather invite—"

"Can I get some punch?" someone asked loudly. I turned to see yet another woman and two friends standing to my right, holding up empty cups.

At that moment, my temper got the best of me. Of course, we Cooper girls are known for our tempers. Sometimes it's cute. Sometimes it's ugly. Today I knew it was about to get full-on, *what-the-fugly*?!

"Help yourself," I snapped. I then left the stunned foursome and walked purposely into the center of the room, searching . . .

"Do you have any more of those crab cakes?" a woman in an emerald sweater and brown leather skirt asked as she walked up to me.

"How the hell would I know?" I said angrily.

She put a hand to her chest. "You're rude!"

I laughed in her face. "I'm just gettin' started, honey. Where's Heather?"

The woman looked me up and down as if she could hardly *believe* I had the nerve to address her like that, so to speed things along, I snapped my fingers in her face and said, "Heather. Where is she?"

At last, the woman pointed across the room, where an archway led to yet another room.

With a brisk nod, I set off.

I found Heather, standing with four other women, all impeccably dressed in vivid colors, but Heather herself stood out even among that crowd. Clad in a persimmon leather skirt with a wide gold belt, an amethyst blouse, and turquoise, knee-high suede boots, she looked like something fresh off the Gucci runway.

For a moment, I was so mad I simply stood there, seething, and trying to decide what choice words I could hurl at my host for setting me up so despicably. As I was formulating my speech, however, the woman with the emerald-green sweater that I'd just left hurried past me and made a beeline for Heather. Nudging her way into the center of the crowd gathered around the host, I saw the woman lean in and whisper into Heather's ear.

For her part, Heather appeared surprised, but then her gaze found me, and her brow furrowed as if she couldn't place me at first. Then recognition lit up her features, and she adopted a puzzled expression.

My teeth ground together as I glared at her. She pretended not to notice but simply smiled to those gathered around and said, "Excuse me one moment, ladies."

The group parted to allow Heather to pass, and she walked toward me with the practiced bounce of a model. Opening her arms wide, she pushed a giant smile to her lips.

I didn't trust her for a second. "Catherine!" she said warmly.

"Don't you 'Catherine' me," I growled, my hands finding my hips. No way was I going to allow any kind of friendly embrace.

Heather stopped in front of me and allowed her arms to hang there awkwardly for a moment. The women she'd just left were watching us, and I could see the puzzled expressions on their faces too.

"You set me up!" I hissed.

Heather's arms dropped dramatically. "Catherine, whatever are you talking about?"

I waved a hand down my front. "This."

"It's a lovely suit, dear, but why would you come wearing black and white to a jewel-tone themed luncheon?"

The ladies behind Heather edged closer toward us, completely engrossed in what was obviously about to become a scene.

"I'm wearing this because you told me this was a black and white themed affair." I was aware that I was speaking through clenched teeth, likely giving me the appearance of snarling at our host. I didn't care.

"What?" Heather said loudly. "Oh my goodness, no! Black and white is what I require the staff to wear. It helps my guests to identify them at these affairs, you know?"

I narrowed my eyes to mere slits. Heather's tone and manner were conciliatory—gentle even. There wasn't a trace of snark or snide amusement. Bitch.

"Well, Heather, *my* invitation noted black and white attire. It didn't say anything about wearing jewel tones."

Heather's gorgeous face fell into a sad pout. "Oh, Catherine," she said tossing up her hands. "Come now, don't be upset. I'm sure there's a logical explanation. Perhaps you misread the invitation."

"I didn't misread it. It plainly stated that I was to wear black and white to your party."

"Well, I personally wrote out all the invitations, and I would never have my friendly neighbor from just next door come dressed as a *servant*, of all things." Heather chuckled merrily, and some of the other women, who had by now gathered around us, also laughed lightly. I was being taken for a fool.

"You clearly treated me like a servant when you texted me just an hour ago to bring punch to the party," I snapped.

Heather put a hand to her lips. Looking troubled, she said, "Oh, my. Now I see what's happened. I believe the caterer's name is Cathy. I must've mixed the two of you up when I was trying to put the finishing touches on the luncheon. Did you bring punch, dear? I have several guests who don't drink alcohol.

And I hope you followed the recipe to the letter. Like I said, I have several guests who don't drink."

I could feel myself seething. Heather was so clearly lying. I could see it in her eyes, but she was playing up this act of miscommunication really well, and all the women around her seemed to be buying her lies. It infuriated me.

"Yes, I brought the punch and I followed your recipe!" I snapped. "Your housekeeper even taste-tested it like I'm some idiot who can't follow simple directions. It was frankly insulting, but not *nearly* as insulting as the fact that when I arrived with the punch, your housekeeper wouldn't even allow me through the front door! She insisted I use the back entrance."

Heather's gaze gave me the once-over. "Well, she probably thought you were staff, dear. I would've directed you to the back as well if you were wearing that outfit and carrying a large punch bowl."

And that's when I knew I had her. I never mentioned anything about bringing the punch over in my own large crystal bowl. Glancing to my right, I spotted the grand window with a view of the front yard. And then I glanced back to the spot where Heather had been first standing before coming over to me. I realized that she'd been perfectly positioned to watch each guest arrive—or, more importantly, to watch for when *I* arrived.

Something else crystalized for me in that moment too: from the many parties and luncheons I myself have thrown, I knew that no party ever has all the guests arriving early. And then I thought about the start time of the luncheon on my invitation. It'd read 12:30 p.m. Not noon, as was more customary, but half past.

That in and of itself had initially struck me as odd because it meant that, with those attendees who'd be late, lunch wouldn't start until closer to one or one-thirty, but I'd passed it off in my mind as just a simple quirk. I now knew that it wasn't nearly that simple. Heather had scheduled her guests to arrive at noon, and she'd written out my invite for twelve-thirty to ensure that I'd be among the last to arrive. Late. Wearing the catering staff's colors, ushered through the back door, and guaranteed to feel embarrassed and out of place when I stepped into a room filled with women wearing vivid jewel tones.

To confirm my suspicions, I turned to a woman to my right and asked, "Out of curiosity, what time was this little affair supposed to start?"

Her brow furrowed, and I could see she felt put on the spot, but she said, "Noon."

"Ah," I said, narrowing my eyes to look scathingly back at Heather. "That's funny. My invite said twelve-thirty."

Heather sighed audibly. "Well, now you're just making things up, Catherine! It couldn't possibly have said that. All my luncheons begin at twelve. Otherwise, we'd be eating far too late."

"Well, *mine* said twelve-thirty."

"Do you have the invite?" she asked me, all sweetness and light.

I wanted to punch her. "No." I'd stupidly left it on the kitchen counter.

Heather threw her hands up in the air like she simply didn't know how to make me happy. "Would you like to go home and change?" she asked, as if exasperated by our conversation. "Lunch is about to be served, but if you're uncomfortable, I suppose we could wait . . ." And then there was a tiny crack in the fissure of her pretense, and she added, "Or you can grab a tray from the back and help serve."

Around us there was a tiny gasp of surprise, and about a dozen muffled snickers. My humiliation was complete.

Still, Heather had yet to learn about the Cooper temper. Abby—my short-fused sister—even has a pet name for when mine flares. She calls me "the Catken."

She may be underselling it.

"You know what, Heather, *dear?*" I said, popping out a hip and placing a hand on it. "I think going home is exactly what I'll be doing, but I won't be returning. We all know you set me up with this little scheme. You *wanted* me to show up in black and white attire. You *wanted* me to arrive a half hour later than your other guests. You *wanted* me to be directed to the back door so that I'd come into your little party and stick out like a sore thumb. Miscommunication my ass, lady!"

"Catherine, please," Heather said, placing a hand to her heart. "It hurts me that you could think I would do anything to jeopardize the good relationship we have as neighbors."

"*Good* relationship?!" I yelled. "Are you *kidding* me?!"

The room turned loud with silence. All murmuring and talking had hushed the second I'd started yelling, and glancing around, I saw how shocked everyone appeared. Even the women who'd been in on the joke seemed surprised that I'd get so mad.

I wanted to laugh right in all of their shocked faces. Meanwhile, Heather had taken a step toward me, her hands clasped together in something of a pleading gesture. "Catherine, I'm very sorry if I've offended you—"

"Oh, cut the crap! You've been nothing but a nightmare to deal with for me and my building crew from the moment we broke ground. You and all your other little flying monkeys can laugh at my expense and eat your lame little lunch or throw feces at one another for all I care, but mark my words, Heather Holland, you've been messing with the wrong woman. I am *done* playing nice!"

Holding up my hand, and curling my fingers, I added, "This cat's claws are coming out, toots, and *you're* going to be the one who ends up a bloody mess in the end!"

With that, I stomped right through the crowd of ladies— mouths agape—and over to the front door, pulling it open hard and making sure to slam it on my way out of the house.

Chapter 3

My moment of triumphant satisfaction for having left the party in a delicious huff lasted maaaaybe ten seconds—or about as long as it took to realize that Gilley had my car. If I called him, I'd possibly have to wait ten minutes or longer for him to show up and drive me home.

"Dammit!" I muttered, thinking that perhaps at least a few of the ladies were craning their necks to look out the window at my departure. Having no other choice, I lifted my chin and proceeded down the steps toward the drive. No way was I going to let a little thing like walking home in high heels stop me, so off I set for the quarter-mile hike.

It took a bit longer than I'd expected, and my feet were a mess by the time I got through the door. "Owwww," I moaned, hobbling over to the staircase to peel one of the Stuart Weitzman booties off my foot. They looked gorgeous on, but they were murder to walk in, especially since the heel was rather high. But that's all I tend to wear, even when I'm more casually dressed.

My sister had gotten the "height" in the family. She was a smidge under five foot five. I was a smidge over five feet even. Sometimes, it's tough being tiny.

Today I'd made up for it with the size of my tempest. No teapot could contain this girl's temper.

Ah well.

The walk home had solidified that I was justified in feeling offended and betrayed, but it'd also solidified the fact that, as usual, I'd overreacted and likely only made a bad situation worse. Nothing to be done about it now, though. I'd just made a town full of enemies, but to hell with them. It wasn't like I especially *needed* friends to live a satisfying life here. After all, I had Gilley and . . .

Crap. Who else *did* I have? "Well, the boys, of course," I told myself. "At least when they agree to visit." Which hadn't been for several weeks, but I was sure they would come home again soon.

And, of course, I had friends back in Massachusetts whom I could invite down for a stay. There were Mel, Susan, Julie, and . . .

I sighed again. I had three very dear friends from college near the town I'd just moved away from, but in the past several years, I'd been so busy with my own corporation that the four of us weren't as close as we once were.

Feeling suddenly very homesick, I hobbled up the stairs and into the master suite—a giant room, eighteen feet by twenty, with a California king bed, a spacious seating area, a giant-screen TV, an enormous closet, and a bathroom most spas would envy. The room itself was done in shades of camel and bone white. I'd wanted a very neutral space to rest my often whirling-dervish mind.

The suite was mostly complete, save for a few decorating touches and some wiring that I'd be having done the following week.

Still, as lovely as it was, I suddenly disliked it the way one regrets the buying of something supremely expensive that just doesn't live up to the hype.

I stood in the doorway to the bedroom for about ten seconds before I blew out another sigh, moved to the bureau in the closet, and pulled out a set of silk pajamas with matching robe and fuzzy slippers. Then I moved to the bath and grabbed a few items there before I made my way back to the stairs again.

After easing my feet into the slippers, I headed down the steps and out the door, crossing the drive to Chez Kitty, where I let myself in using the master passcode—no key required.

The guest house was quiet and peaceful. I leaned against the door and smiled. "Sebastian," I said softly.

"Good afternoon, Lady Catherine. How may I assist you?"

Sebastian is a wonder of technology. When I'd been looking at plans for the house, I'd stumbled across a company that specialized in wiring homes with an electronic butler—similar to a system like Amazon's Alexa, but Sebastian was so much more. He could of course do the simple things like play music or order things off the web, but he could also do more complicated things like adjust the temperature of any room in the house based on that individual's body temperature rather than some preferred prerecorded setting. He controlled the temperature, the lighting, the ambience, the sprinkler systems, the inventory of both the pantry and the refrigerator, the TV, the security system, and even the plumbing. The house was almost totally dependent on him.

But perhaps I was especially partial to him because he always greeted me as "Lady Catherine." It made me feel queenly.

"I'd like a bath please, Sebastian," I said.

The sound of running water from the master bathroom drifted to my ears. "What temperature would you like your bath today, ma'am?"

"I'd like it warm, Sebastian, but not too hot."

"Your current body temperature is ninety-eight point four. Based on your body temperature, may I recommend a setting of one hundred and four degrees?"

"Perfect," I said. Moving away from the front entrance and over to the fridge, I added, "And I'd like some lunch, Sebastian." Opening the door, I took out a perfectly chilled bottle of chardonnay. "Can you arrange for a salad to be delivered?"

"Of course, ma'am. Would you like your usual Caesar salad from Guairmo's?"

"Yes, please. And have them leave it at the door. I'll get it after my bath. But please remember to tip the delivery man twenty percent."

"Of course, ma'am."

Sebastian would place my order over the web, supplying my address, credit card number, and the authorization of a tip, and I didn't even have to power up my computer.

As I started to walk out of the kitchen with my glass of wine, Sebastian stopped me. "Lady Catherine?"

"Yes, Sebastian?"

"Might I recommend some strawberries to go with your chardonnay? There is a fresh quart of strawberries in the refrigerator. Bottom drawer. On the left."

I smiled before turning back toward the fridge. "Sebastian?"

"Yes, ma'am?"

"Have I told you lately that I love you?"

"It's been three days, ma'am. I'd almost thought you'd forgotten."

I soaked in the tub for nearly an hour and a half. Sebastian monitored the water to ensure it was a constant one hundred and four degrees by letting out a little water and running the faucet every now and again.

Meanwhile, I sipped my wine, nibbled on the strawberries, and tried not to stew about Heather.

When my fingers began to prune, I got out of the tub and dried off, donning my silk pajamas and matching robe before heading to the door to retrieve my salad. I stumbled a little at the door—the product of too much wine. "Are you well, Lady Catherine?"

"I'm fine, Sebastian," I said, bending to retrieve the salad, which remained perfectly chilled given the fall temperature. "But I forgot my book." Setting the salad on a side table by the door, I said, "I'll be back in a minute. Empty the tub, and put on some soft music for me, would you?"

"Of course, ma'am."

Breathing in the cool air as I crossed the drive back over to the main house, I tried to clear my head, but the wine was hitting me much harder than usual. When I got inside, I had to clutch the railing tightly as I headed upstairs, and I also had to place my feet carefully. As I crested the landing and wobbled into the master suite, I found my book right where I'd left it on the nightstand. "Hello, Ms. Blackwell," I cooed, picking up the book. Juliet Blackwell was one of my favorite authors. "What letters from Paris might you be writing for me today?"

I hugged the novel and wobbled some more as I stood there. "Good lord," I said to myself, "I'm thinker than I drunk." This sent me into gales of giggles, and I fell forward onto the bed, which was soft and warm and oh so inviting. "I'll just rest my eyes for a minute, Sebastian."

He didn't answer, of course, because the crew had yet to install him in the main house. That was the wiring to be done the following week. "I should call them and tell them to hurry up and get over here," I mumbled, my lips rubbing thickly against the pillow. Closing my eyes, I added, "I love my sweet Sebasty . . ."

That's the last thing I remember saying for the next four hours.

I woke up to a pounding, both in my head and downstairs. "Wha?" I mumbled as I pulled my face away from the pillow. The pounding continued. Putting a hand to my head, I rolled to a sitting position, blinking rapidly. "Catherine!" I heard Gilley's voice call. "Honey, are you in there?"

"I'm here," I called, but it came out as a croaky whisper. Clearing my throat, I tried again. "I'm here!"

"Let me in!" Gil yelled.

I wobbled on the bed for a moment, dizzy and out of sorts. "Coming!"

With effort, I got to my feet, cinching the belt of my robe before stumbling out of the bedroom.

The house was gloomy in the fading light, and I realized I'd slept the afternoon away. I made my way downstairs much like I'd made my way up them . . . carefully. At last, I reached the door and unlocked it, letting Gilley in. "Ohmigod!" he gasped when he saw me. Gripping me by the shoulders, he added, "Are you okay?"

"More or less," I told him.

"You look terrible!"

I frowned and pushed at a stray bang. "Thank you?"

"No, Cat, I mean it. You look awful."

"Please do continue, Gilley. My ego needed some pumping up."

He let go of me and stepped back. "Sorry. It's just that I've been worried sick about you, and when you didn't call me or answer your phone, I raced back here to check on you, and then I saw all those lights at Heather's house and thought the worst—"

My anger from earlier returned. "Don't even get me started on that hateful, horrible hag!"

Gilley placed an arm around me. "Tell me," he said. "Tell me what happened."

My stomach gurgled loudly. "Let me eat something first."

"There's a salad from Guiarmo's on the table in the foyer at Chez Kitty," Gil said. "Sebastian said he ordered it for you hours ago when he also said you left to retrieve a book from your bedroom."

"Ooo, the salad. That'll be perfect," I said, following him to the door. Fishing around in my pockets, I couldn't locate my phone, then I remembered it was in the bathroom at the guest house. "What time is it?"

"Quarter to six," Gil said, closing the door behind us and taking my arm to steady me.

I leaned against Gilley as we walked across the drive, grateful for both the steadying presence and his company. "Wow," I said. "I slept most of the afternoon. I must've been really tired."

"Or it could've been the chardonnay."

I eyed him sideways as we reached the guest house. "You saw that, huh?"

"The nearly empty bottle next to the tub with the wet towel draped over the edge? Yes, Cat, I saw it. I concluded that it must've been a rough lunch if it demanded most of a bottle of chard and a bubble bath."

"Rough doesn't even begin to cover it."

"Judging by the number of strobe lights over there, I bet you're right."

By now, we'd stepped inside the guest house, and I paused by the delivery bag from Guiarmo's to consider Gilley. "Strobe lights?"

He tilted his head slightly and thumbed over his shoulder. "Yeah. You know. The ambulance and police cars."

My mouth fell open. "Ambulance?! Police cars?!"

Gilley's brow furrowed. "You didn't know?"

"Of course not! What happened?"

"No clue. I was hoping you could tell me."

I raced to the window facing Heather's house and pulled back the drape. Sure enough, a series of flashing red lights flared in the dimming daylight. "Ohmigod!" I gasped. "I wonder if it was one of the guests!"

"So . . . you didn't cause that?" Gilley said.

I whirled around. "*NO!* How could you think that?"

Gilley shrugged sheepishly. "Can you blame me? You once ran over a guy's car with a bulldozer."

I waved a hand dismissively. "It wasn't like he was *in* it at the time, Gilley."

"Still," he said.

I sighed and went back to the kitchen counter, sitting down

heavily in one of the gray suede-covered chairs. "What could've happened over there?"

Gilley went into the kitchen and took down a plate from the cupboard along with a set of utensils. Dishing out my salad onto the plate, he said, "I'm wondering that too. What went on at the luncheon?"

I sighed dramatically and pulled the plate he offered close. Poking at the lettuce with my fork, I said, "I was sucker punched."

"Somebody hit you?"

"No, no. Not literally. Heather set me up."

I proceeded to tell him all about what'd happened, and Gilley stood across from me with a shocked expression on his face. "That bitch!" he said when I was done.

"Yes," I said, taking a bite of the salad. "She's as rotten as they come."

"What're you going to do?"

"I'm not sure yet. I may hire a private detective to look into her background and dig up some dirt. I'd like to expose her to the community and rub that smug smirk right off her hateful face."

"You think Heather has dirt?"

I shrugged. "Most people—especially most rich people—have dirty little secrets they don't want the general public to know."

Gil considered me thoughtfully. "Do *you* have dirty little secrets?"

"I once ran over a man's BMW with a bulldozer, Gilley. And on another occasion, I, along with my sister and her best friend, was a fugitive from the law. Both of those things aren't common knowledge, and I'd like to keep it that way, okay?"

Gilley's expression turned contrite. "Point made. But is it really worth the effort, Cat? I mean, wouldn't it be easier to ignore her and get on with your life?"

"No," I said, getting up to retrieve a water from the fridge.

"Heather Holland is a bully, my friend, and the only way to truly handle a bully is to come back swinging. If she put that amount of effort into embarrassing me, I can only imagine what she's done to others in this town. She's probably had a reign of terror going for as long as she's lived here."

"But what if it comes back to bite you in the butt, Cat?"

"I'll make sure it doesn't by finding a way to expose her without it connecting back to me."

"How're you going to do that?"

"Well . . . I don't know yet, but I'll figure it out. First, we need some dirt to work with, and then I'll worry about the details."

Gilley eyed me slyly. "Catherine Cooper, such a vengeful sly fox you are. I like it!"

"There's a reason nobody messed with me in the corporate world, my lovey," I said. "I never forgot a betrayal, and I always got even."

"You should've been a litigator," Gil said. "You'd would've made a great shark."

"You know, I considered going to law school when I was fresh out of college."

"Why didn't you?"

I shrugged. "I had a marketing idea that took off before I was twenty-three. After that, all my focus went into building an empire and raising the boys. There was never enough time for law school."

"How're you going to find a private investigator?" Gilley asked me next.

"Well, I could hire the P.I. I had following Tommy around when he was schtuping that bartender from the country club, but the man reeked of day-old onion sandwich with a healthy side of liverwurst."

Gilley made a face. "Eww."

"Yeah. It always surprised me that Tommy never smelled him coming."

Gilley chuckled. "You know, Cat, I'd be willing to snoop around a little. I could follow Heather and see what she's up to."

"You?"

"Yes. Moi."

"Can you be stealthy?"

"Can I be stealthy . . ." Gilley repeated mockingly. Crossing his legs and picking at a spot of lint on his pants he said, "I can become invisible at a moment's notice."

"Are you invisible right now? Because I can see you. In fact, I'd be hard pressed *not* to notice you, my friend."

Gilley rolled his eyes. "I cannot help it that I'm beautiful. It's the curse no one appreciates."

"Ah, yes," I said. "The beauty curse. How *do* you live with it, Gilley?"

Gil ran a finger along his hairline. "I simply put on a brave face and soldier forward."

I opened my mouth for a rebuttal, but at that moment, there was a loud pounding on the front door.

"Who could that be?" Gilley said.

I put a hand to my forehead, feeling the first pangs of a hangover headache coming on. "They need to knock more softly."

The pounding came again. It was the sort of knock you answer, holding your breath.

Gilley and I exchanged looks of concern, and we both moved to the door. He pulled it open, and on the doorstep stood a great-looking man in jeans, gray shirt, and a dark charcoal blazer. Tall, with light wavy brown hair and eyes the color of topaz, he stood with an air of confident—but cold—authority.

I felt my already nervously fluttering heart beat a little faster.

"Well, hello," Gilley said, his voice brimming with flirtatious interest. "How may I help you?"

The man eyed Gilley up and down before his gaze shifted to me. "Catherine Cooper?" he asked, all but dismissing Gil.

"Yes?" I said, a little unsure if I should admit that, given the man's super serious demeanor. "What can I do for you, sir?"

With the practiced hand of a gunslinger, the man whipped out his billfold, flipped it open, and revealed a shiny bronze badge. "Detective Shepherd from the East Hampton Police Department. I'd like to speak with you privately, if I may?"

My first thought went to the boys, and I clutched the collar of my robe to my throat. "Ohmigod! What's happened? Are my sons all right?"

Shepherd's brow flashed with confusion before he shook his head. "I'm not here about your children. I'm here about your neighbor."

I turned to look at Gilley, and he stared back with wide eyes, mouthing, *Heather!*

"What's happened?" I repeated to the detective, not knowing what to think.

He pocketed his ID and said, "I'll wait out here while you get dressed, ma'am."

My face burned with embarrassment. He'd said that like I was dressed in an unseemly way. "I took a bath," I said, offering an excuse.

He merely nodded and replied, "I'll wait here."

Needing a moment to think, I shut the door in the detective's face. Rude? Yes, but I was still a tiny bit inebriated and totally out of sorts. "That's not gonna win him over to your side," Gilley said as I leaned against the door.

"What could've happened, Gilley?"

"To Heather?"

I nodded.

Gilley shrugged. "Maybe somebody finally put her in her place?"

I bit my lip. "I had nothing to do with any sort of violence against her."

"Duh," Gil said, and he added a grin to reassure me, but his eyes were pinched with worry.

50 Victoria Laurie

I pulled the collar of my robe tighter around me. "Should I call my lawyer?"

Gilley made a face. "I'd wait before I did anything drastic, Cat. That might make you look guilty."

My eyes widened. "Guilty of what?"

Gilley shook his head, his own eyes wide. "Dunno. But with a detective out on the front step, waiting for you to change so he can talk to you, it can't be anything good."

I rubbed my throat nervously. "I didn't have anything to do with anything bad, Gilley. There were witnesses at that party. I left even before lunch was served, and I was here taking a bath and a nap for the rest of the afternoon."

"Which is all you have to tell Detective Heartthrob out there."

Taking a deep breath, I gathered my nerve and opened the door. Shepherd was still on the front porch, his arms crossed impatiently. He frowned when he saw that I remained in my silk robe.

"I live over there," I said, pointing to the main house. "I was only over here visiting with my guest."

Shepherd blinked, but he didn't say anything or stop frowning.

"I'll just go change then," I said, scurrying around him and over to my front door. After letting myself in, I didn't immediately head upstairs to change; instead, I went to the downstairs bath and searched through the medicine cabinet for something to relieve my pounding headache.

It wasn't until ten minutes later that I felt ready to face Shepherd again. Opening the front door to my home, I found him standing impatiently in the courtyard, looking a bit chilled in the early-evening air.

I realized that I'd left him outside to wait, but I'd thought Gil would've at least invited him into the guest house. Which, now that I thought of it, might suit us better for a conversation. I could have Sebastian record every word, just in case something I said was later twisted and used against me.

"Shall we?" I said, motioning back toward the guest house.

At first, Shepherd appeared confused, but then he seemed to understand, and his features next held the hint of an eye roll, but he managed to hold back. Just barely.

I went through the door first and found Gilley sitting at the table scarfing down a bag of Milano cookies. He stared at me and Shepherd as we entered, while a few crumbs tumbled down his chin and hit the kitchen table.

"Oh," he said. "Hewow."

"Hey," I replied. "I thought we could conduct the interview in here."

"Is there a reason you'd prefer to be interviewed here versus your house?" Shepherd asked, his voice laced with suspicion.

"There is."

"And that is . . . ?"

I pointed toward the ceiling. "I'd like Sebastian to record our conversation."

Shepherd's brow furrowed, and then he looked around the room until his gaze settled on Gilley. "You Sebastian?"

Gil swallowed his mouthful before answering. "Nope."

"Sebastian isn't a person," I said. "He's an AI butler."

Shepherd scratched his head. "A what now?"

"Think of Amazon's Alexa, but waaaay cooler," Gil told him.

For a demonstration I said, "Sebastian?"

"Yes, Lady Catherine?"

"Can you make it a little brighter in here?"

The four recessed lights in the living room brightened.

"Ah," Shepherd said with a nod. "And he can record our conversation?"

"He can."

The detective crossed his arms. "Why do you think it's important to record our conversation, Ms. Cooper?"

"For the same reason I suspect you'd like to record it, Detective. You don't trust me."

Shepherd's eyes narrowed, but there was the slightest twitch at the corner of his mouth. Not quite a smile, but it was at least a break from the frown. "Okay," he said, taking a seat at the kitchen table.

I sat down too, and Gilley of course stayed where he was, wearing an expression of indecision. "Um . . . should I give you two some privacy?"

"Stay," I said.

"Go," said Shepherd.

Gilley's head turned from side to side, looking to me, then to Shepherd, then back to me. "I have no idea what to do."

"Stay," I said.

"Go," said Shepherd.

"Oy," said Gil.

"I'd prefer to talk to you in private, Ms. Cooper," Shepherd said.

"And I'd prefer if Gilley stayed."

"I'd prefer to not be in the middle of this," said Gil.

I turned to Gilley and glared. "You're staying. End of story." Then I looked up slightly and said, "Sebastian, please record our conversation."

"As you wish, ma'am."

Shepherd shrugged and got out his cell phone. Placing it on the table, he tapped at it for a few seconds, and I saw a recording app come up. He hit the red button and looked at me expectantly.

So I returned the look.

"My stomach hurts," Gil said as the detective and I sat there in stony silence.

"Ms. Cooper," Shepherd began, "I'd like to know about the party at Mrs. Holland's."

"What about it?" I asked. Truthfully, I didn't feel it was a good idea to answer such an open-ended question without a lawyer present. I was worried that I'd talk myself into a trap.

"What can you tell me about it?"

"What, specifically, would you like to know about it?"

"You were there, right?"

"I was. Briefly."

"What happened when you were there?"

"What happened?"

"Yes."

"What do you mean what happened?"

"I mean, when you were there, what took place?"

"Took place?"

"Yes."

"Yes?"

Shepherd sighed and rubbed at the scruff of his neck. Turning to Gil he said, "Is she always like this?"

Gilley smirked. "No . . . sometimes she's *difficult*."

I glared at Gilley, but I wasn't really mad. I was stalling. I couldn't figure out how to get Shepherd to tell me what'd happened to Heather without having to answer his questions first, and I knew how it must look from his vantage point. I'd been angry and vocal at a gathering of women who would pledge no loyalty to me.

Shepherd turned back to me. "I'm not the enemy here."

I cocked an eyebrow. "No?"

"No. If you've done nothing to harm Mrs. Holland, then I'm your ally."

There! That was my opening, and I pounced on it. "Harm? Heather has been harmed? What's happened?"

"I'd like for you to tell me about the party," he said smoothly.

Damn him. He'd turned it back to me as deftly as a tennis pro taps at a ball just at the net. "I have no idea what this is all about or why you're suggesting she's been harmed. The last time I saw Heather, she was standing among a group of women hosting a party. I left her home even before lunch was served, so whatever she told you I did to her, I didn't."

"How do you know she told me you did something to her?" Shepherd said.

My brow furrowed. "Why else would you and your hostile attitude be here, Detective?"

Shepherd looked taken aback. "My hostile attitude?"

"Yes."

"What about my attitude seems hostile?"

"Oh, boy," Gilley mumbled.

"Well, how about that perma-frown you've worn from the moment I opened my door?"

Shepherd's brow darkened. "That's just my face."

"Really?" I said. "Well, *that's* unfortunate."

Shepherd made a sound that resembled a growl. "Can we get back to discussing Mrs. Holland?"

"That would be wonderful. I believe you were about to tell me what she's claiming I did to her."

Shepherd rubbed his face. "Jesus, lady, Heather Holland isn't *telling* me anything. And she's not telling anybody else anything either. She's permanently silenced, if you get my drift."

I felt the blood drain from my face, and I stood up abruptly. "*What?*"

Gilley jumped up too, his chair rocking violently from the move. "She's *dead?*"

Shepherd remained seated while he calmly considered the two of us, as if assessing the authenticity of our reaction. "I'd like to ask you again, Ms. Cooper. What happened today at Mrs. Holland's house? Why did you leave? What did you say? And what did you do?"

I sat back down heavily. I couldn't believe this turn of events.

It hadn't yet dawned on me how much trouble I might be in. I think I was too stunned to fully appreciate how precarious my situation truly was.

"I . . . I was invited to the luncheon by Heather. She was very specific in her invitation. She wanted me to wear black and white, which I did. Then, when I got there, I realized that I was the only invited guest wearing the same color scheme as her staff. Everyone else was wearing jewel tones. Heather did that on purpose. She wanted to humiliate me in front of her other guests, and I got angry. And I yelled at her. Then I left."

Shepherd nodded like he'd already heard the story from others. "Did you threaten her?"

"Of course not!"

It was Shepherd's turn to cock an eyebrow as he pulled out a small notebook from his blazer pocket and flipped it open. "Really?" he said to me, lifting the notebook to read from it. "You didn't say, 'Mark my words, Heather Holland, you've been messing with the wrong woman. I am done playing nice,' and then add something about leaving her a bloody mess in the end?"

Gilley let out a small gasp and put a hand to his mouth.

I ignored him and focused on Shepherd as a cold sweat broke out across my brow. "That was just talk. I was legitimately upset, so, yes, I made a public outburst. But then I came home, had a glass of wine, took a very long bath, ordered my lunch, and passed the rest of the afternoon trying to forget about the entire incident."

Shepherd tapped the table. "You came here."

"Yes."

Shepherd shifted his gaze to Gilley. "And you were here too?"

Gilley bit his lip and eyed me nervously. "Um . . . maybe?"

Shepherd narrowed his eyes. "What does that mean?"

"He wasn't here," I said for Gil.

"So no one witnessed that you were in this house for the entire rest of the day?"

I rolled my eyes. I didn't like the fact that he was pressing me on the point. It felt like I was being set up to take the fall, which I probably was. And then I thought of something. "I wasn't *entirely* alone. I had Sebastian."

"Sebastian? You mean your virtual butler?"

"Yes. Sebastian monitors my every move to ensure that the rooms I'm in are always comfortable. He ran my bath and ordered my lunch too."

Shepherd shook his head, a wry smile on his lips. "Ms. Cooper, unless your virtual butler can be deposed, I don't see how he could back up your alibi."

While Shepherd was speaking, Gilley had gotten up to retrieve his laptop. Opening it, he began to type furiously. "You don't understand, Detective," Gil said excitedly. "Sebastian has a log, and I can access it. He keeps track of Cat and anyone else in the house at all times."

"That's creepy," Shepherd said.

I glared at him. "Sebastian is *not* creepy. He takes care of me."

"If he can confirm you were here between four-thirty and six-thirty, then that's all that matters," Shepherd replied.

Gilley suddenly stopped typing and looked up triumphantly. "I've accessed the log. I'm printing it now."

Gil got up to retrieve the log, but I was starting to feel the first hint of nervousness. I hadn't been in this house from about three to six p.m. I'd been in my own home, and Sebastian wasn't there.

I looked at Gil as he crossed the room to the printer and retrieved the document. He began to read it as he came back toward us, and I knew immediately that he was seeing what I already knew.

Stopping midway back to the table he looked at me, as if uncertain about what to do.

"What's the matter?" Shepherd asked.

I focused on Shepherd. "It's true that I was home between one and six p.m., Detective. But I wasn't in this house. I was in the main house. I took a bath here, then I left to take a nap in my own bed, so Sebastian's tracking of me would've ended around two-thirty p.m., I think." I looked to Gilley to confirm, and he nodded and came back to his chair, setting the log facedown on the table.

Meanwhile, Shepherd appeared puzzled. "Can't you just grab the log from that house?"

"Sebastian isn't wired over there," I said. "He will be next week, but for now he's only here."

"So you have no alibi?"

"No," I said. "I definitely have an alibi. I was home. I haven't left my home since arriving back from Heather's party."

Shepherd nodded, and at first, I thought he believed me. But then he said, "The party where you threatened to kill her, and then she was murdered a few hours later."

"I *didn't* threaten to kill her," I said sternly.

Shepherd sat back in his chair and crossed his arms. Looking at me squarely, he said, "I have a room full of witnesses that say otherwise, Ms. Cooper."

"I was angry, and I misspoke. There wasn't anything else to that. Certainly not a threat."

"Really?" Shepherd said, unconvinced. "Leaving her a bloody mess sure sounds like a threat to me—especially when she turns up dead."

"This is ridiculous! Detective, I had nothing to do with her murder! I don't even know how it happened! I mean, how do you *know* she was murdered?"

I suspect that Shepherd had been waiting for me to say something exactly like that because his mouth quirked into a knowing smile, and he said, "She was found facedown with a large open wound to the back of her head and shards of crystal from a punch bowl all around her. We have witnesses that say the punch bowl belonged to you."

I gasped. Beside me, Gilley reached for my hand and whispered, "Molly, you in danger, girl!"

Chapter 4

The conversation with Shepherd ended abruptly after he shared the news about the punch bowl. Actually, it ended with a panicked call to my attorney, who told me to shut my mouth and not say another word until he arrived.

When I relayed the message to Shepherd, he put away his notebook, gave me a twisted smile, and said, "I'll be in touch."

With that he was gone.

And I was left shaking.

"I'd offer you some wine, but I'm not sure you'd be able to get it down," Gil said.

I'd been staring off into space when he spoke, and the sound of his voice caused me to jump. "Yeah. I think I would like a glass of water, though."

Gil was up in a flash, tending to me. I took a sip of the glass of water he offered, and I will admit, my throat was so tight, it was hard to swallow. "You're shivering," Gil said, and off he was again to fetch me an afghan.

"Thank you," I said when he laid it around my shoulders. Then I looked up at him. "Gilley? What just happened?"

Gil sat down and reached for my hand again. "Someone is using your outburst at the party to frame you for murdering Heather."

His words were like a sock to the stomach. "Who?" I asked. It came out as a hoarse whisper.

"Don't know, lovey. But I have a bad feeling that if we don't find out, you might have to think about how to accessorize prison orange."

I actually smiled. It was so absurd. "Thanks for sugarcoating it."

"I think it's best to be blunt," he said, but he grinned and squeezed my hand.

I took a deep breath and let it out slowly. It helped a tiny fraction. "My lawyer will be here soon. He'll know what to do."

Gilley sat back in his chair and furrowed his brow. "Will he, though?"

"Of course. Tony is an excellent attorney."

"I'm sure he's the best that money can buy, but is he a criminal defense attorney?"

"A . . . what? No. He handles all my real estate interests."

"Then why the hell is he coming over?"

"Because I have him on speed dial," I said sharply. Too sharply. Gilley winced.

"Sorry."

"It's okay," he said. "What I mean, Cat, is that you're going to need a criminal defense lawyer."

I started shivering again.

"Lady Catherine," Sebastian said. "I've noticed a dip in your body temperature. Shall I turn the heat up?"

I pulled the afghan around me tighter while I noted that Gilley—who definitely ran a few degrees warmer than me—had a slight sheen across his brow. "No, Sebastian, I'll be fine. Thank you."

Gilley smiled at me and tucked the afghan around my shoulders and feet; then he got up to pace the room. "Even after we find you a good defense attorney, we'll still need to work on solving this case."

I blinked. "Work on what now?"

"Cat, your attorney will defend you in court, should it come to that, which, given the evidence that Shepherd just talked about, I can't imagine why you haven't been arrested yet, but that'll probably change once they get the coroner's report."

"*Coroner's* report?"

Gilley waved his hand dismissively. "Coroner, medical examiner, whatever they're calling them these days. Anyway, the point is that I think an arrest is imminent."

I felt my chest constrict in a spasm of fear. "You do?"

"Yep. That's the way these things go. The cops always look to the most obvious suspect, and if there's enough to build a case, they rarely bother looking at any other potential suspects."

The constriction grew worse.

"The good news is that you're ridiculously wealthy, and posting bond shouldn't be a problem, but they may limit your movements, and you'll probably have to give up your passport."

I opened my mouth, trying to inhale, but only a sliver of breath came into my lungs.

Gilley continued, unaware of the panic overtaking me. "Now, I've been on a few of these investigations with M.J., so I know how to get to the bottom of a case like this. We could always hire our own private investigator, of course, but we should still cover some of the legwork ourselves. All we need are a few really good suspects to help create reasonable doubt, and hopefully that'll sway the jury enough to acquit you, but if not, at least we're not in a death-penalty state."

Darkness began to close around my vision. Sparks of light flashed in the periphery, and I felt myself falling forward. I tried to lift my arm to the table to steady myself, but I couldn't seem to manage it in time to prevent myself from falling forward onto the floor.

The pain of the hard wood against my shoulder was stunning, and I finally managed to inhale a gulp of oxygen that cleared my

vision for all of two seconds—long enough to see Gilley's terrified face hovering above me. A searing pain in my chest distorted
the image, however, and I slipped away into darkness.

I came to, still on the floor, to find myself being cradled by
Gilley and aware of a second presence in the room. "Why the
hell would you *say* that to her?" shouted a voice I recognized.

"I was just talking through what's likely to happen! I was trying to prepare her!" Gilley cried.

I blinked. It took effort, but at least I seemed to be breathing
with ease again.

"You don't say that to someone who's just been questioned by
the police, you dolt!"

Tony Bianchi—my attorney—came into view; he laid a cold
compress on my head. "Catherine?" he said when he saw me looking up at him.

"I'm sorry!" Gilley wailed.

I raised a feeble hand and laid it on Gil's arm. "It's okay," I
mumbled.

Gilley bit his lip. "Cat? Oh, Cat! Don't move. I've called an
ambulance."

"You what?" I said, trying to sit up. The world spun a little,
and I laid my head back in Gilley's lap.

"Catherine, lie still," said Tony.

"Thanks for coming," I said to him.

"Sorry I got here too late to intercept Detective Columbo," he
said, glaring at poor Gil.

"I said I was sorry!"

"Boys!" I said, making another effort to sit up, and this time
succeeding. "Stop. I'm fine."

In the background, the sound of an approaching siren made all
of us turn toward the door. "Send them away," I told Gil.

"I think it's best if they check you out," Tony said.

I pushed myself to a better seated position on the floor. "I'm fine. I am. Just a little overwhelmed by the possibilities."

Gilley sniffled, and I noticed that he'd been crying. "Cat, I'm so, so sorry!"

The siren drowned out any further chance at conversation, but right when it was at its loudest, it abruptly stopped, and three short moments later, there was a knock on the door. Tony answered it, and two paramedics entered.

"For heaven's sake," I said after Tony pointed to me and they approached. "I'm *fine!*"

"Hello, ma'am," said the first paramedic with a nod to me as she set down her black medical kit. "You know, you actually do look fine, but would you mind if we just made sure of that?" She had an easy smile, and it calmed me immediately.

I sighed. "What do I have to do?"

"Well," she said, opening her kit and reaching for a blood-pressure cuff. "How about you let us do all the work and you just sit there and relax?"

"Okay," I said on a sigh.

The two medics worked for a solid twenty minutes to determine whether or not I was worthy of transport to the hospital. In the end, the lead medic said, "Well, it looks like you've only had a panic attack. Your blood pressure is normal, and your EKG reading is also well within the normal range. I'm not a medical doctor, though, so I think it might be wise to transport you to the hospital and let them have a more thorough look."

I offered her a half-hearted smile. "I bet you say that to all your patients."

She raised her right hand. "Guilty as charged."

At the sound of the word "guilty," I flinched again but tried to hide it. "I'm fine. Really. It's just been a stressful day."

"All right," she agreed, pulling out her iPad, which had what looked like a legal document on it. "Then I'm going to ask you to sign this release form, which states that you're refusing our recommendation to be transported to the hospital."

"Catherine," Tony began, but I was already reaching for the iPad and doodling my name with my finger.

"Thank you very much for coming," I said to the medics. "I'll await your bill in the mail."

Gilley helped me to the sofa, and Tony walked the medics out. Gil fussed over me for a few extra moments, no doubt driven by guilt.

"Gil," I finally said, as he tucked, and tucked, and *tucked* the afghan around my legs and feet.

He stopped and stepped away, blushing. "Sorry. I just feel bad."

"You should," Tony snapped.

I rubbed my temples. "Can we all just please have some peace?"

"Sorry, Catherine," Tony said.

When the silence carried on a bit longer than it should've, I looked up and saw Tony fidgeting with his wedding ring. "What?" I asked him.

His hands fell to his sides. "Nothing. It's nothing. I don't want you to worry. I have a good friend, Raymond Kovac, who's an excellent defense attorney. I've just left him a voice mail."

"You've already reached out to a defense attorney on my behalf?" I asked.

Tony's face reddened ever so slightly. "I have."

"Then you think I'll need one."

He tugged at his tie. "I do."

I went back to rubbing my temples. "So, what Gilley said might happen—actually could?"

"If the synopsis he gave me about your conversation with Detective Shepherd is true—"

"It's true," Gilley said, vouching for himself.

"Then worst-case scenario, yes, it could happen. Which is why I called the best criminal defense attorney I know."

I looked up at him. "I didn't do it, Tony."

He softened and said quickly, "Of course you didn't."

That statement from someone I trusted was so heartening. "What's my next move?" I asked.

"Well," he said, gathering up his coat; he pulled a card out of his pocket and laid it on the table. "For now, you sit tight and wait for the police to come back to you for more questioning. If they come back tonight, you call me before you even answer the door, and if they arrest you, you don't say a word without either me or Ray. If they come back tomorrow, call Ray. His cell and office numbers are on the card."

After Tony left, Gilley and I sat in silence for a long time. My mind was spinning, and I couldn't seem to stop shivering. At last, Gilley called out to Sebastian to turn up the heat, and then he got up and headed into the kitchen. I heard him fussing in there for a while, but I didn't turn my head to look. I was too wrapped up in my worried mind to do much more than stare listlessly out in front of me.

"Here you go," Gil said, setting a plate of cheese and fruit in my lap.

"I'm not hungry," I told him, trying to push the plate away.

He pushed it back into my lap. "Yes, I know you're not hungry, but you've had a terrible day, and you need to eat something before I hustle you off to bed."

I looked up at him. "What time is it, anyway?"

"It's after nine."

"Whoa," I said. "I had no idea it was so late."

"Eat," he insisted.

I sighed and picked up a piece of melon. Taking a small nibble, I had to admit that the fruit was at least sweet and easy to swallow. "Thank you," I said after a few more bites.

"You're welcome, sugar," he said, before trotting off toward the bedrooms.

Alone with my spinning mind, I ate the plate of fruit and cheese and was surprised to see that I actually felt much better for it. I stopped shivering, and my headache went away.

Gilley finally returned to the living room, wearing a set of silk pajamas and matching robe. "You're probably as tired as I am," I said, stifling a yawn. "I should head on home and let you get some sleep."

"You're not going anywhere," he said.

"What do you mean I'm not going anywhere?"

Gilley stretched out his hand toward me. "Come," he commanded.

I took his hand, and he led me to the master bedroom. The bed looked freshly made with clean sheets, and there was a small chocolate bar on the pillow. A glass of water sat on the nightstand, and a book I'd left here before moving to the main house was on the nightstand. "You're in here tonight, Cat," Gilley said. "I'm taking the spare bedroom."

"What? Why?"

Gil eyed me seriously. "Because someone out there is using you to get away with murder, and until he or she is caught, I'm not letting you out of my sight."

I felt woozy all over again, and my mouth went dry. "Oh," I managed. I hadn't even considered that I might be in any kind of danger.

Gilley leaned in and hugged me tight. "Try not to worry," he said as he let go and left the room.

"Too late," I whispered.

I found Gilley up and busy in the kitchen early the next morning. "Hey," I said in greeting, adding a yawn.

He turned away from the stove to look me up and down. "Did you get *any* sleep?"

I sat heavily in the chair at the table and rested my chin on my hand. "Maybe an hour or two, but mostly I just tossed and turned all night."

"Oh, honey," he said. "We'll figure this out."

"How?" I asked. "I mean, how *exactly* are we going to figure this out, Gilley?"

He looked a bit lost for a second and turned back toward the stove. "I'm making crêpes," he said. "With Nutella. Everything tastes better with Nutella, and it'll be the perfect food to fuel us while we come up with a plan."

"I don't know that I can eat anything."

Gil flipped a crêpe onto a plate and hustled some Nutella into the center. I watched as he carefully rolled the crêpe and opened the oven door, where he added it to a plateful of identical siblings. "Coffee?" he asked after a bit.

I yawned. "Yes, please."

Gil came to the table carrying a French press and two mugs. He set the press in front of me. "You can work the plunger. Pour me a cup too, would you?"

I poured both of us a cup of steaming hot coffee, and it smelled heavenly.

"Is there cream?"

Gilley loaded the last crêpe onto the stack from the oven and brought the plate to the table, along with a small pitcher of cream. He then returned to the counter for powdered sugar and a platter of bacon.

After setting everything down, he settled into a chair and took up the empty plate in front of me. Loading it with three crêpes, he set the plate back down, then sprinkled the crêpes with powdered sugar and used a pair of tongs to dish out two pieces of bacon.

"This looks entirely too decadent," I said.

"Which is fair. It's the least you deserve, sugar."

My eyes misted. Gilley didn't always say the right thing . . . okay, he almost never said the right thing, but sometimes he'd come up with the exact perfect thing, said in the exact perfect tone at the exact perfect moment, and I rather loved that about him. "Thank you," I said, reaching for his hand and squeezing it.

"You're going to be okay," he told me, and I was further heart-ened that he looked me straight in the eyes as he spoke.

I nodded, wanting to reply, but I didn't trust that I could, so I let go of Gil's hand and reached for my fork. The least I could do was nibble a little at his delicious-looking breakfast.

As it turned out, I did more than nibble. The crèpes were so delicious that I ate all three and most of the bacon to boot. "That was heaven," I said, sitting back in my chair with a satisfied sigh. "Crèpes make everything better."

"I thought Nutella made everything better."

"Pardon me," Gilley said, laying a hand to his chest. "What I meant to say was, Nutella crèpes make everything perfect."

I poured more of the coffee into each of our cups. It was only lukewarm by now, but I didn't care. I loved the silky-smooth fla-vor of it. "I feel like I should be doing something."

"We still have to shop for the perfect outfit for your hot date," Gil suggested.

A jolt went through me, and I sat up straight. "Ohmigod! I for-got all about Maks!"

"Aw, sugar, don't worry. We've got the whole day to shop."

"No, no," I said. "I can't go now, Gilley."

"Okay. We'll go after lunch."

I shook my head, frustrated and flustered at the same time. "No, what I mean is, I can't possibly go out with Maks now."

"Why not?"

"Are you kidding?"

Gilley appeared confused. "I never kid about a hot man. Why can't you go out with him?"

"Because I'm a suspect!" I shouted. I hadn't meant to. The stress of the situation and the lack of sleep were getting to me.

Gilley's eyes widened, but he recovered quickly. I think he understood. "Cat," he said reasonably, "right now, the police have only a small piece of the puzzle that includes you. At most, you're a person of interest, among probably at least a few others. I'm positive they'll figure out very quickly that you had nothing to do with Heather's murder."

"That's not what you said last night."

Gilley dipped his chin and put a hand to his heart. "I misspoke. I'm sorry that I frightened you. I think I was just freaked out."

"Imagine how I feel."

"Actually, I can."

And then I remembered Gilley telling me the story of how he'd once been accused of murder, and that made me soften a bit toward him. "I'm sorry," I said.

"Think nothing of it. But you *are* going out on that date. It'll be the perfect distraction."

"You got that almost right. I'm going to be far too distracted to have any fun. Or to be any fun."

"I doubt that. Now, no more arguing the point. You're going on the date, and we are going to find you the perfect outfit right after you scoot home and change into something fabulous enough for Bloomingdale's!"

Many hours later, Gilley and I were in my bedroom, surrounded by shopping bags and tissue paper. "Black pumps or red?" I asked, standing in front of the mirror with a skeptical eye toward the perfect shoes and handbag to go with the absolutely gorgeous Sachin & Babi black A-line dress adorned with bursts of red poppies placed almost randomly about the skirt and bodice.

"Wear the Louboutins," Gil suggested. "That way you'll cover both colors without looking like you're trying too hard."

I smiled at him while I headed to the closet. "You're so right." Once there, I grabbed the black pumps with the distinctive red sole along with three choices for a handbag. Gilley immediately pointed to the clutch in my left hand. "That one."

I tossed the other two on the bed, slipped on the pumps, and considered my reflection. "Well?" I said to Gilley as I saw him also looking over my shoulder.

"Honey, if gorgeous were currency, you'd be *rich!*"

I giggled. "I'm already rich."

"Which makes you even *more* gorgeous!"

I rolled my eyes as Gilley chuckled, but he knew I was pleased by the compliment. Turning my wrist to catch the time, I said, "Ooo! He should be here any min—"

The sound of the doorbell cut me off.

"He's here!" Gilley said, dashing out of the room.

"Gilley!" I called, but there was no stopping him.

With a groan, I reached for my wool coat and hurried after him.

By the time I reached the stairs, Gilley was already opening the door. "Well!" he said almost breathlessly. "Hello there, handsome. Those for me?"

I had to descend a few stairs before I could see Maks in the doorway, holding a small bouquet of white roses in his hand and a completely confused look on his face. "Uh . . . er . . . I believe I might have the wrong address," he said, reaching into his pocket to pull out his phone.

I descended the stairs a little faster. "No, you've arrived at the correct address, Maks. My friend Gilley is a bit too mischievous for his own good."

"I was just having a little fun," Gil said, winking at me in that way that suggested he approved.

When I finally stood in front of Maks, I could understand why. Not only was the man even more sexy than he'd been the day before, but he smelled even more wonderful. "Oh, my, what *is* that scent?" I asked, taking in a whiff of the citrus mixed with a hint of musk that subtly enveloped him.

Maks smiled sweetly at me. "It's called Pure White by Creed. I purchased it in Toronto. I wear it only on the most special occasions."

"It's very nice," I said, feeling a teensy bit flushed.

"Speaking of nice, you, Catherine, are breathtaking."

A full blush bloomed across my face. I did a small curtsy, and Maks chuckled.

"So, where y'all goin'?" Gilley asked, letting the full scope of his southern accent out to play.

"Pierre's," Maks said. "I've reserved the upstairs just for us. It's quite cozy."

My eyes widened, and I knew that Gilley was also surprised. Pierre's was basically *the* place to see and be seen in the Hamptons. And I'd been to the lounge upstairs before. It was indeed lovely, but it was also almost always jam-packed. I wondered how Maks had ever convinced Pierre to let him reserve it exclusively for us. "That sounds perfect," I said, taking Maks's arm when he offered it. Looking over my shoulder as we left the house, I said, "Bye, Gil. Don't wait up."

"Bye, Cat. I won't. You two have a good time."

Stepping out onto the drive, I noticed a large, burly-looking character standing next to a gorgeous silver Rolls-Royce. Internally, I was very impressed. Outwardly, I tried to keep calm and act like this sort of seriously hot date happened to me every weekend. "Hello," I said to the man, who bowed formally to me before reaching to open the door to the back seat. "Ma'am," he said, with another bow.

"This is Frederick," Maks explained. "My driver."

"Lovely to meet you, Frederick."

I got into the car, and Maks came around to the other side. Immediately after getting in, he said, "May I offer you some champagne?"

It was then that I noticed the ice bucket set neatly near Maks's feet and the bottle of Dom chilling in the bucket.

"Yes, please," I said. I'm not a big drinker, but I do love a good glass of champagne.

Maks poured me a glass and handed it over. I took a small sip and shivered with delight. It was divine. "Sipping champagne always makes me feel like I should be celebrating something."

"Aren't we?" Maks said, clinking his glass to mine.

"Celebrating?" I asked. "What?"

"Well, I'm not sure if you're aware, but I've recently acquired the perfect space for my local office here in the Hamptons. And the landlord is gorgeous."

I felt a little breathless and took another sip to cover for it. My God, this man was charming. And sexy. And he smelled amazing.

It all made me feel a little less wicked about shaving above the knee.

"Speaking of office space, I received your e-mail with the scanned application, and everything looks in order. I should have the lease agreement ready for you to sign on Monday morning."

"Excellent," Maks said, his rich voice reverberating through my senses like a warm breeze on a cool day. "I'd tell you to e-mail it to me, but I'd rather come by your office and sign it in person."

"I'll be there by nine." And then I thought better of that. "No, wait, I have a client at nine. Best make it any time after ten."

"Done," Maks said with a clink to my glass. "I hope your other client isn't anyone interested in renting my office space."

"Oh, no. It's not a potential tenant. It's a client from my other business."

"What other business?" he asked, and I could see that he was genuinely curious.

"I'm a life coach, and she's a client."

Maks seemed surprised. "A life coach, really? That's fascinating. How did that become your profession?"

"Well," I said, "it's been a pretty circuitous route. I founded a marketing and brand-management company when I was in my early twenties that ultimately grew into a very successful business. It was headquartered in Boston, but I also had branch offices in D. C., L.A., and Austin, and about five hundred employees nationwide. But when the right offer came along, I decided to sell the firm and take up the next chapter in my life."

"I'm surprised you didn't start another company," Maks said.

"I thought about it. And I also thought about consulting, but I really wanted a break from the corporate world. I wanted to dig into life, you know? And since I've always been good at giving advice to people—something that runs in my family, actually—I decided to focus on the personal touch by offering my wisdom to real people struggling with real-life issues."

Maks nodded, and in his expression I thought I detected a hint of approval. "You must have a packed schedule," he said. "I would think everyone would want advice from you."

I felt that blush touch my cheeks again, and for the first time, I looked away from Maks and fidgeted with my skirt. "Not really. At least, my schedule isn't exactly packed yet, but I'm very new at this. Still, I have a feeling that it'll happen. It'll just take some time."

"I have no doubt you'll be very successful, Catherine," Maks said sweetly.

I looked back up at him, grateful for that. "Thank you."

"Sir," said Frederick. "Sorry to interrupt, but I wanted to make you aware that we have a situation on our hands."

I studied the back of Frederick's head. *Situation?* I thought. *What could that be about?*

Maks leaned forward and said, "What is it, Frederick?"

"The car behind us, sir. It's been following us turn for turn since we left the house."

Maks and I both turned to look out the back window. All we could see was a pair of headlights about three car lengths behind.

"Do you know who's back there?" Maks asked his driver.

"No sir. It's a black sedan. That's all I've been able to see."

"Well, that's odd," I said.

"Are you quite positive they're following us? And perhaps not merely going in the same direction, Frederick?"

"Quite positive, sir. I've already made two turns away from Pierre's just to see if they would continue on, and they've stuck to us like glue."

I turned to Maks. "Should we be concerned? I mean, what if they're drug dealers or something, and they want to take your car?"

The corner of Maks's mouth quirked. "I don't think we have to worry about drug dealers, stealing this car, Catherine, but we should take care until we reach the restaurant. Frederick, how much farther?"

"Just a mile, sir. Straight down this road, and there's enough traffic that I don't think we're in danger."

"Should we call the police?" I asked.

"We could, but what would we tell them?" Maks said. "No, I think it's best to continue on to Pierre's and keep to an area with a lot of people. Besides, it may simply be a case of curiosity. This car is a rarity, even for the Hamptons."

I sat back in my seat and tried to breathe a little easier. It probably was exactly that. Just some curious car enthusiast who wanted a better look at the Rolls.

In short order, we arrived at Pierre's, and I was relieved to see it crowded. Frederick pulled forward just past the valet, parked, and exited the car quickly, his hand noticeably reaching inside his blazer to his waistband.

It was a move that reminded me of some of the crime shows I've seen, where the cop takes up a defensive posture and places his hand on his weapon.

And that thought made me very nervous indeed.

"Should we get out?" I whispered.

Maks pasted a calm smile on his lips, but there was a hint of concern in his eyes. "Sit tight just for a moment," he said. "Frederick will make sure we're secure."

I watched through the windows as the driver moved to the trunk and looked toward the road. He seemed to be following the progress of a car as it passed the restaurant, and he waited a few extra beats before opening up Maks's door for him. "They've driven past," he said.

"Excellent," Maks said, reaching for my hand to help me out of the car.

I had to scoot over a bit, but I managed, and the second I exited, I realized how close Frederick was standing to us. It was a distinctly protective move, as if he was using his great bulk to shield us.

"Shall we move along inside?" Maks asked me casually.

"Yes, please." I wanted that very much.

We headed inside, and almost immediately upon entering, I had a delightful moment when I nearly ran into Kendra Tillerman—one of the women from Heather's party who had given me the cold shoulder on numerous occasions. She seemed *quite* taken aback by my appearance, but that was nothing compared to the look on her face when she spotted the man holding my hand. And she held that look even as her head swiveled from her husband—who closely resembled Severus Snape in both facial features and hairstyle—and then back to the gorgeous Mr. Grinkov.

I wanted to take a picture of her face, frame it, and mount it on my wall, but instead I sighed happily, tilted my nose in the air, and walked right on past her.

As we approached the stairs leading up to our private area, Maks leaned in and said, "Did you know that woman?"

I smiled wickedly. "The one with the big, round, ogling eyes and the greasy-looking husband?"

Maks smiled too. "Yes. That's her."

"Nope. No idea who she was."

Maks turned to look over his shoulder. "She seems to know you."

"Why? What is she saying?"

"I don't know, but she's pointing at us and talking to the people around her."

I sighed happily and stopped at the foot of a man, wearing a white coat, black vest, and matching tie who appeared to be guarding the stairs. "Maybe she's jealous," I said to Maks. "I mean, look who I'm with and look who she's with."

"Hello," said the waiter. "I'm sorry, folks, but the upstairs is reserved for a private party tonight."

"We're the party," Maks said, extending his credit card to the young gentleman.

The waiter read the name on the card, nodded courteously, then stepped to the side and waved us upstairs. "After you, Mr. Grinkov. Ma'am."

Maks once again offered me the crook of his arm, which I was grateful for, because of the rather tall heel on my pumps, and we headed up. The stairs were lit with small votive candles on either side of a deep burgundy runner, and I marveled at the extra touch of romance at our expense.

When we crested the landing, I was delighted to see it lit mostly with candles and decorated with overstuffed white couches, off-yellow side chairs, oriental rugs, and dark walnut side tables. On almost every available surface there was a small vase with three perfect white roses. A table for two had been set in the center of the space. It was covered in an embroidered tablecloth, gold-rimmed crèpe-colored china, and what appeared to be sterling-silver flatware. The centerpiece was a gorgeous flower arrangement of more white roses and greenery.

I turned to Maks and shook my head. "You realize you've set the bar ridiculously high, don't you?"

"What do you mean?"

"Well, this is the date to which I'll compare every other date I ever have. You've ruined it for any future man who may want to take me out to dinner."

Maks's eyes flashed with something unexpected—I couldn't say exactly what, but in a moment that flash was replaced with something playful and perhaps . . . smoldering. He reached for my waist and pulled me to him, and at first, I thought he meant to kiss me, but then I realized he had grabbed my left hand and was holding it high. "Catherine," he said as his hips (and, in turn, mine) started to sway in rhythm to the smooth jazz filling the room. "I haven't even *begun* to ruin you."

I let out a breath and chuckled. "Do you even *get* how sexy you are?"

He shrugged one shoulder. "I have my moments."

We danced in a small circle in front of the large picture window for a few moments, saying nothing but simply looking at each other. And I really liked looking at Maks—his square, masculine features, the obvious care he took with his appearance, the firm muscles of his bent arm causing his blazer to ripple, and, of course, that glorious aftershave. It was all a little intoxicating.

"Would you like a cocktail?" he finally asked.

"I would," I said, but it came out a bit strained. I cleared my throat. "Sorry. Yes. A cocktail would be perfect."

Maks danced me expertly over to the bar, where the same waiter who'd greeted us at the stairs stood sentinel.

"What's your name?" Maks asked the waiter.

"Jacob, sir. What may I prepare for you this evening?"

"Jacob, the lady will have . . . ," Maks paused to give me a questioning look.

"I'd love one of your lavender martinis," I said, remembering the drink I'd had here a few weeks before.

Maks considered me curiously. "That's an interesting choice."

"If you're nice to me, I'll let you try a sip," I said coyly.

He pulled me a little tighter to him, his eyes casting that same smoldering glow. "I'll be nothing but nice to you, Catherine." To Jacob he said, "Vodka. Neat."

"Yes, sir."

Jacob moved behind the bar, and Maks and I continued to dance cheek to cheek around the room. It was silly, and fun, and romantic, and I thought that if the rest of the evening was anything like this, then I'd never ever want it to end.

Maks's blazer made a small vibration against my abdomen, and I said, "I think your phone is buzzing."

"Let it buzz," he said. "I'm presently occupied."

I sighed happily and closed my eyes as we continued our sashay around the room.

"Catherine Cooper?" someone said loudly from the stairwell.

Startled, I pulled back from Maks and peered over toward the stairs. Seeing who'd called my name caused me to abruptly stiffen, and then I felt all the blood drain from my face.

Detective Shepherd stood at the landing, accompanied by two uniformed officers.

"Oh, no . . . ," I whispered.

Maks was looking too, and I saw him turn toward the police approaching us, then look sharply toward the window. Reflexively, he tightened his hold on my waist and my hand, and my gaze pivoted to the window as well.

Below, I could see Frederick, leaning up against the Rolls-Royce, his hands clearly cuffed behind him, while yet another uniformed officer was making his way through the driver's pockets.

On the hood of the Rolls was a gun, and I had two immediate thoughts. One: what the hell was Maks into that his driver needed to carry a gun, and two: if the police wanted Maks, and/or his driver, then why had they called my name?

My answer came almost immediately when Shepherd reached our side and took me by the arm. "Come with me please," he said.

Maks moved as if to block Shepherd, but an officer stepped right up to Maks and physically pushed him back. For an incredibly tense moment, it looked like things were going to escalate, and in a panic, I said, "Maks! Don't. Please."

Maks's gaze swiveled to me, his expression cold and unreadable, but I could still feel the tension wafting off of him.

Meanwhile, Shepherd had me spinning around and was pulling my arms behind my back. "What's happening?" I said desperately.

"Catherine Cooper, you are under arrest for the murder of Heather Holland. You have the right to remain silent. Anything you say can and will be used against you in a court of law. You have the right to an attorney . . ."

Shepherd's voice droned on with the Miranda rights ringing in my ears. I closed my eyes when I felt the cold steel of handcuffs click shut tightly against my wrists. I was then marched forward, with Shepherd still speaking loudly, and we made our way down the stairs.

Somehow, I managed not to trip, but that might have been because I was staring so hard at the ground as the shame and humiliation of the moment rose up to meet me head on.

I felt like I might faint again, so I simply focused on taking each step carefully and inhaling and exhaling deeply.

At last we reached the ground floor, and Shepherd finished the last words of the Miranda speech. When he stopped speaking, I realized the entire restaurant was so quiet you could hear a pin drop.

I happened to glance up only once and was immediately horrified to realize that every single person in attendance was staring at us with mouths agape and wide eyes.

Well, all except for one woman. Kendra sat at a table nearby, and she was smirking for all she was worth. And then, to add to the humiliation, Kendra began to clap. It was one of those slow, deliberate claps, but other than my heels on the floor, it was the only other sound in the restaurant.

I hung my head to hide the tears that had formed and begun to leak down my cheeks, while Shepherd marched me out the door.

Chapter 5

I was processed through the East Hampton police station, which is housed in a larger building than you would expect.

For the record, there is no way to prepare for a mug shot. If you're ever unlucky enough to pose for one, you'll want to fix your hair and wipe the mascara smudged on your cheeks, but there's no mirror and no sympathy from the officer behind the camera. As he told me gruffly, "It's not a glamour photo, lady."

I was then given a gray cotton top and matching bottoms—they reminded me of scrubs—and my personal belongings were taken and cataloged, then shoved into a large, clear plastic bag. I asked them to be careful with my new dress, but truly, I knew that even if they hung it inside a garment bag, I'd likely never wear it again. It would always be the dress I was wearing at my most humiliating moment.

After I changed, I was placed in a room and handcuffed to a table. That was uncomfortable for several reasons, but the worst was that I had to keep bending my torso forward to wipe away my tears, which brought me far too close to the stained and dirty tabletop. And no matter how hard I tried, I couldn't seem to stop crying.

How did I get here? I wondered. How had I gone from the pinnacle of success, ripped from the most romantic night of my life, to wearing an ugly, gray prisoner's uniform in a windowless room, handcuffed to a dirty table?

I stared at my hands and kept thinking back to that moment when I'd yelled at Heather. How good it'd felt in that moment to rip her a new one. How righteous I'd been, and how determined to get even.

I had a few moments then to actually consider if I was capable of murder, and it was a thought I felt I *had* to entertain, because if someone asked me if I had killed her, I needed to be sincere in my reply, or they might misinterpret my answer for a lie.

In the end, I decided that I couldn't murder Heather. I couldn't murder anyone. Save for defending my sons, I knew I wasn't capable of that level of violence.

And then I had another, horrifying thought.

"The boys!" I whispered. "Oh, God!" And the tears came again in earnest. What would they think of me? What would they believe? Would they visit me, even if I were wrongly convicted? "They will!" I told myself, but still there was a tiny trickle of doubt in the pit of my stomach that bothered me greatly.

My sons love me, but they'd also been through so much with the divorce and my constant legal battles with their father. This could be the straw that broke the camel's back for them.

My thoughts continued down these same, terrible paths for what felt like an eternity, until the door opened and Shepherd appeared, looking smug.

Well, at least he looked smug until he got an eyeful of me, and then, for a moment, I swear he looked almost . . . guilty.

Pulling at his tie, he came over and sat down across from me. "Something you want to tell me, Catherine?"

"Yes," I whispered.

Shepherd leaned in. "What's that?"

I lowered my chin and mumbled something unintelligible.

Shepherd leaned in further. "What's that?" he asked.

I mumbled again, making a show of wiping at my cheeks with my cuffed hands.

"I didn't catch that," he said, leaning forward a little more.

Finally, I looked up at him, and in as loud a voice as I could muster, I yelled, "*Lawyer!*"

Shepherd jerked and pivoted back in his chair, crossing his arms and glaring hard at me. He wasn't happy that I'd suckered him in so I could yell in his ear.

"I. Want. My. *Lawyer!*" I yelled again, my despair suddenly replaced by a deep ember of fury.

Shepherd's flinty stare was ice-cold. Then, with a sneer, he reached into his blazer and pulled out my cell phone. Sliding it over to me, he said, "I'll give you ten minutes. Then I'm taking back your phone."

As he was getting up to walk out, I protested. "Hey! You've got to un-cuff me so I can use it!" I wouldn't be able to hold it up to my ear with my wrists handcuffed to the table.

"Use the speaker function," he said, without even bothering to look back.

And then he was gone, and I was left alone to shake with fury and frustration.

It took me a minute or two to collect myself. Finally, I pulled the phone close and squinted at the screen. I was surprised to see that it was nearly eleven o'clock. Maks had picked me up at seven-thirty, which meant I'd probably been arrested at Pierre's at around eight-thirty, which *then meant* that I'd been throwing myself a pity party for a solid two hours.

"Which is an hour and fifteen minutes too long, Catherine," I said to myself. My personal opinion is that no pity party should ever last longer than a quarter of an hour. It was time to pull myself together and solve the problem. "But where do I even start?"

Closing my eyes, I tried to remember the name of the referral that my attorney had given me. "What did Tony say his name was?" I muttered. "Ray? Or maybe Ron something?"

I couldn't remember. But then I did remember that Gilley was currently at home in my guest house, and Tony had left the card of the defense attorney on the table. I was positive it was still there.

I clicked on Gilley's number in my favorites and heard it ring loudly from the speaker function. "Come on, Gil," I said impatiently.

The call slid to voice mail. "Dammit!" I swore. "Dammit, dammit, *dammit!*"

My sister is well known for her sailor mouth, while I'm much more circumspect, given the fact that I'm a mother and former corporate figurehead, but tough times called for tough talk, and I gave myself a pass on the salty lingo.

I tried the number again, and my knee bounced with anticipation as the phone rang another four times.

Then it slid to voice mail. After the tone, I said, "Gilley! It's Cat. I need help. I've been arrested! The police think I murdered Heather, and they're holding me at the East Hampton police station. I need you to call that attorney that Tony recommended. His card should be on the table, okay? I need you to do that right away, Gil. I know it's late, but I need him to come down here—"

The beep of Gilley's voice mail cut me off, and the call hung up. I stared at the screen for a long time, willing it to ring. Or *bing* with an incoming text. Something to let me know I'd been heard.

In desperation, I called Tony's cell, but it also went to voice mail. Still, I left him a message and kept my fingers crossed that somebody out there would hear my plea. I didn't want to spend the night in jail, which is exactly where I knew I was headed.

My eyes welled with tears again as I realized that ten minutes had already passed. Shepherd would be coming in at any moment.

But the minutes continued to tick by, and no one came in to retrieve my cell or to cart me off to jail.

I tried Gilley again—still no answer. Then Tony—and couldn't get him on the line either. And then I wondered if I should call my sister.

Or better yet, my brother-in-law.

Dutch, Abby's husband, is an FBI agent. He and I aren't necessarily close . . . I've heard that he finds me a little overwhelming, and I find him . . . a little dull. I mean, he's definitely a beautiful man, yes, on the inside but especially on the outside, and he takes care of my sister better than anyone else ever could, but as far as personality goes, he's a little too vanilla for me.

Still, Dutch had connections, and I wondered if a call to him via my sister would yield me a little latitude.

But that was going to be a tough call to make.

I'd also heard that there was a betting pool going around Dutch's bureau as to when I'd get arrested. I had always found that notion hilarious until about three hours ago. Now it just made me want to cry.

And what would Abby say about all this? My guess was that she'd either be judgmental or sympathetic, and if she started out as judgmental, I'd remind her that she'd been arrested more times than I had at this point.

Also, I reasoned, her intuition could prove invaluable to me right now.

My finger hovered over her name in my list of favorites. I couldn't really tell you what my hesitancy was; maybe it had to do with being the older sibling and always being the one never to cause trouble but instead always being able to solve it. Abby was the troublemaker in the family, and I'd spent nearly forty years sitting on my high horse about it.

I looked around the bleak little room, noticing a camera up in the corner of the ceiling and wondering how many police were gathered round a monitor, laughing at my expense.

I offered the camera the finger, and then used the same middle digit to tap on Abby's name in my phone.

To my immense relief, she picked up on the third ring. "Cat?" she said loudly. There seemed to be a lot of noise in the background.

"Abby!" I sang, overjoyed to hear her voice.

"What're you doing calling me so late?"

"Well," I began, "it's an interesting stor—"

"Listen," she interrupted sharply, "Cat, I can't really talk right now. I'm in the middle of something."

For a second, I was taken aback. How could my own sister be so dismissive? "I wouldn't have called if it weren't an emer—"

Three loud pops cut me off. They sounded like gunfire. "Holy shit! Cat, I gotta go, okay? Call me tomorrow, and we'll talk."

"Wait! Abby! Was that a gun?"

The phone beeped, and all sound on her end of the line went dead.

"Abby?" I said desperately, my voice choking with emotion. "Don't go . . ." I hit on her phone number again, and the call went immediately to voice mail. "Why?!" I cried. I tried her one last time, but just as her voice announced that I'd reached her voice mail, the door to the room abruptly opened and Shepherd came in, followed by another man in a charcoal suit and burgundy tie.

At first, I thought he might also be a detective, but then I got a better look at him and knew he wasn't.

For starters, his suit was perfectly tailored. Exquisitely so. The tie was definitely top of the line as well, and he wore a solid-gold Rolex and what I suspected were Movado cufflinks. His shoes were Italian leather, and he carried a briefcase that was likely also Italian leather.

He had dark skin, a bald head, and the most gorgeous almond-brown eyes. I found him quite striking.

And maybe a little intimidating too.

"Ms. Cooper?" he said softly.

"Yes?" I said, my voice cracking.

"I'm Marcus Brown. Your attorney."

I blinked. I was fairly certain that Tony had offered me a different name. Then again, I realized that the man in front of me—though a stranger—was still willing to help me at nearly midnight on a Friday, and no way was I in any position to turn that down. "Thank you so much for coming at such a late hour," I said, my lower lip quivering with the emotional relief of the moment.

"Least I could do," he said with a warm smile.

That warmth vanished, but the smile remained when he turned to Shepherd. "Has she eaten?" he asked bluntly.

"Has she eaten?" Shepherd repeated. "What do we look like, a bed and breakfast, Counselor?"

"You arrested her before she'd had a chance to have dinner, didn't you?" Marcus replied calmly.

"How should I know?"

"I have it on authority that it was prior to her meal being served. She may be your ward, Detective, but she still has rights. Bring her a sandwich and something cold to drink."

Shepherd stood there, looking stunned. He opened his mouth to reply, but Marcus cut him off.

"I'll need some time with my client, Detective," he said, turning away from Shepherd dismissively to walk over and sit across from me.

I watched with wide, greedy eyes as Shepherd stood there in the doorway as if he didn't quite know what to do.

"That'll be all, Detective," Marcus said, the soft manner of his voice disappearing for a deep, resonating baritone.

Shepherd's eyes narrowed, and his lips pressed tightly together, but he still stepped out into the hallway and slammed the door shut.

After he'd gone, Marcus seemed to notice my cuffed hands. "How long have you been like that?"

I held my hands up feebly. "Since they put me in here. Probably a couple of hours."

Marcus's own eyes narrowed, and he pushed back from the seat with an "Excuse me for one moment."

He left the room but was back in less than a minute with a uniformed officer. "Turn your wrists up, please," the officer said.

I did, and he produced a key. I wanted to cry when the handcuffs clicked open and dropped loudly to the tabletop. "Thank you," I said to both of them.

The officer offered me the hint of a smile and left the room.

"Better?" said Marcus.

"Yes," I said. "Much."

"Good," he said. "Let's get started, shall we?"

As Marcus settled his briefcase onto the table and worked the latches to open it, I reached over and touched his wrist to get his attention. "Can I ask you something?"

"Of course," he said, pulling out a yellow legal pad and setting it in front of him.

"I don't mean to be rude with this question, but I am actually wondering . . . who are you?"

There was a twinkle in Marcus's eyes as he answered me. "I'm your attorney, Ms. Cooper."

I bit my lip. "So you say, but, Mr. Brown, I didn't call you, and I have no idea who did."

"I was retained by someone who is looking out for you, Catherine," he said gently.

His soft tone and his confidence gave me such courage. Still, he was a puzzle I couldn't quite put together. "Did Gilley call you?" I pressed.

Marcus studied me for a long moment. It didn't feel like he was trying to stare me down, quite the contrary. It felt more like he was trying to figure out how best to put me at ease. "I've been retained by someone who cares about you, ma'am. That's all you need to know for the moment. Now, why don't you tell me what this is all about, in your own words, and please start from the beginning."

What felt like a very, very long time later, interrupted only by the scarfing down of a sandwich and cola that Shepherd had sent in, I finished telling my story, and Marcus finished asking me a plethora of questions, going over, and over, and over the events of two days before at least a dozen times, until I felt I'd be hearing my own voice reciting the same story in my dreams.

At last, Marcus said, "All right. We're ready. I'm going to call for Shepherd, and he's going to ask you lots of questions. At the end of every question, I want you to turn to me, and if I nod, then you may answer that question. Under no circumstances should you answer a question before checking with me. Is that clear?"

"Yes," I said wearily.

"Excellent," Marcus said.

He got up and went to the door. Opening it, he spoke to the same uniformed officer outside who'd unlocked my handcuffs and brought me the sandwich, and then he came back to sit next to me rather than across from me.

"How was your sandwich?" he asked.

"It was fine," I said. Actually, it'd tasted like cardboard, but for some reason I'd found myself famished when it was placed in front of me.

"Good," Marcus said. Then he studied me again critically. "You must be tired."

"Exhausted, actually."

"I bet. It's after midnight, so hopefully Shepherd will be tired too. It's better when the guy asking questions isn't as sharp as he could be."

I rubbed my eyes. They were dry and gritty. "I never would've thought such a lovely evening was going to turn out to be one of the worst nights of my life."

"I heard that Shepherd arrested you at Pierre's in front of the dinner crowd."

"It was humiliating." For the first time I thought of Maks, and what he must be thinking. "Marcus?"

"Yes, Catherine?"

I stared at the table, unable to meet his eyes as I asked my next question. "I was out to dinner with a genuinely beautiful man at the time that Shepherd decided to ruin my evening. Could I trouble you to contact him and explain all this? And maybe apologize on my behalf for the ruined night out?"

"You don't want to call him yourself?"

I bit my lip. It was hard to even think of ever having the courage to reach out to Maks again. He'd no doubt never want to see or hear another word from me, but for some reason, I felt I owed him an apology. "No," I whispered. "I don't think I'm brave enough. And I don't think that he'd really care to be contacted by me, either."

Marcus didn't say anything, so I looked up, and his expression was unreadable. I was about to ask him what he thought when Shepherd entered the room, carrying his own legal pad.

"Let's get this party started, shall we?" he said.

I glared at him, loathing the man with a passion.

He looked down at his notes for a moment, then up at me. "Who were you out with tonight, Catherine?"

I turned to Marcus and was surprised to find his brow furrowed as he stared at Shepherd.

"How is that relevant to the charges you've filed against my client, Detective?"

"Your client has been arrested for murder, Counselor. *Everything* associated with her is relevant at this point in the investigation."

Marcus's jaw clenched and unclenched, but finally, and without taking his steely glare off Shepherd, he nodded for me to answer.

I tugged at the gray scrub top I'd been given, uncomfortable with how emotional I felt at the mention of Maks and how much I was afraid my voice would break as I spoke about him. I decided to keep it as simple and short as possible. "He's a business associate."

Shepherd cocked an eyebrow. "A business associate?"

"Yes."

Shepherd scratched his chin, which was clearly showing a five o'clock shadow. "You two seemed pretty chummy for business associates."

"Well, I can't really speak to what you find chummy, Detective," I said. "For all I know, you weren't hugged enough as a child and as an adult you find a handshake promiscuous."

Out of the corner of my eye, I saw Marcus duck his chin and clear his throat as a cover for the chuckle that had started to escape him.

Shepherd, on the other hand, was staring at me with surprise. Good. I liked that I'd rattled him, if only a little.

"Do you normally dance with your business associates?" Shepherd said next.

"Only if they're good dancers," I replied, and then I remembered that I'd forgotten to look to Marcus, but he covered another laugh and sat back in his seat as if he were enjoying this.

Shepherd tapped his finger on the table. "What business do the two of you have in common, exactly?"

I looked at Marcus, and he nodded. "The gentleman I was about to have dinner with is interested in available office space in the building I own here in town. At least, he was interested before you showed up to ruin our evening."

"Yeah," Shepherd said, "he did look pretty interested."

I glared at him, and he glared back. "Are you insinuating something, Detective?" I said icily.

"Nope," he replied. "Well, maybe. I just find it curious that you're dating so soon after your divorce, Catherine."

"I've been divorced for eight months, and prior to that, separated for six more. Should I wear a black veil and pretend to be in mourning for another year or so to satisfy your high societal ideals?"

"Speaking of your divorce," Shepherd said, referring again to his notes, "your husband was a little concerned about your temper, was he not?"

I looked at Marcus, who was again studying Shepherd. He nodded, but I had the feeling that I'd need to tread carefully with my answer here. "My ex-husband is an adulterer. You can't be an adulterer and not also be a liar, Detective. If you're referring to the statement he made when he was attempting to procure sole custody over my twin sons, the court decided his statements had no merit, and we retained joint custody."

"But they don't live with you, right? They attend boarding school near New York City, correct?"

"They do."

"Why don't they live with you, Catherine?"

"What the heck does any of this have to do with the charges?" Marcus interrupted, and his tone wasn't so gentle anymore.

"I'm trying to identify a pattern," Shepherd said.

"What pattern?" Marcus demanded.

"A pattern that suggests that when your client doesn't get her way, she turns violent."

"That's absurd!" I said.

Marcus laid a hand on mine, and I bit back the argument I'd wanted to launch at Shepherd.

"I'm going to ask you again, Detective," Marcus said. "What. Pattern?"

"We found an incident report," Shepherd said. "It's a statement given by a bakery that refused to bake a cake for Ms. Cooper, and she proceeded to demolish two other cakes on her way out the door. The report notes that Ms. Cooper threw a wedding cake against the shop window, ruining the display."

I felt my insides go cold. Oh, God, I'd all but forgotten about that.

When I'd planned Gilley and Michel's wedding, I'd ordered a cake from a local bakery here in the Hamptons that made the most beautiful wedding cakes. But when I went to personally place the order, the man behind the counter got angry at me when I said that I wanted two grooms for the top of the cake. He was a religious man, he explained, and he absolutely refused to bake a wedding cake for a gay couple.

I'd felt so indignant on Michel and Gilley's behalf, and so furious at the bigotry of the proprietor that I had indeed lost my temper, but I hadn't thrown a whole cake. In fact, I had only thrown a piece the size of a brownie, which had been served to me before the proprietor and I got into an argument. I had indeed thrown it at his window on my way out the door, but that was it. It'd been nothing more than that.

Marcus turned to me. "Is any of that true?"

"Only the part about me throwing some cake, but it wasn't a whole cake, Marcus. It was a piece *this* big." I used my fingers to indicate how small the piece of cake was.

"That's not what the bakery owner said," Shepherd told me.

"Of course it's not," I said. "Because he's a *liar.*"

"Yeah, well, it's a pattern. And it says something about your temper."

I sighed and sat back in my chair. "So you've arrested me for murder because I threw a piece of cake at a window?"

"No," Shepherd said. "I've arrested you for murder because of *this!*"

Shepherd slapped a crime-scene photo on the table in front of me, and I was so startled that I jumped in my seat, but I also stared at the photo as if it had a tractor beam for my gaze.

What I saw was disturbing. It was what looked like Heather Holland's body, lying facedown on the floor. All about her were shards of glass, and clearly they were pieces of crystal, judging from the way they reflected the light in the room and from the camera.

On the back of Heather's head there was a rather large gash that definitely looked lethal. Whoever had murdered Heather had been in a violent rage—the wound was clearly evidence of that.

I shoved the photo away and averted my eyes. "That's dreadful," I said.

"That's your punch bowl," Shepherd replied.

And that made me think of something. "You know, Detective, for someone so smug in assuming he has all of the answers to this crime, you seem to have missed the fact that I loved that punch bowl. It was a gift from a dear friend of mine, and I would never, ever use it, even in a fit of rage against someone else. It was far too precious to me."

"If it was the only thing handy, I'm sure you were willing to use it," Shepherd said back.

While Shepherd and I were arguing, Marcus had pulled the photo forward, and he seemed to be studying it carefully. "Detective," he said.

"What?"

Marcus held up the photo and tapped at the gaping wound on Heather's head. "Explain that to me, would you?"

Shepherd's brow darkened. "Okay. Your client threatened Mrs. Holland at a luncheon that Mrs. Holland had been kind enough to invite her to. Once there, your client had trumped up some lame reason to feel offended and she lashed out verbally at the victim before storming out the door, leaving her punch bowl behind. Sometime later, your client decided to retrieve her punch bowl, but when she arrived at Mrs. Holland's she decided to feel offended all over again, and in a fit of rage, she waited for Mrs. Holland to turn away from her before striking out with her precious punch bowl hard enough to crack Mrs. Holland's skull."

Marcus eyed Shepherd with heavy lids, giving the impression of a parent about to lose patience with a child. "That's not what I'm talking about," Marcus said. "I'm talking about the wound itself."

"What about it?" Shepherd said.

I was curious too. What was it about that awful wound that Marcus found so interesting?

"Where's the blood?" Marcus asked.

I gasped and immediately looked again at the photo. "Ohmigod, he's right! There's barely any blood!"

Marcus nodded. "Exactly. Head wounds bleed, and they bleed bad."

"The M.E. thinks she was killed almost instantly," Shepherd said, but there was doubt in his voice.

"Even if she was killed instantly," Marcus told him, "there would still be a pool of blood about her head. At best, you have a wound here that looks like it was delivered postmortem."

Shepherd's jaw clenched and unclenched, and for the first time, I could see the smokescreen he'd put so much effort into.

"You knew that," I said, anger making my voice sound sharper than I'd intended. "You *knew* that wound was delivered post-mortem!"

"We have nothing confirmed yet," Shepherd said. "The M.E. has yet to receive the toxicology report back. The most likely cause of death is still blunt-force trauma."

"That's a load of crap, Detective," Marcus said, his own voice rising angrily. "Why did you arrest my client on such flimsy evidence that you know I'll destroy in court?"

"She *threatened* the victim with violence," Shepherd snapped. "And just a few hours later, the victim came up dead, surrounded by shards of glass from a punch bowl owned by your client."

Marcus turned to me, and he was now ignoring Shepherd. "Catherine. We're not answering any more questions. If the detective continues to question you, you simply say, 'On the advice from counsel, I refuse to answer that question.' Do you understand?"

"I do."

"Excellent." Turning back to Shepherd, Marcus said, "Your move, Detective."

"She'll be in here until tomorrow," Shepherd said angrily.

Marcus looked at his watch casually. "I'll pull some strings. Her bond hearing will be in front of Judge Cartwright first thing in the morning, and since it's already close to one a.m., I'm pretty sure my client is tough enough to handle a few more hours in your . . . charming establishment."

I gulped but tried to put on a brave face. I wanted to go home more than anything I'd ever wanted in my life, but I knew it wasn't going to happen until morning.

Shepherd folded his notes back up and stood up. "Fine," he said. "I'll send someone in to take her to lockup."

With that he was gone.

Marcus stood after the door closed. "Will you be okay in here tonight?"

"I don't know, will I?"

He offered me a crooked smile. "I think you'll be fine. If anything goes sideways, you demand to speak to me, okay? I can be here in less than twenty minutes."

"Where do you live, Marcus?"

"Sag Harbor."

"Ah," I said. It was a relief knowing he lived nearby.

Moving to the door he said, "Sit tight, Catherine. I'm going home to get a few hours' sleep, and I'll be back at nine a.m. We'll have you out of here by noon."

"Noon?" I said, my voice quivering. "You can't get me out any sooner than that?"

Marcus walked back to put a hand on my shoulder in an effort to calm me. "Try not to worry. I'll be pushing for an open dismissal tomorrow. The evidence they have against you is so flimsy it'll disintegrate in court."

I put my hand over his. "Thank you, Marcus. Sincerely."

"You're welcome."

The door opened again, and a female uniformed officer waved to me. "Let's go," she said. I walked toward her, and she put up her hand in a stopping motion, then expertly swiveled me around and said, "Hands behind your back."

I sighed as I was handcuffed a third time, then moved through the door and to an awaiting cell down the corridor.

Chapter 6

Surprisingly, I actually slept rather well for the next few hours.
I was the only one in my jail cell, and the cot was a little hard
but not unbearable, and honestly, I was so exhausted from the
entire ordeal of being arrested and interrogated that I was out the
moment my head hit the prison pillow.

I was then awakened at six-thirty, offered a surprisingly decent
breakfast of eggs, toast, and coffee, and allowed to shower and
call Gilley again. He answered his phone frantically. "Ohmigod,
Cat?! Is that you? Are you okay? What the hell happened?"

"Hey," I said wearily. "Shepherd arrested me. At Pierre's. In
front of everyone." My voice squeaked a little as I spoke. I had
no idea how I'd ever live down the humiliation.

"Holy four-star dinner!" Gilley replied. "What the hell was
Shepherd thinking?"

I sighed. "I have no idea, other than it seems everyone in this
town wants to take a crack at me."

"Where are you right now?"

"In jail."

"Ohmigod . . . of course. Right. You've been arrested. Should I
call your sister?"

"No," I said, remembering the commotion on the other end of
the phone line when I'd reached out to her. "I already reached out."

"Is she getting Dutch to pull some strings?"

"No."

Gilley seemed a little confused by my monosyllabic responses, but I was too tired to elaborate. "Do you need me to call that lawyer from the card Tony left here?"

It was my turn to be confused. "You mean you didn't send an attorney over here last night?"

"Um . . . what? No. I was asleep when you called, and I didn't get your message until about two minutes ago. I've been calling your cell ever since."

"Well, an attorney showed up here for me last night. And he seems very good."

"What's his name?"

"Marcus Brown."

I heard the telltale clicking of a keyboard, then a lengthy pause, then, "Whoa."

"What's whoa?"

"Marcus Brown is some kind of fabulous legal eagle, honey."

"Tell me," I said. Gilley had obviously Googled Marcus and I was anxious to hear the details.

Gilley recited his résumé. "Stanford undergrad, Harvard Law, graduated magna cum laude, and spent time clerking for a New York Supreme Court justice before joining the firm of Latham and Watkins . . ."

"Ooo, I've heard of Latham and Watkins. They're among the best firms in New York."

"Yep. Brown worked there for nearly a decade before leaving with two other associates to open his own firm in Sag Harbor of Brown, Duvall, and Kirkpatrick, and they come very highly rated for criminal defense."

"So I'm in good hands."

"I'd say you're in some of the best. And if he's as gorgeous in person as his photo, then I'd say you're in *very* good hands."

"He is beautiful," I said. "But it wouldn't matter to me if he were a troll. As long as he can help me."

"I think he can help you. And speaking of helping you, how can I?"

"I need some clothes, Gil. Something appropriate for court."

"On it. Give me twenty minutes, and I'll have a suit for you."

"Great. Thanks."

True to his word, Gilley pulled a charcoal-gray pantsuit out of my closet and hustled it down to the jail so that I could change for my court appearance. Marcus had already sent a message through to one of the officers guarding me that he'd meet me in court by ten.

At the appointed time, I was handcuffed once again and loaded into a van with two other prisoners, and we were driven to the courthouse just a short distance away.

After being unloaded, I was placed in a small room with a table and two chairs. The cuffs remained on, which bothered me more than I could say.

Marcus walked in a short time after, and he looked as if he'd gotten a full night's sleep, though I suspected he'd gotten even less rest than I had.

"Good morning," he said to me with a smile.

There was such confidence in his voice and his manner that in an instant I felt buoyed and hopeful. "Morning, Marcus. Can you walk me through how this is going to go? If they set bail at anything over five hundred thousand, I'll need some time to call my broker and liquidate some stock."

Marcus smiled wider. "I'm thinking you won't need to make that call, Catherine."

I blew out a sigh of relief. "Thank goodness. I don't mind bailing myself out of jail for a crime I didn't commit, but I hate the thought of tying up so much cash for an extended period."

He nodded like he understood, but there was something else that he seemed to be keeping close to his chest. "First, I need to know if there's anything you haven't told me that you think could be used against you today."

My brow furrowed. "Like what?"

"Like the thing with the cake at the bakery. What was that about?"

I blushed. "My dearest friend was getting married, and I was helping to plan his wedding. I found a baker here in the Hamptons that made the most beautiful wedding cakes, but when I ordered two grooms for the topper, he said that his religion wouldn't allow him to accept our business. In this day and age, it just infuriated me. I took the sample piece of cake he'd offered me when I arrived at his shop and threw it at his window on the way out the door."

Marcus nodded. "Got it. Has anyone else ever pushed you to lose your temper like that?"

I shook my head automatically, and then I gave it a little more thought and . . . "Oh, no."

"What's oh, no?"

I bit my lip. "Well . . . there was this one time . . ."

"Yes?"

"It was a long time ago," I prefaced, wondering what this man would think of me once I told him.

"I'm listening."

"It was a very stressful time in my life."

Marcus simply looked at me expectantly.

So I took a deep breath and dove in. "I was visiting my sister. It was during a time when I was still attempting to gain the approval of my parents . . . this was before I realized through a great deal of therapy what horrible people they are, and how toxic and abusive they'd been to me and especially to my sister."

"Did you harm them, Catherine?"

"No!" I said. "It was nothing like that."

"Good. Tell me what happened."

I took a deep breath. "My sister, Abby, was having a very hard time with a rental property she owned. It was haunted."

Marcus squinted at me. "Haunted," he repeated.

"Yes. I don't know if you believe in ghosts or not, but I swear it was haunted, and it was causing my sister a significant amount of strain. I just wanted to help her, you know?"

Marcus didn't say anything. He didn't nod or in any other way acknowledge that he understood what I was getting at. He simply stared at me.

"Anyway," I continued, flustered at the thought of how I must sound to him. "I wanted her nightmare with the house to end, so I went to a construction site, borrowed one of their bulldozers, and headed over to the property."

Marcus's jaw dropped. "You *borrowed* a bulldozer?"

I shrugged. "For the right price, you can borrow just about anything. I also paid the guy to show me how to work the gears, so I knew what I was doing."

Marcus pressed a finger to his lip and studied me for a moment before he said, "You bulldozed the house?"

"No."

He let out a breath. "Good."

"I bulldozed a BMW."

His eyes widened. "You got into an accident?"

"Um . . . not exactly."

"Tell me the exactly part then."

"My future brother-in-law's best friend arrived at the scene and attempted to block my efforts to bulldoze the house. I might have accidentally run over his car."

"You *accidentally* ran over his car?"

"Yes. Two or three times."

Marcus stared at me with big wide eyes, and then he let out a bark of laughter, and he quickly pressed his hand to his lips, but his shoulders shook, and his eyes watered, and then he couldn't seem to stop. And then he actually got up, held his finger up to me in a "wait a sec" manner, and left the room.

The sound of his laughter from the hallway echoed into the room, and I felt both mortified and a tiny bit giggly myself. Maybe it was the lack of sleep. Maybe it was the ludicrous situation I was in or the ludicrous situation I'd created all those years ago with the bulldozer, but I too allowed myself a few moments of levity.

At last, the laughter subsided, and Marcus opened the door and came back in. "I'm very sorry," he said, and I could see he genuinely meant it. "You caught me off guard with that one. I mean, I've heard some stories, but I've never heard one quite like that."

"Not one of my finer moments."

Another giggle escaped Marcus's lips, and he cleared his throat to cover it. "Is that the end of the story?"

"Yes," I said. "Well, not exactly."

Marcus made a hand gesture and said, "Lay it on me."

"Milo—that's the best friend of my brother-in-law whose car I wrecked . . ."

"Yes?"

"He was a detective with the Royal Oak Police Department."

Again, Marcus's eyes widened, and he pressed his lips together tightly, but another round of giggles made him stand up and exit the room.

I sighed and rolled my eyes, waiting for him to return. He did in a matter of moments, and I could tell he was really trying to hold it together. "Catherine, please accept my apology. That was unprofessional and discourteous of me. I can only say that you have surprised me like no other client ever has."

"It's okay. There were plenty of people in the Royal Oak P.D. who found it pretty hilarious too."

"So, charges were brought against you?"

"Oh, no. Nothing like that. I paid for the car, of course, and Milo was a close friend of my sister and her future husband, so after we all calmed down and Milo had his brand-new car, all was forgiven."

"Then there's no record of you destroying the BMW?"

"None that I know of."

"That's good. We don't need that to come up today in court."

"It shouldn't. No one here knows about it—well, besides my dear friend Gilley, but he wouldn't have mentioned it to anyone."

Marcus tapped his pen on his legal pad. "You said last night that you were recently divorced, is that correct?"

"Yes. Why?"

"Does your ex know about you running over the BMW?"

I tensed. "He does."

"If Shepherd called him to get some dirt on you, would your husband share that story?"

I thought about that for a long moment, and then I said, "No. If Tommy were going to use that against me, he would've brought it up at any number of custody hearings we had over who should get the boys. Of course, he knew that if he mentioned the bulldozer, then I'd tell the judge all about the time he rammed his golf cart into a parked car at the country club because the owner had purposely coughed during a critical moment at the tournament Tommy was playing in. Oh, and then there was the time Tommy threw a set of golf clubs into the lake on the course because he said that the owner was taking too long on each hole and wasn't allowing Tommy and his buddy to play through."

"So your ex has a temper as well?"

"Yes," I said. Isn't it funny that I had a half a dozen stories like the two I'd just told Marcus about Tommy and I'd never really considered that Tommy had an anger-management problem too?

"Good. That's good."

"It is?"

"Yes. I just want to be prepared for any scenario where we could be surprised this morning. Is there anything else you think I should know?"

"Nothing I can think of."

"Good. Okay, then let's get to court. I can promise you—I will be bringing my A game, and if all goes well, you won't have to say a word and you'll be home very soon."

*   *   *

True to his word, Marcus brought his A game, and I didn't have to say a word. I sat in my seat looking as innocent as possible, but it turned out I didn't even need to do much of that. The judge seemed to be very much on my side.

"I must say," she said, looking over her reading glasses at Detective Shepherd, who sat behind the prosecutor, "I expected better from you, Detective." Shuffling the crime-scene photos and tossing them aside, she added, "Counselor Brown is correct. This is the flimsiest evidence I've ever seen for an arrest. One photo of a broken punch bowl that has Ms. Cooper's fingerprints on it and a few witness statements about a threat Ms. Cooper may or may not have issued to the decedent do not a murder case make."

"Your Honor—" the prosecutor said.

"I do not want to hear it, Counselor!" the judge snapped. "You've got no eyewitness, no confession, no sign of forced entry, and not one shred of evidence linking the accused to the death of Mrs. Holland except for a punch bowl that got left behind at a party!"

"Your Honor," the prosecutor tried again.

She put up her hand and glared hard at the man at the table next to ours. "Don't even with this, Dashiell. Seriously. Your ace detective here arrested Ms. Cooper before the M.E. could file his official findings and issued only a preliminary report, calling the death of Mrs. Holland 'suspicious' *without* citing an *actual* cause of death in lieu of the toxicology report, and while noting that the wound to the back of her head was *most likely* delivered postmortem. Are you serious with bringing me this nonsense?!"

This time, the prosecutor remained mute, but his face reddened to near purple, and I could tell he was equal parts furious and humiliated.

Meanwhile, Detective Shepherd looked as if he was trying

very hard to become one with the chair he was sitting on and disappear from view.

"This is nothing but a waste of the court's time and a possible civil case for you if Ms. Cooper chooses to sue, and I might even be inclined to encourage her," the judge said before raising her gavel and adding, "Defendant's motion for dismissal is granted. Ms. Cooper, you are free to go."

My heart swelled with adoration for the judge in that moment. She saw the truth!

I got up as she did, and after she left the courtroom, I turned to Marcus and hugged him fiercely. "Thank you!" I said. "Thank you, thank you!"

He gave me a quick pat on the back and released me. "You'll have to sign some paperwork and be processed out from the jail, but you should be on your way home in an hour. Two at the most."

"I have to go back to the jail?"

"Yes," he said, packing up his briefcase. "But it's only to collect your personal items and have them process you out. It should go smoothly, but if it doesn't, call my cell."

Marcus handed me his card, and I stared at it. "You're leaving me?"

He chuckled. "Yes. Which is a good thing. But, Catherine, you should understand that we won here today only because the police rushed their case. The prosecutor was also humiliated, and he's not going to take that lying down. My concern is that they will want redemption, and they're going to be working hard to build a case against you."

I put a hand over my heart and felt suddenly queasy. "So it's not over?"

"Probably not," Marcus said. "The good news is that they've already tipped their hand, and I still can't understand why Shepherd—a seasoned detective—would do that. Dashiell Tanning is the new boy on the block, and he obviously didn't know any better when Shepherd brought him the case and pushed for the arrest warrant, but I can tell that our young prosecutor over there isn't going to take this lying down. He'll push Shepherd to find better, more damning evidence just so he can haul you back into court and shove it right back in the judge's face."

"So, no matter what, you think I'm coming back here?"

"Yes. Unless they find the actual murderer, which, given how quick they were to peg you for the crime, I doubt they'll be motivated to look elsewhere for."

"Cat!" I heard behind me. Turning, I saw Gilley approach. "Ohmigod! You won!" he said, smiling from ear to ear.

I sat down heavily in the chair. "Hardly," I told him.

Gil looked from me to Marcus. "What's happening? What'd I miss? Didn't the judge dismiss the charges?"

"She did," Marcus said. "But it's likely only a delay." Turning back to me, he said, "Try not to worry, Catherine. We beat them once. We can do it again."

With that he began to walk away, and I called out to him. "Wait, Marcus, don't I owe you a check or something?"

He glanced at me over his shoulder. "Not this time. It's been covered."

And then he was gone.

I stared at his retreating back for a long moment, wondering what the heck *that* meant. Had someone else paid him? Had he been working pro bono?

As I was trying to figure out an answer to that cryptic question, a uniformed guard stepped up to me. "Ms. Cooper, I'm here to walk you through processing. Please come with me."

I stood, but before I left with the guard, I said to Gil, "Meet me at the police station in an hour. And have Sebastian order me another Caesar salad for when I get home, would you?"

"Will do," Gil promised.

* * *

I don't know that I'd ever been so happy to walk through the door of the guest house as I was that day. Sebastian even greeted me as I entered. "Hello, Lady Catherine. Did you enjoy your time away?"

"No, Sebastian," I said to him, heading straight for the couch. "I definitely did not!"

"Sorry to hear that, ma'am," Sebastian said. "I have taken the liberty of ordering your usual lunch."

The doorbell rang at that moment, and Gilley opened the door to the young man delivering our meal. Gilley took the food, tipped the kid, and brought everything to the couch.

Sebastian chimed in again with a helpful "There is a chilled bottle of Pellegrino in the refrigerator. Would you like me to play some music?"

I sighed. "No. Thank you, Sebastian. I think I simply want to sit and talk to Gilley for a while."

"As you wish, ma'am," Sebastian said.

Gilley waited on me like the sweet, lovable, doting friend he is, and after handing me my salad, he set his own lunch aside to take the time to lift my feet into his lap and massage them.

"You're an angel," I said, feeling weary down to my bones.

"I'm so sorry you're going through this mess."

With a long sigh, I said, "And the nightmare doesn't seem to be over."

"Maybe Shepherd will find someone else to pick on?"

"That's not likely."

"You never know," Gil insisted.

"I may not have my sister's intuition, lovey, but I know enough about men to know that Detective Shepherd has no intention of looking anywhere else but in my direction when it comes to identifying suspects."

"Why do you think that is?" Gil asked.

I shrugged. "Who can say? But I do think we shouldn't take it lying down."

"You mean, 'cause we're sitting here basically lying down?"

I chuckled. "Yes."

"What're you thinking?"

"I think we'll have to take a page out of Abby and M.J.'s books and turn ourselves into amateur sleuths."

Gilley stopped rubbing my feet. "You're joking."

"Nope."

"Cat, I was part of the M.J.'s super-sleuthing team for almost a decade. It was a lot harder than you might think."

Undeterred, I asked, "How many mysteries did you guys solve?"

Gilley looked up at the ceiling. "I don't know. Eight? Ten? Something like that."

"So, basically, you're telling me that you're a subject-matter expert, right?"

Gilley scrunched up his face. "Um . . . I guess . . ."

"So all we have to do is rely on your expertise and my can-do attitude, and we should be fine."

"See, now when you put it like that, you make it sound easy, and, Cat, you should know, I almost *died!* Like, *several* times! Nearly. Dead . . . me!"

I grinned winningly. "But you didn't. In fact, you look none the worse for wear, my friend."

Gilley rolled his eyes. "I'm serious!"

"So am I. In all those cases, weren't you also battling some sort of evil demon? And weren't *they* the reason you were in danger?"

Gilley frowned. "Not in *every* case. Some were just spooks, and the people were the ones who wanted to murder us to death."

"Well, no one wants to murder you to death in this case. They just want me to go to jail for the rest of my life. But if helping me out would be such an *inconvenience* to you, then, I guess we know where our friendship stands."

Gilley glared at me. "Really, Cat? You had to pull out the friendship card?"

I glared back. "Yep."

He sighed dramatically. "Fine! Have it your way. We'll poke around and see what we can see, but if things get dicey, your Sherlock will be less one Watson."

I reached out and took his hand, squeezing it with relief. "I can live with that. I just want to live, Gil. I don't want to go to jail for a crime I didn't commit. I don't want to lose my sons. I don't want to lose my life. I don't want to . . ." My voice trailed off as the emotional toll caught up to me, and I had to settle for ducking my chin and shaking my head because I couldn't go on.

Gilley patted my hand, then got up and headed toward the bedrooms, arriving back by my side carrying what looked like a thick comforter. "Here," he said, draping it over me.

I was shocked by the weight of the thing. It felt like it weighed about fifteen pounds. "What's this?"

"It's a gravity blanket."

The weight of the comforter surrounded and enveloped me, and in an instant, I felt a sense of incredible calm come over me. "Oh my God, what's happening?" I asked. Was this some kind of mind trick?

"How do you feel?" he asked.

My eyes misted at the immediate effect the gravity blanket had on me, and I looked up at him and said, "I feel . . . safe."

He grinned. "Right? Isn't it crazy?"

"Where did you get this?" I asked.

"Michel gave it to me a few months ago. For some reason, I'd been having panic attacks. I think it was a latent effect of all the scary stuff that M.J. and I used to do. For as long as we were both working on the *Ghoul Getters* set, I was able to keep all that stuff from affecting me, but then a few months after M.J. and Heath moved to Santa Fe, I started to wig out a little."

"Oh, my goodness, Gil. I had no idea."

"Yeah. I was able to keep it a secret from everyone but Michel. He encouraged me to start seeing a therapist, and I did, and it helped, but that blanket was the game changer. Michel discovered it on a blog he read about natural anti-anxiety methods. I would've never known about it if he hadn't read that blog, and I think that blanket just about saved my life."

"I'm so glad," I told him. "And I wouldn't have believed you if I weren't actually under this thing right now and feeling its effects. I can't believe the difference." I snuggled farther under the blanket. "I mean, one minute I was almost in a panic, and right now I feel like I could doze off."

"Go for it," Gilley said, tucking the blanket around me.

"But we have to come up with a game plan," I said, adding a yawn.

"Later," he assured me. "For now, sleep, Cat."

And I did.

Chapter 7

"Where do we start?" I asked Gilley. It was Sunday morning, and I was feeling much better. I'd caught up on my sleep, I'd gone on a long walk that had bolstered my resolve, and I'd spent the evening cuddled with Gilley on the couch, huddled under the gravity blanket, watching old movies and eating popcorn.

We'd both worn tiaras.

Life is just better wearing a crown of jewels.

But by Sunday, I was anxious to get the super sleuthing started, so I'd woken early, made Gilley and me a delicious basket of raspberry scones, and was now seated at the table with my tablet and stylus, ready to crank out a game plan.

"Good Lord, woman, can I finish my coffee?"

"Sip while you talk," I said impatiently.

"Mamehminiffmybrmfst?" Gil replied, his mouth crammed full of scone.

I sighed. "Fine. Eat, chew, swallow, *then* talk."

"Thank you. This scone is *divine*."

"My grandmother's recipe. She left all her recipes to me, actually. Which is good, considering that had she left them to Abby, they probably would've burned up in a kitchen fire."

Gilley giggled. "M.J. can't cook either. Well, I shouldn't say that. She's gotten better since the baby came along, but I swear, Heath is a saint for choking down some of the gruel she serves up."

"At least she's not on a first-name basis with the local firemen."

"I'd like to be on a first-name basis with our local firemen," Gil said, smiling wickedly.

I rolled my eyes. "Can we get back on track here, please?"

"Yes," Gil said, popping another large piece of scone into his mouth before reaching for his own tablet. Swiveling it around, he showed me the screen. "I managed to worm my way onto this page this morning."

I squinted at his tablet. "That's Heather's Facebook page?"

"Yep. She had it set to private, and I couldn't crack her password, so I spent an hour combing through her friends' accounts until I finally found one that had an easy password, and I was able to hack into *that* account, then log onto Heather's page to see what we can see."

"Wait, you *hacked* into someone else's Facebook account?"

"I did," Gilley said. "And I'm not sorry. We need information, and the best way to get that info is through social media."

"Whose account did you hack?" I asked nervously. "Seriously, Gilley, we could get in major trouble for that!"

"Joyce McQueen."

I blinked. "Who's Joyce McQueen?"

Gilley rolled his eyes. "Some eighty-two-year-old woman who has twenty-six friends—total—and she hasn't posted on Facebook in over a year. I'm not sure she's even still alive. We're not gonna get caught, Cat."

"Oh," I said, relieved. "You're sure someone won't catch on that we've hacked into a private account?"

"Honey, do I look new at this?"

"No. Which worries me."

"Relax. I do this kind of thing all the time."

"Wait, you're telling me you illegally hack into stuff all the time?"

"What do you think the term 'computer hacker' means, Cat?"

I blinked some more. "Okay, I know you used to hack into stuff in college, but I had no idea you were still doing it."

"How do you think M.J. and I solved most of those mysteries?" he asked me next.

"I don't know," I snapped. "M.J.'s a psychic. Didn't she do most of the sleuthing?"

Gilley lowered his lids to half-mast. "Girl," he said levelly, "in the first place, M.J. isn't like your sister. She's a medium. She talks to dead people, who're not nearly as forthcoming with information as you might think. In the second place, we both brought our skills to the super-sleuthing table. She talked to the dead, and I hacked into databases and whatnot. I never stole anything, and any private information I got, I never passed on. No one was put in danger. No one got hurt. Well, at least not from my hacking."

I sat with that for a minute, still unnerved by the obvious lawbreaking. But then I also had to consider that I trusted Gilley. He'd never once lied to me. And he'd never once betrayed me. So if he said that he only used his skills for good, then I suppose, given the circumstances, I had to be okay with it. "Okay," I said. "Just please make sure to reset Joyce's password back after we're done poking around."

"Of course," Gilley assured me, adding, "I had every intention of restoring her password. What was it again?"

My eyes widened, and I sucked in some air. "You don't remember it?"

Gilley adopted a knowing smile. "Of course I remember it. It's PASSWORD."

I laughed. "Wow. That must've put your hacking skills to the test!"

"I know," he said. "She made it too easy."

"What'd you change it to?" I asked, genuinely curious.

"DROWSSAP," Gil said.

At first, I thought I misheard him—that hadn't even sounded like a word, and then I realized he'd simply changed it to PASS-WORD spelled backward. "Clever," I told him.

He smiled. "After we're done snooping, I'll change it back and send her an anonymous e-mail to let her know that her security is at risk and she needs to change it to something more challenging ASAP. But I digress. What's *really* important here is that we can look all through Heather's Facebook pages and see what we see."

I scooted closer to Gilley to peer over his shoulder as he scrolled down the page. "Is that Joyce?" I asked, pointing to a photo of a little old lady with silver-blue hair, leaning heavily on a cane.

"It is. She looks like a crafty one, if you ask me."

"She looks sweet and trusting," I said, poking him in the arm.

"Stop with the guilt trip. I'll do no harm to sweet and trusting Joyce."

"Good. Now that that's settled, what do we see?"

"Well!" he began, and I could tell he'd been snooping for a while. "Not only do we have a fantastic suspect pool with her friends' list—"

"Excluding poor Joyce, of course."

"I'm not excluding anyone yet, sugar."

"You really think an eighty-two-year-old killed Heather?"

Gilley eyed me seriously. "See, this is where my experience really comes in handy. I think anyone is capable of anything."

"Gilley, she was smashed over the head with a crystal punch bowl that I personally know weighed about six pounds. That thing was heavy! No way could an elderly woman with a cane accomplish that."

Gilley continued to eye me skeptically. "We'll clear Joyce of all suspicion once we've identified the real killer."

"Fine. I don't want to argue. How many names do we have in the suspect pool?"

"Three hundred and sixty-eight."

I stared at Gilley for a long moment. "Please be kidding."

"I never kid about suspect pools. I only kid in the kiddie pool."

"Ba-dump-bump, shhhhh," I said, adding an eye roll.

"Thanks. I deserved that."

"Can we get back to work here?" I asked, pointing again to the screen.

"Of course. Sorry. As I was saying, we have over three hundred suspects to look at."

"Wait. You're saying that you suspect *every* name on Heather's friends' list?"

"Yes."

"Gilley, I'm sure some of those people don't even *live* here in New York."

"Doesn't mean they didn't fly in to do the deed."

I rubbed my temples. "You're giving me a headache."

"Look, all I'm saying is that it's likely that Heather knew her killer. And if she knew her killer, then it's likely that the killer has a social-media profile and was friends with Heather."

I moved my hand over to the touch pad on the computer and tapped at something that caught my eye on Heather's personal page. "Hold on a second," I said.

"What?" Gil asked me.

"This post," I told him, clicking on it. "That's from the party. And that's . . ." My voice trailed off as I looked in horror at the screen.

"That's you," Gilley said breathlessly.

The image was obviously taken right in the middle of my angry outburst, and the caption was the one that was most hurtful. Heather had written,

Yikes! This cat clearly needs to be checked for rabies!

"Well, that's just mean," Gilley said.

A deep, dark anger took hold of my insides. "I'm going to say something, and I don't want you to judge me, Gilley."

"Go for it," he said.

"I'm not sorry she's dead."

"I know, Cat. You and at least one other person feel the exact same way."

I closed my eyes and forced myself to take some deep breaths. "*Why* was she so mean to me?"

"You know, that's actually one of the questions I think we need to have answered."

I opened my eyes again. "We do?"

"Yes," he said. "She *was* particularly vicious toward you. And we both have no idea why, right?"

"Right."

"But at least some of her friends seem to be in on the joke. See? Ten women commented with laughing emojis or stuff that was supportive of Heather. That's telling, because in my experience, most women just aren't that bitchy to each other. I mean, it's risky, especially on social media, to be that blatantly mean. So, they must've felt justified in their support of Heather's comments."

"That's a really good point."

"And what's even more important is that someone is obviously using Heather's hatred of you against you, by basically framing you for murder."

"But we don't know that yet, do we? I mean, yes, she was hit with my punch bowl, but that could've been just because it was handy. Plus, we're not even sure that that's how Heather died. To Marcus's point, the photo of the crime scene doesn't indicate Heather bled to death, and the M.E.'s report said the blow likely came postmortem. So how did Heather die?"

Gilley scratched at his chin. "That's the second question we need to focus on."

"I think that's the first one, Gilley. I think the answer to that question is where we should begin."

"How're we going to answer that?" Gil asked. "The M.E.'s official report is probably at least a week away."

"Ah. Good point," I said. "But it does beg the question: What *do* we know about the way Heather might've died?"

"For all we know, it could've been natural causes," Gilley said.

I shook my head. "Not from the crime-scene photos I saw. She died violently. She was facedown on the floor surrounded by the shards of my crystal bowl."

"But there was no blood, Cat," Gilley reminded me. "And I'm not a medical expert, but I think I can still hazard a guess that the reason her head wound didn't bleed is because she was already dead when she hit the floor."

I got up from the table and paced back and forth for a moment, and then I had a thought. Reaching for my cell phone and my purse, I took out Marcus Brown's business card and punched in the numbers. I then came back to the table and put the phone on speaker.

"Marcus Brown," the counselor said, answering on the first ring.

I smiled. I liked a man who was willing to answer a call right away. It spoke to his take-charge character. "Marcus, it's Catherine Cooper."

"Catherine, how are you?" he said smoothly. "Don't tell me that moron disguised as a detective arrested you again."

I laughed. "No, no. Nothing like that. I'm calling because Gilley—you met him at the courthouse—and I want to look into Heather's murder and—"

"Hold on, you want to what now?" Marcus interrupted.

"We're looking into Heather's murder," I repeated.

There was silence on the other end of the line. I had the feeling I'd surprised Marcus once again.

Because he didn't speak, I decided to plunge ahead. "I was

hoping that, in the stack of papers you brought to the courthouse during my bond hearing, you might have some documentation regarding the M.E.'s findings. Even if they're the preliminary findings."

"I do," Marcus said, sounding careful with his wording. "But I still don't understand why you think it's a good idea to go poking around the investigation. That could bring you a world of trouble, Catherine."

"I'm already in trouble, Marcus. And if we don't start identifying other suspects who had more cause to do Heather harm than myself, I'm telling you, it'll only be a matter of time before they haul me off to jail again."

"So why not hire a professional?" he asked. "I know of at least two very good private investigators. They could do all the legwork and keep you from drawing the attention of the E.H.P.D."

"As it turns out, Gilley has quite a bit of investigative experience," I said. "Besides, I think it's within my best interests to be seen as someone attempting to solve the crime."

"You could just as easily be seen as someone trying to obstruct justice," Marcus warned. "If you go poking your nose into this, the prosecutor could make a case that you're attempting to shift suspicion from yourself onto someone else."

"I am attempting to shift the blame off myself and onto someone else. I just don't know who that someone else is at the moment."

"I think it's a bad idea," Marcus warned.

"I appreciate that," I said, and I genuinely meant it. "But this is something I need to do. If I'm going to live in this town as a free woman, I now know I'll need to *earn* my reputation back; otherwise, assuming I'll be acquitted, I'm likely to forever be known as the woman who got away with murder."

"All right," Marcus said after another lengthy pause. "I guess I can't stop you. But do me a couple of favors."

"Of course. What?"

"Number one: don't become a pain in the ass. You're not well loved in that community, and the last thing we need are people coming forward with fabricated stories about the terrible feud between you and Heather Holland that will get created out of annoyance and the hope that you'll go away."

"Noted, and granted."

"Number two . . ." Marcus continued.

"I'm listening."

"Keep me in the loop about your progress. If you find out anything that you think might be relevant to your defense, shoot it to me."

"Also noted and granted," I said.

"Number three: stay away from Shepherd. *Do not* even *think* about questioning him about any of his findings or suspicions— especially those that involve you."

"That's one promise I can easily keep," I assured him. "But at some point, I would like to talk to the M.E. At least as soon as he finishes his report."

"Larry Beauperthy," Marcus said.

"I'm sorry?"

"The M.E. His name is Dr. Larry Beauperthy, and as it so happens, you may be in luck, having retained me as your attorney."

"Granted, I do feel lucky that you've been defending me, Marcus, but I'm still confused as to how I retained you and what you're actually referring to here."

"A benefactor set up enough of a retainer for you to cover your bond hearing. Going forward, I'll be billing you directly."

"Good to know, and I'm assuming that billing will start with this phone call?"

"It will."

"And just how much will this call cost me?"

"One hundred and fifty dollars."

My eyes widened. "Your hourly rate is only a hundred and fifty dollars?" I asked. I was floored. With Marcus's credentials, I'd have thought his rate was triple that.

"No. My services come at six hundred dollars an hour. I'm hanging up the moment we reach the fifteen-minute mark."

"Ah," I said. Even I'd lowballed his rate.

"Try not to worry," Marcus said. "It's money well spent. And here's why: Dr. Beauperthy was my college roommate at Stanford. We go way back."

"Get out of here," I said, and Gilley bounced his eyebrows.

"It's true. And I already have a call out to him on your behalf. That will also be included in my bill."

"Isn't that some sort of conflict of interest?" I asked.

"No," Marcus assured me. "Our friendship will have nothing to do with his findings, and to preempt any protest from the D.A.'s office over it, I'm already planning to record every single conversation with the good doctor."

"So you can probably find out what he thinks about the way Heather died," I said.

"Yes. I think I can."

Gilley nodded and flashed me two thumbs-up. "That's fantastic. And you'll share that with me?"

"I will," Marcus said. "As soon as your retainer check clears the bank."

"What retainer check?"

"The one you're sending to my office. I think a twenty-five-thousand-dollar retainer should get us started."

Gilley and I exchanged a look. "Very well, Marcus. Let's hope I won't actually need defending again and you'll be returning most of it back to me."

"Honestly, Catherine? Nothing would make me happier. Especially since I drive a BMW."

With a chuckle, he clicked off the line.

"What did he mean by that?" Gilley asked. "Lots of people drive BMWs."

"Inside joke," I told him. "Okay, so, hopefully we'll be getting at least a few answers about the manner of death in Heather's case. Let's look again at where we should start."

"I think we should start with the crime scene," Gil said.

"Good. I like it. But how do we do that?"

Gilley smirked wickedly. "I know a way . . ."

"I'm nervous, but listening."

"Hold on, let me show you," he said, getting up from the table and disappearing into the hallway leading to the bedrooms. A minute or two later, he returned with a small, black drone. "Ta-da!" he said.

"That's very nice, Gilley. What do we do with it?"

"We use it to spy on Heather's house."

"How will we be able to see anything?" I asked.

Gilley pointed to a good-sized lens on the underside of the drone. "This camera can rotate three-hundred-sixty degrees, and the image quality is fantastic."

I frowned. "Again, I ask you, how will we be able to see anything? Heather died *inside* her house. That drone will only give us a good look at the outside."

Gilley placed the drone on the floor, keeping the remote control in his hand. He then moved to the front door and opened it wide.

"Watch," he said.

Moving back toward the drone, Gilley fiddled with the controls on the remote, and the drone came to life with a high-pitched buzz. It then lifted off the ground and zipped out the front door. Using his free hand, Gilley pointed to his tablet on the table, and I immediately saw the view of the drone as it elevated into the sky. It then moved over the roofline of the guest house, pivoted, then began to descend back down, keeping close to the exterior wall.

A few seconds later, I was watching myself watch the video of the drone watching me through the window. "Wow," I said, turning to see the thing hovering at eye level. "That's seriously creepy, Gil."

"It's the future," he said. "But do you see, Cat? We can look in through the windows at Heather's house and get a surprising amount of detail."

For emphasis, Gilley pivoted the camera back and forth, and I realized that he was right. We could see quite a lot of detail about the room we were standing in.

"Can we fly that thing from here over to Heather's?" I asked. I was worried we might get caught if we had to stand out on the road or something. It would definitely look suspicious.

"No," Gil said. "The range is just a little too far. But I have a solution."

"Excellent. What?"

"You know that patch of woods at the far end of Heather's property?"

I thought back. I almost never drove in that direction as my office was the other way, but on the few occasions when I had driven past Heather's house, I did think I remembered a large patch of dense woods edging close to the road and bordering Heather's property. "Yes," I said.

"If we head in there and I have you hold the tablet, I can navigate the drone to peek in all the windows, and we can record the video for further analysis."

"Who owns those woods?" I asked, worried about trespassing.

"Probably Heather," Gil said. "They practically butt up to the south end of her house."

"Yikes. I'm not sure about that plan, Gilley."

"Come on, Cat. It's not like she's going to be around to catch us. And by now, I'll bet the police have cleared out the crime-scene tape. The place is bound to be abandoned."

I tapped my finger against my thigh nervously. But then I decided that, as a life coach who should be setting an example for her clients, I'd need to take some personal risks every once in a while. "Fine. But we should go at night."

"The camera won't be able to see anything if it's dark out."

"Crap. Okay, I get it. When do you think we should go?"

"Now," Gilley said.

"Now?"

"Yes, Cat. I mean, why not? It's Sunday morning. Who's going to be around and curious about what we're up to on a lazy Sunday morning?"

I took a deep breath and let it out slowly. "All right. Yes. You're right. Let me just change into something more appropriate . . ."

"More appropriate. What does that mean?"

"It means I'm not wearing a silk blouse and dress slacks to go hiking in the woods on a secret spy mission."

Gilley grinned. "I can't wait to see what you're gonna change into."

As it turned out, I had very little in my wardrobe that was appropriate for such a mission. I finally settled on a pair of black leggings, a black sweater, and a black raincoat. I topped the ensemble off with a pair of black sunglasses and a dark gray beret.

Shoes were another matter entirely. The only thing I had that could hold up to the wet, woody conditions were a pair of rain boots with little hot-pink paw prints on them. They went against my more refined style, but I giggled every time I wore them. Well, except today. I wasn't giggling much when I thought of all the laws we might be breaking.

Arriving back at the guest house, Gilley met me at the door, gave my look an up-down, and said, "You do know it's raining, right?"

"Yes, which is why I'm wearing a raincoat and boots."

"The boots," Gil said. "Loooove them, but you might want to rethink the sunglasses."

"I'm trying to be inconspicuous."

"Yes. Nothing says 'don't notice me' like a pair of sunglasses on a rainy day."

I pulled off the glasses. "There. Happy?"

"Ecstatic. Shall we?"

We left the guest house and began walking up the road. It wasn't raining hard, more of a drizzle, but it was chilly, and I shivered in my raincoat.

Gilley wore a backpack, and I assumed the drone was inside. He and I didn't talk as we walked; I think we were both a little nervous.

As we strolled past Heather's estate, I wondered if she had any next of kin to take over the care of the grand house. Surely she'd have a relative who would inherit the property. Or maybe a member of her staff would care for the place until the estate was settled. Craning my neck, I looked for any signs of life, like a light on or a car in the driveway, but the estate seemed abandoned. At least as far as I could tell.

That gave me a bit of relief at least. The last thing we needed was for someone inside the house to spot the drone.

"Have you heard from Maks?" Gilley asked me.

I started at the sound of his voice. "No," I sighed. "But I didn't expect to. The poor man. Being hauled away in handcuffs at Pierre's was mortifying for me. I can only imagine it must've been incredibly embarrassing for him as well. For all he knows, he was on a date with a murderess. And if that weren't enough, I think his driver, Frederick, was arrested."

"Why would his driver have been arrested?"

"I'm not quite sure, but I do know that Frederick was carrying a weapon."

"Why would Maks's driver be carrying a weapon?"

"I think because he was doubling as a bodyguard."

"Why would Maks need a bodyguard?"

"You're full of questions today," I said.

"Color me curious."

"I don't know, Gilley," I said impatiently. Thinking of the other night was almost too upsetting to bear. Even in the cold, I could feel my cheeks burning with humiliation.

"Sorry," he said softly.

"It's okay. I'm just embarrassed. I really liked Maks."

"I liked him too," Gil said. "Maybe after this is all over, you can reach out to him and tell him that you've been cleared of the crime."

I laughed, but there was no humor in it. "I'm sure he'll *jump* at the chance to take me out again."

"You never know, Cat. People can surprise you."

I stared at the pavement as we walked. "And sometimes they're as predictable as they seem." I was a good judge of character. I'd seen the look in Maks's eyes as they'd hauled me away. He'd never want anything to do with me again. Which reminded me . . . "I'll need to look for another renter for the upstairs office space."

"You're positive Maks won't want it?" Gil asked.

"Yes," I said. "Mark my words: we'll never see that man again."

By that time, we'd reached the woods, and Gilley led the way to a path that was all but obscured.

"I had no idea there was a path here."

"You'd miss it if you didn't walk the road," Gil said.

"I wonder who could've used it," I said.

"Anyone who knew about it," Gil told me. "It leads right up to Heather's house."

I tried to think back to anytime I'd ever seen Heather taking a walk along the road, and I couldn't think of a single instance.

Then I tried to think about anyone else who might've taken walks along the road, and no one came to mind. Well, maybe a dog walker here or there, but no one I could actually picture.

Gilley led the way deeper into the woods, and I followed, making sure to stick to the path lest I trip over a fallen branch or a log. My boots squished on the wet earth and, loud and somewhat silly as they were, I was glad I'd worn them.

At last, we came to a small clearing where Gil stopped to unload his backpack and dig out the drone, the controller, and his iPad.

Handing me the tablet, he said, "Hold that so I can see where I'm going with the drone."

"Got it," I said, turning it to the landscape view and angling it so that he could see the screen.

Gilley placed the drone on the ground, clicked the control, and in an instant, the drone had come to life and was lifting up, up, and away.

Gilley focused his attention on the drone until it'd cleared the trees, then he turned his focus to the iPad to fly the contraption toward Heather's.

I watched the screen with him in silence and couldn't help but be impressed with not only his idea but his remote flying skills.

In short order, the drone moved past the woods and over to Heather's house. Gil zoomed around the south end, over to the ocean side. He then lowered the drone to ground level and moved it carefully toward the massive series of windows that all but completely made up the back of the house.

"Wow," I said as the drone moved in for a close-up. "We can see everything."

"Yeah," Gil said. "But the place is neat as a pin. Do you see anything out of place?"

I squinted at the screen. "No."

Gilley moved the drone up and down the line of windows while we searched for anything that might offer a clue. There was nothing.

"I don't think she was murdered in any of the rooms at the back of the house," I concluded. "I mean, surely we'd see *something* out of place if that were the case."

"You'd think so," Gil said.

Abandoning the back of the house, Gilley moved the drone over to the north end. There were a few windows here, and we peered into what looked like a master bedroom—also neat as a pin—a guest room, a bathroom, and a sitting room.

Nothing appeared out of place. "I guess we should be thankful at least that the blinds are open."

"True that," Gil said.

Flying the drone around to the front of the house, we looked in window after window, trying to find any sign of a struggle or remnants of a crime scene. There was nothing.

Even the front dining room and adjoining parlor, where Heather had thrown her luncheon, were tidy and neat, with nothing out of place. It bothered me that there was no trace of either the luncheon or any kind of altercation. It was as if the luncheon—the setting for my original humiliation—had never taken place.

And then, as Gilley was winding the drone back toward our direction, he paused at a room at the far-south side. There appeared to be a gritty substance on the window. "What is that?" I asked.

"I think it's fingerprint powder," Gil said.

He hovered the drone in front of the window as we tried to peer through the smudges. "I think there's something on the floor," I said.

Gilley moved the drone over slightly, and we found a clear patch of window to peer through. Able now to make out the room, I could see that it was a library, with a desk, shelves of books, and a seating area.

On the floor was an outline that faintly resembled the body outlines you'd see taped off in old crime-scene photos.

"Is that what I think it is?" I whispered.

"I believe so," Gilley whispered back. And then he sucked in a breath and said, "Look! There's another window and a door on the other side of the room. Let me move the drone to that side. I think we can get a better look."

I pulled my focus back from the screen as Gil zipped the drone around to the other side of the house; the effect was slightly dizzying. He then found the window and lowered the drone. "This is a better angle," he said.

"And there's less smudge on the window," I agreed.

Peering at the screen, I looked all around the room. It was darkened by the gray day, but we were still able to make out everything with good clarity.

I could even see a few pebbles of broken glass on the floor that no doubt came from my punch bowl.

To the right was an overturned chair, and I found that disturbing. It either indicated signs of a struggle or the police had toppled it during their investigation. I had a hunch it was the former, though.

On the desk was a pair of black latex gloves that'd been peeled off and cast aside, but other than that, there wasn't much litter about the place.

"It appears this room was the focus of the police investigation," Gil said.

"She must've died in this room."

"Let me move over to the door," Gil said. "There's a window at the top there. We might be able to see something else from that angle."

Gilley moved the drone about again, and I looked away, feeling dizzy again at the sudden movement. "There," he said when he'd settled the drone at the door.

I peered at the screen and could see the room, but then something suddenly moved in front of the camera and the screen darkened.

"What the—?" Gilley said, as he maneuvered the drone back a foot or two.

It was then that a face came into view.

A very angry, familiar face.

"Ack!" I squeaked.

"Gah!" Gilley exclaimed, pulling hard on the handle of the remote control.

For a few moments, the drone spun in a dizzying circle, and because my eyes had been locked on the screen, I immediately felt a wave of dizzying motion sickness take over. "Ack!" I repeated, twisting away.

Unfortunately, I moved the iPad with me, and Gilley couldn't see the screen.

"I can't see!" he exclaimed. "Cat! I can't see where I'm going!"

Recovering myself, I pushed the tablet toward him and shook my head, trying to clear it. Inadvertently, I caught the image of that angry face again, only this time it was attached to the rest of the body, and it was armed with a large paperweight.

"Lookout!" I cried, just as Detective Shepherd launched the paperweight right at the camera.

But it was too late. There was a jarring motion, the screen went blank, and the remote control emitted a loud beep of alarm.

Gilley swiftly turned off the remote control, shoved it into his backpack, and grabbed the tablet out of my shaking hands. "Let's go!" he said, taking me roughly by the elbow.

Belatedly, I realized that Shepherd would be looking for the drone's owner and likely head right for the woods to conduct a search.

I ran with Gilley down the path, focusing on keeping my footing but moving as fast as possible.

We gained the road much sooner than I'd expected. "Thank God!" I said as we jumped onto the road and slowed our progress to a quick walk.

Gilley hitched his backpack up and attempted to smooth out his jacket. "Look cool," he said, slowing my pace a little more.

No sooner had he said that than we spotted a black sedan pull out of Heather's driveway, onto the road, and come straight for us.

"Son of a . . ." I whispered.

"Hey!" Gil said, to get my attention. "Cat. You've got to be cool, okay? We're just out for a stroll."

I nodded and reached into my pocket for my sunglasses. I couldn't resist the urge to hide behind *something*.

Shepherd pulled up to us and stopped. I didn't know if we were simply going to ignore him and move on past, or stop when he rolled down the window to speak to us, but Gilley paused, nodded to the detective and said, "Morning!" in a bright, cheerful voice.

"What're you two doing out here?" Shepherd demanded.

Gilley did a wonderful job of appearing confused. "We're out for our morning walk, Detective. Why?"

Shepherd reached over to grab something off the passenger seat and held it up toward us. "This belong to you?"

"What's that?" I asked, attempting to sound as innocent as possible.

"It's a drone," Gilley said. "I've seen those offered for sale in the hobby shop in town. We saw one flying around here a little earlier." Turning to me, he added, "Do you think that's the same drone that cruised over our heads about ten minutes ago, Cat?"

"Hmm," I said, "It sure looks the same. I hope it's not causing you any trouble, Detective."

Shepherd glared at us. It was obvious he thought we were fibbing. Which, we were, but still . . .

"I found this thing snooping around my crime scene," Shepherd said. "I could charge the owner of it with obstruction, and I'll remind you that I have your prints on file, Ms. Cooper."

"Oh?" I said, pushing at my sunglasses, and thinking about whether or not I'd ever touched the drone. I concluded that I hadn't, and that made me feel a bit better, at least. "Well, your job certainly sounds challenging, Detective. Best of luck to you."

Taking Gilley by the arm, I moved away from Shepherd's car.

The detective didn't much care for my obvious dismissal. He

put the sedan in reverse and started moving slowly backward alongside us. "Were you looking for something you left behind, Catherine?"

"I don't have any idea what you're talking about, Detective."

"At Heather's. Was there something that maybe you forgot that you think I'll find and would point to your guilt?"

I stopped and stared at Shepherd in open astonishment. "You genuinely think I murdered her, don't you?"

"Duh," he said, adding a sneer.

I let go of Gilley to put my hands on my hips. "You know what, Detective? You're an idiot."

Shepherd's sneer vanished, and it was replaced with a look that was also a bit shocked.

"I'm Catherine Cooper," I said boldly. "I'm a highly success-ful, self-made woman, who's *exceptionally* well respected in my industry. True, I'm new to *this* community, and also true, I wasn't well liked around here due to Heather, but *none* of that would've been motive enough for me to cause harm to a relative stranger. You think I'd throw my relationship with my sons away for a mere social snub? You think I'd throw my *life* away for the petty excuse of getting even with a woman who merely *embarrassed* me? How *dumb* are you, Detective Shepherd?!"

I'd yelled that last part. I hadn't meant to. It was the strain and anxiety of the moment.

"Cat," Gilley whispered, tugging on my arm. "He's not worth it."

"Of course he's not worth it!" I snapped. "But I am! I'm sick of being looked at as the *only* suspect in this case. It's ridiculous!"

"Cat!" Gil said with more urgency. "Stop, okay?"

I inhaled a deep breath and shook my head. I was so frus-trated. "Good day, Detective," I said firmly and set off toward my home.

Shepherd backed up the car again. "I don't think you mur-dered Heather because she embarrassed you," he said. "I think there was another reason, and I'm digging into your history to find it, Catherine. For now, I better not catch you anywhere near my crime scene ever again, or I'll haul you back to jail, and I'll make sure to make it just as public as last time."

With that, he shifted gears and zipped away down the road, leaving me shaking from head to toe.

Chapter 8

The call came about two seconds after we came through the door of the guest house. "Hello, Marcus," I said, not at all surprised.

"What did you do?" he demanded.

"Nothing," I told him. I wasn't going to own up to anything if I didn't absolutely have to.

"Catherine," he said, his voice calm but firm. "What did I tell you about getting into it with Shepherd?"

"Not to."

"So you *were* listening."

"Yes. Of course. I always listen to counsel on important matters like these."

"Then why didn't you do what I asked?"

"I didn't intend to have a confrontation with the man, Counselor. Gilley and I were merely out for a walk, seeing what we could see."

"And the drone?"

"Could have been flown by anyone."

There was a pregnant pause before Marcus spoke again. "If you haven't already dropped that check in the mail, I'm going to ask that you alter the amount. Make it a fifty-thousand-dollar retainer, okay?"

"Noted," I said crisply.

The line clicked, and he was gone.

"That sounded rough," Gil said.

I put away my cell. "Sorry about your drone."

"It's fine," Gilley said.

"Do you think they'll be able to trace it back to you? Through fingerprints or something?"

"My fingerprints aren't in the system," Gil said.

"Weren't you once arrested for murder?"

"That was in Scotland," he said. "I doubt the East Hampton P.D. has a relationship with Interpol. Plus, it's raining."

"Why does that matter?"

"Rain would've washed away or obscured most of my prints. It'll be fine, don't worry."

But I was worried. Very, very worried.

"What do we do now?" I asked. "Other than discovering that Heather was probably murdered in her library, we got nothing."

"I wouldn't say that," Gilley said.

Moving to the table with his backpack, he pulled out the tablet and tapped at the screen. I realized belatedly that he'd recorded the video feed from the drone. Using his finger, he scrolled along the feed quickly to the last few moments. I blinked several times in order not to get sucked into the dizzying effect caused by the footage, but then Gilley paused on one frame and sat back in his chair as if he'd just discovered something big.

"What?" I asked him, staring at a still of the back door with Shepherd's blurry image about to step over the threshold.

Gilley pointed to the upper-right portion of the screen. "See that?" he said.

I looked at the screen. "What is that?" I asked.

"It's a security camera," Gilley said.

I sucked in a breath. "A security camera? Why aren't the police analyzing the footage? If Heather had cameras over the doors of her home, then the footage would totally exonerate me and point to the killer!"

"This was the only camera I saw on the drone's tour of the house, Cat," Gil said. "But if the killer used that door to enter and murder Heather, we might be in luck."

"Again, I'm asking why the police haven't analyzed the footage and cleared me of any wrongdoing?"

"Either there's nothing on the tape around the time of the murder or they missed it in their investigation, which I don't think is likely."

"Since they're only looking at me as the murderer, I'd say it's possible. How do we get a copy of that footage?"

Gilley leaned back in his chair and studied me seriously. "Given some time, I think I could hack into the system and get us a copy."

"No way," I said immediately. "Gilley, we're already riding the fine line of obstruction here. Shepherd now suspects that I'm trying to tamper with the crime scene to obscure any clues that might indicate me as the killer. If we got caught, it'd be a nail in my coffin."

"I know," he said. "And if we got caught, it would look pretty bad. But it could also completely exonerate you, Cat."

I sat with that for a bit. "I hate this," I said. "It's an impossible choice."

"Not for me."

"You want to take the chance."

"I do. I'm good, Cat. I'll make sure I hack in and get out fast, before anybody is the wiser."

"But you couldn't even hack into Heather's Facebook account. How are you going to get into her security camera feed?"

"I couldn't hack into her account before I had access to what was on her profile page," Gil said. "Now that I know what's on her personal page, I'm pretty sure I can figure out a password for her camera system."

"How does that make a difference?"

Gilley shrugged. "Most people create passwords that they know they'll easily remember. Like a pet's name or a nickname they go by combined with their birthday. Some people even use their spouse's name as a password."

I reddened slightly. I'd used my ex's middle name with his birthday as a password for years. In fact, I still had at least a few sites in my system that bore that particular password.

"But how do you even know where to start?" I asked. "I mean, where would that kind of footage be stored in the first place?"

"Probably on Heather's iCloud account," Gil said.

"And that's what you're going to hack into?"

"Yes," Gilley said. There was a gleam in his eye that suggested he found this to be a challenge he was eager to take on.

"Won't the police be looking into her iCloud account?" I pressed. I was scared of Shepherd seeing Gilley hack into Heather's iCloud account in real time and tracing it back to us.

"I doubt it. They'd need her password, which they might be able to get, but if—worst-case scenario—they do notice a hack, I can make sure that it'll look like it's coming from Russia."

My eyes widened. "You can do that?"

Gilley laced his fingers together and flexed them. "Child's play."

While Gilley was busy trying to crack Heather's iCloud account, I busied myself with a little of my own business, paying some bills, re-posting the listing for the upstairs office space, and replying to some e-mails, and then I thought I'd check in with the boys.

I called my son Mathew first, but it went to voice mail. I tried Michael, and it also went to voice mail, but a few moments later, I did receive a text from him.

S'up?

I know all you mothers out there are simply *envious* of the obvious love my son shows me.

I decided to respond with an example of how one should talk over text when speaking to a loved one.

"S'up?" Are you serious with me right now, Michael? No, "Good morning, Mother. How are you? May I assist you with something?"

Three bubbles appeared immediately, and I smiled. No doubt my message was received, and I'd get a proper response from him.

S'up?

I glowered at the screen. "You little *beast!*"

"Did you say something?" Gilley asked.

"No," I told him. "Not yet at least." I then began poking out a new message with emphasis.

Shall I remind you that your phone is registered to MY name, and one call to Verizon will put your phone in lockdown?

Bubbles again.

I waited with a tapping foot until they dissolved.

Good morning, Mother. How are you? May I assist you with something?

I sighed. I'd had trouble getting pregnant. Tommy and I had tried for years until we'd gone to see a specialist who'd recommended fertility drugs. I'd taken the injections for months, and my rear end had often looked like a pincushion. When that didn't work, we moved to IVF, which required yet more injections and one very painful procedure. When my sons were born, the feeling was so euphoric. It was almost as if I'd fulfilled the most important promise I could've made to myself. It was a life's wish granted, and as I read my sweet, beautiful, blond-headed son's text, I wondered what the heck I'd been thinking those fourteen years ago?

How's school? I tried.

Good

Your classes going well?

Yeah

Do you still like all your teachers?

Yeah

Anyone giving you trouble?

Nah

Do you need anything? Clothes? Shoes? Food? Snacks?
Nah. I'm good.

Goodness. A two-sentence response. *With* punctuation. How *would* I contain myself?

I just tried reaching your brother. He didn't answer.
Sleeping
All right. Well, give me a call sometime, my sweet boy. I'd love to hear your voice now and again.
K

And that was it. Our "conversation" was over.

"Who're you texting?" Gilley asked.

"Michael," I said, my voice squeaking with emotion while I looked through the text exchange, hunting for any hint of the little boy who used to shout, "Mom! Mom! *MOM!*" as he jumped off the school bus after school and dashed into my arms. Between the lines and letters, there seemed to be no hint of him. He'd been replaced by a cold, listless, alien creature.

"Aww, you miss them, huh?"

"Yes, and no."

"Yes and no?" he pressed.

I knew Gilley could tell I was upset. Mostly I was hurt, injured by the fact that my sons no longer saw me as a superhero and often saw me more as the villain. "I miss feeling like I matter," I said to Gil. "I miss feeling like they care how I am or what I think."

"They care," Gilley assured me. "They just forget how to express it between the ages of fourteen and twenty-two."

I looked up at Gil. "Is that true?"

"It was true for me," he said.

That surprised me. "You're kidding."

Gilley worshiped the ground his mother walked on. I'd met his mother at Gilley's wedding, and I'd found her to be extraordinary—and absolutely delightful.

"Not kidding," Gilley assured me. "I don't think I discovered how cool and fabulous my mom was until I was in my mid-twenties."

A small weight lifted off my heart. "That's a relief."

"Hang in there," Gilley said. "You've got a few more tough years of being treated like the enemy. Then you'll see your sons turn into doting young men who brag about how amazing you are to all their friends."

"I look forward to it," I said, tucking away my phone. "How's the hacking coming?"

Gilley rolled his head from side to side. His neck cracked, and I winced. "This may take some time," he admitted.

"How much time?"

"A day or two."

"That long?"

He regarded me with heavy lids. "That long? Gurl, please. In the hacking world, that's light speed."

"Ah. Okay, well then, I'm going to head across the courtyard to Chez Cat and read for a bit."

"Have fun," he said.

I headed over to Chez Cat and entered the front door, feeling a bit melancholy. Thinking of my book upstairs, I retrieved it, then settled down in the sunroom at the back of the house that offered glorious views of the ocean on all three sides.

The day was still gloomy, with a steady drizzle, but visibility out on the ocean wasn't compromised, and the view was worth taking in.

For a long time, I simply watched the water, allowing its calming, hypnotic effect to settle around me. My thoughts at first were occupied with Matt and Mike, but then they drifted to the events of the past few days, and even the calm of the rolling seas couldn't settle my nerves. It felt wrong to be sitting comfortably in my home while Detective Shepherd did everything he could to build a case against me.

Setting the unopened book aside, I got up and moved to one

of the windows. I felt unsettled and stymied. There had to be something I could do to move our investigation forward while Gilley was busy working his hacking magic.

And then I had a thought, and as an upstanding citizen (well, mostly), it wasn't one I really should've entertained, but it wouldn't go away. I debated with myself for a good ten to fifteen minutes but finally gave in to the impulse and went in search of my laptop.

Finding it in the kitchen, I brought it back to the sunroom and powered it on. After a few clicks, I was at Joyce McQueen's login to Facebook, and I typed in "drowssap." It gave me an error message. Frowning, I tried again, typing out the word slowly and carefully, but again it gave me an error message.

"Did Gilley already change it back?" I said to myself.

I tried "password" and "Password," but neither of those two worked. Then I tried "Drowssap," and it still wouldn't take. As a last resort, I tried "drowssaP," and to my surprise, I was logged in.

"Eureka!"

Quickly, I moved over to Joyce's friends' page and scrolled down to Heather's personal page. Hopping over, I began to read through her posts, and it was shocking to me how much personal information Heather shared among her three hundred friends and acquaintances.

That's when I discovered something I hadn't known before, and the revelation sent me to my feet and racing for the door.

"Gilley!" I said, coming into Chez Kitty.

"*What?*" he shrieked, jumping up and looking ready to race out the door.

"Sorry," I said. "Didn't mean to startle you."

Gilley put a hand over his heart. "Then *why* did you come bolting in here shouting my name?!"

I'd been clutching my laptop, and I hastily moved it over to the table to open it up and show him. "Look!" I said, triumphantly.

COACHED TO DEATH   141

Gilley's hand remained over his heart as he squinted at the screen.

"What?"

"I've discovered the *reason* Heather hated me! She used to date Nigel Fitzpatrick!"

"Um . . . okay?"

"Look!" I repeated, pointing to a man in the photo that Heather had posted on her Facebook page with a caption that read, "Thanks for the memories, loser! Nigel and I are over!"

"Who's that old geezer?" Gilley asked.

"Nigel Fitzpatrick," I said, waiting for him to get it.

Gilley's gaze pivoted from me, to the screen, to me, to the screen, then back to me again. "I don't get it."

I sagged dramatically. "*Nigel . . . Fitzpatrick!*"

Gilley did that whole pivot, pivot, pivot thing again and repeated, "I. Don't. Get. It."

I sighed and rolled my eyes. "You don't remember me going on and on about a Nigel Fitzpatrick?"

Gilley's brow furrowed. "Okay, so that name actually does ring a little bell."

"Nigel!" I yelled at him, wanting him to put it together.

And then Gilley's eyes widened, and he stared at me in shock. "The old man you bought the lot from? The one who took you to lunch and said that a woman with eyes the color of the sea should live by the sea?"

"Yes!" I said, so relieved that he remembered.

"Wait, Heather *dated* him?"

"For two years!" I said, hopping over to her photos page and scrolling down through the months to the section that showed her and Nigel in what appeared to be happier times.

"Ick," Gilley said. I couldn't agree more. "Tell me again what all that was about?"

"Nigel sold this parcel to me. His best friend is on the board with me at Camp Hope for Kids—"

"The kids with leukemia camp charity you organize every year?"

"Yes. Me and four others. Anyway, Tyrone—my fellow board member—heard I was looking for property in the Hamptons, and he said that he'd just been speaking to his best friend Nigel about selling off a parcel of land that had been in his family for years and years. He owns a house on the south side of town, which he's always adored, and he never wanted to bother with the hassle of building a new home here just for the view. He said he was tired of paying the taxes, and it was time to sell, and Tyrone would never recommend anyone less than stellar to him, so he was willing to part with the parcel for a very reasonable price."

"Aww," said Gil. "He sounds like a sweet old geezer."

"He was quite sweet, but far too old for me. He asked if I'd like to see him socially, and I politely declined, even though I was worried he'd retract his offer, but he never did. He was a true gentleman and honored the verbal agreement."

"So you never saw Nigel again after buying the lot?"

"No. I never did."

Gilley tapped his lip. "So *why* would Heather have cared? I mean, the old man sold you the lot fair and square. So what?"

I frowned. "I don't know. But there has to be a reason, and I believe that reason is connected to Nigel somehow. Maybe she saw me meeting him for lunch, got jealous, and they split up because of it."

Gilley continued to eye me skeptically. "What's the date of her breakup post?"

I squinted at the screen. "She broke up with him shortly after I submitted my plans to build on the lot."

"Hmm," Gil said. "Okay, the timing is a tiny bit suspicious— maybe the two events are linked, but I have to ask again, why would she care?"

"Well, maybe it's simply the fact that Nigel sold this lot to me and I put a big old house on it." When Gilley's brow furrowed, I added, "Hear me out. When we were headed into the luncheon the other day, I happened to notice that the ocean view from Heather's house on the north side would've been obstructed when my home was built. This was vacant land before I came along, and the view must've been spectacular."

"So she hated you for an obstructed view?" Gilley asked skeptically.

I sighed. Even I thought that was a bit of a stretch. "Well, it has to be *something*."

"I know this might be a terrible suggestion, Cat, but have you ever thought about asking someone in Heather's crowd why she had it out for you?"

I stared openmouthed at Gilley for a beat before managing to say, "No."

Gil turned back to his screen. "Well, *Joyce*, maybe you should look through Heather's friends' list and find someone willing to talk to you about it."

I stood there for a long moment just staring angrily at Gilley. At last I said, "They won't talk to me. They all know I was accused of her murder."

Gilley continued to gaze at his screen. "And you know this for certain because you've already reached out to a few of them?"

Again, I could only glare at Gilley.

"Sugar," he said, sitting back in his chair to regard me, "what're you always telling me are the three tenets for being a good life coach?"

My brow furrowed. Where was he going with this? "Listen, learn, lend."

Gilley nodded sagely. "Yes. Listen and learn. Those are the things you need to be a good investigator too. Funny how they overlap."

I rolled my eyes. "Point taken. But for the record, sometimes I hate it when you're right."

"I know, puddin'. But I only say it because it's for your own good."

"Fiiiiine," I sighed. "I'll go change and start calling on people."

"Good. That's great," he said, getting back to his hacking.

Back at Chez Cat, I changed into neutral tones—brown slacks, brown sweater, and chocolate pumps, adding a small punch of color with an orange beaded choker—then sat down once again and surveyed Heather's list of friends.

One face I recognized from Heather's party was the pregnant woman I'd first met at the punch bowl. She'd seemed nice. Maybe I could reach out to her.

"Okay, Sunny D'Angelo. Let's see if you're willing to talk to me."

A Google search gave me Sunny's address, and before I had a second to reconsider or lose my nerve, I grabbed my keys, coat, and purse and headed out the door.

Chapter 9

I parked on the street and stared at Sunny's stately home for a good five minutes before working up the courage to approach her front door. I had only a vague idea what I might say, and I hated that I was so nervous about even starting a conversation with her. I mean, I used to run a multimillion-dollar firm. I'd stood before world leaders and attended parties with famous celebrities, and I'd spoken to a group of over a thousand businesswomen once, and none of that gave me the butterflies in my stomach like working up the nerve to speak to a woman who might already consider me a murderer.

Still, like my former congresswoman, old E.W., I persisted. With a shaking hand, I rang the bell, and a few moments later the door was opened by Sunny herself.

She gasped when she saw me on her doorstep. "Catherine," she said. "Oh, my goodness! What a surprise. I heard what happened to you the other night at Pierre's, you poor thing. Are you all right?"

Her greeting left me speechless. I mean, I'd been prepared for a number of reactions, but genuine concern for my person was not one of them, and without warning, I found myself welling up. "Hello, Sunny," I said, blinking furiously in an attempt to chase away the tears.

"Oh, honey," she said, stepping to the side. "Come in, and I'll fix you some tea."

I swallowed hard and dipped my chin slightly as I stepped carefully past her rounded belly. I found it hard to speak, and even more difficult to know what to say other than a hoarse "Thank you."

She shut the door behind me and then moved ahead, waving me forward. "The kitchen is this way."

We walked the length of a long hallway that gave way to a large, beautifully lit gourmet kitchen with a white marble countertop, gray cabinets, and a black slate floor. "Take a seat at the table," she instructed, and I did, finding an upholstered chair to sit in.

Meanwhile, Sunny busied herself by filling the teakettle and getting down a teapot and two china cups from the cupboards. "You know, it's so funny that you're here; you've been on my mind so much this morning," she said.

"I have?"

She smiled kindly at me. "Yes. I heard all about Pierre's. I'm so sorry they did that to you."

I bit my lip at the mention of the memory. "So . . . you don't think I'm guilty?"

She laughed lightly. "Oh, honey, of course I don't think you're guilty! No one does!"

"That's a surprise," I said.

She nodded knowingly. "I'm sure it is. You were treated so unkindly by Heather and her posse, I think that if the situation were reversed, I'd probably think everyone thought I'd done it too."

"Can you tell that to the police?"

"You mean my brother?"

It was my turn to gasp. "What?"

"The detective who arrested you. Steve Shepherd is my brother," she said. "He's my twin, although technically I'm older than him by almost twelve minutes."

I stared at Sunny with large, unblinking eyes for at least thirty seconds. "But he thinks I'm guilty!" I finally said . . . perhaps a bit louder than I'd intended.

The whistle of the teakettle drowned out much of my outburst, however, and Sunny spent a moment in silence pouring the hot water into the teapot before coming over to sit down across from me. "Maybe," she said. "And maybe he doesn't."

I stared at her in confusion. "That's a little cryptic, Sunny. Could you be more specific?"

"What you have to know about Steve, Catherine, is that he's very, very clever. I know he doesn't always let on that he's the sharpest tool in the shed, but he is. And sometimes he likes to run a good ruse to root out the real culprit, which I believe—and, mind you, I only believe it to be true, because he hasn't spoken specifically to me about it—is what he's up to with the whole public arrest thing at Pierre's."

I rubbed my forehead. "I still don't think I'm following you."

Sunny got up and moved over to the simmering teapot, bringing it over to the table with the two cups; then she also retrieved a small pitcher of cream and a matching sugar bowl. "Steve is trying to root out the real murderer by making it look like he's focused only on you. It's why he made your arrest so public, and why he pushed to have the D.A. file charges so quickly."

My jaw dropped. "But that's so unfair!" I exclaimed. My goodness, I was having a hard time controlling my emotions.

Sunny eyed me with sympathy. "I know it seems that way, Catherine, but if it works, then it might all be worth it."

"But you haven't talked to your brother about it, right? So you don't really know that's what he's up to."

"Correct. I haven't spoken directly to him about the case. But I do know him well, and that's what I suspect he's up to with all of this public attention on you as the suspect."

Sunny poured me some tea and then offered the cream and sugar. I spent a little time trying to sort out all this new information by filling my tea with a bit too much cream and sugar. The tea was light and delicious all the same. "Can I ask you something that may sound weird?" I said at last.

Sunny grinned. "You want to know why I don't think you did it, right?"

"Yes."

"Well, because, what's the motive? I mean, you're going to kill Heather over a misunderstanding? That doesn't make any sense to me."

"It wasn't a misunderstanding," I said. "Heather meant for me to show up looking and acting like the hired help."

"Well, of course she did. That bitch was just plain mean, Catherine, and everyone thought so, but we were all a little afraid of her, so no one was ever willing to stand up against her. And she'd hazed all of us at some point or another. Even me, and I'd known Heather since grade school."

"So that's what you think that stunt at the luncheon was all about? Just a hazing?"

"No," Sunny said. "No, I think it went a little deeper than that. She really did hate you."

"Do you have any idea why?"

"Well, I think it's because you got to Nigel."

"I got to Nigel? You mean her ex?"

"Yes."

"What does that mean, though. That I 'got' to Nigel?"

"The oceanfront lot," she said simply. "You got him to sell it to you. What you might not realize is that Heather tried for years to get him to sell it to her. She was furious that he'd sold it to someone else when she'd done everything she could think of to entice him into selling it to her."

"Why was that lot so important to her? I mean, isn't her estate big enough?"

"I sure thought so. But I believe Heather had other plans for it. She was going to build one of those awful mega homes—you know, a real pig-mansion—or maybe even squish two houses onto the lot and turn a nice profit."

I blinked again. "Heather was in construction?"

"Yes. After her ex—Tony—met with an untimely end, Heather took over her husband's construction firm, and she's been building these god-awful homes all over the area ever since."

"What do you mean by Tony's untimely end?" I asked. This was one of the most interesting conversations I'd had in a very long time, and I felt like someone asking to be read the Cliff Notes on an engaging saga.

"Well," Sunny said, taking a sip of her tea, "there were rumors that Tony was involved with the wrong kind of people, if you get my drift." For effect, Sunny pushed at the side of her nose.

"Ahh," I said. "The kind that likes to fit their enemies with cement shoes?"

Sunny winked. "Exactly. A few years ago, Tony was found dead at the base of a bridge on the other side of the Hamptons. His car was parked and still running by the side of the bridge when his body was found. The M.E. ruled it a suicide, but no one—including my brother—thought he'd killed himself. Steve spent a lot of time looking into Tony's business dealings, trying to find something that would point to evidence of foul play, but he could never find anything substantial, and Heather flat out refused to cooperate.

"In fact, for a long time after that, I remember Heather ran pretty scared. Always flinching at loud noises, declining social engagements. And she was seen very little in public. When she was spotted, she was always wearing last year's fashions. My housekeeper even told me that she let all but one of her staff go, indicating she'd fallen on hard times. But then things seemed to improve for her, and she started socializing again and boasted that her business was booming.

"The jewel in her crown was going to be Nigel's lot and the new houses she'd build on it."

"It's hard to imagine more than one large home on that lot." I said. It was a short trip from my back door to the beach—maybe only a hundred feet, so it was impossible to picture two large homes on the site.

"Trust me," Sunny said, "Heather would've found a way to cram in more than one home on that lot. At some point, I think that Nigel figured out Heather was just using him, and he did an end run around her by selling the property to you. At least that's my theory. She was absolutely furious when she found out. She dumped him the second the news reached her, and then she went around town issuing threats and vowing revenge against him. It was as if she was coming unhinged, and it scared Nigel enough to pack up and leave the Hamptons."

"Wait, he left?" I asked. I'd had no idea.

"Yep. I heard he headed to Florida. Now that she's dead, I don't know if he's coming back, but I wouldn't count on it."

"Wow," I said, stunned by these revelations. "And here I thought the bad blood between me and Heather was because I'd blocked her view of the ocean."

"Oh, she was pretty ticked off about that too, but by then that was just adding insult to injury," Sunny said. "She had several reasons to hate you."

I shook my head. I'd had no idea the ill will had run so deep, but it helped clear up a lot of questions. "Sunny?"

"Yes?"

"Do you know who might've killed her?"

My host shrugged. "Pick any name out of a hat, Catherine, and they're as likely to have killed her as the next person. Heather was deeply disliked, but revered. Nobody crossed her if they could avoid it. All these years, we put up with her crap because when she turned on you, she went for blood."

"Besides me, who do you know that she had turned against?" I asked.

Sunny made a derisive sound. "That list is long. She turned on business partners, construction workers, friends, family, neighbors, staff, service people, city workers . . . and, rumor has it, some of the people that might've had a hand in her husband's death."

"Really," I said. "Wow. That's intense."

"Yep. Just like Heather."

I left Sunny's home a short time later, feeling like I'd had several important questions answered, but then I realized that they weren't the most important questions I should've been asking. I'd had no idea that Heather had so many enemies, and from places much more sinister than the local Junior League.

I drove back to Chez Cat more frustrated than I'd been when I'd left it. The other thing that bothered me was this whole arrest thing with Detective Shepherd. I found myself furious that he'd arrested me in public like that when he *knew* I hadn't killed Heather.

I mean, what the hell had I ever done to him?

As I pulled into the drive and waited for the garage door to lift, the seed of an idea came to my mind. It was a bold idea for sure. And it could totally backfire. But it was one I felt I needed to see through.

Lifting my phone, I dialed the now-familiar number.

"Catherine," Marcus Brown said, his voice warm, possibly amused. "What's happened?"

"Hello, Marcus. So sorry to disturb you on a Sunday."

"Not an issue. What do you need?"

"Information."

"What kind?"

"The self-revelatory kind."

"Intriguing. Continue."

"How good of a defense attorney are you?"

"Exceptional."

I exhaled in relief. He hadn't even hesitated, and I felt that Marcus wasn't the kind of man who issued falsehoods about himself to pump up his own ego. No, I had the feeling that he was someone who held himself to a very high standard and worked to uphold that standard at all costs.

"Perfect. Can you meet me at the East Hampton Police Department tomorrow?"

"What time?"

"Let's say around eleven?"

"May I ask why?"

"I'd rather you didn't."

"Fine. See you tomorrow, Catherine."

Marcus hung up, and I pulled into the garage, my palms feeling sweaty on the wheel. I was about to make either an absolutely brilliant move or an impossibly stupid one, and the only way to know which was to see it through to the end.

The next morning, I headed to my office to meet Erma. All the drama in my own life aside, I was anxious to see how she was faring after I'd given her what I was sure was terrific advice.

I hadn't woken Gilley when I left; I'd seen that the kitchen light in the guest house was on when I'd gone to bed at ten, and I knew he'd likely stayed up late trying to hack into Heather's iCloud account. I could handle Erma on my own.

"So, how've you been?" I asked when she and I were seated across from each other.

"Good," she said, in a voice that sounded only a little unsure. "Mostly good."

"Excellent," I said, beaming at her. "Did you take my advice, Erma? Did you start asking for help from others?"

"I did!" she said, using that booming voice of hers.

I winced. My goodness, the woman was loud. "And how did that work out for you?"

"Good. Mostly good."

I nodded, hoping she'd be forthcoming with the details, but apparently the woman needed to be prodded. "Sounds fabulous. Any examples you'd care to share?"

"Well, after I left here last week, I went to the grocery store and bought a lot of stuff."

"Wonderful! I love a well-stocked fridge, don't you?"

"For sure. But not much of what I bought would go in the fridge."

"Really? What did you buy?"

"Mostly doughnuts."

My eyes widened.

"That guy who works here?"

"You mean, Gilley?"

"Yeah. Well, he just got my mouth watering for doughnuts even after the six he brought me. And there was a sale at the supermarket. So I bought a couple dozen more."

"I see," I said, feeling my smile tighten. "But how does that work into the advice that I gave you?"

"Well, there was this sale on Mr. PiBB, and I just *love* Mr. PiBB, so I bought a couple cases. Anyway, my grocery cart was really loaded down, and when I left the store, I passed by these kids sitting on a bench outside the grocery store, so I asked if they would help me load the groceries into my car, and they said, 'Sure!' That's not something I ever would've done if you hadn't told me to."

I clapped my hands. "Excellent! See, Erma? When you ask for help, good things happen!"

Erma nodded with enthusiasm. "Yeah, I know, right? It was good. Well, mostly good."

My brow furrowed. "Only mostly good? Didn't the kids help you load the groceries into your car?"

"Not exactly."

"What does that mean?"

"It means they mostly helped load my groceries into *their* car, and then they took off."

I blinked. "They . . . *stole* your groceries?"

"Um . . . yeah. They did."

"Did you call the police?"

"Um . . . no. I didn't."

"Why not?"

Erma shrugged and shook her head. "I guess I didn't think about it. Plus, it would've made me late for work, and I had another chance to put your advice to work."

I perked up again. "You did?"

"Yeah. So my boss, Mr. Gutworth, likes to dump a lot of stuff on my desk. Like, my job description doesn't cover half of what he gives me to do, and I always do it, even though most days he makes me get there by seven a.m. and there's so much work that I don't get to go home until about seven at night."

"That's a twelve-hour day," I said. I was impressed. I didn't know Erma was such a hard worker. "What do you do again, Erma?"

"Mostly it's data collection. I work for an attorney who specializes in tax-lien relief. I do all the background research—like tax logs, credit checks, etc., etc."

"Sounds . . . interesting," I said.

Erma laughed and waved her hand dismissively. "It's dull as dirt. But I'm going to miss it."

I shook my head, thinking I hadn't heard her right. "You're going to miss it?"

"Yeah. I got fired on Friday."

My jaw dropped. "You got *fired?*"

Erma's eyes welled up. "Yes. Yes, I did."

"Why? I mean, did your boss give you a reason?"

"Well, after I got to the office and saw the stack of work on my desk, I decided to take your advice, so I marched right into my boss's office and told him I couldn't do these twelve-hour days anymore and that I needed help with the workload."

"He fired you for that?" I asked, incredulous.

"No. He fired me because I walked in on him and Mrs. Mandlebam. She's one of his clients. They're both married to other people. And while that might not've gotten me fired on any *other* day, last Friday Mr. Gutworth's wife showed up just as he was yelling at me and pulling up his pants. I'd left the door to his office wide open, and Mrs. Gutworth came running when she heard yelling, and well . . . she kind of saw everything."

"Oh, Erma, I'm so, so sorry!"

Erma shrugged. "I spent the weekend crying—and packing, of course."

I gulped. Could this story get any worse? "Packing?"

Erma nodded. "My roommate moved out of the trailer we share in Islip last week in the middle of the day while I was at work. She didn't tell me she was leaving, and she hadn't coughed up her end of the rent before she left. I was already kind of scraping by, and now without a paycheck I can't make my rent this month. But I remembered your advice, so I went to the trailer park owner and asked him to help me out, you know, maybe give me a few extra weeks to find a job or another roommate and get the rent in, but he said that because my roommate didn't pay her share, I'm one and a half months behind, so he wants me out by next Tuesday."

My eyes widened yet again.

"Anyway," Erma continued while I was left absorbing all of *that*, "I think this is going to have to be my last session, Ms. Cooper. I really only came today to give you back your car and thank you very much for all your advice. Even though it didn't really help me in the end, I'm sure you meant well."

Erma started to get up, extending her hand to offer me the keys to the Audi, but I put my hand up to stop her. "Hold on, dear," I said firmly. "You're not going anywhere just yet."

Erma sat down and stared obediently at me.

Taking a deep breath, I said, "First, what happened to your car? Did you get it out of the lot?"

"Oh, that's the other thing I forgot to tell you," Erma said. "When I called my bank to see how much I owed, they said that due to penalties and interest, it all came to about five hundred dollars more than you'd given me. So I can't afford to get my car out of impound, and truthfully, I owe more than that piece of junk is worth, so I told them they could keep it. Oh, but I did bring you back your check."

Erma began to dig in her purse for the check I'd written her, and I stopped her again.

"Erma," I said gently. When she looked up, I continued with, "Deposit that check and use it to pay your rent. We need to keep a roof over your head until we can find you a job. And one that pays you enough to make your rent each month without having to rely on roommates. Given how hard you're willing to work, it's a crime that you're not being paid enough to meet your needs."

Erma's mouth dropped open, and she stared at me in shock. "You mean it?"

"Yes, dear. Also, you may keep my car as long as you need it."

"I was gonna look for something closer to where I live," she said. "I can take the train if I can just find something four or five stops away."

"Of course," I said. "But for now, keep the car and cast as wide a net as you need to look for another job. Third, we work on updating your résumé to help find you decent employment as soon as possible. Forward your résumé to my assistant, Gilley. He and I can take a look at it and polish it up if need be. Fourth, I'm going to reach out to a few of my contacts and see if we can't get you something—even temporary—to tide you over."

Erma's eyes misted again, and she put her fingers to her lips, appearing unable to speak. She then let out a sob and crumpled forward. It broke my heart to see her in such a state. She was a mess, this one, and she knew it, and because she knew it, she was willing to accept every cruelty thrown at her, offering nothing in return but a nod and a forced smile. I could only imagine how many people had mistreated her over the years. It angered and affected me to think about anyone being unkind to her simply because she wasn't as together as some of the rest of us.

"Fifth," I said gently, nudging the box of tissues closer to her. "I don't want you to worry, Erma. This will not be our last session, and there is no charge for today, and I'm refunding you your session from Friday." She started to shake her head no, and I felt I had to insist. "Listen," I said softly, "sometimes you need to ask for help, and sometimes you simply need to accept it when it's staring you in the face. Do you understand?"

Erma lifted her chin to look up at me, and I stared at her intently—making my point. "Accept the help, Erma."

"It's too . . . too . . . too much," she stammered, tears making her words sound thick.

"No. No, it's not. It's probably only a tiny fraction of what you deserve, in fact. I have no doubt that you're a good person, Erma. Just think of this as the universe's way of letting you know that you have value and that it recognizes what a good soul you are." I stood up and motioned for Erma to get up too.

She did, and I was taken completely by surprise when she launched herself at me, lifting me in the air for a gigantic hug. She squeezed hard, and the air rushed out of my lungs. "Errrma . . . ," I squeaked. "Erma, I can't breathe!"

At that moment, the door opened, and in walked someone I never expected to see again.

"Is this a bad time?" Maks asked, a bit of a bemused smile on his lips.

Erma whirled around, still clutching me, and said, "Oh, hey!"

"*Erma!*" I tried, again in a choked whisper. "Put . . . me . . . down!"

Abruptly, she did, and I nearly sank to my knees. Taking in a huge lungful of air, I was grateful for the hands that reached out to support me.

"Gosh, Ms. Cooper! I'm so sorry! I didn't realize how itty bitty you are. I hope I didn't break anything!"

"No," I said, bent over and touching my ribs. "I'm fine. Really."

"Would you like to sit down?" Maks asked.

It was in that moment that I realized his were the hands supporting me. "That would be good."

He moved with me back to my chair, and I got my breathing under control. Meanwhile, Erma continued to stand there and wring her hands. "What can I do?" she said.

For her sake, I gathered myself together and pushed a reaffirming smile onto my lips. "Nothing, dear. I'm fine."

Erma continued to look worried, so I reached out and squeezed her hand. "Truly. I'm fine."

She let out a big breath of relief and said, "I should go. I've got lots to do now that you're helping me out."

"Yes," I said. "Yes. We'll talk very soon, Erma."

After she'd gone, I stared up at Maks with a mixture of emotions ranging from embarrassment to joy. "What could possibly have caused you to come here today, Maks?" I asked him. It wasn't accusatory. I genuinely couldn't fathom why he'd arrived at my office.

In turn, he seemed puzzled. "We had an appointment," he said. Reaching into his coat, he withdrew a checkbook. "Remember?"

My brow furrowed. "Wait . . . you still want to lease the upstairs office space?"

"Of course," he said easily. "And, of course, I wanted to see you."

I rubbed my temple. "Were you not there last Thursday night? Do you not remember my arrest?"

Maks waved his hand as if that was nothing. "A trumped-up charge and an overly eager detective, trying to make a name for himself. That much was obvious."

I stared at him for a solid thirty seconds before speaking. "Hold on," I said, putting at least one of the puzzle pieces together. "Marcus Brown . . . know him?"

Maks smiled. "In fact, I do."

"Hire him lately?"

Maks's smile grew bigger. "Perhaps. A friend was in need of representation, and I may have made a call and done a small favor."

"That was incredibly kind of you," I said. I didn't even know what else to say.

"The least I could do. The detective should never had treated you that way. He should be fired."

"Not to worry. I plan on getting my revenge."

"Do you now?"

"Yes."

"How?"

"By beating him at his own game, but let's not talk anymore about him. I want to hear about you, Maks. What happened after they hauled me away for a crime I didn't commit?"

"Well," Maks said, taking a seat on the couch that Erma had vacated. "I missed dinner, of course, which is a shame because I so like the food at Pierre's. We should go there again, you know. This time without interruption."

Butterflies took flight in my stomach. Still, I wasn't eager for a return date there. "I don't think I could ever show my face at that restaurant again."

"Somewhere else then?"

"Yes. That would be lovely."

Maks leaned forward, his eyes gazing into mine, and I felt like I'd turned to liquid under his stare. "Shall we attend to some real business now, Catherine?"

"Real . . . real business?" I stammered. What did *that* mean? Was he asking for . . . for . . . sex?

"Yes," he said, continuing to stare at me with that smoldering gaze. "You know, our *real* business together."

Oh, God. He *was* hinting at something sexual! What a pervert! I stood up angrily. "Mr. Grinkov, I will have you know that I'm not *that* kind of woman. While I appreciate—very much—your assistance the other evening and your generous donation to my legal defense, I'm afraid you're assuming far too much about me in this moment."

Maks blinked at me in confusion. "So, you *don't* want me to sign the lease after all?"

I sucked in a surprised breath. Putting up a hand to cover my mouth, I then began to giggle, but I was also mortified. "Oh, God! Maks, I'm so sorry! I . . . I don't know what I was thinking!"

"You were thinking I wanted to do something inappropriate with you?"

I shook my head vigorously, but then nodded too. "No! Well, maybe. Okay, yes, but please forgive me. It's been a very long and trying weekend."

Maks stood and came over to me; taking up my hand, he said, "Catherine, please know that I would never push you to do something you didn't want to do. I simply enjoy your company and look forward to spending more time with you."

I stared at him, my head shaking involuntarily. Could a man really *be* this genuine? Putting my free hand on his shoulder, I asked softly, "Are you for real, Maks Grinkov?"

"I am very real," he assured me. "Just ask your sss—" Maks seemed to catch himself and, instead of finishing his sentence, he put the hand he was holding to his lips and kissed it.

"Just ask my who?"

"Your solicitor," he said, quickly. "Or, as you call them in this country, your attorney. Marcus. He's known me a little while, and he can vouch for me."

I didn't think Maks had been referring to Marcus when he'd first spoken, but I let it go because I didn't want anything to ruin the good impression I was forming of Mr. Maks Grinkov. I liked him. Probably too much, but at the moment, I didn't care. "Did you bring the completed application?" I asked, changing the subject.

Maks released my hand and moved over to the leather bag he'd carried in with him. Digging around in it, he lifted out a manila folder and handed it to me. "I've included a credit report and three references for you," he said.

I took the folder, opening it to survey the documents. "Wonderful. This all looks in order." I then moved over to Gilley's desk to riffle through the drawers for a few moments until I located the lease agreement I'd prepared for Maks the other day. "Here we are," I said, handing it over to him. "If you'd like to take a day or two to look over the terms, feel free. I'll hold the office space until I hear from you. I'm asking for a twenty-four-month lease, but if you insist on a shorter term, I'm sure we can find a compromise."

Instead of replying, Maks placed the lease on Gilley's desk, reached into his coat pocket, and withdrew a pen. He spent maybe thirty seconds skimming the lease with his fingertips before turning to the last page and scrawling out a signature. Handing this to me, he then opened up his checkbook, scribbled out a check, tore it off, and handed that to me as well.

I looked down at the dollar figure written on the check in confusion until I realized he'd just paid for the entire twenty-four-month-term in one payment. "Goodness," I said. "Are you sure you want to pay all your rent up front, Maks?"

"Positive," he said, tucking his pen away. "This way, we'll never have business get in the way of a personal relationship."

I felt myself blush, and that squiggly butterfly feeling returned to my insides. My God, what this man did to me . . . "Let me get you a set of keys, then," I said, flustered and not knowing what else to do.

I handed Maks the keys, and he reached forward to take them from me, but his fingertips lingered on mine. "Have dinner with me," he said.

"When?"

"Tomorrow."

I bit my lip. "I'm sorry, I can't tomorrow. I'm taking my sons to dinner."

"Oh, and I'm traveling again the day after tomorrow, and I'll be gone a week. What about late next week?"

"That would be lovely," I said.

"This time we'll dine in," Maks said. "At my home. That way we'll have no interruptions."

I cocked my head. "You cook?"

"Not at all," he admitted. "But my chef is excellent."

"You have a chef?" I asked, impressed. Even I didn't have a chef.

"I do. He's from Paris, and a bit of a snob, but I don't hold that against him because his cuisine is magnifique!"

I laughed. "I look forward to it."

"Excellent," Maks said, turning to the door. "I'll send my driver. Fredrick will pick you up at . . . seven?"

"Perfect," I said, and I wasn't talking entirely about the time.

Maks bowed his head. "I should allow you to carry on with your day."

"Yes, thank you," I said, glancing at my watch and noting the time.

Maks picked up his bag, and I walked with him toward the door. "Busy day?" he asked, obviously noticing that I'd glanced at my watch.

"Very."

"Clients to coach?"

We paused in front of the door. "No," I said. "I simply have an errand to run at the pharmacy, and then I'm getting arrested."

Maks's eyes widened, and then he burst out laughing. "Oh, Catherine. You are delightful!"

He thought I was joking. I laughed too and didn't have the heart to tell him I was dead serious.

Chapter 10

I was escorted to a room at the back of the station. It wasn't the same interrogation room where Shepherd had first put me, but it was every bit its twin. I was told to wait and that Shepherd would be in just as soon as my attorney arrived.

I'd purposely gotten to the police station thirty minutes before Marcus, and I'd kept my fingers crossed that they'd put me in a room with a camera.

"Lucky me," I whispered, eyeing the camera over the door. "Showtime."

Reaching into my purse, I took out a small prescription bottle and lifted off the lid. I hadn't had the script filled in nearly three months, but I was glad it was still valid. Tapping out two capsules, I popped them into my mouth and took a swig from the bottled water I'd also purchased at the pharmacy. Leaving the prescription bottle on the table, I waited. Soon my head wobbled a bit on my neck, and a goofy smile pushed its way onto my lips.

The door opened at exactly eleven a.m., and Marcus walked in. He came over to my side of the table and took a seat next to me. I saw his gaze wander to the prescription bottle on the table and the bottled water before he addressed me. "Catherine."

"Marcus."

"Care to tell me what this is about?"

"Not yet," I said, unable to suppress a small giggle. Sometimes I giggle when I'm nervous.

Marcus again eyed the prescription bottle on the table. "You okay?"

"Glorious," I said, my grin even wider.

Marcus appeared like he wanted to ask me something else when the door opened and Shepherd breezed in. "Morning," he said without even a hint of warmth.

"Detective," I said, my head bobbing up and down.

Shepherd checked himself before sitting, and I noticed that his gaze also went to the prescription bottle on the table. He then stared at me. "What're you here for, Ms. Cooper?"

I turned to Marcus and smiled. He frowned. I think he might've had an inkling as to what was coming, and I almost felt bad that I hadn't let on beforehand, but I'd been afraid he'd try to stop me.

"I'd like to confess," I said.

"Confess?" Shepherd said carefully.

I turned my attention to him. "Yes. I'm here to clear my conscience." Marcus's hand landed on my arm in caution, but I ignored it. "I murdered Heather Holland."

For a solid fifteen seconds, nobody spoke and nobody moved. Finally, however, Shepherd spoke. "You murdered Heather," he said. He seemed angry. Which was fabulous.

"Yep. It was me." For emphasis, I pointed to myself with a big jabbing gesture.

"Catherine," Marcus said softly, his hand tightening on my arm. "Stop talking."

"I murdered her," I repeated, totally ignoring him.

Shepherd's gaze shifted back and forth between me, Marcus, and the prescription bottle. I leaned forward so that he could see my eyes when I said, "You shoulda kept me locked up, Shepherd."

Shepherd's fingers drummed on the tabletop. "Okay," he said. "Walk me through it. How did you murder her *exactly*, Catherine?"

COACHED TO DEATH 165

"Oh, you know," I said. "It's like you said. I came up behind her, and—whammo!" I made a show of pretending to hit Heather over the head with a large object.

Shepherd shook his head and pressed his lips together. He was obviously furious. "This some kind of a joke?" he asked Marcus.

"I've got no idea," Marcus said, reaching for the prescription bottle to peer at the label.

"No joke!" I said, a bit too loudly. "It's what you wanted, right, Shepherd? You wanted to get a confession out of me and close your case, right?"

Shepherd worked his jaw for a minute. "This is a waste of my time."

"Or *is* it? I should think it's the opposite of a waste of time for you, Detective! I should think that you'd want a nice tidy end to a puzzling case like this, which is why I'm here as your *number-one* suspect to make it soooooo easy for you!"

Shepherd ignored me and focused on Marcus. "What'd she take?"

"Xanax."

I held up two fingers. "Twice," I said, then pointed to the camera above the door and grinned for effect. Holding forth my wrists, I added, "Ain't cha gonna arrest me now, Shepherd?"

The detective got up and began to move to the door. I stopped him in his tracks when I said, "No? Gee, won't the press wonder what the deal is when I have Marcus here phone in a tip that a person of interest in the murder case of Heather Holland showed up to confess to the crime and wasn't even arrested!"

Shepherd turned back to me, furious. "You want me to arrest you, Catherine?" he snapped, before hauling out a set of hand-cuffs.

"I do!" I yelled, and I held my wrists aloft to make it easy for him.

"She's clearly under the influence here, Detective," Marcus said, getting to his feet as well. "If this goes to trial, I'll get the whole confession thrown out."

"She should've thought of that before she came in here to confess!" Shepherd said angrily, and then he seemed to think of something, and his jaw dropped a little before he turned to stare at me.
"You did think about it before you came here, didn't you?"

"Yep," I said. "I thought about how you arrested me at Pierre's
so publicly when you had *nothing* but some flimsy circumstantial
evidence, and how you proceeded with the charges even though
it was clear that the judge was going to toss the case out for lack
of evidence, and how you've been so intent to make *me* the focus
of your investigation when you *know* I didn't do it . . ."

"You just confessed that you did," he reminded me.

I rolled my eyes. "Right. And you *totally* believe that, huh,
Shepherd? You totally believe I did it."

"Maybe you did!" he snapped.

"Maybe I did," I agreed. "And that means that you can close the
case on Heather. *And* put away that file on her dead ex-husband
too! His death can just remain *suspicious*."

Out of the corner of my eye, I saw Marcus turn his head
sharply toward me. I think he was starting to put it together as
well.

Shepherd stood there, holding the handcuffs for a good couple
of beats, and we waited him out. At last, he came calmly back to
the table, pulled out the chair again, and sat down. "What do you
want, Catherine? An apology or something?"

"That would be a nice start," I said.

"No."

I glared at him. "You and your stupid pride," I spat. "You *owe*
me an apology, Detective. You know you do." Waving my hand in
a circle, I added, "That whole stunt at Pierre's was just one giant
ruse to keep the real killer from thinking you were onto them.
And I know you believe the two deaths are related, so as long as
you can dangle me to the public as a person of interest, you can
dig deeper into Heather and Tony's murders. And Tony Holland
was murdered, wasn't he?"

"You done?" he asked.

"With you? Not by a long shot." I stood, and Marcus got up with me. "I'm going to do a little digging myself, Detective, and if you cause me even one more *ounce* of public humiliation, I'll make sure the press hears that I came here today and confessed to murdering Heather. Marcus, of course, will get me off because I popped two anti-anxiety pills half an hour ago, and no judge in her right mind would allow a confession made by someone hyped up on so much Xanax, and while it might all be terribly inconvenient to me to be thrown into jail again, I'd still sleep well knowing I'd ruined your chances of ever bringing the real killer to justice because the other defense attorney would have it on public record that *I* confessed to the crime."

Shepherd eyed me moodily. I had him. I knew I had him. And I expected him at any minute to jump to his feet, lose his cool, and arrest me on the spot, but what he did next wasn't any of that, and it surprised me a great deal. He stood calmly, tucked the handcuffs into his back pocket, and said, "She was poisoned, Catherine. That's why there was no blood at the scene. She was dead long before that punch bowl broke over her head. We don't know what the toxin was that killed her, but we do know that her central nervous system shut down rapidly. You didn't kill her. Sorry about the other night."

With that, Shepherd strolled out of the room, and Marcus and I were left to stare at each other.

A bit later, Marcus walked me out of the police station. "I think I should drive you home," he said.

"Why?"

"Because you've taken two Xanax, and I'm not comfortable with you driving under the influence of that much prescription medication in your system."

I lifted my arm to access my purse and dug around for a moment, coming up with some breath mints. Using my thumb to pop the top, I offered the container to Marcus. "I had two Tic Tacs. Not Xanax."

His eyes widened.

"I swapped them out in the car before I went in," I explained.

"Clever," he said. "But don't tell anyone else that. Ever."

Saluting with two fingers, I said, "Noted."

Marcus looked around suspiciously. "Still, Catherine, to keep up the ruse, it might be a good idea to take an Uber or a taxi home. The last thing we want is for some cop to pull you over on suspicion of being under the influence."

"But I just told you that I'm fine to drive," I said.

"Oh, I know. It's not you I don't trust. It's Shepherd. It wouldn't surprise me if he sent word out to his patrol buddies to keep an eye out for your car."

I rolled my eyes. "Don't the police in this town have better things to do than pull over innocent people?"

Marcus shook his head. "I'm the wrong person to ask. I've been pulled over three times in this town."

That floored me. "For what?"

"DWBBMW."

"What does that stand for?"

"Driving while black in a BMW."

My mouth dropped. "Please be kidding."

Marcus chuckled. "Funny," he said. "That's exactly what I said to the police the first time they pulled me over for a report of a suspicious driver in a BMW."

I stood there for a long moment, trying to get a handle on my anger. Outright racism, bigotry, misogyny, and hatred are all trigger points for me. They're trigger points for my sister too. Heaven help the fool who pulls such shenanigans in front of the two of us—our wrath unfolds in tag-team *waves* of anger. "I'm so sorry," I said to him, at a loss for anything else I could say. "It means all the more that you were willing to come here so late to help me the other night."

"I owed a friend," he said with a one-shoulder shrug.

"Ah," I said, nodding. "Maks."

"I see he's confessed to being the benefactor."

"He has. He's incredibly kind, don't you think?"

Marcus looked at me curiously. "Kind? Maks? Hmm. I don't know that I'd describe him *that* way, Catherine, but he has gone out of his way to be kind to you."

"That's an odd thing to say."

Marcus shrugged again. "Maybe it is."

Marcus did not come forth with any further details; instead, he changed the subject. Lifting his watch, he said, "I should go. I have a meeting at one."

"Thank you again, Marcus."

"Just doing my job," he said, already moving away. "I'll refund your retainer just as soon as I subtract my hourly rate for today's counsel."

"Thank you," I told him, and then I thought of something and added, "Marcus, do you happen to know of any tax attorneys looking for some administrative or clerical help?"

"Actually," he said, looking surprised, "I do. You know of someone?"

Picturing Erma, I cleared my throat nervously but pressed on. "Yes. One of my clients recently found herself laid off. She's got a rather big presence, but she's a hard worker and eager to please."

"Big presence?" Marcus asked. "Is that code for something unpleasant?"

I attempted a laugh, though it came out a bit strained. "No . . . ahem . . . No. She's just a big energy, lots of enthusiasm, you know the type."

Marcus cocked a skeptical eyebrow.

"Please?" I said. "I need this, Marcus."

He nodded slowly. "In truth, that could work. The attorney I'm thinking of has an . . . *unusual* personality."

I blanched. "Is that code for pervert?"

Marcus chuckled—his laugh was genuine. "No. Not a pervert. Dwight's a geek. Harmless, but he's definitely on the spectrum."

"On the spectrum?"

"Asperger's. He struggles with social interactions."

"Erma—the woman I'm recommending—struggles with those a touch too."

"Send me her résumé, and I'll forward it to Dwight."

I let out a sigh of relief. "Thank you, Marcus."

"You're welcome."

Waving good-bye, I left him and moved in the opposite direction, heading toward my car, which was in a church parking lot two blocks down. As I was rounding the corner and about to cross the street to the side where my car was parked, a movement out of the corner of my eye caused me to turn my head, and what I saw stopped me in my tracks.

Bursting out of the church door came none other than the dreadful housekeeper who'd given me such a hard time at Heather's.

While I stood there in shock, she came dashing straight toward me, and I'll admit to raising my arms up defensively as she drew close. In that moment, she seemed to recognize me too, and just as she seemed set to collide with me, she shifted slightly and scrambled past my stunned form.

Confused, I spun around and watched her continue to run toward a sedan that'd definitely seen better days. The door was open, and the housekeeper launched herself inside, and before she even had a chance to close the passenger-side door, the car was speeding away.

I don't know what compelled me, but I took a few hurried steps in the car's direction and took note of the license plate, saying it out loud to myself over and over long after the car had sped away.

Reaching into my purse, my hand shaking, I pulled out my

phone and tapped the license number onto the screen of a new e-mail that I would send to myself. I then jotted a few words about the car, its bronze color, the rust on the right-front fender, and the shape of it. I wasn't clear on make or model, but I didn't think I needed to be, having gotten the full license plate number.

I then realized that my heart was racing and a cold sweat had broken out across my brow.

"What on earth was that all about?" I mused.

My gaze turned toward the church, and I approached it, wondering if that was a good idea. I hadn't witnessed a crime, but the woman's actions were certainly suspicious. I wondered if she'd been questioned by the police . . .

"Certainly she has," I said to myself.

But what if she hadn't.

Reaching the door of the church, I pulled on the door, but it was locked. "Strange," I said. I'd just seen the woman come out of the building. How could the door be locked so quickly after she'd appeared?

Unless someone who had been in the church with her had locked the door right after her escape.

With a bit of reservation, I knocked on the entrance. No one appeared, so I put my head to the door and listened, but no sounds came to me.

"Odd," I said.

At last, I turned away to walk down the steps toward my car again, and after reaching the sidewalk, I glanced back at the door one last time. To my surprise, another figure appeared from the doorway, and she casually descended the steps as if she were completely oblivious to the scene of the housekeeper racing away from the church only moments before.

Adding to the strangeness of the moment, the woman descending the steps was dressed like someone who'd just stepped out of the sixties. Clad in a patterned dress that was cut three inches above the knee and colored bright orange, lime green, neon yellow, and pink, the woman casually walked down the stairs and toward me, her hair bound in a high-volume coif, a chunky white necklace with a big peace sign at her neck, and her hands covered in white leather gloves. Her look was topped off with a pair of thick Jackie O sunglasses and bright-pink lipstick.

I winced taking all of her in; it was quite retro, but overall it didn't really work. Perhaps it just seemed that she was trying too hard to get some attention.

Still, I couldn't let her go without asking her about the housekeeper. "Excuse me!" I said, waving to her.

The woman's head jerked when she realized someone was calling to her. "Yes?"

I approached her and asked, "Were you in there with that other woman?"

"Other woman?" she said.

"Yes, the one that just came running out of the church."

The stranger appeared to consider me suspiciously. "I don't know what you're talking about."

Thinking fast, I reached into my purse and pulled out my wallet. "The woman who came out of the church dropped this. She left in a car before I could call out to her. I was hoping you knew her and could help me track her down."

The stranger looked from me to the wallet, then back again. "I don't know who just came out of the church," she said. "I was in there to pray for my mother. She's having gallbladder surgery tomorrow."

"Oh, I'm so sorry. I hope your mother will be all right."

"Thank you," the woman said, about to turn away.

Quickly I said, "Is there anyone else inside who might have known her?"

The woman's lips pursed in a pout of impatience. "Father Stephan was the one giving the sermon today, but he left twenty minutes ago for lunch. Otherwise, it was just me, praying." She tapped her finger to her lips and added, "You know, I thought I did hear a door close. Maybe that was this other woman you were talking about. I'd tell you to take the wallet inside and leave it on the pulpit with a note, but the door locks automatically. Father Stephan should be back from his lunch by one o'clock or so."

I smiled and put the wallet back into my purse. "Thank you. You've been most helpful."

She nodded and went on her way, while I waited until she was out of sight to move to my car and get in.

On another impulse, I called the East Hampton Police Department and asked to speak to Detective Shepherd.

"Shepherd," he said gruffly.

"Detective, it's Catherine Cooper."

There was an audible sigh, then, "You wanna come back in and confess to another crime you didn't commit?"

"No, I believe my limit of one confession per day has been reached. Speaking of confession, however, I have a question for you: Did you ever interview Heather Holland's housekeeper?"

Shepherd didn't answer for a beat or two, which I found a little telling. "We're still attempting to locate her."

"Ah. Well, you might want to ask the owner of a bronze-colored sedan with the license plate number V, L, A, one, six, seven, six."

Another pause, then, "How do the two connect, exactly?"

"That's the license plate number of the car that I just witnessed Heather's housekeeper jump into. She came barreling out of a church two blocks from your station, in fact, to throw herself into that waiting car, and it took off before she even had a chance to close the door. Now, I'm no *detective*, but I'd call *that* suspicious."

Shepherd swore, and I heard the sound of snapping fingers, then "Thanks." And then he hung up.

Satisfied that I'd done my duty as a concerned citizen, I sat still and watched the church for a while. I can't really explain why—call it a hunch.

My hunch paid off five minutes later when Shepherd showed up in an unmarked black sedan. I watched from the shadows of my car as he pulled up on the other side of the street, all his attention focused on the church and not me, thank God. After parking, he got out of his car and hurried up the steps to the door, which he attempted to pull open, but which I knew to be locked. He then settled for knocking, but there was no answer.

Shepherd then walked around to the other side of the church and back again. I smirked as I watched him and sunk a little lower in my seat so as not to be seen.

I needn't have worried; he was entirely too preoccupied with trying to get inside the church.

Finally, just when I thought the detective was ready to abandon the effort, a priest appeared, walking with haste toward the church. Shepherd stood at the base of the steps until the priest got to him, and then a verbal exchange between the two took place. And then an argument.

"So it's not just me," I muttered. "Shepherd can even try the patience of a priest!"

The priest kept shaking his head at Shepherd, but I couldn't hear any of their conversation. Still, given their body language, I felt I was able to suss out that Shepherd wanted to go inside the church to look for evidence that Heather's housekeeper had been there. He took out a photo from the folder he'd been holding, and the priest had looked at the photo and frowned. I had the feeling the priest knew the woman, but he didn't appear to be very forthcoming with information.

And if Heather's housekeeper had used the church as a sanctuary, then I could understand the priest's lack of cooperation.

Finally, the priest had had enough of the conversation, and he walked past the detective, inserted a key into the lock, and let himself inside the church without even a glance back.

"Ha!" I laughed softly. "Priest one, Shepherd zero."

For his part, Shepherd stood in front of the steps leading to the church with his hands on his hips, clearly frustrated.

And then it was almost as if he knew I was watching, because he swiveled on his heel and turned in a half circle to stare directly in my direction.

"Shit," I swore and ducked way down in my seat, not even daring to look in his direction.

A moment or two later, the rapping sound on my car window caused me to jump.

With a sigh, I turned the car on and rolled down my window. "Yes?" I asked innocently.

"What're you doing?" Shepherd demanded.

"Sitting in my car."

"Why?"

"It's a nice day. I was taking in some afternoon sun."

"In your car?"

"Yes."

"Step out, please," he said, his tone suggesting that it wasn't a request.

"Am I under arrest?"

"Step out of the car, Catherine."

Rolling my eyes, I did as he asked and stood in front of him, trying my best not to shake in fear.

"Tell me exactly what you witnessed with Ms. Kuznetsov."

"Who?" I asked, even though I knew full well who.

"Don't play coy," he said sharply.

"Don't be an ass!" I replied, turning away from him and reaching for the door handle to my car.

"Catherine," he said with the same sharp tone. And then, much more softly, he added, "Wait."

I pulled the door open and turned sideways, but I didn't get in. Instead, I stood there waiting to see if he'd be nice or stick to being a jerk and make it easy for me. I'd committed no crime, but I was still a little nervous about getting behind the wheel of the car when he thought I might be too high from the Xanax I'd pretended to consume.

"Can't we be civil about this?" he asked me.

"I've been more than civil. *You*, on the other hand, have been a royal prick."

Shepherd pursed his lips and squinted at me. "Royal prick?"

"Yep."

"That the best you got?"

I spent the next thirty seconds taking a page out of my sister's salty-sailor-speak handbook. I called him everything I could think of, combined lots of adjectives and at least one verb, and topped that all off with the Portuguese phrase for "to pleasure oneself anally," which, ironically, was about the only Portuguese I still remembered from my one year in college spent abroad.

At the end of it, I stood breathing hard and simmering with anger.

"Huh," he said when I'd finished. "That last one sounds like it'd hurt."

"You speak Portuguese?"

"I spent a year in Portugal when I was a junior in college."

"You *did?*" Before he could answer, I pointed to myself. "Me too!"

"No way," he said. "What school?"

"UMass Amherst. Class of ninety-eight. You?"

"Same, but I was class of ninety-seven," he said.

"Huh," I said.

"Huh," he replied.

And just like that, most of the tension that'd fueled our previous encounters vanished. "I don't remember ever seeing you," I said. "But then, the school was huge."

"Yeah. Funny. A year earlier or later, and we could've been in Portugal together."

I stepped to the side and closed the car door. Leaning against my sedan, I said, "What do you want to know about Ms. . . . what was her name again?"

"Kuznetsov. Carmen Kuznetsov."

"Yes. Her."

"What exactly did you see?"

"I saw her come out of that church like a bat out of hell. She ran right past me and jumped into an awaiting getaway car."

"How did you know it was a getaway car?"

"The motor was running, the passenger-side car door was open, and the second she jumped in, it sped away."

"Okay," Shepherd said. "I'll give that one to you. Can you describe the driver?"

"No. I was startled at first, and by the time I thought to take note of anything, the car was in motion. I only had a chance to get the license number."

"It's bogus," Shepherd told me. "It's a retired plate."

"What does that mean?"

"It means it was retired by the DMV, replaced by a guy from Schenectady a year ago. He claims that he threw the old plate in the recycle bin, where we think it was picked up and resold to someone closer to here."

"Wow," I said. "Resourceful."

"Criminals are definitely that."

"So you think she's a criminal?"

"We haven't been able to track her down since her employer's murder. She wasn't at the house when the body was found, and the address on her green card is currently being occupied by a couple in their thirties who've never heard of her."

I crossed my arms. "You mean to tell me you had all of *that* information, or lack of information, and you *still* thought to arrest me?"

"I needed the ruse," Shepherd said simply.

"Ruse? You needed a *ruse?* Who even uses that word anymore?"

"Guys who graduate with a liberal arts degree from UMass."

I shook my head at him. "You owe me an apology A *sincere* one this time."

Shepherd looked at the ground and kicked at a pebble. "That's not really my strong suit."

"Practice makes perfect."

He offered me a lopsided smile. "You're tough, ain't ya?"

"When it comes to holding people responsible for their appalling behavior, yes, you could say I'm tough."

Shepherd blew out a sigh. "Fine, okay. Look, Catherine, I'm—"

At that moment, the door to the church flew open, and out ran the priest. "*Detective!*" he cried. "*Detective! Help!*"

Shepherd was in motion far more quickly than I could take in. Before I realized what was going on, he was flying across the pavement, up the sidewalk, and toward the door. The priest saw him coming and turned back to the door too, catching it before it could close and lock them out.

As Shepherd launched himself up the stairs, the priest shouted, "In there! In there! So much blood! Oh, my heavenly Father! There's so much blood!"

Shepherd flew into the building, and the priest ran in after him. All this happened while I stood dumbly next to my car and tried to process what the heck was going on.

Without thinking, I headed toward the door myself; it was instinctual, really, but I didn't hurry. I think I was simply in a state of shock. When I got to the door, it opened abruptly, and the priest stumbled out. He was pale, bent double, and I had the distinct feeling he was about to retch.

"Oh my goodness, Father, are you all—?"

That's as far as I got before the poor man bolted down the steps and around the corner, finding a bush to duck behind before the awful sounds of him becoming sick reached my ears.

It was then that I realized I was holding the door open, and as my own stomach turned uncomfortably, I moved inside and allowed the door to close to block out the sound from the bushes.

I stood against the door for a long moment, my eyes closed and my chest taking in big lungfuls of air. You would think that after raising two boys, I'd be immune to the effects of the sound of gagging, but not so. It's an instant trigger of nausea for me, and it took me perhaps a full minute to fend off that queasy feeling.

Finally, I opened my eyes and looked around. The church was dim. There appeared to be only two windows at either end of the large room, and both were of stained glass, which caused the light to be filtered and muted. I took a step away from the door and listened as the sound of someone talking came to my ears.

It was Shepherd, and I quickly gathered that he was speaking to someone on the phone. "I need a forensic crew here ASAP. And the M.E. No paramedics and no sirens, though, Trish. The vic is past the point of saving."

I moved toward the sound of Shepherd's voice, drawn there by perhaps a morbid curiosity. Peering cautiously around the corner, I saw him standing next to a confessional. The door was open, and a figure was slumped inside. A large pool of blood that covered the floor of the confessional had leaked out onto the floor near where Shepherd was standing.

I put a hand to cover my mouth and stood there staring. Dumbstruck, I couldn't seem to move or look away.

And I didn't even notice when Shepherd ended his call and came over to me. Putting a hand on my elbow, he said, "Look away, Catherine."

My head jerked up, and as I stared at him, my eyes became cloudy with tears, but still I couldn't seem to move.

"Come with me," he said, placing an arm across my shoulders and physically turning me away from the scene. I leaned against him, unsure of my footing until we got to the door of the church. Shepherd let go of me and propped the door open with a nearby folding chair; then he guided me out of the door, down the steps, and onto the sidewalk.

"Hey," he said, to get my attention. "You okay?"

"What . . . happened?" I asked. My hands were trembling, and I felt weak in the knees. I'd never seen so much blood before, let alone a murder victim up close like that.

"Someone killed the priest."

"Who?" I asked. It was a silly question, but it escaped my lips anyway.

"If I had to guess? I'd say a woman in need of a getaway car."

"Heather's housekeeper," I whispered.

"Yeah. Could be."

"What should I do?" I asked.

Shepherd eyed me silently for a few moments. Then he said, "Go home. Have that guy in your guest house look after you until I can swing by to get your statement."

"My statement? What statement?"

"You saw Kuznetsov fleeing the scene of a murder, right?"

"Um . . . I guess."

"I'll need an official statement for that."

"Should I call Marcus?" I asked. Again, it was a silly question to ask Shepherd, but my mind didn't seem to be working so well.

"That's up to you," he said. "But at this point, you're not at the top of my suspect list."

Shepherd turned away to head back inside the church, and I was left to shiver on the sidewalk.

Chapter 11

"**M**ore soup, sugar?" Gilley asked.

I was curled up on the couch in Chez Kitty, staring numbly into space, my mind still processing the sight from earlier in the day.

"No," I said, shaking myself out of the disturbing memory.

Gilley came to stand next to me. "How about if I just warm up what you've still got left in the bowl?"

I looked down. The bowl of homemade minestrone was full and cold. I'd taken only a few sips of the broth. "Thank you, but I don't think I'm hungry," I said, offering it back to him.

He took the bowl and walked it over to the microwave. I heard the door open, the clink of the china on the glass turntable, and then a sequence of beeps as Gilley programed the soup to heat up again.

I sighed. My houseguest was a stubborn one.

When he brought back the steaming bowl to me, I refused to take it from him. "Cat," he said sternly.

"Gilley."

"You have to eat."

"I will, just not now. Later."

Gilley sat down next to me. "I think you're in shock, sugar."

I nodded. That felt about right.

"And you know how they treat people in mild cases of shock?"

"No, how?" I asked almost absently.

Gilley shoved the bowl at me. "They get them to eat."

Sighing, I took the bowl again and lifted the spoon he'd brought to me earlier. Dipping it into the soup, I took another sip. I was surprised at how flavorful it tasted this time. "It's good," I said, dipping my spoon again.

"Damn skippy it's good," he muttered.

As I finished the soup, and felt better for it, Gilley chatted me up. It wasn't a conversation that required any deep concentration; he was merely discussing the storyline from a Netflix series he liked, and I quickly understood that this was his way of giving me a little therapy. It was a way to keep me out of my head for a few minutes, and I found myself deeply grateful to him.

Handing the empty bowl back to him when I'd finished, I said, "Thank you. That honestly helped."

Gilley took the bowl to the sink and brought me a fresh cup of hot tea. "Okay," he said, sitting back down on the other end of the couch. "Tell me, from the beginning, what happened."

When I arrived at Chez Kitty, I'd given Gilley a grossly disjointed story, starting at the end with the dead priest in the confessional and backtracking to the interview with Shepherd. I'd left out so much in my effort to explain why I was so rattled, and I wasn't surprised that he was asking me about it again.

So I started at the very beginning and was working my way through the encounter with the woman at the church who'd come out after Kuznetsov when there was a knock on the door. Gilley got up to answer it, and I said, "I think that might be Shepherd."

"*What?*" Gil asked, spinning around midway to the door. Pointing to the hallway, he lowered his voice and said, "Go hide in my closet! I'll tell the detective you're not here!"

I got up, waving my hand at him. "It's all right, Gilley. He told me he was coming."

"To arrest you? I'll call Marcus! What's his number?"

"Gil," I said, reaching the door. "Chill."

Pulling it open, I found Shepherd on the front step, looking tired and grumpy. "Detective," I said with a nod.

"Catherine," he replied, dipping his chin. "This a good time?"

"Of course. Please come in."

I stepped to the side and allowed Shepherd to enter. Gilley stood there with his hands on his hips, glaring, and then he seemed to realize that his laptop was open and the screen wasn't hidden. His computer was still running passcode variables, trying to hack into Heather's iCloud account. Launching himself toward his computer, Gilley slammed the lid shut and practically laid on top of it from the effort.

"That's not suspicious," Shepherd said.

"It's for work," Gilley told him. "Proprietary stuff."

"What do you do?" the detective asked.

"I . . ." Gilley's face went blank, probably much like his mind.

"He's a computer coder," I said. "He's working on a new app. Right, Gil?"

"Oh, yes. Sure. That's it. An app. That's what I'm working on. An app for the Apple phone. I mean the Apple iPhone. The iPhone."

A sweat broke out across Gilley's brow.

Shepherd turned to me. "He's kind of goofy, huh?"

I frowned and glared hard at Shepherd when I saw the hurt on Gilley's face. "He's my dearest friend in the world, Detective."

An awkward silence followed. Shepherd finally dipped his chin again, and with a hand on his chest, he said, "Noted."

I believe that was as close to an apology as either Gilley or myself was going to get. Gilley gathered up his laptop and the notebook he'd been scribbling notes into and stomped off toward the bedroom.

I motioned to a chair at the kitchen table, and Shepherd took a seat. "Can I get you something to drink?" I asked. I always try to be a good hostess, even when my guest is a horse's ass.

"Water, if it's not too much trouble."

I got him some ice water and set down the glass next to him, and that's when I heard his stomach rumble. Shepherd cleared his throat loudly, trying to cover it, but I'd heard the gurgle, and it made me smile. "You hungry?"

"No, I'm good," he said. Shepherd's stomach rumbled again. It said different.

Moving away from him again, I went to the counter next to the stove, got down a bowl, and filled it with some of Gilley's soup. I brought it over to the detective with a spoon and a napkin; after setting it down in front of him, I said, "Eat."

"I don't want to impose," he said, eyeing the soup hungrily.

"Then don't decline my offer to feed you. Now eat."

Shepherd took up the spoon and tasted the soup. "Man, that's good."

I pointed toward the bedroom. "Gilley's."

"I almost feel bad for insulting him."

"Almost?"

"I insult a lot of people on a regular basis. You develop an immunity after a while. It's part of being a cop."

"Or a terrible person."

Shepherd's spoon stopped midway to his mouth. "You think I'm a terrible person?"

"I don't know you well enough to have a concrete opinion, but you *have* actually been terrible to me, so . . ."

"How have I been terrible to you?" he asked, and I was flabbergasted that he seemed genuinely puzzled by my accusation.

"Are you kidding?"

"No. I really want to know."

"Um, how about, oh, I don't know . . . the night you *arrested me* at Pierre's?"

"What was so terrible?" he asked. "You were a suspect, we had some solid evidence against you, the arrest was legit."

"The arrest was *not* legit," I snapped. "You *used* it as a way to trick the real killer into thinking you were only focused on me."

"Well, that night, maybe I was only focused on you."

"What the hell does that mean?" I demanded.

"Who's the guy?"

"What guy?"

"The guy from Pierre's?"

"Maks?"

"Yeah. Maks."

"He was my date," I said.

"Yeah, I already know that. Who is he, exactly?"

I blinked. What the hell was he getting at? "Why is that relevant?"

Shepherd shrugged. "Just curious. He's Canadian, huh?"

I frowned. I had no idea. His accent was more Russian or Croatian, but perhaps he could've had Canadian citizenship. "Don't know," I said crisply. "I haven't asked."

"So you don't know each other very well, then? Which is surprising given how chummy you seemed that night."

And that's when I saw a hint of something in Shepherd's eyes that I swear looked a whole lot like that green-eyed monster jealousy. Which was ridiculous. Absurd. Impossible. And yet . . .

"Can we stop with the third degree on my social life for a minute?"

"Fine," he said, setting aside the bowl of soup. "I just thought it was odd that you were out with a guy who travels around with an armed bodyguard. People like that are usually trouble."

I glared at Shepherd. "You know what you are?"

"What I am?"

"Yeah."

"I'll bite, what am I?"

"You're that guy that likes to get a rise out of people. The guy that pushes people's buttons just to watch their reaction, and while you probably have a few acquaintances, I doubt you have many friends, because no one can stand to be around someone like that for long."

It was Shepherd's turn to look hurt. After chewing on the inside of his cheek for a minute, he said, "That's probably fair."

I crossed my arms. I felt a tiny bit bad for having said that, but I wasn't about to apologize. The man was insufferable.

"My ex-wife used to tell me I was the reason we never got invited to parties in this town. And I'm pretty sure that's why she left me. I think she got tired of being lonely."

I sighed as my anger dissipated. Damn him. Why'd he have to play the pathetic divorcé card? "My ex-husband blamed me for the divorce too. He said that I worked too much."

"Did you?"

"Yes. But now that I've had time to think about it, I don't agree with him that that's why we split. I think that we split up because we stopped connecting. We stopped being friends. We didn't so much fall out of love with each other as we fell out of like."

"Huh," Shepherd said. "Yeah. I know exactly what you're saying."

"It doesn't mean that your ex didn't have a point, though. You should try to be nicer. It might get you further in life."

"Homicide detectives aren't supposed to be nice, Catherine. We're supposed to get results."

"Why are those two things mutually exclusive?"

"Because people lie."

"I don't."

"You don't lie?"

"Nope. Not if I can avoid it."

"Right."

"I'm serious. Go ahead, ask me something. Anything. I'll tell you the truth."

"Was that your drone the other day?"

I smiled. "No. It wasn't." And that was the truth.

Shepherd narrowed his eyes. "Whose drone was it?"

"A friend's," I admitted. No way was I going to tell him it was Gilley's, and without that part of the confession, I doubted he could arrest anyone.

"Okay," he said, and I was surprised that he was willing to leave it at that. "Now can we talk about what you saw today?"

"You mean when Kuznetsov came running out of the church?"

"Yes."

I told him everything I could think of about the encounter while he took notes. At the end of my speech, he looked over his notepad and said, "You say that you thought she recognized you. How would she know you?"

"From the party. She opened the door when I got to Heather's and made me walk around to the back to bring in the punch."

"Did you talk to her at the party?"

"No. Not really. She simply asked me if I'd followed the recipe for the punch, and I said I had, and she asked me if the punch had alcohol in it, and I told her no, and then she taste-tested it to be sure, which I found incredibly insulting, and after that she instructed me to carry the punch out to the party. I never spoke to her again after that."

"Why was she so worried about the punch being spiked?"

I shrugged. "I don't know. Maybe because it was just about the only refreshment available for the guests who don't drink. Like your sister; she had some punch and can vouch for me."

Shepherd seemed taken aback. "Sunny?"

"Yes. She asked about the punch too—it being spiked, I mean—and because I'd made it with Gilley's help, I knew it was safe for her to drink."

"Got it. I'll follow up with her just to close the loop. Now, let's go back to the church; did you see anyone else come out of the church with Ms. Kuznetsov?"

"Well, not with Ms. Kuznetsov, but after her a woman did come out."

"A woman?"

"Yes."

"Did you get her name?"

"No, but I did talk to her."

"What'd you say?"

"I asked her if she'd seen the woman who'd run out of church ahead of her, and she claimed that she hadn't. Her mother is having surgery or something, so she was inside praying."

"Who let her into the church?"

"Um, I think she was there for the sermon at eleven."

"What sermon at eleven?"

"The sermon that Father Stephan gave," I said.

"You mean the dead priest?"

My jaw dropped. "What? No! Father Stephan came back from his lunch, and he alerted you to the body, Detective."

"No, that was Father John. Father Stephan was at the church and alive up until about eleven a.m., we think."

"That can't be right," I insisted. "The woman who came out of the church, she said that she saw Father Stephan leave for lunch."

"He never left for lunch, Catherine. He never left the confessional."

I shook my head, trying to sort it all out. "Maybe she was mistaken then," I said. "Maybe she saw Father John and thought he was Father Stephan."

"No," Shepherd said again. "Father John was coming back from his mother's house, where he'd spent the night. He hadn't been at the church since yesterday, and he was going there to relieve Father Stephan."

"Well, you'll just have to talk to the woman then to get a clear answer."

"But you don't know who she is, right?"

"I've no clue."

"And we're supposed to get in touch with her how?"

"With her fashion sense, it shouldn't be hard. The woman stood out like a sore thumb."

"What does that mean?"

"It means that she was dressed in the most god-awful retro outfit. It practically screamed 'Notice me!' And anyone who wears something like that to church probably dresses like that all the time. I'm sure if you tell Father John you're looking for a woman who dresses like she's stepped out of the sixties, he'll be able to tell you exactly who she . . . Detective? What's wrong?"

While I'd been speaking, Shepherd's face had noticeably paled. "Catherine, I'm going to ask you a question, and I want you to be as detailed as you can be with your answer, okay?"

"Okay."

"What did this woman look like, *exactly*. And by exactly, I mean, I want you to close your eyes, picture her face, and tell me what you see."

"You want me to . . . what?"

"Please," he said. His tone was a touch sharp, and I got goose bumps at the sudden shift of his energy. "I need the details of her person, not what she was wearing."

Closing my eyes, I called up the image that I had for her. "She had brown hair."

"How long?"

"I don't know; it was pulled back and up in this beehive chignon."

"What does that mean?"

"Think Audrey Hepburn in *Breakfast at Tiffany's*."

"Got it. What else?"

"Well, she had . . . ," I paused. What else could I recall? My mind easily remembered the hair, the sunglasses, the beads at her neck, the dress and the shoes, but as for the details of her face . . . I couldn't seem to pull them up in my mind's eye.

As I continued to struggle with a description, Shepherd tried to help me out. "Was she white?"

"Yes."

"Pale? Or darker-toned skin?"

"Kind of in between," I said, but I wasn't sure. How could I not be sure?

"What color were her eyes?"

"She was wearing sunglasses. Jackie O's. They were big frames."

"Okay, can you describe her nose? Her mouth? Her chin?"

"Um . . ." I bit my lip. Those details weren't clear to me anymore because all I could see in my mind were the iconic things she'd been wearing.

"You can't picture them, can you?" Shepherd said.

I opened my eyes. "No. Every time I try to fill in what she looked like, I keep picturing only what she was wearing. But how did you know?"

"Because she's an assassin."

I laughed. I truly thought he was kidding.

"I'm not joking," he said, and I quickly fell silent again. "She's an assassin, Catherine, and honestly, I'm surprised you're alive."

It was my turn to grow pale. "Are you serious?"

"Yep. This woman has hit this area three times. The first person we suspect she murdered was Tony Holland, Heather's husband. The witness who found the body said he saw a woman walking away from the bridge, wearing a blue and white dress with white go-go boots and big sunglasses. He said he noticed her because of how loudly she was dressed, but when he sat with a sketch artist, he couldn't remember any of the details of her face, and when I asked him how tall she was and what her build was all he could say was 'average.' "

"But how do you know this woman is an assassin?" I asked. "I mean, couldn't it just be a case of her being at the wrong place at the wrong time? Isn't it more likely that Ms. Kuznetsov killed the priest?"

Shepherd scratched at his chin, where a five-o'clock shadow had formed. "A year ago, a prominent realtor was murdered during an open house she was hosting here in town. A couple, who were on their way inside for the open house passed a woman leaving the scene, wearing those Jackie O's—on a rainy day—and they also described her as wearing a bright neon-green raincoat with an orange scarf and a yellow dress topped off with white go-go boots.

"Just like you and my other witness, they also didn't remember anything significant about the woman's facial characteristics other than that she had light brown hair. Or maybe dark blond. They weren't sure."

I put a hand to my throat. The same woman clad in vividly memorable attire at all three murders wasn't a coincidence.

The detective nodded. "Anyway, we know she was the killer because the realtor had sent a text to her business partner only four minutes earlier. So, she was alive just a few minutes before the couple arrived on the scene and saw the assassin leaving."

"That's horrible," I said, but what truly struck me was how haunted Shepherd seemed to be by the story he was telling. Maybe that's why I asked him, "Did you know the realtor?"

His gaze focused intently on me. "Yes."

"A friend?" I prodded.

"No," he said. "She stopped being my friend when we divorced."

I gasped. "Your ex-wife?"

He nodded.

"Why would anyone want to kill your ex-wife?"

"That's the question I've been asking myself for the past year, Catherine. And one I still haven't found an answer to."

"And you're convinced that this retro-clad woman is some kind of professional assassin?"

"I am."

"But I thought assassins were supposed to blend in, be inconspicuous, not draw attention to themselves."

"See, that's the brilliance of this woman's m.o. She dresses so loudly that you can't help but notice her, except that all you're taking in are the things she's wearing, not anything about her face."

"Ohmigod, that's absolutely genius."

"It is. It's the perfect disguise."

"And she probably doesn't dress like that all the time, so there'd be no way to spot her at the grocery store."

"Exactly."

A chill went up my spine when I realized how physically close I'd come to a professional killer. "Do you think she lives here?"

"Hard to say."

"Do we know why she killed the priest?"

"No. But I have my suspicions."

"Care to share?"

He inhaled a deep breath, and I had the feeling he was weighing the pros and cons of discussing the case with a civilian, but finally he said, "I think Father Stephan was hiding Ms. Kuznetsov. I think the church was giving her sanctuary, and I think this woman knew she was hiding somewhere in the church, tried to get Father Stephan to tell her where she was, and when he wouldn't tell her, she killed him.

"I also think that, when you saw Kuznetsov running out of the church, she was literally running for her life."

"So you don't suspect that she killed Heather?"

"I don't know what to think about that," Shepherd confessed. "Like I told you, Heather Holland was given some sort of toxin. Her organs showed signs of shutting down—she was in renal failure and her lungs were full of fluid. The M.E. has concluded that she suffocated from the buildup of fluid in her lungs. And, whatever happened to her, it was quick. According to every witness I've spoken to, she was perfectly healthy at the party, but four hours later her system was in total shutdown. So, whatever the toxin was, it spread through her fast."

"And you suspect Ms. Kuznetsov because it was likely some-one close to Heather who offered her the toxin, right?"

"Yes."

"But anyone at the party could've offered her something."

"True, but no one else at the party became sick or died, and the M.E. thinks that whatever she ingested caused an immediate shutdown of her system. He thinks that anything she'd had at the party would've been noticeable. She would've collapsed within minutes, possibly even moments."

"So she died immediately after ingesting the toxin?"

"That's the weird part," Shepherd said. "The M.E. thinks she died about twenty minutes or so after ingesting the toxin. That's how long it would've taken her internal organs to shut down and her lungs to fill with fluid."

"Twenty minutes? So why didn't she dial nine-one-one if she knew she was in distress?"

"Either she couldn't, because the effects of the toxin com-pletely overwhelmed her and she was too weak or too out of it to call for help, or someone waited there to prevent her from reach-ing for the phone."

"That's pretty twisted."

"In general, most murders get pretty twisted."

"So why hit her over the head with my punch bowl after she was dead?"

"That's a piece of the puzzle we don't have an answer to."

"Among all the other pieces you don't have answers to."

"Yep."

"Hmm," I said, thinking about how tangled Heather's murder seemed. "Could it have been to frame me?"

"Sure," Shepherd said. "It could also have been to make sure that Heather was dead. Or an attempt to cover up the use of the toxin. Or to make it more difficult for us to collect forensic evi-dence. Pick a theory. One's as good as the others."

"But why would this assassin be after Heather?" I asked. "Or your ex-wife?"

Shepherd's shoulders dropped a little. He looked weary and, for the first time, vulnerable. "One of my sources in the city said that Heather wasn't making all of her payments to someone big."

"Someone big?"

"In the organization."

"In the organization?"

"In the organized crime organization."

"Heather was involved in organized crime?" That shocked me. Sunny had hinted that Heather's husband had those kinds of connections, but I hadn't thought they would've extended to Heather.

"We don't know for sure, but we suspect that she could have been. Her husband was being investigated by the FBI at the time of his . . . death, and there was some good evidence that he was laundering money for one of the larger Chechen mafia groups in New York."

"So you think Heather took over for her husband?"

"I do."

"But you have no proof."

"I don't. And except for the appearance of this mysterious woman at all three crime scenes, I don't have any solid links to all three victims."

"Do you suspect your ex-wife was involved in organized crime?"

Shepherd shook his head. "No. That would've been a leap for Lenny. She just wasn't the type to get caught up in that."

"Did she know Heather?"

"Everybody knew Heather," Shepherd said. "But to my knowledge, the two didn't mingle. Heather stuck to her affluent circles, and she would've considered my ex-wife part of the working class and, as such, beneath her notice. The irony is that, in any other zip code, Lenny would've been part of the upper class. She did very well for herself as a realtor, but by East Hampton standards, what she made was probably paltry."

"So why did this assassin murder her?"

"Wish I knew," Shepherd said softly. I could see in that moment that he was a man haunted by the murder of his ex-wife. And the fact that he hadn't been able to solve her murder made it clear why he was working so hard to solve Heather and her husband's cases. The three were seemingly linked, but how?

The whole thing was making my head spin, and I had a moment where I considered calling my sister and asking for her intuitive insight when Gilley's voice rang out from the bedroom.

"*Eureka!*" he shouted.

Shepherd and I both turned toward the hallway leading to the bedrooms.

"Who's the grand wizard? Huh? Who's your daddy? Huh? *Me!*"

Gilley appeared from the hallway holding his laptop and wearing an excited grin. The moment he realized Shepherd was still in the house, however, he came up short.

Gil and I locked wide eyes, and I shook my head subtly. It was obvious that he'd been successful hacking into Heather's iCloud account—which was a crime. Perhaps even a federal crime.

"What's going on?" Shepherd asked curiously.

Gilley's big eyes rolled toward Shepherd.

Then back to me.

I shook my head again.

Gilley opened his mouth to speak, but nothing came out, and for a long, panicky minute, I could sense he was about to blurt out something that could've implicated us.

"Mr. Gillespie?" Shepherd asked again, a hint of suspicion in his voice. "Care to share what all the excitement is about?"

"Um . . ." Gilley said, his voice cracking. "I . . . I . . ."

"You, you . . . ?" Shepherd said.

"I just saved fifteen percent on my car insurance!"

My eyes widened. A long moment of silence followed Gilley's

declaration; it lasted until I lifted my watch and exclaimed, "Oh my goodness, would you look at the time? Detective, I'm so sorry to have kept you so long. I didn't realize how late it was getting, and I have an important call to a client I simply *must* get to."

Jumping up from my chair, I moved hastily toward the door, shooting Gilley an irritated look in the process.

For his part, Gil turned on his heel and headed quickly back into the bedroom, while Shepherd got up and walked to me.

"What am I missing?" he asked, clearly onto the fact that we were trying to cover up something.

"Well, that depends. Have you checked your car insurance premiums against any major competitors lately?"

The edges of Shepard's lips quirked in a smile. "No. Can't say that I have."

"Well, then, you might be missing out, Detective." Reaching for the door handle, I opened the door and offered him my most congenial smile.

Shepherd stood there for a moment, staring out the door to the drive while the wheels turned in his mind. I sincerely hoped he wouldn't start grilling us about the obvious ruse. "Thanks for giving me your statement."

I felt a wave of relief wash over me. "You're welcome. If I think of anything to add, I'll call you."

"That would be good," he said, looking at me intently.

I pushed the smile a little harder onto my lips.

He started to walk out the door, but then hesitated one last time. Turning back and wiggling his finger between where Gilley had disappeared to and me, he said, "Whatever's going on with you two, be careful."

I didn't say anything, because any acknowledgment would have also been an admission.

Shepherd nodded, as if he understood, and then he looked me in the eyes with that same intensity again. I felt a flicker of heat spark between us that caught me somewhat off guard. "I'd hate to see anything happen to you, Catherine," he said softly.

My breath caught. The way he'd said that sounded oddly sincere. Intimate even, and all I could do was nod.

Shepherd nodded too, and then he walked down the steps and over to his car. I closed the door before he could look back, although I wasn't sure if I was afraid of him looking back as a suspicious cop or looking back as a man who'd just sparked a wave of electric heat to surge through me.

I didn't have long to dwell on it because the minute the door closed, Gilley reappeared in the hallway, still holding his laptop. "Is he gone?"

"Car insurance?" I hissed in reply. "*That's* the best you could come up with?"

Gilley winced. "I forgot he was here!"

I sighed dramatically and moved back to the table. Gilley came with me. "I'm assuming you hacked your way into Heather's security camera footage?"

"Yes! Take a look at *this!*"

Gilley swiveled the screen of the laptop toward me and pushed a button. A black-and-white video appeared, and immediately I understood that the footage was taken from the camera hoisted above the door, leading to Heather's library. "That's the security footage you were talking about," I said.

"Yep. Heather's camera is set to record a week's worth of info, which is then uploaded to her iCloud account, and then it's deleted and replaced with a new week's worth of info. This happens every Friday at midnight, which meant that I had to fastforward through a *lot* of dead space before I got to this from last Tuesday a little after five."

As I watched the screen, something curious appeared in the bottom right corner. "What is that?" I asked, pointing to the square object.

"I didn't know at first, but now I think I do. Just watch it for a few more seconds, and I'll explain."

We watched together as, at first, nothing happened, and then all of a sudden the camera angle changed dramatically. It went from being angled directly toward the door to being angled down to the ground, revealing only the front step at the top of the screen.

"What happened?" I asked.

"I think the square object we saw appear in the camera frame was the foot of a step ladder, which someone placed out of view before they climbed it and purposely moved the angle of the camera."

"Oh, no," I said. "So all your effort of trying to hack into Heather's iCloud account to see who might've murdered her was a waste of time?"

"Not necessarily," Gilley said, using his keyboard to fast-forward through the video again. "Watch this section taken almost exactly twenty-four hours later."

The grainy detail of the fast-forward motion disappeared when Gilley pressed PLAY again, and I waited, as not much happened. But then a set of white boots appeared at the top of the camera frame.

I actually gasped when they came into view. "Ohmigod! That's her! That's the assassin!"

"The one you and Shepherd were talking about, right?" Gilley said, practically giggling with excitement. "Overheard that part of the conversation before I went back to my hacking efforts."

"Yes. Those are the same boots worn by the woman I encountered at the church. The woman who could've murdered Father Stephan."

"I knew it!" Gilley said. "The go-go boots must be her signature accessory."

"So she *did* murder Heather."

"It looks like it. See? The boots definitely go inside the house, and then about four minutes later, they appear again. Here, I'll fast-forward a touch . . ."

Gil began to fast-forward the tape, but I put a hand on his shoulder. "Wait. You're saying that she was in and out in only four minutes?"

"Uh, yeah. See? Here they come out again."

The still setting of the camera aimed directly at the ground was disrupted again by the appearance of the go-go boots as they crossed the front steps away from the library.

"Well, then, she might not have been the one who murdered Heather, Gil."

"What do you mean?"

"Is there a time stamp on any of this?" I asked, rather than answer Gilley's question.

He pointed to a series of small numbers at the bottom right of the screen. "This was at five-thirteen p.m."

I shook my head. "Heather was already dead by then, Gilley. Shepherd said she died sometime before four-thirty."

Gilley's brow furrowed. "But according to the tape, nobody entered the house until this moment."

"Nobody entered the house from that door," I corrected. "Somebody could've definitely gotten in at any one of the other doors."

"Okay, so why was the camera tilted down a full twenty-four hours before the go-go murderess entered the house?"

"I don't know," I said. "Maybe the assassin had already entered the house an hour before, forcing Heather to take the toxin, then came back to make certain that she was dead."

"So why not just hang out at the house for an hour?" Gilley asked. "I mean, that's a lot of coming and going, which is risky because it'd be at least two opportunities to be seen and reported to the police."

"I agree. Especially if she's wearing white go-go boots and some crazy loud outfit. Still, maybe she showed up on Tuesday, found Heather and her housekeeper out of the house, tilted the camera down, and planned on coming back a day later."

Gilley frowned. "Okay, *that* part could be true, but does *any* of the rest of this make sense to you?"

"No. It's like some crazy hard jigsaw puzzle where we keep looking for a corner piece—something to tie some of these things together—and we can't seem to find anything but regular pieces with no real link to each other."

"What else did Shepherd tell you?" Gil asked next.

I took ten full minutes to give him the lowdown on my conversation with the Detective.

"Whoa," he said when I'd finished. "So his ex was murdered too?"

"Yes. Same description of a woman seen at the site of where Heather's husband was murdered. He believes Tony Holland was murdered because he'd done something to piss off the head of the organized crime ring he laundered money for."

"And Shepherd has no idea how his ex was mixed up in all of this?"

"No clue."

"And we don't know if the go-go assassin murdered Heather or not, even though she was at the scene, because of the timing."

"And the cause of death," I reminded him. "Heather was poisoned, not shot, but all the other victims were killed with a gun, including poor Father Stephan."

"You gotta be a special kind of evil to murder a priest," Gilley said with a shake of his head.

"Definitely," I agreed. "Anyway, should we e-mail the footage from the security camera to Shepherd?"

Gilley's face turned to alarm. "What? *No!*"

"What do you mean, no?"

"I mean I'd prefer not to go to jail, thank you, *no* thank you!"

"How would you go to jail?"

"Hello? Hacking is a federal offense, Cat."

"We don't have to tell him that you hacked into Heather's iCloud account. We can simply say that the footage came to us in an e-mail."

Gilley dipped his chin and looked at me the way you look at a simpleton.

"Right," I said, understanding his unspoken point. "He'd want to see the e-mail. Well, there has to be some way to show him this footage. It could be really important to his investigation."

"True, but I can't think of a way to show it to him without implicating myself."

"What if we just sent it to him anonymously?"

"Too risky," Gilley said. "I don't trust that guy not to start digging, and it wouldn't take a super genius to realize someone had hacked into Heather's account."

"Can't you just erase your tracks?"

Gilley rolled his eyes. "I think you've been watching too many movies. I've left a trace. My IP address has been attempting to hack its way into Heather's account for two days. No way am I confident that I could fully erase all of that."

"Well, then what do we do?"

"We let the detective keep digging," Gilley said. "The footage on the camera can't really help him anyway. I mean, the go-go boots don't even appear until after Heather's dead. It's not like this woman could've re-murdered her."

I sighed. "I suppose you're right, but I have to say, it doesn't really sit well with me."

"That might be the least of your worries," Gilley said.

"What does that mean?"

"Well, you're basically an eye witness to the murder of Father Stephan. This assassin might worry that you could identify her."

I felt the color drain from my face, and my mouth went suddenly dry. "Oh, God," I whispered. "I hadn't even thought of that!"

"I know, but it's definitely something to keep in mind," Gil said. "You need to be careful, honey. Very, *very* careful."

I leaned back in my chair and put a hand over my eyes dramatically. "Move to the Hamptons, they said. It'll be swell, they said . . . Oh! I hate my life!"

"Sorry, sugar. What can I do?"

I lifted my hand and looked over at him. "Help me solve this murder."

"You still want to dig around in all this, knowing how dangerous it is?"

"Yes," I said. "Otherwise, I'll always be looking over my shoulder."

Gilley sighed. "Fine. But we'll need to be discreet."

"Agreed."

"Where did you want to start?"

"At a place I don't think Shepherd has thought to look."

"Where's that?"

I pointed to Gilley's laptop. "Google any vintage dress shops in the area, Gil. Let's see who's bought a pair of white go-go boots in the past year or so."

Gilley smiled. "Oooo," he said. "That's good."

I pointed again to his keyboard, and he got to typing.

Chapter 12

There were seven vintage clothing stores within twenty miles of East Hampton. Gilley and I hit four of them before five the day Shepherd took my statement, and we got an early start the next morning, covering the next three. It was at the very last one that we hit pay dirt.

At first, however, it looked like it was going to be a bust. At ten-fifteen, we walked into Vintage Is the New Black and immediately spotted a perky twentysomething with stringy long hair, clad in a yellow poncho with red bell-bottoms and a leather headband. She could've walked right out of Woodstock.

When we entered, she was fussing with something in the display case. "Hey!" she sang as we came through the door. "Everything on the back rack is fifty percent off today."

"Wonderful," I said, plastering a friendly smile onto my face. "I'm actually on the hunt for something specific."

She looked up from her task. "Cool. We probably have it or can get it, whatever it is."

"Well, I'm looking for a pair of white go-go boots. A friend of mine purchased some about a year ago, and she thinks she bought them from here."

"White go-go boots are super popular. We usually can't keep them in stock when we get them in. What size are you?"

"Um . . . size six and a half," I said. The other stores had simply told me that they didn't have any and couldn't remember selling any within the last year.

"Yikes," the clerk said. "You have tiny feet!"

I felt my cheeks heat. I was petite right down to my toes, and I'd always wanted to be taller. It cut a little deep anytime someone commented on my size.

"So, you sell a lot of go-go boots?" Gilley asked, taking over.

The clerk shrugged. "A couple pair a year. Last year I think we sold three pairs. This year I've already sold four."

I frowned. That wasn't good. "You know," I said, hoping to jog her memory a little more, "my friend also bought the most amazing outfit to go with them. It was this patterned dress with black lines in bright orange, neon yellow, pink, and lime green."

The clerk's brow furrowed. "Yeah, we get a lot of great stuff. Maybe look around and you'll find something close? I can help you as soon as I put this back in the case."

I moved over to the counter while Gilley made a show of pretending to look around. Or maybe he actually was looking around. Gilley did love to make bold fashion statements.

"Darn, I was really hoping to pick up a pair of those go-go boots," I said, waiting for her to stop fiddling with the item in the glass case.

"If you'd like, I can take down your number and size, and if we get a pair in, I'll call you."

"Thank you," I said. She did seem sweet.

"Grrr!" she grumbled. "I can't get it to clasp right. I hate returns. They're always a pain in the butt."

It was then that I really looked down at the necklace she was struggling with. "*Ohmigod!*" I exclaimed.

She jumped, and the necklace went flying.

"Sorry!" I said.

The clerk looked rattled, but she covered it with a smile. "It's cool," she said, bending to pick up the necklace.

"*Don't touch it!*" I shouted.

Again, the poor clerk startled, and this time she actually yelped.

"What's going on?" Gilley said, coming to my side wearing a pair of chaps, a vest with an Andy Warhol–inspired print, and a cowboy hat.

Ignoring his alarmingly quick fashion statement (and *my*, what a statement!), I pointed to the necklace. I would've recognized that big white peace sign anywhere. "The woman with the go-go boots! She wore that necklace when she was coming out of the church!"

Gilley peered over the counter where the necklace lay. "What? How could she have worn that, Cat? It's here in the store for sale."

"No! The clerk just told me that someone returned it." Turning to the clerk, I added, "That's right, right? You said someone just returned it, correct?"

I was speaking in a rush, stringing my words together, and I was quivering in both fear and excitement.

"Yeah," she said cautiously, her eyes flickering back and forth between me and the necklace on the floor. "A customer retuned it right before you guys came in."

I turned to Gilley, and he turned to me. He looked like he'd just seen a ghost, and I knew exactly how he felt. "She was here!" I said.

"Just a few minutes ago!" he said.

"She could've seen us coming!"

Gilley turned back to the clerk. "Do you think she saw us coming?"

The clerk looked super confused and perhaps even scared of us. "No," she said. "She left, like, a couple of minutes before you guys walked in."

"We need that necklace," I said. "There could be fingerprints on it."

The clerk held up her hands in surrender, and now she really did look freaked out. "Whoa, I don't know what you've heard, but I did *not* know there were gonna be drugs at that party."

I shook my head. "Not your fingerprints, dear."

"But we will need yours to single out hers," Gilley said.

If possible, the clerk seemed even more alarmed, and she backed up against the wall away from us like a caged animal. "I think you guys should go," she said.

"We've upset you," I said. "I'm so sorry. It's just that I believe the necklace was worn by someone who committed a pretty terrible crime—"

"What kind of crime?" she interrupted.

Gilley and I looked at each other, both of us unsure how much to reveal. He made the call. "Did you hear about that priest that was murdered?"

"The one in East Hampton?" she asked.

"Yes," Gilley and I said.

"Ohmigod! You think that the lady who came in here to return that necklace was the one who murdered that priest?"

"Maybe," I said carefully. "But she also just as easily could've been a witness. Either way, we need to find her." Then I had a thought and looked around the corners of the shop. "Do you by any chance have security cameras?"

"Uh . . . no," the clerk said. And then she asked, "Hey, are you guys cops?"

"No," I said.

"Yes," Gilley said.

I eyed him sharply, but he simply stared confidently at the clerk. "Can I see some ID?" she said to him.

Gilley rolled his eyes and made a sweeping motion down his front. "I don't have it on me, sugar. I'm undercover today."

"Oh," she said, and to my surprise, she seemed to accept that explanation. "Okay, so what do you want me to do?"

"Well," I said, jumping in before Gilley could make any more false statements. "We need that necklace, but please don't touch it with your bare hands."

The clerk looked around her counter, and her eyebrows bounced when she spotted a pen to use to pick up the necklace. She maneuvered the necklace carefully onto the counter, and I used a tissue to lift it into my purse. "We'll also need something with your fingerprints on it to rule you out when we send this to the lab," I said, trying to sound official.

"That Dixie cup should work," Gil said, pointing to a cup of water she had by the register.

Our helpful clerk downed the water and handed over the cup, which I also handled with tissue and set it inside my purse.

"And you said the necklace was a return. Did the woman who returned it pay for it with a credit card, perhaps?" I crossed my fingers hoping our assassin had left some kind of a trace.

"No," said the clerk, dashing my hopes. "She paid cash, and I refunded her in cash."

"Darn it," I said, before thinking through what we'd need from the clerk next. "I suppose the last thing we'll need is a physical description," I said. "Can you describe this woman in as much detail as possible?"

"Um, sure. She was, like, a little taller than me—"

"How tall are you?" Gilley asked.

"Five five and a half," she said. "And she was maybe a few inches taller, but then she was also wearing heels."

"That's great," I said, eager for the details. "Now, describe what she looked like for us."

"Okay, um, she was pretty, and well-dressed."

"In vintage?" Gilley asked.

"No," the clerk said. "She was definitely designer label material. I'm not sure who she was wearing, but it was expensive. She wore a sand-colored, full-length fur vest, with a matching sand-colored turtleneck tunic, and a long scarf in the same tones trimmed with fur. Oh, and she also wore these killer stone-colored leather boots, gloves, and matching fedora."

"She wore gloves?" I asked. She'd worn gloves at the church too.

"Yeah. They were gorgeous."

"And a hat?" Gilley pressed.

"Yep. And sunglasses."

My hopes were beginning to fade. "But you could tell she was brunette, right?"

The clerk appeared confused. "She was blond."

Well, that was a new twist. "Did she take the sunglasses off?" I asked, already knowing she hadn't.

"No. She wore them the whole time she was in here."

"Can you describe her face?" I pressed.

"Um, well, she had on bright red lipstick, and like I said, she was wearing big round sunglasses."

Dammit! I thought. The woman had used another outfit to distract from and obscure her features. Everyone who encountered her seemed to notice everything about her outfit, but almost nothing overly descriptive about her facial features.

And the leather gloves worried me: I had a feeling that the only prints we'd find on the necklace would be the clerk's.

Gilley must have been thinking the same thing, because he sighed heavily and said, "Is there anything, and I do mean *anything*, that you can tell us about her appearance that was distinctive? I mean, other than what she was wearing?"

The clerk pursed her lips and thought for a moment. "Not really."

"She's foiled us again," I said to Gil. "She wears vintage in a town known for designer labels and designer labels in a store that's vintage. This woman is beyond clever."

"Hey, guys?" the clerk asked meekly.

"Yes?" Gilley and I both said.

"What if . . . what if she comes back?"

I realized that all this talk of murder had frightened the poor clerk. "I doubt very much that she'll come back here, so please don't worry, but on the off chance that she does, don't say a word about what we've told you. Wait on her, and be on your best behavior. If she wants to return ten things, take them all back; then the moment she leaves, you call the East Hampton police and ask for Detective Shepherd."

"Shepherd," she repeated. "Okay, got it."

I nodded and turned to Gil. "Are you taking those home with you?" I asked him, referring to the hat, the chaps, and the vest.

"Uh, uh," he said with a sigh. "Although I look fabulous in them, no?"

"No," I said, but added a playful grin.

"Humph," Gilley said, turning away. "*Every*one's a critic."

While Gilley shuffled out of his getup, I thought of something and asked the clerk, "How much was the necklace?"

"Um, it was twenty-eight dollars."

I took out a hundred, laid it on the counter, and said, "You've been very helpful. Please keep the change."

With that, Gilley and I left the shop and headed straight to the East Hampton police station.

Shepherd met us in the waiting area, and we explained where we'd been and what we'd discovered. He took the necklace and the cup from me, placing both in plastic baggies.

After we'd finished telling him all about the visit to the vintage shop, however, he moved us over to a bank of chairs and asked us to sit. I had the feeling a lecture was coming.

Holding up the baggie with the necklace, Shepherd said, "This was good work."

"Thank you," Gilley said, and he did look pleased.

"But . . . ," I said, because I knew where this was headed.

Shepherd offered me a lopsided smile. "But . . . I need you both to stop."

"Stop what?" Gilley asked.

"Stop snooping around this case. This isn't a civilian matter. It's a matter for the police."

Gil crossed his arms, his pleased smile fading into a frown. "With all due respect, Detective, you should be happy we're helping you out. Without us, you never would've been led to the necklace."

"True, but what have you really given me? I mean, we'll look for prints on this thing, but I think we all know that it's more than likely to have been wiped down."

"You don't know that for sure," I said, irritated that he was so quickly dismissing us when we really had done some good detective work.

"True, which is why I'm going to send the necklace and the cup to the lab, and pay a visit to this vintage-shop girl, but I want to make it clear that this assassin is dangerous. She's careful, she's smart, and she's met you, Catherine. If you continue to snoop around in her business, I'm worried that it could have . . . consequences."

Gilley reached out and squeezed my hand. "Yikes," he whispered.

Gazing directly at me, Shepherd said, "Promise me you'll stop snooping around, looking for the woman," he said.

I glared stubbornly at him; maybe it was the thrill of discovering the trail of the assassin, or maybe it was that it felt empowering to be investigating someone dangerous. Or maybe, just maybe, it was because after twenty years of knowing *exactly* who I was and what I wanted in life, I wasn't so sure of either myself or my purpose anymore, and this felt like a clear and distinct direction for a change.

"Fine," I said at last.

"You'll butt out?"

I got up in a little bit of a huff and began to walk out. "I said *fine*, didn't I?"

From behind, I heard Gilley scramble up and after me. And then Shepherd called out, "You never lie, right, Catherine?"

I shook my head and pushed my way out the door without a backward glance or another word.

* * *

"He didn't even thank us," Gil said, sitting down next to me at the kitchen table of Chez Kitty.

I spooned some sugar into the tea he'd made for us and picked up a cookie. "He's insufferable," I agreed. "He's rude, he's arrogant, he's stubborn, he's . . ." I was suddenly at a loss for what else the man was, so I looked to Gilley to see if he could fill in the blank.

"I think that about covers it," Gil said, swirling his tea with his spoon. "And I'd absolutely hate him except that he's gorgeous."

My mouth fell open. "You're *kidding* me, right?"

"Come on, Cat, you know he's pretty."

"He is most definitely *not* pretty."

Gilley sipped his tea and cocked a skeptical eyebrow at me.

"He's not," I insisted. "You want pretty, all you have to do is look at Maks."

"Maks is devastating," Gilley agreed. "But Shepherd could hold his own in a beauty contest between the two."

"No way," I said.

"What I find curious is why *you* are so insistent that he's not beautiful when he so clearly, clearly is, sugar. Why, mercy me, might you be a tiny bit attracted to our lonesome detective?"

Sometimes Gilley's southern accent comes through a little more distinctly in his speech. I've noticed this happens when he's tired or has had too much to drink or, like now, when he's trying to make a not-so-subtle point. "You read too much into everything, you know that, Gilley?"

Propping his elbow on the table and resting his chin lazily in his hand, Gilley said, "Do tell."

I rolled my eyes and tapped the table. "Can we please talk about something relevant?"

"Shepherd is definitely relevant."

I sighed. "He's not the only one who's insufferable at the moment."

"Fine. What would you like to talk about?"

"The case."

"I thought we'd quit that."

"What gave you that idea?"

"Well, probably the moment when the gorgeous detective we're no longer talking about ordered you to butt out and you said you would."

"I did no such thing."

Gilley slanted his eyes at me. "Catherine Cooper, I heard you with my own ears. You agreed to butt out."

"No, you heard me say 'fine,' which isn't quite an agreement, is it?"

Gilley giggled. "You're a sly one."

"Not as sly as this assassin. But you're right, we probably can't go snooping around inquiring about her lest we provoke the ire of the E.H.P.D.. But I was thinking of a different angle, anyway."

"What angle would that be?"

"Well, the one piece of this puzzle that really doesn't fit is Heather's housekeeper. She did come running out of that church as if her life depended on getting away, and she did look terrified. Something spooked her, and I have a feeling it was our go-go-wearing hitwoman."

"Do you think the assassin is after Heather's housekeeper?"

"Maybe. And if she is, the question is why?"

"Indeed," Gilley said. "Especially since it appears that the housekeeper may have been the one who killed Heather."

"Yes," I agreed. "As a trusted employee, she could've easily slipped Heather some poisonous substance, then waited around to make sure she was dead."

"And we still don't know what the toxin was, huh?"

"No," I said. "At least not according to what Shepherd told me yesterday."

"Okay, so, what's Heather's housekeeper's name?" Gil asked, as he pushed his tea to the side and reached for his laptop.

"Kuznetsov. I don't remember her first name."

Gilley grunted as his fingers began to type. "Was it Sasha?"

"No," I said.

"There's a Sasha Kuznetsov who lives in West Hempstead."

"West Hempstead . . . that's near JFK, right?"

"Yes."

"Any other Kuznetsovs nearby?"

"She's the closest one."

"Carmen!" I said as the name suddenly flashed into my mind. "I remember now: her first name is Carmen."

"Hmm," Gilley said, typing. "She's not coming up anywhere on social media."

"Do you think that Sasha is related?" I asked.

"Possibly." Gilley eyed me sideways. "Why do I feel there's a road trip involved here?"

I got up from the table, taking my teacup with me. "Tomorrow," I told him. "Tonight I've got a double date, and I gotta get moving if I'm going to make it."

"It's not even two o'clock," Gil said. "And who's the double date with? You, Maks, and another couple?"

"No. Me, Matt, and Mike. I'm meeting them in the city for dinner. It's almost a three-hour drive, and I still have to change."

"Good for you," Gilley said, getting up to take his teacup to the sink as well. "It'll be nice to spend an evening with your sons."

"Yes, if one enjoys scintillating conversations of me saying many, many words and getting monosyllabic responses."

"The joys of parenting," Gilley said. "Remind me never to try it."

I laughed and looped my arm through his. "It does have its joys," I said. "Years four through twelve were wonderful. And, according to you, they'll be wonderful again when they're twenty-two."

"Only seven and a half more years," Gil said.

"Why do I have a feeling they'll fly by?" I sighed wistfully. "I can't believe how quickly they're growing up. Both boys are now taller than me."

"Honey," Gilley said. "They passed you by when they were eight."

I pretended to glare at him. "Ten, and I wouldn't mock, Mr. Gillespie. Mathew is already two inches taller than *you*."

"Which is why I think I'll spend the evening shopping online for some new boots. Something with a heel. Put a little of my own go-go in my step!"

"Have fun," I said, letting go of him. "With luck, I'll make it back here before midnight."

"Drive safe."

I left Gilley to cross the courtyard to Chez Cat, where I changed into something "motherly" and was on the road within the hour. I was meeting the boys in Manhattan at a favorite restaurant of theirs where the slabs of prime rib were thick, the prices were high, and the all-female waitstaff were gorgeous. The restaurant was always teeming with businessmen, and I likened it to Hooters for the upper crust.

As I was getting onto US-27, my phone rang. Caller ID said Marcus Brown was on the line. "Marcus?" I said when I picked up the call.

"Catherine," he said warmly. "I have news to share."

"Good news?"

"No. Just news. I spoke with Dr. Beauperthy—the medical examiner—and he said that he's still unable to identify the toxin that killed Heather, but he also relayed that there was nothing unusual or lethal in her stomach contents, although her blood-alcohol levels were elevated. He attributes that to her having had at least three martinis between noon and four. He also found some of the Cobb salad from the luncheon, and he noted that your punch was clearly the last thing she ingested as there was still some liquid found in her esophagus, but he tested all of the ingredients and found nothing chemically toxic in it.

"He also did a thorough examination of her body and could find no puncture wounds where a needle might've delivered a fatal dose of some kind of poison. He's actually stumped at how she came into contact with the toxin, whatever it was."

"Well, I guess that's good news after all," I said. "I mean, good news for me, but not so good for Heather. She was still murdered."

"True."

A thought occurred to me. "Does Shepherd know all this?"

"Beauperthy e-mailed him his report an hour ago."

"Can he still come after me in light of this?" I asked, hoping the M.E.'s report would put me in the clear once and for all.

"He could, but he'd get laughed out of court again. There's no evidence connecting you to Heather's cause of death. At most, he could bring a charge of causing harm to a corpse, but even that's highly circumstantial. Truthfully, I don't think he's that stupid, Catherine."

I let out a sigh of relief. "Me either," I said. I'd gotten to know Shepherd a little better, after talking to both him and his sister, and I didn't feel that he was legitimately targeting me as a suspect anymore.

"Thank you for the update, Marcus," I said.

"You're welcome. If I hear any further updates, I'll contact you, but I think you can rest easy for now."

I smiled. Just hearing Marcus say that did make me feel much better.

After hanging up with the attorney, my mind drifted to all of my encounters with the detective, and then to what Gilley had said about Shepherd. I didn't like that Gil had accused me of being attracted to him. I mean, the man truly was insufferable. And annoying. And he'd arrested me in public!

But there was a side of Shepherd that spoke to me. It was his sad side, I suppose. No one tells you this if you've never been through it, but divorce is as much a death as losing a loved one.

It's the death of your identity as a married person, as someone's partner, as a member of a team.

But it's also the death of the future you were certain you would have. That image we all create of being one half of an old couple, shuffling along in some bucolic park, hand in hand . . .

And that death will hit you hard, even when you can't wait to be free of the person you're married to. There's still a mourning process that comes with the vow of "I no longer do . . ."

So I could understand Shepherd in a way that made me sympathize with him. It seemed to me that his grumbly, cantankerous nature was due to the fact that he was still in mourning. For his divorce and for his murdered ex-wife.

Still, the man was *insufferable!* And my attentions were currently being pointed toward a certain lovely, charming, sincerely nice man named Maks.

So why was I spending so much time thinking about Shepherd?

"Damn you, Gilley Gillespie," I muttered.

With a sigh, I prepared to change lanes by checking my rearview mirror. Finding the lane open, I maneuvered over and noticed the car behind me did as well. It wasn't anything alarming, just something I noticed. But then a car in the lane to my right moved over into my lane and slowed down, which meant I had to move back to the left again.

"Annoying," I said as my gaze glanced in the rearview. It was then that I caught that the car behind me also moved over.

Now, it could've been because the car in front of me had in fact slowed down, and maybe the car behind me saw that and moved over to pass that car, like I was doing, but something about it felt a teensy bit off.

So I began to glance every few seconds in my rearview mirror, and when I got the chance, I moved over two lanes to the right and took my foot off the accelerator, effectively slowing down myself.

Wouldn't you know it, the car behind me copied the move.

"Uh oh," I said, as a frightened tremor went down my spine.

I looked around me and felt better when I realized that there was fairly heavy traffic surrounding my car. And there would be heavy traffic all the way to my destination at this hour.

Still, I was traveling to see my sons, and while I didn't know who was behind me, I did know that I didn't want to expose them to even the smallest possibility that someone nefarious was on my tail.

"Stay calm, Cat," I said to myself. "It might be nothing. Give it a few minutes in this lane, then change again and see what happens."

Having talked through the plan with myself, I waited exactly three minutes, then changed lanes without using my blinker.

The car behind me followed suit.

"Ohmigod," I said, the tremor moving from my spine to my voice. Using my car's hands-free option, I called out for Siri to place a call.

"East Hampton Police Department," said a raspy female voice.

"This is Catherine Cooper. I need to speak to Detective Shepherd right away!"

"Hang on. I'll see if he's still here," she said.

I bit my lip while the line played some hold music, and then Shepherd's voice boomed out of my car's speaker. "Shepherd," he said.

"Detective? It's Catherine Cooper. I'm on US twenty-seven headed west, and there's a car behind me that's been following me for several miles."

There was a pause, then, "How far out of town are you?"

"I'm . . . I'm . . . ," I scanned the road, searching for a road sign. "I'm coming up to Patchogue!"

"You're sure it's following you?"

"I'm ninety-five percent certain."

"Okay, here's what I want you to do: take the Waverly Avenue exit and head south for about a quarter of a mile. The Suffolk County police station will be on your left. If the car behind you continues to follow you, park in the lot, and I'll send an officer out to meet you. Stay put until I get there, okay?"

"But . . . ," I said, as my eyes misted. I was so scared I was shaking.

"But what?" he asked gently.

"I'm supposed to meet my sons for dinner."

"Call them," he said. "Tell them you can't make it."

"Tell them I can't make it? But this is their one night to spend with me!"

"Catherine," he said. "Come on. You're a witness to the assassin. She might think you can identify her. Until she's caught, you'll need to rethink your family get-togethers."

I wiped my cheeks because I'd started to cry. I was so scared. "Yes, of course, you're right. I'll call them. How soon can you be at the Suffolk County station?"

"At this time of day, probably over an hour. Just wait there until I can escort you safely home, okay?"

"Okay."

I hung up with Shepherd and called my son Michael.

"Hey, Mom," he said.

It broke my heart that he actually sounded pleased to hear from me for a change. "Bood," I began, using the pet name I'd called him since he was an infant, "I have bad news."

"What?"

"I can't make it to dinner tonight."

"Okay," he said, like I'd just given him the weather report.

"Try not to sound so disappointed."

"Naw, it's cool, Mom. Matt and I wanted to hit a Game Stop anyway."

I bit down on my lip to stop the small sob that threatened to bubble up. I suddenly missed my boys more than I could say. "Okay, love. Call or text me tonight when you get back to school, all right? And don't you dare miss your curfew."

"I won't, Mom. See you in two weeks, okay?"

"No," I said quickly. "This is my weekend with you. Your father had you last weekend."

"Yeah, but we're going to Washington for that class trip, remember? You said it was okay to go on your weekend. You even signed the permission form."

A tear slid down my cheek. "Oh, of course." I hadn't remembered. "Yes. We'll talk before you leave for that."

"Okay, Mom. Bye."

"Love you!" I called out, but he was already gone. I spent a minute or two crying in the car, my gaze periodically going to the rearview mirror. Seeing that the car behind me was still on my tail made me cry even harder.

I pulled myself together, though, because the exit for Patchogue came up fast. I took it without using my turn signal, and I was so relieved to see the green light at the bottom of the exit that I sped up to get through it in time. The car behind me stayed right with me as we cruised through the intersection.

Turning left at the light, I continued down Waverly until the large sign indicating the Suffolk County P.D. came into view. I let out a sob of relief and gripped the steering wheel tighter. When I pulled into the lot, the car behind me slowed and passed the station by.

The second I pulled into a space right near the door, panic fueled my actions and I decided not to wait for an officer to come out to meet me at the car. Instead I bolted from the car and dashed inside. I was met by a large, barrel-chested officer with a bushy mustache and meaty hands who took my arm and led me to a bank of chairs. I was sobbing so hard I couldn't really speak.

"Are you Catherine Cooper?" the officer asked.

I nodded and worked to take a deep breath so that I could at least get a few words out. "I . . . she . . . followed . . . here!" and I pointed toward the lot.

The officer called out to another uniformed cop, and she came running. "Check the lot," the officer sitting next to me and still holding onto my arm said. Turning to me he asked, "Can you describe the car?"

"Silver . . . S . . . U . . . V."

The female officer dashed out the door, but she was back within a matter of moments. "There's no car like that in the lot."

"Can you tell us anything about the driver?" the first officer asked me.

I shook my head. It was approaching dusk, and the SUV's lights had been on. Plus the car had never gotten close enough for me to get a look at the driver. I hadn't even been able to tell if it was a man or a woman tailing me.

"Okay," the officer said. "Can I get you some water, ma'am?"

I wiped at my cheeks, finally calming down. "Yes. Yes, that would be very nice, thank you."

The male officer got up, and I saw him point to me as he passed the woman cop. She sat down next to me and patted me on the back. "How far did he follow you?"

"I think all the way from East Hampton."

"And you have no idea who he was?"

"No. But it could have been a woman. I couldn't tell a gender."

"Could it have been a case of road rage? Did you cut the driver off or anything?"

"No," I said. "Absolutely not."

"Okay, we'll send a patrol out and have a look around, but he or she is probably long gone now that they've seen you turn in here."

I nodded. "I hope so."

The first officer came back, handing me a bottled water, and then the pair traded places again. The female officer said, "I'm gonna cruise around the block."

"Okay, Sinclair," said the first officer. I finally looked at his name tag. And the stars on his lapel. He wasn't an officer; he was a sergeant, and his name tag read Alfonsi.

"Can I get you anything from the vending machine?" he asked after Sinclair had gone.

I offered him a weak smile. "No. Thank you. You're very kind, Sergeant Alfonsi. I'm sorry to be in such a state."

"Don't sweat it," he said. "That must've been a heck of a scary ride."

"I think I'm also emotional because I had to miss dinner with my sons. They're at the Masters School in Dobbs Ferry."

"You were headed all the way to Dobbs Ferry?" he asked.

I shook my head. "No, I was headed into the city. The boys took the train. We were going to meet at their favorite restaurant in Midtown. I'd really been looking forward to it."

"That's rough. What grade are they each in?"

I realized that Alfonsi was making light conversation to calm me down and settle my nerves. I wanted to hug him, because it was working. "They're twins, and they're in the ninth grade. They've grown up so fast."

"I've got two of my own," Alfonsi said. "One in sixth grade, one in fourth. And I know what you mean. It feels like just yesterday that my boys were toddlers."

I nodded. "The hardest thing about their being at boarding school is not being part of their nightly ritual anymore, you know? The Masters School is terrific, and they love it there, but . . . well, I miss them, you know?"

"I do," he said. Then he pointed to his chest. "Divorced. I get them every other weekend and every Wednesday."

I tapped my bare ring finger. "I'm divorced too."

"Splitting up is rough, huh?"

"It's the worst. But the alternative is being married to someone who makes you unhappy. I wouldn't take my ex-husband back for all the tea in China."

"That's the way I feel too," he said.

At that moment, Officer Sinclair came back into the building. "I cruised around the block. There's no sign of your stalker."

Alfonsi said, "Would you like to file a report?"

"What can I report?" I asked. "I was followed here from East Hampton by someone I can't describe in a silver SUV. That could be any one of probably ten million cars."

"Probably more," he agreed. "Still, if there's ever another incident involving this particular car, you'll have something on record showing it's a pattern."

I considered that and then nodded. "All right. I'll file a report."

It took about ten minutes for Alfonsi to walk me through the paperwork. After that, I did visit the vending machine and got myself a snack. A good twenty minutes after that, Shepherd arrived, looking decidedly weary from the rush-hour traffic.

"You okay?" he asked me.

"Yes, thank you."

"Did you get a description of the car or the driver?" he asked.

"It was a silver SUV, and I never got a glimpse of the driver."

"Damn," he said. Then he headed over to speak with Alfonsi, and it was obvious that the two knew each other and were friendly.

While the men talked, I sat in my chair and nibbled at my cheese and crackers. They were stale and dreadful, but by now, I was quite hungry.

Finally, Shepherd came back, handed me his card, and said, "Okay, Catherine, let's head out. Follow my car, and call the cell number on my card if anyone tracks too close to your car."

"Shouldn't you follow me?" I asked as we headed out.

"I know a shortcut," he said.

I sighed wearily as I got into my car and followed Shepherd out of the lot. We drove for probably forty-five minutes and were close to Water Mill when Shepherd put on his turn signal. I stuck to his tail as he exited US-27 and led me along a winding series of streets edging closer and closer to Mecox Bay. At last we pulled into a parking lot for what appeared to be a run-down restaurant named Moe's.

Parking next to Shepherd, I got out and stared at him expectantly.

"We gotta eat, don't we?" was the only explanation he gave me before turning away to walk toward the door to the restaurant. "Come on, Catherine, I'll buy you dinner."

It wasn't the worst dinner invitation I'd ever had.

But it was far from the best.

With another sigh, I followed after him. At least he was gentleman enough to hold the door for me.

We entered a dimly lit room, paneled in dark wood and dusty oil paintings of the mostly seascapes and fishing themed variety. Tan leather booths lined three of the walls, but the center was cluttered with four-tops that were mostly empty.

"Charming," I said, with only a slight curl to my lip.

"Aww, come on, give it a chance," Shepherd said, grabbing two menus from a bus cart and motioning for me to follow him.

We wound our way through the chairs and tables to a booth in the back. Shepherd sat down first and handed me a menu. "The ribs here are out of this world."

"I smell seafood," I said. The smell of fried fish hung thickly in the air.

"They have great seafood too."

I opened the menu tentatively and scanned the fare. I was a little surprised to find pecan-crusted crab cakes and avocado and crab guacamole on the starters menu, and as I read on, the menu got even more interesting.

"The mahi-mahi sounds very tempting," I said.

"I'm telling you, the ribs are the way to go," Shepherd said. "Order it with Moe's roasted potatoes and collard greens, and you'll thank me later."

I cocked a skeptical eyebrow.

"Will you just trust me?" he said wearily.

I closed the menu and nodded. "Fine. Ribs it is."

Shepherd clapped his hands enthusiastically. "Now we're talking!"

The door to the kitchen opened, and out stepped an elderly man who could've been anywhere between seventy-five and a hundred and five—it was impossible to tell. He was bent with age, had an almost crippling case of osteoporosis that gave him a sizable hunchback, and shuffled more than he walked, pivoting stiffly to the right so that he could angle his gaze at us. "Steven!" he croaked.

"Hey, Moe," Shepherd said.

The old man's shuffle got ever so slightly faster as he made his way over to us. "And you brought a pretty girl too! Is she for me?"

"Not this time," Shepherd said with a laugh. "Besides, she's way too young for you."

"Does she have a grandmother?" Moe asked.

I laughed too. Okay, the old man was charming. "Hello," I said, extending my hand to him. "I'm Catherine. It's a pleasure to meet you, Moe."

Moe took my hand and brought it to his lips for a quick peck. Then he focused on Shepherd. "What's your poison, son?"

"The usual," he said.

"Right. One light beer with no gusto and no taste, coming up."

"Actually, Moe, give me a regular beer. I'm off the diet."

"Oooo, look who's gotten himself all fancy," Moe said. "Alrighty, one regular beer for the adventure seeker." Pivoting to me again he said, "And for the lady?"

"You know, a beer sounds pretty good, Moe. I'll have one of those."

"Right away," he said and shuffled off at the speed of snail.

When he was out of earshot, I leaned toward Shepherd and said, "I haven't had a beer in ten years."

"That doesn't surprise me."

I pulled my chin back. "What does that mean?"

Shepherd tapped the menu with his index finger. "You strike me as part of the fancy drinking crowd. I would've pegged your first choice to be a crisp chardonnay, a dry cab, or dirty martini."

My face flushed with heat. He'd pegged me well. "Do I really come off as that much of a snob?"

He shrugged. "Yeah."

"Wow," I replied. I didn't quite know what to say. "I wasn't always a snob, you know."

"Money changes people."

"I wasn't always rich, so that much is probably true."

"Let me guess, your ex was some heart surgeon or hedge-fund manager or rich oil tycoon, right?"

I laughed heartily. "No. He played golf."

"Professionally?" Shepherd said, with a hint of interest.

I rolled my eyes. "Yes, but he wasn't ranked very high. Tommy didn't have the talent it takes to play in the majors. He just liked to play. A lot. And he sponged off me the entire length of our marriage."

"Sponged off you?" Shepherd said. "*You* were the money-maker?"

I smiled confidently. "You betcha."

"Huh," he said. "And here I had you pegged for a gold digger."

"Thanks."

He shrugged again. "East Hampton's full of them. So what do you do, Catherine?"

"I'm a life coach."

That got me a jaw drop. "You made your money coaching people about life?"

"No," I said. "I made my money building a marketing empire, which I then sold, and now I'm a life coach."

Shepherd pressed his lips together hard, but then a small bubble of laughter escaped.

"What's so funny?" I demanded.

"Here we are," said Moe, approaching our table one slowly shuffling foot at a time. I realized he'd gone to get our drinks several minutes earlier. I could only imagine how long it'd take to get our dinner.

"Thanks, Moe," Shepherd said, picking up his bottle. Waiting until I took up mine, he clinked the necks and said, "Cheers."

I took a sip, still a little miffed about him laughing at my newfound profession, but I figured I'd let it go because I was tired of arguing with the man.

The beer tasted wonderful. It was bitter and bubbly and suited my mood perfectly. "That's good," I said, setting it down.

"What can I get for ya?" Moe asked.

We ordered our rib dinners, and after Moe shuffled away again, Shepherd said, "So how did you get into the life-coaching biz?"

I narrowed my eyes at him, waiting for another bubble of laughter, but he wasn't showing any signs of still being amused at my expense. "I don't exactly know," I said. "I think that my marketing experience has taught me a lot about what motivates people, what inspires them to behave in certain predictable patterns. And because that's been my life's work, I thought I could bring that experience to helping people figure out why they act in a certain way that might be limiting them, and how I can redirect them to new patterns of behavior that they'll benefit from."

Shepherd looked surprised. "That's kind of brilliant," he said.

I smiled. "Thank you."

He tilted his beer at me. "Those qualities would make you a good detective too."

"They come in handy when I'm trying to read what motivates a person."

Tilting his chin slightly, Shepherd said, "What do you think motivates me?"

I chuckled. "You don't want to know what I think about what motivates you, Detective."

He smiled—almost overconfidently. "Sure I do. Come on, tell me, oh brilliant marketing whiz, what motivates me in life?"

I took another sip of beer. "Well," I said, "for starters, I think you have a giant chip on your shoulder."

Shepherd rolled his eyes, like he understood that was obvious.

"But I don't think that came from your childhood. I think that chip formed when you decided to become a police detective in your hometown."

"How would that form a chip on my shoulder?" he asked, and I could see the doubt in his eyes.

"Because no one in East Hampton takes you nearly as seriously as you take yourself," I said. "And you interpret that as a lack of respect. So you're hard on people in every way you can be because you're constantly trying to prove to them that you're good at what you do, and that they should respect you."

Shepherd's eyes widened, and for a moment, he was totally speechless.

I continued. "So what motivates you is a desire to get a little recognition for doing a good job in a town where respect and recognition are hard to come by for anyone without a trust fund."

"Huh," Shepherd said. And I knew in that moment that I'd nailed him.

I smiled slyly. "See? I would make a good detective."

"Yeah," he said, his face reddening. "I could've used your input on a few cases I've worked on."

"Speaking of which," I said, "do you think I was being followed tonight by the assassin?"

"Hard to say, but someone was interested in where you were going and what you were up to."

"Why would the assassin be interested in me, though?"

"You saw her up close," he said. "And I'll bet anything she waited around to see what you'd do after she left the church."

"So she would've seen me get in my car, make a call, and wait; then when you showed up, she would've seen us talking."

"Yeah. A lot of ifs, but still plausible. She also would've known with your public arrest and bond hearing, that you were my number-one suspect."

"So . . . what? She's keeping tabs on me to make sure you're still interested in pointing to me as Heather's killer?"

"Maybe," he said.

And then I had another thought, a very unsettling one. "You don't think she wants to kill me too, do you?"

He shook his head. "If that was her behind you and if she did want you dead, trust me, you'd be dead."

I gulped. "Comforting."

Moe arrived at that moment to drop off some rolls. Shepherd took up the basket, unfolded the cloth napkin covering the rolls, and offered me one.

"No thank you," I said. Bread goes right to my hips.

He frowned. "You're not one of those are you?"

"One of *those?*"

"Yeah. One of those people who denies themselves the pleasure of a dinner roll because you're worried about the carbs or that the gluten is some kind of poison."

I took a roll from the basket. "Nope."

Tearing a small bit of the warm pastry off the end, I popped it into my mouth, and my taste buds lit up. The roll was soft, buttery, and deliciously sour. I nearly moaned. Shepherd bounced his eyebrows and bit into his own roll.

We chatted then about other things: my sons, his family, life in East Hampton. Our food did eventually arrive, and the restaurant started to fill up too. More staff arrived in the form of two high school girls who waited on tables and brought food out.

Pushing my plate away after I'd eaten more than I should've of the delicious dinner, I said, "This is an odd little place, isn't it?"

"Moe's?" he said.

I nodded.

"Yeah, I guess. The service is slow, but the food is the best. I hang out here a lot. Moe takes good care of me."

"You two kind of look alike," I said, teasing him.

"He's my granduncle—the youngest of my grandfather's brothers—so that's not surprising."

"He is?" I said. "I meant that as a joke."

Shepherd chuckled. "Joke's on you then. You ready?" he asked next.

I nodded. Shepherd motioned for me to gather up my things, which I did, and while I was doing that, I noticed that he took out a hundred-dollar bill and left it tucked under his dinner plate. He then got up and walked with me over to where Moe was standing, talking to two men who were also eating ribs.

Shepherd draped his arm over Moe's shoulder, leaned down, and said softly, "Gotta go, Uncle Moe. Can you spot me dinner?"

"Don't I always?" Moe said, turning to hug the younger man. Moe then stepped back and held his grandnephew at arm's length, considering him with a worried frown. "You doin' okay, squirt?"

"I'm doin' great," Shepherd assured him. "Thanks for dinner."

"You betcha!" Moe said. "Stay outta trouble, you hear?"

Shepherd gave him a cool two-finger salute before motioning me to walk in front of him out the door.

"He calls you squirt?" I asked as we passed through the doorway.

"I was a late bloomer," Shepherd said. "I was the shortest kid in class until I was about seventeen, when I finally got a good growth spurt."

"I know all about being the littlest kid in class," I said.

He eyed me sideways. "You turned out just fine."

I felt myself blush. "Why, Detective, was that a compliment?"

Shepherd ignored the question and instead cleared his throat and pointed to his car. "I'll follow you to your house to make sure you're safe."

"Okay," I said. We got into our respective vehicles, and I

pulled out of the lot first. As I drove home, I kept glancing in the mirror, where I could see Shepherd's lights a respectful distance behind me.

It was comforting that he had my back. It was also comforting to simply have him nearby, and that wasn't something I wanted to analyze overmuch.

Finally, I pulled into my drive, and Shepherd did too. I waited for the garage door to go up and eased inside; and that's when Shepherd appeared at my door and pointed to the house, as if asking if he could enter. I then noticed that he had his free hand on his holstered weapon, and I gripped the steering wheel tightly as I realized he wanted to go in and check to make sure the assassin wasn't lurking in the shadows.

Sebastian wasn't yet wired to the house, so it was a source of vulnerability for me. Still, there was an alarm, and I rolled down the window. "The code is 0710," I said, pointing to the alarm panel. It was the twins' birthday.

"Got it," Shepherd said. "Sit tight."

I watched as he moved to the panel, punched in the code, then entered through the door. A light flipped on inside and I waited in anxious silence for what seemed like eternity. At last, Shepherd reappeared, and approached my window. "All clear," he said.

I let out a breath of relief. "Thank you."

"Set the alarm tonight," he said, moving away toward his own car.

I got out and stood for a moment by my car door. "Goodnight," I called.

He waved over his shoulder without looking back. I moved to the door and punched the button to close up the garage again. Shepherd was by now in his car, but he hadn't backed away yet. There was a moment where I stood there in the beams of his lights and had the strangest urge to call him back and invite him inside. For what I didn't quite know, and the thought was truly just a momentary flash of . . . I don't know. Maybe just loneliness.

It'd been nice to spend an evening with him. Even though it hadn't been a date, it'd still been nice.

At least I didn't think it was a date.

Had it been a date?

Shepherd's car began to back up as the door to the garage got to about knee level. I moved inside but paused in the back hallway leading to the family room. "Nah," I said, laughing at myself. "Definitely not a date." And then I stopped again. "But what if it had been?" I considered that for a lengthy moment. "Oh, my," I said. "Oh, my . . ."

Chapter 13

I found Gilley sipping coffee at the kitchen table in Chez Kitty, still looking sleepy.

"Good morning," I sang as I breezed into the cottage.

He looked up. "Coffee's hot," he said.

I moved to the counter and took a mug from the cupboard. Pouring myself a cup from the French press, I loaded in some cream and sugar and brought it to the table to sit down next to Gil. "No breakfast this morning?"

Gilley frowned, and his lower lip quivered. "I Skyped last night with Michel," he began. "It didn't go well. We got into an argument, and he . . . he . . . he threw the F-bomb at me!"

I gasped. Knowing Michel, that was nearly unfathomable to me. "He called you . . . ?"

"Fat!" Gilley wailed. "He actually called me *fat*, Cat!"

"Wait, a fat cat, or just fat?"

"Just fat. Not a cat. You're the cat, Cat."

"Got it." Placing my hand over his, I said, "You're not fat, Gilley."

"Tell that to Michel."

"What were the exact circumstances surrounding his . . ."

"Calling me fat?"

"Yes."

Gilley's lower lip trembled again, and I squeezed his hand in comfort. It took him a moment before he could speak. "I wanted to do something nice for him, so I thought a little strip tease would be appropriate, you know, because he's in London, and I'm all the way over here, and it's been forever since we've seen each other, if you get my drift."

"I do," I said, hoping he wouldn't go into detail.

"So, anyway, I was doing my sexy dance, which is part Brit-Brit, part Bey, part Madge—"

"Britney, Beyoncé, Madonna," I said.

"Mmm hmm," Gilley said. "And I was full on vogueing it up like all the single ladies in a 'Slave 4 U' tribute when I heard Michel . . ." Gilley paused to lower his chin and emit a tiny sob.

"You heard Michel what?" I asked.

Gilley looked up at me, his expression so pained. "I heard Michel . . . giggle."

"Oh, no," I said. "Oh, Gilley . . ."

"Can you *believe* that?"

"Well, maybe Michel wasn't laughing *at* you. Maybe he was laughing *with* you. Maybe it was simply a case of him thinking you were joking, only to discover that you were serious."

But Gil shook his head. "No," he insisted. "No. He laughed *at* me, Cat. *At!*"

"I'm assuming you told him you were offended?"

"Oh, I did, sister. I did!" Gil said. "I let him have it. Unfortunately, I was shirtless while I was yelling at him, and at the end of my yelling he pointed to me and said that it was hard to take me seriously when I'd gotten so fat!"

"So he was merely being defensive," I said. Michel was typically so even-keeled; it was hard to imagine him losing patience with Gilley enough to resort to that kind of an insult. "He simply uttered it during an argument. I'm sure there's no truth to it, Gil. You're fine!"

Gilley stood and pulled up his shirt. A roll of blubber had settled nicely around his waistline. "Still think I'm *fine*, Cat?"

It took all of my willpower, and I do mean *all* of it, not to laugh at the ridiculous image of Gilley with his shirt pulled up, the roll of blubber splooging around his middle, and the pained and furious expression on his face.

Still, I managed to hold it together. "We all have a little extra junk somewhere on us, Gil. It doesn't make us fat," I said gently.

Gilley lowered his shirt and slumped back into the chair. "No," he said. "He's right. I've been snacking on far too many carbs lately."

"What can I do?" I asked him. I hated seeing Gilley so upset.

"I don't know. Distract me from the thought of food."

I got up from the table and headed to the fridge. I took out some eggs, some blueberries, and some strawberries. "What're you doing?" he demanded.

"You're going to eat a sensible breakfast of eggs and fruit, Gilley," I told him. "Starving yourself isn't the way to keep yourself healthy. You need to fuel your body properly with good foods, add in a little exercise, and you'll be trim again in no time."

Half an hour later Gilley pushed his plate away. "Thanks, Cat."

"Of course," I said. "You're always taking good care of me. It's nice to take care of you for a change."

"So how was your night last night with the boys?" he asked.

I shook my head. "It never happened."

"What never happened?"

"Dinner with Matt and Mike."

"Don't tell me they blew you off?"

"No, no. Nothing like that. On the drive to the city, I was followed."

Gilley leaned forward. "Followed? By who?"

"Whom, and I don't know."

"Do you think it might've been Shepherd?"

"No. Definitely not him."

"How do you know if you don't know?"

"Because I called Shepherd and told him I was being followed, and he sent me to the Patchogue police station, where I waited for him to come and escort me back."

"Wow," Gil said. "That was nice of him."

"It was. And he even bought me dinner."

Gilley leaned forward again. "You guys went on a date?"

"No," I said firmly, having decided sometime between two and four a.m. that we had most definitely *not* been on a date.

At least I thought so.

"So who did he think was following you?"

"He didn't know either. We're both hoping it wasn't the assassin."

"Do you think it *was* the assassin?"

"Maybe," I said. "And that's terrifying me."

Gilley gulped. "You know, the crazy thing is, Cat, whoever this woman is, she could basically walk right up to your house, knock on your door in plain clothes, and you'd never know it was her. She could shoot you before you even had a chance to process who she could be!"

I felt the color drain from my face, and I gripped my coffee mug tightly. "Gee, Gil, thanks for that absolutely *terrifying* thought."

Gil's expression turned regretful. "Sorry. I'm sure that won't happen, though. I mean, now that I think about it, it's a pretty far-fetched scenario."

Suddenly, the doorbell rang.

Gilley and I both looked at each other in alarm.

"Who the hell is that?" I whispered.

"How should I know?"

"Well, go look through the peephole!"

"It's your guest house! *You* go look through the peephole!"

I shook my head.

Gilley shook his.

We both glared hard at each other.

The doorbell chimed again.

Slipping out of the chair and pulling Gilley with me toward the kitchen, we ducked down behind the counter, and I called out, "Who is it?"

"It's UPS, ma'am," came the faint reply. "I have a package here that requires a signature."

"Oh! My new drone!" Gilley sang happily, and he bounded out from behind the counter and skipped over to the door.

"Gilley!" I said in a harsh whisper. "Look through the peephole first!"

Gilley paused in front of the door and tilted forward on tiptoes. "It's really him," he said with a relieved sigh. After opening the door and signing for the package, he came back to the table and began to pry open the box.

It was about then that he realized I was still ducked down behind the counter. "What're you still doing over there?" he asked. "It was only the UPS guy."

"This time," I said. I stood up slowly and rubbed my shoulders as a cold shudder went through me. "I can't live like this, Gilley."

He frowned and set aside the box to focus on me. "What do you think we should do?"

"I think we have to find Heather's murderer. I was up most of last night mulling this whole thing over and over, and the more I think about it, the more I think that maybe Carmen really did kill Heather. And that's why she was fleeing the scene at the church. I think she might've confessed to Father Stephan that she killed Heather, and, nervous that he'd break the oath of confession and talk to the cops, she killed him. I'm also thinking that the getaway car she hopped into was driven by someone she trusted. Maybe a relative."

"Sasha," Gilley said. "She lives in West Hempstead. That's a little bit of a hike from here, but drivable in a little less than two hours."

"Yes. We need to find where Sasha lives and see if Carmen is a relative of hers, and if so, if she's taken refuge with her."

Gilley shrugged. "I'm game. Give me ten minutes to make myself presentable, and we're off."

True to his word, Gilley was ready exactly ten minutes later, and we set off toward West Hempstead.

Still feeling a little wary about being followed the night before, I drove my sedan to a storage facility on the west side of town, making sure to double-check my rearview mirror every few seconds along the way.

"What's here?" Gilley asked me as I entered my security code.

"Another mode of transportation," I said.

Gilley furrowed his brow, but I waited to show him when we got to a set of garage doors. Using the remote I'd brought along, I opened the doors and put the car in park.

"Ohmigod!" Gilley squealed. "We're taking the Ferrari?"

I chuckled. "No, dear. We need to be a little more inconspicuous. We're taking the Mini Cooper."

Years earlier, my sister had won two Mini Coopers and ten grand in Las Vegas. She'd given one of the cars to me as a thank-you for my help in getting her out of a sticky situation that had nearly gotten us both killed.

In the years since I'd owned the Mini, I'd barely used it, but I couldn't bear to part with it because, truth be told, that week in Vegas with my sister had been one of the most thrilling of my life.

As Gilley and I approached the car, Gil said, "Is there room enough for the both of us?"

"Ha, ha," I said, opening the door and slipping behind the wheel. Mini Coopers are deceptive—they're actually quite roomy inside. "I haven't started it in months. I hope it still runs," I said, turning the ignition and smiling when the engine turned over. "Ahh," I said, petting the dashboard appreciatively. "Who's a good little Mini? Hmm? You are!"

"Wow," Gilley said, looking around the interior. "There's more legroom in here than I thought."

"Buckle your seat belt," I told him, and we set off.

It took a good hour and a half to reach West Hempstead—a community not far from JFK Airport. We had to rely on my app to locate Sasha's address, and after several turns and what felt like a few misdirections, we came upon a duplex that'd definitely seen better days.

A gutter hung down from the roof, draping itself like a dead snake across the front of the garage. The windows were covered by blinds that had whole sections missing—giving the house the impression of a gap-toothed old man, and an orange flowerpot still holding some sort of long-dead plant gave the only spot of color to an otherwise dreary scene.

"Yikes," Gilley said, looking out at the house.

I sat in the car, parked at the curb, and worked up some courage, then tapped Gil on the shoulder and said, "Come on. We might as well get this over with."

We walked up to the front door, and Gil depressed the doorbell, but no sound came out. "Did it ring?" I asked him.

He shrugged. "I didn't hear anything."

"Yeah, maybe it's best to knock." I rapped on the door three times, and we waited. And waited. And waited.

"Nobody's home," I said.

"Ugh. We drove all this way too."

"We could wait," I suggested.

"We could," Gilley agreed, but I could tell he didn't really want to.

"Just for a little while," I told him.

"Yeah, okay," he said.

We got back to the car, and Gilley reached into the rear seat and pulled out his drone. He'd been fiddling with it and putting it together since we'd started our journey. "I think it's ready for a test flight," he said.

"What? Here?"

"Sure," he said. "Don't worry. I won't fly it far."

Gilley opened the car door and set the drone on the sidewalk; then he closed the door and opened the window. Next, he propped his iPad against the gearshift and used the remote control to launch the drone.

"That's a nice picture quality," I said, eyeing the screen as the drone lifted off into the sky.

"It is," Gil said. "I upgraded to more pixels."

"Good choice." I was fascinated by the bird's-eye view. "How far is the range?"

"On this model it's fifteen hundred meters, or about a block and a half."

"That's not very far," I said.

"Yeah. The price jumps significantly once you get above two thousand meters."

I put my hand on Gilley's arm as his drone looped around a tree and started coming back to the car. "Wait. Go back."

"Go back?"

I pointed to the screen. "Yes! Go back!"

Gilley pivoted the drone around and directed it away from us again. "Why?" he asked, working the joystick.

"Stop!"

"What?!"

"There!" I said, pointing to a car on the street. "Can you move the drone lower?" Gilley did and I gasped. "That's it!"

"What's it?"

"That's the car that I saw Carmen jump into!"

"That beat-up rust bucket?"

"Yes! I remember the gray paint on the back quarter panel, and the dented front fender! Quick, lower the drone to the license plate."

Gilley lowered the drone to the rear of the car, and I lifted up my phone and scrolled through my notes until I found the plate number. It matched. I then looked down the street, but I couldn't make out the drone. "How far away is that?"

"Seven hundred meters," he said.

I started the engine and pulled out into the street. There was no traffic either coming or going, which was good, because Gilley's drone was now hovering about car height, and an oncoming car could've taken it out. "There!" I said, pointing to where the drone hovered in the street.

"Uh, Cat?" Gil said, his voice unsteady.

"Hang on," I said. "I gotta find a parking spot."

"No . . . Cat . . . you should really look—"

"There's a spot!" I said, zooming past the drone to a small space that would just fit the Mini.

"Cat!" Gil said, as I slipped into the space.

"What?"

"*Look!*"

I glanced to where Gilley was pointing, down at the screen of his iPad, and for a moment, I couldn't really tell what I was looking at.

"Is that . . . ?"

"Yes. Yes, I think it is," Gil said, a wobble still in his voice.

"Oh . . . my . . . God," I whispered. "She's dead, right?"

"I don't think there's any question."

With shaking hands, I parked the car and sat there silently with Gilley while we stared at the iPad in stunned silence. Slumped over to the side in the front seat of the vehicle was the figure of a woman, her clothes stained with dried blood, her hair covering her face, and her blue and bloated hands limp at her sides.

"What do we do?" I whispered.

Gilley maneuvered the drone away from the car, sending it up before bringing it straight back to us and in through the window, to settle gently in his lap. Rolling the window up, he turned to me and said, "We get the hell out of here."

"You're kidding, right?"

"No. Not even remotely. We need to go."

"We need to call the police!" I said, reaching again for my phone.

Gilley slapped it out of my hand. "Cat, listen to me! If we call the police, that makes *three* murder scenes that you've been involved in. Given that statistic alone, I think it's only a question of time before you land not only back in jail, but are accused once again of murder and held without bond."

I winced. "I hadn't even thought of that."

"I know. So put this car into gear, and let's get the hell outta here!"

With mounting panic, I pulled hard on the wheel and zoomed out of the space, bolting down the street, past the sedan with the dead woman's body. I didn't even break for the stop sign at the end of the block.

And that was a rather unfortunate maneuver, because no sooner did I blow the stop sign than I saw flashing reds in my rearview. "Oh, no!" I cried.

"*Really?*" Gilley said, craning his neck to look back. Turning to me, he said, "What karmic goddess did you piss off to have this kind of run of bad luck?"

"I don't know!" I wailed. "What do I do?"

"What do you mean what do you do? You pull over!"

"But the dead woman!"

The burst of a siren accompanied the flashing red lights behind us.

"That cop doesn't know about the dead woman!" Gilley yelled. "Pull over, tell him you didn't see the stop sign, and take the ticket!"

I nodded and flipped on my turn signal, but I was shaking so hard it was difficult to ease the car over to the curb. "What do I say if he asks what we're doing around here?"

"He won't," Gilley said, although his voice had gone up an octave, which meant he too was nervous and scared. "He'll ask for your license and registration and write you a ticket. Just chill."

"My registration should be in the glove box," I said.

Gilley opened the box and began to rummage around. "Where?"

"I don't know!" I snapped, leaning over to push his hands out of the way and search myself.

A hard wrap on my car window caused both Gilley and me to shriek. I sat up more calmly, my registration in hand, and rolled down the window.

"Ma'am," the cop said, "do you know why I pulled you over?"

"Um . . . no?" I said meekly. "Was I speeding, Officer?"

"Yes. And you ran a stop sign."

"*I did?*" I asked, maybe a weeeeeeeeee bit too forcefully.

The cop gave me a look that said, *Really?*

I dropped the innocence act. "I'm terribly sorry, Officer. Here are my license and registration."

I handed over the docs, and the cop walked back to his car, got in, and proceeded to run my information. I tried not to stare anxiously into the rearview mirror as Gilley and I waited in silence, but it was really hard. My heart was thundering in my chest, and I felt a trickle of sweat at my temple. "Come on," I muttered. "What's taking so long?"

"Be cool," Gilley said. "Just be cool."

Finally, the cop got out of his car, and I could see the ticket in his hand, flapping in the breeze. I had an almost overwhelming urge to put the car in gear and take off at top speed; the anxiety of the moment was really getting to me. At last, the officer reached my window and handed back my identification, the registration, and the ticket.

"Again, I'm very sorry about that, Officer," I told him after he'd given me instructions about how to pay the fine.

He nodded and started to turn away when a garbled message came over the microphone, attached to his lapel.

I didn't catch all of it, but the dispatcher clearly said "body" and "automobile," and I thought I heard the name of the street we were on.

In that moment, the cop's eyes met mine, and I knew immediately that he saw the guilt in my expression. Standing at my window, he spoke into his microphone. "Unit seven eighty-two responding." And then he stared at me for a little while longer, as if trying to memorize my face.

I tried to cover for myself by pushing a shaky smile to my lips and offering a, "Well, you seem busy. Have a good rest of your day!"

With that, I rolled up the window and eased forward a bit, my hands gripping the wheel so tightly they hurt. "Does he look like he wants me to stop?" I whispered to Gilley.

Gil was looking back at the cop. "No, keep going, Cat. Keep going!"

I put a little more pressure on the accelerator, and we moved slowly away from the officer. "What's he doing?" I asked, keeping my eyes forward.

"He's watching us."

"Dammit!" I swore. I pushed the accelerator a little bit more, and we continued to move slowly away from the officer. "Has he turned away yet?" I said, a bit too loudly, my nerves sending tremors through my whole frame.

"No," Gilley squeaked. "He's still watching us!"

"*Why?*" I cried, not to Gilley but to the universe. "Why did that stupid call have to come in right before he was letting us go?!"

"Oh, no!" Gilley gasped.

"What?"

"He's raising his hand! He's waving to the curb again!"

"Do you think I can pretend not to notice?" I said, the tremors leaking into my voice.

"No! He sees me looking right at him, Cat!"

"Ohmigod, ohmigod, ohmigod!" I exclaimed as I pulled over to the curb again.

Looking in the side mirror, I saw the cop trotting toward us. I took several deep breaths and let them out slowly. When he was at my door, I lowered the window again. "Yes, Officer?" I asked, adopting the innocent routine again.

"Quick question," he said. "I noticed your address is in East Hampton. Want to tell me what you're doing in this neck of the woods?"

"Not really," I said.

"Is that so?"

"We've been scouting the neighborhood," Gil said. "Catherine is thinking of investing in some rental properties, and there's quite a few for sale around here," he said. And then, like a blessing, Gilley offered up the screen of his phone to the officer. "I've tagged all our favorites on Zillow."

I don't know how he managed to do that so quickly, but I was incredibly thankful.

The cop surveyed Gilley's screen for a long moment. Then he said, "Why didn't you want me to know that?"

I opened my mouth, but Gilley was quicker. Picking up his drone he said, "We were using this to scout out the houses we're interested in. It's just under the half-pound limit, so I don't have it registered, but I think we might be too close to the airport to fly it, even though I've kept it at twenty feet or lower."

The cop's eyes flickered from Gilley to me and back again. Finally, he said, "Keep the drone inside the car. If I see it flying around, I'll cite you another ticket."

"Yes, Officer," Gil and I said together.

"You can go now."

With that, he trotted back to his car.

I blew out a huge breath of relief. "Ohmigod, Gil. That was some incredibly quick thinking."

"Thanks," he said, and I could tell he was proud of himself. "M.J. and I used to get ourselves into all kinds of pickles. I learned to think fast on my feet."

I wiped away the beads of sweat on my forehead. "Which is what makes you a terrific sidekick. Come on. Let's get out of here."

Gil and I arrived back home and walked into Chez Kitty spent and hungry. Neither of us had the energy to cook, so we had Sebastian order us a carryout. While we waited for the delivery, Gilley and I sat at the table and talked about the body in the car. We were both also thoroughly convinced that Carmen and Sasha were related.

"Was it Sasha or Carmen dead in that car?" I asked Gilley.

"It could have been either, with the other in the trunk," he said.

I made an *eww* face. "Why would someone be trying so hard to kill Heather's housekeeper?"

"I have no idea," Gilley said. "Why would someone want to kill Heather?"

"Because she was hateful," I said. "And underhanded. And her husband was supposedly tied to the mob."

"Yeah, but didn't he die a few years ago?" Gilley asked.

"He did. And he was shot, like Shepherd's ex-wife. But Heather wasn't shot. She was poisoned."

"With some unknown toxin," Gil said, "that the coroner can't detect."

"It's all so strange," I said. "According to Marcus, the only thing Heather had in her stomach were traces of the three martinis, Cobb salad, and some of my punch, but there was no sign of any toxin in any of that. Although Marcus did note that my punch was the last thing Heather ingested before she died, but the M.E. tested all the ingredients, and there was nothing toxic or poisonous in it."

"What if someone spiked your punch with an untraceable toxin?"

"If that happened, then why was Heather the only one who died? Why didn't at least *someone* else get sick?"

"Maybe no one else drank it after it was spiked," Gilley offered.

I pointed at him. "See, but how likely is that, Gil? I bring the punch to the party, and the killer simply *hopes* that no one but Heather drinks the punch? Plus, she was hammering away on those three martinis throughout the luncheon. Heck, she even had one in hand when she and I were trading words. Anyone who drinks a martini as an appetizer to lunch is a pretty hard-core drinker. No way could the killer have anticipated that Heather would've swapped the martinis for punch later. Although . . ."

"Although what?" Gil asked.

"Although there's the very odd occurrence that Carmen was all over me about the punch from the moment I arrived, but not in the way I suspect you're thinking. She wanted to know if I followed the recipe exactly to the letter, and then she taste-tested it in front of me like she was making sure I *didn't* spike it."

"Okay, now that *is* weird," Gil said.

"Right?" I said. "If Carmen wanted to poison Heather, why would she grill me about the punch being made exactly to spec?"

"That almost sounds like someone who would want to make sure Heather *wasn't* poisoned," Gilley joked.

I eyed him keenly. "Exactly," I said. "Yes, Gilley, that's it *exactly!*"

"That's what exactly?"

I began to pace back and forth, tapping my lip as I thought. "We need to talk to Carmen."

"We might as well call Heath then, Cat, because if that body in the car was Carmen, the only way to reach her would be through a medium."

I eyed Gilley sharply again. "Would he *do* that?"

"Oh, he might, but M.J. would kill him . . . and me, if she

found out. She wants the both of them *out* of the murder-solving business."

"Hmm, we probably don't want to upset M.J. during her pregnancy, do we?"

"We don't really want to upset her at any point, actually. The only person scarier when they're angry may be your sister."

I laughed. "We'll call it a tie. Still, I wish there was *some* way to know if it was Carmen in that car, or if maybe her cousin was the one murdered and Carmen is still on the run."

At that exact moment, there was a knock on the door. And by *knock* I mean that someone took their fist and pounded Chez Kitty's door hard enough to rattle the hinges.

Gilley and I traded looks of alarm. "That can't be good," he said softly.

I tiptoed to the door and squinted through the peephole. Shepherd's angry face glared back at me. "Uh oh," I said softly.

"Who is it?" Gilley asked, just as softly.

"It's Shepherd!" he yelled through the door.

Gilley made a *yikes* face. "Should we pretend we're not here?" he whispered into my ear.

"Don't even try pretending you're not here!" Shepherd yelled.

I gulped.

Gilley's *yikes* face turned into an *EEEEEK!* "Don't let him in!" he mouthed.

"You better let me in!" Shepherd shouted.

I turned to the door. "How are you doing that?!"

"So you *are* home!" Shepherd said.

With a sigh, I smoothed out my features and opened the door. "Detective," I said pleasantly, "to what do I owe this delightful surprise?"

"Cut the crap, Catherine. I know you and your sidekick were in West Hempstead earlier. Care to explain why I've got you connected to *another* murder?"

I pressed my lips together. The man was *beyond* intolerable. "I'm quite sure I don't know *what* you're talking about, Detective."

His expression went from angry to downright dangerous. "You're 'quite certain,' are you?"

"Yes," I said, feeling a spark of anger ignite in my own belly as my defenses went up.

Shepherd rubbed his face with his hand. And then he did something I'm sure was quite difficult for him. He took a deep breath and softened his tone. "I know about the ticket in West Hempstead."

"So I got a ticket?" I said, not giving him an inch. "So what?"

Shepherd simply stared levelly at me.

"Lots of people get tickets."

Without blinking, he continued to stare.

"I'm sure I'm not the only person in this town who's received a ticket in the last week. Or even today!"

"You done yet?" Shepherd asked.

It was my turn to take a deep breath and let out a sigh. "Yes."

"Can I come in?"

I was surprised by the request and looked to Gilley, who seemed just as surprised. He shrugged, so I opened the door wider, and Shepherd stepped in. "Thanks," he said, before pointing to the table and raising his brow in question.

"Of course," I said, a bit thrown by his sudden congenial manner. "Please take a seat. Would you like something to drink?"

"Is there any tea left?" he said, pulling out a chair and sitting down.

"I'll put the kettle back on," Gilley said, trading another look of disbelief with me.

I sat down at the table carefully, like you'd sit down next to an unstable person. "I would've pegged you for a coffee drinker," I said.

"You would've pegged me right. My sister got me hooked on an afternoon cup of tea, though. It's sort of become our ritual ever since Lenny died."

· "That ritual must bring you a bit of comfort," I said.

"It does," Shepherd agreed, "I was a train wreck in the weeks that followed Lenny's murder. I couldn't solve the case, and it drove me to say and do some . . . shall we say, stupid stuff at work. And, because I was being a little reckless on the investigation, my lieutenant ordered me to take a few weeks off. That was my lowest point, I think. Sunny pulled me out of it by showing up at my door with a couple of tea bags every afternoon around four. And it was nice, you know? Sitting together, drinking something hot that didn't taste like tar. Those afternoons helped me get my head together."

Shepherd had a wistful, faraway look in his eye that moved me. It was odd to find myself moved by the story and the expression of this man—whom I'd recently detested.

"Anyway," he continued, "even after I got my head on straight and returned to work, I still make it a point to drop in on her once or twice a week, and we hang out and drink tea."

I poked him in the arm. "Careful, Detective. You might be showing us your human side."

He shrugged as Gilley set down a steaming cup in front of him. "I think my secret's safe with you two," he said, while pouring in some cream and sugar. As he was stirring his tea he added, "Nice drone."

Gilley and I traded another look, this one definitely alarmed. Gilley laughed nervously, picking the drone up from the table and placing it out of sight on a chair next to him. "I ordered it just the other day," he said. "I got the idea from the one you found last week."

"Oh, yeah?" Shepherd said, clinking his spoon against his cup as if he totally bought that explanation. "The West Hempstead cop I talked to said you'd been flying it near the site of another murder."

"How did you find out about that so quickly?" I asked, dropping the pretense.

Shepherd took a sip of tea before answering. "He ran your license, Catherine. Your arrest record came up, and because the charges were dropped, he had to let you go with just the ticket, but he'd wanted to dig a little deeper given your . . . suspicious behavior, so he called me. That's when I discovered that the same car that you described as Carmen's getaway vehicle was found with a body inside."

I shuddered at the memory of the terrible image on Gilley's iPad when the drone hovered next to the window of that car. "We had nothing to do with it," I said, wishing my voice hadn't quavered as I spoke.

"I know," Shepherd said.

"You do?" Gilley and I asked together.

"Yeah," he said. "I also talked with the detective on the scene. He says the woman's been dead for at least twenty-four hours, and since you were with me twenty-four hours ago, I know you didn't have anything to do with it."

I felt a wave a relief until Shepherd turned his gaze on Gilley. "Where were you yesterday between six and ten p.m., Mr. Gillespie?"

Gilley pointed to the ceiling and said, "Sebastian?"

"Yes, sir Gilley?"

"Where was I last night between six and ten p.m.?"

"You were in the kitchen area between six p.m. and six forty-two p.m. You were in the central bathroom between six forty-two and six-fifty. You were in the living room area at six fifty-one until nine oh-five. You were in the central bathroom between nine oh-five—"

"Okay, I get it," Shepherd said. "Geez, the last thing I want to hear about are your bathroom habits."

"You asked," Gil said defensively.

"You know what? You're right. And you and your robot answered. So neither of you had anything to do with Sasha Kuznetsov's murder—"

"Sasha?" I said. "You're sure it was Sasha and not Carmen?"

"Positive. As I'm sure you've already guessed, the two were related—they were sisters. Sasha was identified through her fingerprints."

"So Carmen wasn't found in the trunk?" Gilley asked.

Shepherd looked at him oddly. "Why would you think she'd be in the trunk?"

"I don't know," Gil said. "One too many *Law and Order* marathons, I suppose?"

Shepherd shook his head. "You're a little weird, ain't cha?"

Gilley sniffed and threw an imaginary scarf over his shoulder. "I'm an acquired taste."

"I bet," Shepherd said. "But to answer your question, no. There's no sign of Carmen, so she's either dead or on the run again."

"Do you think she might've killed Sasha?" I asked him.

"It's possible, but I don't think so. This looks like it's another hit from our assassin."

"I'm beginning to hate this woman," Gilley said.

"Trust me, I know," Shepherd said. "But it's all the more reason for me to try and talk some sense into the two of you."

"What's that supposed to mean?" I asked testily.

"It means that this woman is dangerous, Catherine. And you're putting your nose into her business. First with the priest, then with the vintage store, and now in West Hempstead. She's liable to get ticked off pretty soon, and we all know what happens when she gets ticked off."

I gulped. "Do you think that's why I was followed last night? She might've thought I was headed to West Hempstead and wanted to follow me there?"

"Anything's possible," Shepherd said. "As far as I can tell, you're lucky to be alive."

"Doesn't that also extend to you, Detective?" Gilley asked.

Shepherd frowned. "I can take care of myself. It's you two I'm worried about."

"What would you like us to do?" I asked him.

"I'd like for you two to butt out. And I know I've already asked you that, Catherine, but I need you to understand how serious this is."

"But what if we discovered something that might be important to your investigation?" I asked.

Shepherd immediately opened his mouth as if to protest, thought better of it, and said, "Like what?"

"Like the fact that Carmen grilled me about the punch when I arrived at Heather's."

"What do you mean she grilled you about the punch?"

"She wanted to know if I'd followed the recipe to the letter, what kind of juices I'd used, and if I'd used tonic or Sprite."

Shepherd eyed me like he was waiting for a punch line. "Aaaaaaand?"

"And then she taste-tested it to make sure what I said was correct."

Shepherd looked at Gilley. "Do *you* know what she means?"

"Not yet," Gil said. "But I think we're about to find out."

"Why would Carmen go to such lengths to ensure that the punch was made correctly if she was the one that poisoned Heather?" I said. "If she did the deed, then why would she even care?"

"Maybe because there was a hit out on Heather, and Carmen thought to collect the reward," Shepherd said.

"Wait, what?" I asked. "There was a *hit* out on Heather? Like . . . a *mafia* hit?"

"Yes," Shepherd said. "One of my sources just confirmed it. Heather had a price on her head."

"So she took over more of her husband's business than just the *business*," Gilley said.

"Looks that way," Shepherd replied. "I've got a forensic accountant going over her books, but we think we've spotted a pattern of money laundering going back a year or two. She was definitely padding the costs of her business's construction. But lately her numbers were off."

"Off?" I asked.

"Yeah. She'd been doing about six houses a year pretty steadily for the past four years, and funneling extra money through the builds. Her costs for everything from lumber to light fixtures were usually two hundred percent above average."

"So who was she funneling money for?" I asked nervously. Thinking that the mafia was present in my own backyard rattled me.

Shepherd blew out a sigh and swiped a hand through his hair. "Around here? There're a few organized crime cells to pick from. Most are Russian-based. My source says there were rumors that Heather was working for one organization and wasn't happy with her cut—her percentage of the profits. There are at least a few additional rumors that say she might've been courting a rival family."

"Why would she do something so stupid?" Gilley asked. "Everyone knows that once you're married to the mob, there's no such thing as divorce. It's till death do you part."

"True, but nothing says that if your profits dry up, you can't be asked to leave."

My eyes widened. "Is that what happened? Heather's business dried up?"

"We think so," Shepherd said. "She was having a hard time coming across available land where she could have the lots reparceled and build multiple homes."

"That's what she tried to do with this lot," I said to him.

"Yeah, I know. My sister told me, which is what led me to start digging through Heather's books. This lot looks like it was her last chance to remain profitable for whomever she was laundering money for."

"Would they kill her just for that?" Gilley wondered.

"They've killed for less. But my guess is that she didn't put much effort into it once Catherine bought this plot. I think she was trying to use the fact that she was no longer profitable to her advantage while making it appear that she was furious over losing out on the lot. That way, her bosses would dump her rather than keep her on, and she'd be free to court another family if she wanted. But she would've needed to be careful. She would've needed to appear to be really upset that she lost out on this property."

I inhaled sharply. "*That's* why she made my humiliation so public!"

"Yep," Shepherd agreed. "I think so."

"So this assassin," Gilley said, focusing us back on the killer, "do you think she works for the Russian mafia?"

"I think she works for whomever wants to pay her," he said.

I had a chilling thought and said, "I almost hate to ask this again, Detective, but are you sure your ex-wife didn't have anything to do with the Russian mafia?"

Shepherd inhaled deeply and said, "Not to my knowledge. Lenny wasn't the type to get mixed up in anything criminal."

"Still," Gilley said, "having an ex-husband who's a cop is pretty good cover if you're trying to fly under the radar."

Shepherd frowned. "Agreed."

"What I don't understand is how Carmen fits into all this," I said.

"Me either," Shepherd admitted. "Her last name is obviously Russian, but she's originally from a place called Tura, which is a remote northern settlement, population less than ten thousand. She and her sister left there in the late eighties, settling in New York. They've worked domestically as housekeepers and nannies ever since. And there's nothing in either of their backgrounds that rings any kind of alarm bells."

"Well, there is one thing," I said.

"What's that?" Gilley asked.

"Carmen worked for a lady who worked for the mob. Maybe she overheard something or saw something incriminating, and that's why she's on the run."

"Or," Gilley said, "maybe through her own Russian domestic connections she heard there was a price on her boss lady's head, and she wanted to collect the dough for it."

"Both of those scenarios are possible. And—to Gilley's theory—it could be why the assassin is after Carmen. If she thinks her paycheck was taken out from underneath her, she'd be hell-bent on getting even," Shepherd said.

I knew that all worked in theory, but a lot still bothered me about all of this. Mostly, I just didn't believe that Carmen was a killer. I'd seen the fear in her eyes as she fled the church, where she'd obviously been hiding out.

"A woman who kills her boss in lieu of getting a big fat paycheck doesn't seek sanctuary in a church. She heads to Aruba," I said. Gilley and Shepherd both frowned. They knew I had a point. "I wish we could form a theory that covers all these bases," I mused.

Shepherd shook his head at me. "See now, that's exactly why I'm here, Catherine. I don't want you to form any more theories. I want you to stay out of this investigation until we find either the assassin or Carmen."

"Deal," Gilley said, and that surprised me. I turned to look at him, and he said to me, "Cat, it's enough. We're playing with fire here. I'm too gorgeous to get burned."

I sighed and offered Gilley a grateful smile. "Yes, all right," I said. "We'll stop."

Shepherd let out his own sigh of relief. "Good." Getting up, he walked his mug over to the sink. He then headed to the door and paused before leaving. "As a thank-you for being so coopera-tive, I promise to update you two when we catch either of these women."

"Thank you, Detective," I said.

With a nod, he opened the door and left.

Chapter 14

Gilley and I sat on the couch later that night mostly in silence. Even the volume on the TV was quieter than usual.

I think we were both feeling a little down in the dumps over being asked to butt out of the investigation. "It really was getting too dangerous," I said, breaking the silence.

"It was," Gilley agreed.

"Still . . . ," I mused.

"Yes?"

I sat up and looked at Gilley directly. "I feel like we're missing something obvious."

Gilley wrinkled his nose. "Yeah. I know. That thought has been bugging me too. But what can we do, Cat?"

I got up and began to pace the room, trying to think of a way to stick my nose back into something dangerous without attracting any attention. I then paused and headed over to the window, looking out across my parcel to Heather's.

Her whole house was dark, which was to be expected, but something about my exchange with Carmen over the punch still really bothered me.

And then I thought I had it. "You know what was so weird when I went to Heather's with the punch?"

"What?" Gilley said.

"The fact that Heather assigned me to make the punch, but her housekeeper insisted on tasting it before letting me past the kitchen. Like I said before, it was almost like she *knew* someone might want to poison Heather."

Gilley cocked his head. "I'm listening," he said.

I turned back to him. "So what if she *did* know that Heather had a price on her head?" I said. "What if Carmen was trying to protect Heather, but failed."

"Makes sense," Gilley said.

I tapped my lip. "In a way it does, but in a way it doesn't."

"What do you mean?"

"Well, if Carmen knew that Heather had a price on her head, the obvious route to taking Heather out is probably a gunshot to the head, right?"

Gilley made a face. "I suppose."

"So how did Carmen know that Heather was going to be poisoned?"

"You know the Russians and their love of killing people with exotic toxins," Gil mused.

"Yes. But then why would Carmen risk her life to taste-test the punch? If she knew that someone might try to kill Heather through some sort of toxic poison, why would she risk her own life by ingesting the punch?"

"Maybe Carmen had already taken the antidote?"

"But to what?" I asked. "Aren't there like a bajillion poisons out there that could kill you?"

"At least that many."

"So Carmen would've known that something in the food or the punch could kill Heather, but not her. How is that possible?"

"Well, if Heather were allergic to something, like shellfish, that could be one way to take her out."

I nodded, but then shook my head. "But wouldn't the M.E. have seen signs of that? I mean, wouldn't her lips and throat be all swollen?"

"One would think so," he admitted. "But not all allergic reactions result in anaphylaxis."

I moved over to the refrigerator and peeked inside it. There was some of the leftover fruit juice and the Sprite we'd used for the punch. I got them out and set them on the counter. "Gil?"

"Yeah?" he asked, eyeing me curiously.

"Do you remember the exact ingredients for the punch?"

"Roughly. It called for iced tea, orange juice, Sprite, sliced oranges, sugar, lemon juice, cinnamon sticks, and some cloves."

"Do me a favor," I said, getting all of those ingredients out from the fridge and the cupboards. "Look up allergic reactions to all of the individual ingredients and see what you get."

Gilley began to type into his tablet as I rummaged through the cupboards for the cinnamon and cloves. "Huh," he said.

"What?" I said with a small groan as I stretched to reach the upper shelf.

"This recipe that Heather sent you? I think she took it from a Pinterest board called Let's Do Punch."

"Doesn't surprise me," I said, setting the cinnamon on the counter. "Pinterest would be where I'd go for punch recipes."

"Yeah, the only difference is that Heather used Sprite instead of tonic," Gilley said.

I froze, midway to reaching for the cloves. Turning slowly, I said, "Wait, what did you say?"

Gilley blinked at me. "She substituted Sprite for tonic water. I'd probably make the same swap."

"Quinine," I said breathlessly.

"What?" he asked. He hadn't heard me.

"Quinine!" I yelled excitedly. "It's the active ingredient in tonic water!"

Gilley's jaw dropped. "Ohmigod!" He knew exactly what I meant. "My great-aunt Mable was allergic to quinine! She said she'd had one drink in her whole life. A gin and tonic, and it sent her to the hospital!"

"Quick!" I told him, forgetting all about the cloves. "Google reactions to quinine!"

Gilley plugged that into the search box, and I waited impatiently while his eyes darted back and forth across the screen. "Eureka," he whispered. "Cat, you're a freaking genius. Listen to this, 'In acute cases, patients with severe allergic reactions to quinine can suffer from flu-like symptoms such as chills, fever, headache, nausea, and muscle aches all the way to a sudden onset of acute abdominal pain, loss of consciousness, renal failure, internal bleeding, and system-wide organ failure. And these can all happen within a matter of minutes.' "

I rushed over to my phone and lifted it, ready to call Shepherd and tell him my theory, but Gilley stopped me. "What're you doing?"

"Calling Shepherd."

"Why?"

"To tell him about the quinine."

"But we're supposed to be butting out," he said. "Won't he get mad? Especially if we're wrong."

"We're not wrong," I said, setting down the phone. "At least I don't think we're wrong."

"If Heather were allergic to tonic, wouldn't her friends know?"

"What friends?" I deadpanned.

"Ha," Gil said flatly. "You know who I mean."

I tapped my lip and thought for a moment. "Sunny would know."

"Should we call her? She's Shepherd's sister. She'd probably tattle on us."

"I'll ask her not to," I said, reaching for my keys. "She seems the type to keep some things secret from her brother."

"Wait, you're driving over there?"

"No. *We're* driving over there."

"Why can't we just call?"

"Do you have her number?" I asked.

"No, but I'm sure I could get it."

I sighed. "Come on, Gilley. Let's just drive over there and talk to her like real people."

With a little more persuading, I managed to get Gilley into the car, and we drove over to Sunny's. After knocking on her door, I realized that it was close to nine o'clock. Not super late, but late enough where she might be annoyed at the interruption.

I needn't have worried. Sunny came to the door and smiled when she saw me through the glass insert. "Hello, Catherine!" she said brightly. "What brings you by?"

"Good evening, Sunny. So sorry to disturb you," I began.

"Oh, pish," she said with a wave of her hand. "This baby is giving me such bad heartburn I need to keep busy to keep my mind off it. You showed up at the perfect time." Turning to Gilley, she stuck out her hand for a handshake and added, "Hello. I'm Sunny."

"And I'm charmed," Gilley said, taking her hand and tipping it slightly to kiss the back of it. "But most people call me Gilley. Gilley Gillespie."

Sunny giggled. "Well, Gilley, aren't you adorable?"

"Yes," he said quickly. "From head to toe, or so I've been told. Repeatedly."

I rolled my eyes. "Gilley is staying in my guest house," I said as Sunny laughed. "He's my dearest friend, and he and I were chatting a bit about Heather."

"Ah, the mystery that everyone keeps speculating about," she said. "My brother's had his hands full since this all happened."

"Yes," I said. "I know."

Her brow furrowed. "Is he still bugging you, Catherine? You just say the word and I'll tell him to back the heck off. He and I may be twins, but I'm still the oldest."

I pressed my lips with a finger to hide a smile. Sunny was such a thin, willowy woman. The only large thing about her was the

baby bump under her long sweater. It was hard to imagine her
brother ever being even remotely intimidated by her. "He's not
bothering me," I assured her. "In fact, it might be the other way
around."

"Well, that's good," she said. "About time somebody gave Steve
a good run for his money. But I'm off track. You wanted to ask me
about Heather?"

"Yes," I said. "Do you know if she had any food allergies?"

"Food allergies?" Sunny said.

"Yes," Gilley said. "Did she ever become violently ill due to
something she ate or drank?"

Sunny scratched the side of her head. "No. Not that I know of.
But she did have a bad reaction to some medicine once. But that
was when we were little kids . . . ages ago."

"She had a bad reaction to medicine?" I asked eagerly. "Do
you know what the medicine was?"

Sunny shook her head. "We were at a sleepover. I think we
were, like, twelve, and Heather was having terrible leg cramps.
They were keeping her up and uncomfortable. The girl who was
hosting the sleepover gave Heather a pill from her mom's stash in
the medicine cabinet, telling her that her mom took it for leg
cramps. Heather popped the pill, and literally within just a few
minutes, she's throwing up and doubled over in pain. She had to
be rushed to the hospital. It was super scary at the time, and our
poor friend got into a heap of trouble over it. I'm sorry I don't remember any more than that."

I looked at Gilley, disappointed. I'd been hoping Sunny
would've remembered an incident involving tonic water, but
Gilley began to dance on the balls of his feet with excitement.
"Actually, Sunny, that's *very* helpful. Thank you."

"That's it? That's all you needed to know?"

"It is," Gilley said. "But do us a favor and don't tell your
brother just yet that we were asking about Heather, okay?"

Sunny grinned. "Sure," she said. "Your secret is safe with me."

Gilley offered her his most beaming smile. "Have yourself a lovely night, sugar."

Taking me by the hand, Gilley turned and walked us back toward the car. "Want to explain?" I asked him as we got in.

He waited until we were in the car to say, "Quinine pills are used to treat leg cramps!"

"Oh my God!" I exclaimed high fiving him. "We figured it out!"

"We did!"

"Okay, let's go back and tell Shepherd," Gilley said.

I put the car into drive, and we wound our way out of the cul-de-sac where Sunny lived and over three streets to the one leading to Chez Cat. Before I pulled into the driveway, however, I stopped the car and turned to Gil. "What if they accuse us of the crime?" I asked him.

"What now?" Gil said.

"Gilley, *we* prepared the punch. If someone did put some tonic water into it, and that killed Heather, it's our butts that'll be on the hook for it."

"Oh, no," Gilley said. "Cat, you're right! So what do we do?"

In answer, I turned to look at Heather's house, which was dark and suddenly foreboding. "I think we need to find the smoking gun."

"Come again?"

"If we can find a discarded bottle of tonic water, it might have the killer's fingerprints on it."

"You think the assassin left a bottle of tonic with their fingerprints behind?"

"No, I don't. And I don't think the assassin killed Heather."

"Well, if I were Carmen and I knew that Heather had that severe of an allergy to quinine, I sure as heck wouldn't leave behind a bottle of tonic. It'd be the first thing I took as I headed out the door."

"I don't think Carmen killed Heather either," I said. "I think we're looking for someone we haven't currently suspected."

"Like who?"

"Like anyone who hated Heather."

"That's the whole town," Gilley said. "Anyone who rules with an iron fist the way Heather did isn't exactly beloved."

"Which is why we need to see if there's a used bottle of tonic water at the estate."

"Wouldn't that have been tossed in the trash by now?"

"Yes, which is my whole point. Shepherd's had that place locked up since the day Heather died. Trash is being collected tomorrow, so it's probably still inside the house, in a garbage bag."

"But why would the killer leave it behind? Wouldn't they want to take it with them?"

"Maybe," I said, putting the car into drive again and pulling away from the curb. "But maybe not. I mean, if the killer was at the party and mingling with the other guests, wouldn't it have looked suspicious if they were to walk out with an empty bottle of tonic in their hands? *Especially* given Heather's allergy?"

"They could've easily concealed a small bottle of it in their purse, Cat."

I sighed. "True. Still, Gilley, I think we should have a look around. Peeking in the windows shouldn't get us into trouble, right? I mean, it's not like we can actually get inside."

Gilley looked at me with a small measure of guilt on his face. "Actually, we can."

My brow furrowed. "What does *that* mean?"

"While I was reviewing footage off Heather's security camera, I discovered that she had a hidden camera set up in the kitchen—probably to spy on poor Carmen. Anyway, it points to the back of the kitchen with a clear shot of the back door. No one enters or exits the back door suspiciously, except for one tiny occurrence about three days before Heather was murdered. On that day, Carmen forgot her key. You can see her through the kitchen door's window, searching her purse, coming up empty, then trying the door, which of course was locked. She then appeared to spend some time bent over and looking around on the ground, searching for something. Finally, she came up with the key and unlocked the door before putting it back somewhere on the ground again. My guess is that there's one of those fake rocks near the back door."

I beamed at him, then put the car into gear and hit the gas. "You're good," I told him.

"Duh."

I punched the brakes again, rocking us forward. "Is there an alarm, though?"

Gil put a hand to his chest where the seat belt had pinched him. "Girl, please. The keypad is right by the door. I watched Carmen punch in the code, which Heather programmed—with no imagination as it's just nine-three-four-nine-three-four."

"Our area code twice over," I said.

"Yeppers."

"Okay," I told him. "Let's do this!"

At Gilley's suggestion, I drove past Heather's place and parked the car off the shoulder and right next to the woods. As that area was curbed and traffic this time of night was spotty, I hoped no one reported it as suspicious. "Maybe we should've walked," I said, reconsidering leaving the car in plain view.

Gilley opened his car door. "We're here now. We might as well have a quick look around and get this over with as soon as possible."

Gil and I kept close to the woods as we trotted toward the mansion. The place was dark and definitely creepy at this time of night. "This feels like old times," Gil said softly.

"You mean when you were M.J.'s partner?"

"Yes," Gil said, adding a shudder.

"I'm sure it's not haunted," I told him, without actually feeling very sure. I mean, the place *was* fairly old, and it was also super-foreboding in the dark.

We were silent the rest of the way and at last made it to the kitchen door. Gilley and I used our phones' flashlight feature to hunt for the fake rock hiding the key.

Gilley found it in under ten seconds. "Ah ha!" he said triumphantly.

"Let's hope the key is still inside," I said, taking his phone so that he could use both hands to open the rock.

"Ah *ha!*" Gilley said again, lifting up the key.

I smiled in spite of my racing heart and nervousness. "Okay, let's get inside and look around."

Gilley inserted the key, and we easily entered the kitchen.

The smell hit us immediately.

"Oh, gah!" I said, coughing and nearly gagging above the sound of the beeping alarm panel. "What *is* that smell?"

"Week-old garbage," Gil said, coughing as well. "Plug your nose while I put in the code on the alarm panel."

Gil punched in the alarm, and with a satisfying beep, the keypad stopped dinging. "Should we turn on a light?" he asked me.

"No!" I said, my voice sounding odd because I'd pinched my nostrils closed. "We can use our phones for light. Keep low and away from the windows, though, so we aren't seen from the road."

Gilley looked about the kitchen. "Cat, the only windows in here face the ocean. I think it's okay to turn on a light."

"Good point," I said, flipping on a switch.

The kitchen came into view, and it looked spotlessly clean, but several of the cabinet doors were either fully or partially open. Parked next to the kitchen door were four garbage bags, the obvious source of the smell. They appeared to have been rummaged through as there were pieces of trash all about the bags on the floor, but the bags themselves were still fairly full.

I felt the hairs on the back of my neck stand up on end when I saw them like that. "Do you think the police left the bags like that?" I asked Gilley, who was staring at them with a bit of alarm.

"God, I hope so," he replied.

"Should we look through them?"

"I almost think we have to, but I really, really don't want to."

I moved over to the kitchen sink, covered my hand with my sweater, and pulled open the bottom cabinet. Rummaging around, I found two pairs of latex gloves and brought them back to Gilley. "One pair for each of us," I said.

"Smart," he said, taking the offering and donning the gloves. "Let's get this over with."

Gilley and I each chose a bag and sorted through the waste. It was an awful job. The garbage smelled rancid from all the wasted fare from the luncheon. "This is so gross," Gilley muttered.

I couldn't have agreed more.

Still, we kept to the task until we'd gone through all four bags. "No smoking gun," I said, coming up for air and pulling off the gloves.

Gilley stood up from his crouched position next to the last bag. Wiping his brow with his forearm, he said, "I'm gonna need a shower after this."

"Should we continue to look?" I asked.

Gilley pulled off his gloves too. "For a bottle of tonic? I think we have to, just so we can put this ridiculousness to bed."

I made a face at him. "It's not ridiculousness if we find something."

Gilley rolled his eyes and moved away from the garbage. Walking over to the pantry, he glanced back at me as he pulled on the door and said, "What're we gonna find, Cat? A big empty bottle of tonic water that says 'poison'?"

I gasped as I had a peek inside the pantry. Gilley was still looking at me, and I could see his brow furrow. "No," I told him softly. "But we might find Carmen."

Gilley's head swiveled ever so slowly toward the pantry, and he jumped back when he spotted the elusive housekeeper standing there, her back against the wall of shelves and a terrified look on her face. "Don't kill me!" she squeaked.

Gil and I didn't say anything at first. I think we were both too stunned. Finally, I found my voice. "What're you doing here, Carmen?"

She didn't reply. She simply stared at me with an almost feral look in her eye.

Gil shuffled slowly back to me, and out of the side of his mouth, he asked, "What should we do?"

"Well . . . ," I began. But for a moment I was at a loss. "Maybe we should call the police?"

It was Carmen's turn to gasp, and then something kind of extraordinary happened. Her eyes misted with moisture; then actual tears began to fall.

"I don't think she wants us to do that," Gilley whispered.

I bit my lip. "Carmen," I said gently, "They're looking for you."

"I *know* they're looking for me!" she yelled. "They want to blame me for Miss Heather's murder!"

"She has a point," Gilley said.

Ignoring Gilley, I took a step toward Carmen. "Maybe," I agreed. It wouldn't do any good to pretend that she wouldn't be a suspect in the case. "But mostly they can protect you. We know about the woman who's trying to kill you."

Carmen gasped again and threw her arm across her eyes dramatically. "She wants to murder me too!"

"Yes," I said.

"She killed my sister!"

"Yes," I repeated.

Carmen sank to the floor and wept, emitting huge, wet sobs.

Gilley and I looked at each other. Neither of us quite knew what to do. Wringing my hands, I stepped all the way to her and crouched down. "Carmen," I whispered, "what can I do for you?"

Carmen rocked back and forth, hugging herself with her arms. It was hard to witness. Gilley brought over a box of tissues and squatted down with us. He placed the tissues next to her so that she could see them while she rocked.

After a few more moments, she did seem to spot them and used several to cover her eyes.

With great care, I placed a hand on her back. "Carmen," I tried again, "I'm so sorry for your loss."

Carmen's body shuddered under my hand. But finally her sobs lessened a bit, and she kind of leaned against me while she mopped at her face and took big, gulping breaths.

"Sasha was my savior," she said thickly. "Always the brave one of us. She convinced me to leave Russia and come here, where we could have some opportunity. And we did! We always had jobs, and we were saving our money. We were going to buy a place in Florida and live together when we got too old to work. She and I were going to take care of each other."

I rubbed Carmen's back. "That would've been a lovely plan."

Carmen nodded, and then she sighed so sadly that it broke my heart. "I will miss her."

"What can we do?" I asked her again.

"Don't call the police," she said. "Please. That woman . . . she will find me. She will kill me too."

"She can't get to you if she's in police custody," I said.

"The police want to blame me for Miss Heather's murder!" she yelled at me. "*I didn't kill her!*"

I held up my hands in surrender. "Okay, okay," I said. "I know you didn't kill Heather, and I won't call them. But, Carmen, it's not safe for you out there."

"Why do you think I'm in here?" she said flatly. "It's a good hiding place. No one would think to look for me here now that Miss Heather is dead."

"That's true," Gilley said. "But what're you going to do, Carmen? Live here in the dark? And what happens when the food runs out and the water and electricity get turned off? I mean, winter is coming, you know."

Carmen played with her tissue. "I'll get by."

"Oh, Carmen," I said, "you'll do no such thing." Holding out my hand to her I said, "I want you to trust me."

She looked from my hand to my face, and I could tell she was trying to make up her mind. "Miss Heather really hated you."

"I know," I said. "She was mistaken about how I acquired the property next door. But that's neither here nor there. What's important is that we get you to safety. We'll start with my home, and then tomorrow, after you've had some rest and something warm to eat, I'll settle you someplace very safe. Someplace the assassin will never think to look. But, first, you have to trust me."

Carmen hesitated a few seconds longer, but finally she took my hand. "Don't double-cross me," she said.

"I wouldn't dream of it."

Back at Chez Kitty, I handed Carmen a set of towels, a robe, and a pair of slippers. "The slippers are brand-new, never worn," I told Carmen. "You can keep them if you'd like. The bathroom has extra towels, and there are clean sheets on the bed. I'll bring you some dinner in a bit, after you've had a chance to freshen up."

Carmen hugged the items to her chest. "Why are you being so kind to me?"

"Because I'm a nice person," I said. "And because you need help, and your sister just died. And also because I don't believe you had anything to do with Heather's death."

"I didn't."

"Me either," I told her. "But I want to find out who did. And maybe you can help with that."

"How?"

"Shower first, eat second, we'll talk third," I said.

With that, I left Carmen alone and found Gilley in the kitchen throwing together some dinner for Carmen. "I hope she likes linguini carbonara," he said, stirring a pan of bacon.

"I'm sure she'll love it," I said wearily. Eyeing the clock, I added a sigh. It was nearly ten-thirty, and I was bushed.

Gilley cooked in silence for a bit, but then, after chopping the parsley, he turned to me and said, "We could get into big trouble for not calling Shepherd about her."

"I know."

"She might be safer with him, you know."

"No," I said, "I don't agree. This assassin is a master of disguise. Who's to say she doesn't don a police uniform, waltz into the jail, and shoot Carmen?"

"That'd be insanely bold," Gil said.

"It would. Which is why I'm worried about it. She shot a priest, Gilley. A *priest!* In broad daylight even. Then she waltzed right out of the church like she was heading out for a stroll. She has the confidence of a practiced killer, and that's something you can't be protected from for long."

"So we're keeping Carmen *here?*" he asked me.

"No," I said. "Absolutely not. That's far too close for comfort."

"Then where?"

"I was thinking we could hide her in Islip."

"Islip?"

"Yes."

"Where in Islip?"

I looked meaningfully at Gil.

He sucked in a breath and pointed a finger at me. "You can't mean . . . !"

"She needs something to do, Gilley. And this will give Erma something to do."

"Cat!"

"What?"

"She's a *train wreck!*"

"Agreed. But she isn't someone on the assassin's radar. She's got nothing to do with any of this. And her roommate already moved out, Gilley. This will give her a little company."

"Are you going to tell her she's harboring a fugitive?"

"Carmen isn't a fugitive," I said. "She's a witness. And yes, I'm going to tell Erma that Carmen is in trouble because she witnessed something really awful and she needs a safe place to hide for a bit."

Gilley put a hand on one hip. "And are you going to tell her that, by harboring this *witness*, Erma's life could also be in danger?"

"I was actually thinking of leaving that part out," I said. "I mean, what good can come of it other than totally stressing out Erma?"

"She has a right to know, Cat. Especially after what happened to Sasha."

I winced. He had me there. "Fine. I'll tell her. But first let's get Carmen's story and worry about what we say to Erma later."

"How're you going to sneak Carmen into Islip?" Gilley asked next. "I mean, after you were followed the other day, I should think you'd be super nervous about leading the assassin to Erma's place."

"I was hoping you could sneak Carmen into Islip."

"Of course you were," Gil said with a scowl. "So then I can become a target."

"No," I said. Then I sighed. "The assassin is interested in me, not you. If that truly was who was following me, then it's clear that she's interested in me."

"I think she'd give chase to anybody who leaves this driveway and heads to the highway."

I nodded absently. "You know, you're probably right. Maybe there's a way to work all of this out in the morning that will keep everyone safe." Pulling out my phone, I sent a quick e-mail to Erma, asking if she could drive out to my office in the morning. She answered back immediately that she'd do just that.

Carmen appeared from her shower, with a towel wrapped

around her head and wearing my robe and slippers. She cinched the belt tighter when she saw us. "That was a very nice shower. Thank you, ma'am."

I smiled and patted one of the chairs. "Come and sit at the table, Carmen. Gilley has prepared you a delicious dinner."

Carmen came and sat at the table, and Gilley served her a heaping plateful of pasta while I poured her a glass of wine.

When she saw that we weren't eating and hesitated to pick up her fork, I said, "We ate earlier. Please, enjoy your dinner."

Carmen dug in while Gilley and I cleaned up the dishes, then we each sat down again with some tea and waited for Carmen to polish off the last of the pasta.

Pushing her plate away, she smiled shyly at us. "That was very good. Almost as good as I make."

Gilley snorted, and I could tell he was about to say something snarky, so I quickly said, "So, Carmen, now that you've had a chance to eat and freshen up, is it all right if we ask you some questions?"

"You want to know what happened to Miss Heather. How she died, right?"

I blinked. "Yes. That's correct."

"That woman killed her," Carmen said, her lower lip trembling. "I saw her do it."

"You saw her put the quinine in Heather's drink?" I asked.

Carmen furrowed her brow. "Quinine? What're you talking about?"

Realizing she didn't understand that quinine was the chemical in tonic water that Heather had reacted to, I tried again. "You saw the assassin pour tonic water in Heather's drink, or in the punch, correct?"

Carmen shook her head vigorously. "No. Miss Heather was allergic to tonic water. She said she'd break out in a terrible rash if she had it, and she wouldn't allow the stuff in the house, which was why I wanted to make sure your punch didn't have it, and that's why I taste-tested it. I'm sorry about all that, by the way."

I glanced at Gilley. He seemed as confused as I was. "Don't worry about it," I told Carmen. "It's water under the bridge. Why don't you tell us what you saw, and I'll just stay quiet?"

Carmen nodded. "I had been late getting to church because the cleanup from the party took so long, so I stayed a little later to make sure I said all my prayers. When I got back to Miss Heather's, I cleaned up the rest of the kitchen and was gathering all the garbage in the house—you know, to take to the curb for collection the next morning—and when I approached the doorway, I heard a terrible crash, and someone was cursing and carrying on . . ."

Gilley and I exchanged another look. I had a baaaaad feeling about where this was headed.

"I ran forward, thinking Miss Heather was in trouble, and when I got to the doorway of her library I saw this . . . this . . ."

"Go-go-boot-wearing woman?" Gilley supplied.

"Yes!" Carmen exclaimed, pointing at Gilley. "Her! She was standing over poor Miss Heather! She'd killed her with the punch bowl!"

My shoulders slumped. "No, Carmen," I said wearily. "She didn't."

"Yes!" Carmen insisted. "I saw her, Miss Catherine. I *saw* her!"

Gilley shook his head at me before saying to Carmen, "Continue on with your story, Carmen. What happened next?"

"Well, we both stood there for a minute. I think she was surprised to see me, and I was surprised to see her standing over poor Miss Heather, and then she just looked at me with these dead eyes, reached into her purse, and started to pull out a gun!"

"Oh, my," I said. "Did she shoot at you!"

Carmen's head pumped up and down. "I . . . I think so. It all happened so fast, and I didn't hear anything louder than this dull pop as I turned and started to run. But then something whizzed past me and hit the bookcase."

Gilley leaned over to me and whispered, "It sounds like the assassin was using a suppressor."

"A silencer?" I asked.

He nodded, a grave look on his face.

"Then what happened?" I asked.

"Then I heard more cursing," Carmen said. "I swear she said something like, 'I hate it when they run.'"

A shudder went through me, and Gilley mouthed, *they*.

"But you managed to escape," he said.

"Yes. I know that house like the back of my hand. There's a secret door leading from the parlor right to the kitchen, and the parlor is just down the hallway from the library, so I headed there first, ducked through the door, came out into the kitchen, and ran for my life."

"Where did you go?" I asked.

"I hid in the woods for most of that night," she said. "And then I made my way to the church for the ten a.m. Mass and hid in the basement for a few days—no one goes down there except on Sundays. At night, I snuck food out of the pantry and finally got up the courage to call my sister. I told her everything that'd happened, and we made a plan to run away to Florida together."

"Why didn't you just go to the police?" I asked. I couldn't figure out why Carmen hadn't immediately sought help.

"Because she would've found me and killed me," Carmen said simply. "The Angel of Death always collects."

"What does that even mean?" Gilley asked.

Carmen shook her head and put her fist to her lips. She seemed overwhelmed with fear. "My sister worked for someone," she said softly. "Someone you don't talk about outside of their home, you know what I'm saying?"

"She worked for a criminal," I said, putting some of it together.

"Yes. An important man in his . . . business."

"He's a member of the mafia," Gilley said.

Carmen made the sign of the cross. "We don't *speak* of what he does outside his house!" she snapped.

· "Apologies," Gilley said. "Sincerely," he added when Carmen glared at him.

"Carmen, please continue," I said. "We'll respect your warning."

Carmen took a deep breath, and she seemed to settle down. "My sister, she heard things. Things that I should have paid attention to. She said that she heard that Miss Heather was making people angry with the way she conducted her business, and I told Sasha that that's just how Miss Heather was. She wasn't afraid to push people around. She used to tell me she had to be seen as tough in the construction business because nobody would take her seriously if she wasn't.

"Anyway, after Miss Heather was murdered and I made it to the church, I called my sister, and told her what happened. She told me to stay at the church until she could make sure it was safe for me. I waited two days for her to call me back, and when she did, I almost fainted with shock at the story she told me.

"She said that Miss Heather had definitely angered some very powerful members of her boss's organization, and that they had sent the Angel of Death after her."

"Angel of Death," I repeated. "That must be our assassin."

Carmen nodded. "Sasha said that the Angel had arrived at Miss Heather's only to find her already dead, and they believed the housekeeper had killed her!"

Gilley pointed at Carmen. "The housekeeper, meaning you?"

"Yes!" Carmen said, obviously upset by the accusation. "Me!"

"It's a wonder Sasha's boss didn't think you did it, Cat," Gilley said.

"The Angel of Death must've admitted to them that she was the one who broke the punch bowl over Heather's head, so she knew I hadn't done it," I said. "Only she knew that Heather was already dead."

Carmen stared at us in confusion. "What do you mean?"

"Heather *was* dead when the Angel found her, Carmen," I told her. "The medical examiner concluded that she'd died from some toxic substance being introduced into her system."

Again, Carmen stared at me in confusion. "I don't understand this. Miss Heather was fine when I left for church, and I was only gone an hour and a half."

"That's all that it took," I said gently. "We believe someone laced the punch with tonic water."

Carmen shook her head, "I already told you: Miss Heather wouldn't allow that in the house, and I tasted your punch to make sure there was no tonic water in it."

"Yes," I said. "At the time that you tasted it, we believe there was no tonic in it, but someone at that party must've known about Heather's allergy and laced the punch with some tonic water."

"But why would Miss Heather die from tonic water?" she said. "She could've started itching and called nine-one-one, no?"

Gilley answered her. "We believe that Heather's allergy to quinine—the chemical in tonic water that she was reactive to—was so severe that it would've caused an immediate catastrophic response to her entire system. She probably felt ill almost immediately, and it likely came on her so overwhelmingly that she wasn't able to get to her phone and call for help. She would've collapsed, gone unconscious, and her organs would've started to shut down one by one. Her death would've taken a little while, but she would've been completely incapacitated from almost the moment it passed her lips."

"How do you know all of that?" I asked Gil.

"I did some research while the bacon was cooking," he said. "And from that research I discovered that even the smallest of doses would've been enough to trigger a systematic shutdown of her system."

Carmen's jaw dropped. "All of that from . . . from . . . *tonic water?*"

"Yes," I said. "Carmen, do you remember anyone at the party

bringing a bottle of that in? Or did you perhaps discover a discarded bottle of it in the trash?"

"No," she said. "No, nothing like that at all."

"So the killer took it with them," I said to Gilley.

"Seems like it."

Carmen threw up her hands. "All I know is it wasn't me, and I don't want any of that dirty money for it either."

I blinked. "Dirty money?"

"Yes—oh, I forgot to finish my story," she said. "My sister told me that there was a paycheck waiting for me. They wanted to give it to me for killing Miss Heather."

Gilley pointed to her. "*That's* why the Angel of Death wants to kill you," he said. "She thinks you stole her paycheck."

Carmen nodded. "Yes, but I had nothing to do with it! And still she hunts me like a dog! She killed Father Stephan because he wouldn't tell her where I was, but he didn't even know! I was hiding in the basement, and I heard her arguing with him. I crept upstairs, afraid of how it would end, and that's when I saw her shoot him!"

"He didn't know you'd sought sanctuary in the church?" Gilley asked.

"No," Carmen said. "Like I told you, I kept to the basement and lived on the leftovers from the Sunday school pizza party. No one knew I was down there except my sister. And if she hadn't texted me right then that she was outside waiting for me, I think the Angel would've found me and murdered me too."

"What happened with Sasha?" I asked carefully.

Carmen shook her head, then dropped her chin. Her shoulders shook for a moment, and she put her fingers to her lips. I felt bad for asking about something so painful, but I also knew we needed to have as much detail about the Angel's methods as possible.

"She hid me at her place. I was upstairs getting dressed, and Sasha called up that she was going out for some groceries. I happened to glance out the window as Sasha got into her car, and that's when the Angel of Death appeared out of nowhere, yanked the car door open as my sister was putting on her seat belt and . . . and . . ."

Gilley reached over and put a hand on Carmen's shoulder while she shook her head and dissolved into a puddle of tears. She didn't need to tell us what happened next. We already knew.

Still, Carmen gathered herself and said softly, "She killed her. She killed my beautiful Sasha, who did nothing. She did *nothing*. And now the police are after me! How could they think I had anything to do with that?"

Carmen lifted her chin and looked imploringly at me and Gilley.

I said, "Because they have nothing but some flimsy witness who spotted you running from your sister's house. If you'll let us call the police here, Carmen, I'm sure we can explain—"

"No!" Carmen yelled. "No police!"

I pressed my lips together. I could understand her fear, but she was being a bit unreasonable. Still, I had promised to respect her wishes. "Fine. We won't call them. Not yet. But eventually, we'll need to let them know that you witnessed this Angel of Death breaking the punch bowl over Heather's head."

"But I didn't witness that," she said. "I only came to the doorway after I heard the crash."

"It's basically the same thing," I said. "And we need them to find the bullet that was fired at you. I'm quite certain they don't even know it's there."

"It's there," she said. "I felt it go by me and saw the puff of dust when it went into the bookcase."

"See? If they dig that bullet out and match it to the one that killed your sister, then they'll have something to go on, Carmen. They'll know your story is true," Gilley said.

But Carmen still looked uneasy. She rubbed her temples and said, "I don't know. I still think it's a bad idea for me to talk to them. What if they think I fired the bullet into the bookcase to throw them off? If they match it to the gun that killed my sister, they could lock me up for her murder too."

"Okay," I said. "For now, let's just worry about what to do with you in the next few days."

"Can't I stay here?" she asked.

"You certainly could, but it'd get a little tricky. The Angel of Death has been seen in this area by several people. She might be too close for comfort right now. Plus, one of the detectives on Heather's case often stops by. If he spotted you . . . well, it could be bad."

"That's no good," Carmen said. "Maybe I should go back to Miss Heather's."

"And maybe there's another solution," I told her. "Have you ever spent time in Islip?"

"No," she said.

"Would you like to?"

"As long as it's safe from the Angel of Death, I'd be willing to go there."

"Excellent. I have a plan. Tonight you stay here, and Gilley and I will also sleep here to watch over you. The alarm is on, and my electronic butler monitors my every movement; he'll know to alert the police should anyone attempt to get inside. I think we'll be okay.

"As for tomorrow, we'll move you to a safe location, and then we'll talk to that detective about digging out the bullet and about the quinine. It's a shame we couldn't find any evidence in Heather's house tying someone to the poisoning."

"I'm sorry I couldn't be more helpful with that," Carmen said. "I didn't know Miss Heather was poisoned. Who would've thought that some simple tonic water would kill her?"

I blinked and looked at Gilley. "What?" he asked.

"*Who* indeed," I said to him. "Who would've known about Heather's allergy?"

"Any of her friends might've known," he said.

I pointed to Carmen. "But Carmen didn't even know. Carmen, how long had you worked for Heather?"

"Seventeen years," she said. "I worked for her and her husband, and then just her when he passed away. When she was having money troubles, she let everyone else go but me. She said I was her most loyal and trusted employee."

"Then why did she set up a camera to spy on you six months ago?" Gilley asked.

Carmen appeared taken aback. "How do you know about that?"

"I'm a good investigator," he said and didn't explain further.

Carmen frowned, but she seemed to accept his answer. "She wasn't spying on me. She was going to use the camera to spy on her ex-boyfriend. She thought he was seeing someone . . ." Carmen paused to look meaningfully at me.

"Nigel and I were never a thing," I said. "*Never.*"

Carmen nodded. "Yeah, I believe you. Anyway, the camera was hidden in a little clock. She tested it out in the kitchen for a few days last spring, and then she sent it to Nigel, but after he unwrapped it, he sent it back telling her it wasn't his taste, so she never got any proof one way or the other. She was going to throw the clock away, but I told her I liked it, so she let me put it on a shelf in the kitchen and the camera probably just kept running all this time."

"Do you know why she had a security camera over the door at the far end of the house?" I asked.

Carmen cocked her head. "What camera?"

"Heather had a camera pointed at the door that led to her library."

"She did?" Carmen said. "That's the first I've heard of it. But it was probably because she used to go there every night to work, and it was a little creepy at that end of the house after dark. It was right next to the woods and everything, so maybe it was to make her feel safe."

"That makes sense, actually," Gilley said, adding a yawn.

I looked at my watch; it was nearly eleven. "All right, every-one," I said. "Let's get to bed. We'll all sleep here tonight, and I'll lay out our plan in the morning, okay?"

Gilley and Carmen nodded, and we got up as one and began to troop toward the bedrooms. "Where are you bunking?" Gilley asked me.

"With you," I said.

"Me?"

"Yes. Is that a problem?"

He smiled sideways. "No. As long as you don't get all handsy."

I rolled my eyes. "Jazz hands are the only hands I'd ever get with you, sweetie."

"See?" he said, looping his arm through mine. "*This* is why we're friends. You just get me."

Chapter 15

The next morning, I was up before everyone else, making coffee and pacing the kitchen floor. The thing that was truly troubling me was the fact that, with her story of what happened the night Heather was murdered, Carmen had effectively given the Angel of Death—our assassin—an alibi.

"So who *did* kill Heather?" I muttered.

"What's that?" Gilley asked from the doorway.

I jumped at the sound of his voice. "Nothing. I was just muttering to myself."

Gilley rubbed his eyes and moved directly to the coffee carafe. "Anything good in all that muttering?"

I sighed. "No. Unfortunately. I'm still just really stumped by this mystery about who actually did kill Heather."

"It would've had to have been someone who specifically knew she could die by ingesting quinine," Gil said.

"Exactly. And if Carmen had worked for Heather for seventeen years and *she* didn't know the extent of Heather's allergy—then who did?"

"Maybe someone from that slumber party that Sunny told us about," Gil said.

I scowled. "Come on," I said. "From a million years ago? Who'd remember that? And who'd know to connect quinine to what happened that night? Even Sunny didn't know what kind of pill Heather had ingested."

"Just a thought," Gilley said.

"We'll need to do some digging," I said.

"When are you going to call Erma?" Gil asked, changing the subject.

"I sent her an e-mail last night while you were in the bathroom."

"Did you lay out all the specifics?"

"No. I simply suggested that we had a friend who was in a bit of a jam and needed a place to stay, and did she have any room at her place, now that her roommate had left, to accommodate this friend of ours."

Gilley cocked an eyebrow at me. "Sugar, you're going to have to warn her about what she could be getting herself into. Remember, Carmen's sister was *murdered* for harboring her."

"Yes, I know, Gilley. I'm going to have a follow-up conversation with her at the office, and I'm going to tell her that Carmen is in the kind of trouble that could bring danger. I'll let her decide if she wants to get involved or not."

Gilley shook his head. "Sorry, I don't agree. I think you should come totally clean with Erma. You can't ask her to harbor a fugitive and not tell her that's what she'll be doing."

"Carmen didn't kill anyone," I said testily. "Especially not her sister."

"Technically, that is probably correct, but also technically, at this moment, Carmen is being sought in connection to her sister's murder—and Heather's, for that matter—and as such she is also technically a fugitive from the law."

I growled in frustration. I hated that Gilley was right. "Fine. I'll divulge all to Erma. And we'll both have to hope that she doesn't run screaming to the police and all three of us end up in jail."

"Erma's not gonna snitch," Gilley said, but then I noticed a hint of indecision in his expression. "I'll bring doughnuts."

I pointed at him. "Good plan."

Gilley and I drove separately to the office. We left the driveway at the same time, me driving behind him all the way to town. I checked my rearview every few seconds to make sure we weren't being followed, and as far as I could tell, we weren't.

Still, I didn't rest easy until Gilley had turned into the parking lot behind my office building, and I continued on a bit to park at the curb. Keeping a watchful eye on my rearview mirror for exactly two minutes to see if any other cars entered the parking lot behind Gilley, I then texted him that I was on the move and to give me thirty seconds.

Hurrying out of my car, I dashed to the front door, unlocked it, entered the building, turned to relock the door, then ran to my office door to unlock that and step inside to punch in the alarm code. Once that was disarmed, I rushed to the back and threw open the rear exit to allow Gilley to run in with Carmen, who had a coat over her head.

Not that *that* was suspicious.

"Why'd you throw a coat over her head?" I snapped, pulling it off poor Carmen.

"I didn't!" Gilley snapped back. "It was her idea."

"I didn't want anyone to see me," she said, putting a hand to her hair to smooth it out.

I sighed and made an effort to soften my voice. "I think we're in the clear. Now, come with me."

"Where're we going?" she asked.

"Upstairs to an empty office, where I can hide you while I have a talk with a friend of mine who might be willing to take you to her place."

"Okay," Carmen said.

We headed up the stairs to Maks's office, and I fumbled with my keys until I found the right one to unlock the door. Leading

Carmen inside, I was a bit surprised to find it fully furnished—and elegantly so.

"This is nice," Carmen said.

"It is, isn't it?" I agreed. "Okay, Carmen, you stay here for an hour or so. The tenant I have in this office is out of town for the week, but I still think it would be unwise to make any noise or call attention to yourself in any way while you're here. Also, please don't move anything, okay? I don't want my tenant to become suspicious that I had anyone in here without his knowledge."

Carmen moved to a small love seat and sat down obediently. "I won't move from this spot."

"Good," I said, then waved goodbye to her and headed back downstairs.

I waited by the front door, checking my watch every half minute or so, and finally I spotted my Audi making the turn into the parking lot. "Perfect," I said.

Rushing back to my office, I ducked past Gilley, busy at his computer, and to the back door again to open it for Erma.

She came in wearing a big smile and an ill-fitting knit dress. "Good morning, Erma," I said, holding the door while she squeezed past me.

"Hey, Ms. Cooper!" she sang. "I was so excited to get your e-mail and text this morning!"

I locked the rear door and motioned for Erma to follow me. "I so appreciate you coming so early." Once we took our seats, and Gilley appeared with coffee and a plate full of doughnuts, I began to explain Carmen's situation.

Erma stared at me openmouthed and bug-eyed for the entire time I spoke. Well, save for those three instances where she paused to gobble down a doughnut, but otherwise she paid rapt attention. At the end of my story, she said, "Whoa. That's intense."

"It is," I agreed.

"So her sister really got murdered?" she asked.

"Yes," I said. "Which is why asking you to participate in all this may be asking far too much, but I really don't know what else to do with Carmen. I can't hide her at my house, and she's too afraid to allow me to contact the police on her behalf."

"I can take her in," Erma said.

"Oh, Erma, that would be so wonderful, but are you sure?"

"Of course! I mean, the poor lady just lost her sister! That's gotta be rough."

"It would be," I said, thinking with a pang back to the two times I'd almost lost my own sister.

"Well then, heck yeah, I'm in."

"But you realize you would be harboring a fugitive," Gilley said, handing Erma the remaining plated doughnut.

She took it with a giant, grateful smile. "Yeah, that doesn't scare me."

"And," I said delicately, "you must also take into account that her sister was murdered by the same woman who's after her. We can't guarantee that you'll be totally safe with her in your company."

Erma shrugged. "I live in a trailer park in Islip. I'm used to watching my back."

I looked at Gilley, suddenly unsure. I think it was Erma's willingness to toss aside the danger. It left me feeling that she was perhaps too naïve to be involved.

He shrugged and offered a look that said he understood, but it was her choice.

"Erma," I said. "Are you absolutely *positive* that you're up for this?"

She eyed me quizzically. "Ms. Cooper, I know I may look kinda slow on the uptake, but I can take care of myself. Well, usually. Most of the time. What I mean is, I hear what you're saying, and I understand this is a dangerous assignment, but I still want to help this lady if I can. Nobody's gonna follow me to some run-down trailer park in Islip. I can get her into my place unnoticed, I promise, and she can hide out there as long as she needs."

I let out a breath of relief. "Thank you," I said. "Thank you so much."

Ten minutes later, our three cars left the building at the exact same time, all in a row, all following each other very closely until we were at the intersection just before the on-ramp to the highway, and then, as we'd pre-planned, we split into three different routes. Erma carried on straight, I turned left, and Gilley turned right.

"How's everyone doing?" I asked. I had Gilley and Erma connected on a conference call.

"I'm good," Gilley said. "No one on my six."

"Your six?" Erma asked.

"My tail."

"Ah. Got it. No one on my six either, Ms. Cooper."

"Perfect," I said, eyeing my rearview. "Oh, crap," I whispered as I noticed a car behind me.

"What is it?" Gilley said quickly.

I glanced forward again and gripped the steering wheel. "Listen to me carefully, you two. I need for you to call each other. Gilley, you do the dialing. Erma, you continue on to Islip with Carmen. I'll be in touch as soon as I can."

"Cat!" Gilley called out. "What's happening? Should I turn around?"

"No!" I told him. "No, Gilley, I'm fine. I just have a pesky detective riding my own six. And I think he's about to pull me over. You two go on, now, okay?"

With that I hung up, and no sooner had I done that than Shepherd flipped on the police lights in his unmarked vehicle. "Perfect," I muttered. "Juuuust perfect."

Flicking my turn signal to show him how cooperative I'd be, I pulled into the parking lot of a bank and stopped. I didn't get out or roll down my window, settling for simply sitting in my seat and seething.

He rapped on my window, and I waited a beat before I lowered it. "Good morning, Detective," I said flatly. "What's the charge today? Driving under the influence of too much coffee?"

"Cute," he said. "I need to talk to you."

"So talk."

"Have you had breakfast?" he asked. "Other than coffee?"

His question took me by surprise. "Uh . . . no, actually."

"Good. Follow me. I know a great place."

With that, he turned on his heel and walked back to his car.

I frowned as he pulled out in front of me and led the way to the restaurant. This wasn't what I needed this morning. I was anxious about Erma and Carmen. I had planned to make sure that Carmen was safely holed up at Erma's before dropping in on Sunny again to ask her if she knew of anyone who might've known about Heather's allergy to quinine.

I had a theory that Heather hadn't told a soul about it, except perhaps her own doctor. Someone as mean and cutthroat as Heather wouldn't have wanted something like that to be common knowledge, based on the mere fact that any enemy who knew she could be killed by the smallest amount of tonic water could've easily spiked her drink or her food and gotten away with murder.

In fact, that's exactly what I suspected happened. And though Carmen hadn't seen anyone carrying around a small bottle of tonic, it didn't mean that someone didn't sneak one into the party, hidden in her purse, and empty the contents into my punch sometime after Carmen had taste-tested it to ensure it was safe for Heather to drink.

When I thought about it, it was actually a perfect little murder: neat, tidy, and no sign of a smoking gun.

These were my thoughts as I walked across the pavement to

where Shepherd was holding open the door to a café called Eddy's 80's.

When I entered, I realized what half the name must mean: the whole place was devoted to nostalgia of the eighties. There were framed photographs of high school yearbook photos, featuring young men with mullets and tails, and young women with high bangs, shoulder pads, and extra-glossy lipstick.

Movie posters dedicated to *Sixteen Candles*, *The Breakfast Club*, and *Pretty in Pink* lined one wall, and the jukebox played Tears for Fears.

"Cool," I said. Although I'd been young, I'd loved the eighties.

"This place is one of my favorites," Shepherd said. Pointing to a booth covered in turquoise vinyl, he allowed me to sit first before joining me and handing over a menu.

I skimmed the first page and asked, "So, what's up, Detective."

"I've been given a hot tip about the murder of Heather Holland."

"Oh?" I said, as casually as I could. It wouldn't do to look overly interested, not when Shepherd had ordered me to butt out.

"It came in this morning about a minute after I got to my desk," he said. He paused when the waitress stopped by our table with a hot coffeepot and asked to take my order.

"I'd like the crêpes, please," I said. "Extra lemon."

"Good choice," Shepherd said. "I'll have my usual, Cathy."

"You got it, chief," she said, with a wink as she headed off.

"You order the same dish at every restaurant you go to?"

Shepherd stirred some cream into his coffee. "I do. In case you haven't noticed, I'm not a guy who likes surprises."

"Which is no surprise," I kidded.

"Ha," he said flatly. "Anyway, you can imagine how much I didn't like it when I got to work and was greeted with this surprise tip that really threw a monkey wrench into the Heather Holland murder case."

I leaned in. "What's the tip?"

Shepherd paused to take a sip from his coffee. "Mmm, that's good coffee. Have you tried it yet?"

"Just get to the point, man!" I snapped. He was purposely teasing me, and my patience for it had waned.

He smiled. "The point, or rather the tip, was that someone spotted a red Mini Cooper parked on the side of the road last night, next to the wooded section of Heather Holland's estate."

Uh oh, I thought.

"This same witness also swore they saw three people coming out of Heather Holland's house, headed toward the Mini Cooper."

"Weird!" When in doubt, feign surprise.

Shepherd took another swig of coffee. "Yeah. Major coincidence given *you* have a red Mini Cooper registered in your name, right?"

"Oh, please, there are tons of those cars around here."

"Three, actually."

"Excuse me?"

"There are three. Exactly three red Mini Coopers in this part of the Hamptons."

"Wow, I would've thought there'd be a ton more. It's a fun little car."

"If you're looking for a fun red car around here, you'd have to go with a Ferrari, Porsche, Lamborghini, or even a Tesla Roadster."

"I love those cars. I'm thinking of getting one, you know. If I do, I'll let you take it for a test drive."

"You really gonna ignore the fact that I know it was you who was out at Heather's place last night?"

I did my best to appear taken aback. "Me? You can't be serious, Detective. I was at home all evening."

"Yep. I knew you were," he said, looking relieved.

I didn't buy it for a second and felt my heart rate tick up.

"Well, except for that visit to my sister, right?"

Gulp.

"And that was . . . what? About forty-five minutes before a car similar to yours was seen in front of Heather's and three people were spotted moving toward the car."

"If it looked so suspicious, why didn't this witness call it in at the time he saw the three people leaving Heather's?" I said tartly.

"Because this good Samaritan didn't want to . . . and I'm going to quote him, 'stir up trouble,' so he slept on it and finally decided to phone it in this morning."

"How about I just plead the fifth on this one?" I asked.

Shepherd opened his mouth to reply but was once again interrupted by the waitress, who set down a plate of crêpes for me and some sort of gorgeous-looking omelet for Shepherd.

After she left, Shepherd took up his fork and said, "Who was the third person, Catherine?"

"I can't tell you," I said.

"You have to be kidding me."

"Wish I was. But I made a promise, and I'm going to keep it."

Shepherd squinted at me, and then he seemed to connect the dots. "*Carmen?*"

I don't know how he guessed it—skills like that usually only come from my sister. "I can't tell you," I repeated.

Shepherd shook his head and rubbed his face. He then jabbed his fork angrily into his omelet and sawed off a large piece. "You're killing me, you know that?"

"It's not my intention to kill anyone, Detective."

Shepherd chewed his food and glared at me. "You have to bring her in."

"I made a promise. I can't."

"She's in danger, Catherine!" he yelled, dropping his fork in anger. Several people in the café looked over at us.

"She's safe," I replied. "She feels that if she came in, she'd be in even greater danger."

"The assassin's after her."

"Actually, her name is the Angel of Death."

"Is that supposed to be funny?"

"No. That's what a certain person told me her handle was."

"What else do you know?"

"A great deal," I admitted.

Shepherd crumpled up his napkin and threw it on the table, clearly pissed off. "So this whole time you've been holding out on me?"

"No. I've only been holding out on you for about the past twenty-four hours. Ever since you decided our collaboration was over."

Shepherd sighed. "So it's *my* fault."

"Great of you to admit it," I said with a smile.

He shook his head. "Seriously, you're killing me."

Feeling a bit sorry for him, I decided to tell him what I knew. "Heather was allergic to quinine."

He eyed me sharply. "Quinine? Like the active ingredient in tonic water?"

"Yes."

"How do you know that?"

"Your sister."

"My sister told you Heather was allergic to quinine," he said doubtfully.

"No. She told me about a slumber party she attended with Heather when they were young girls. At the party, Heather was having severe leg cramps, and the girl hosting the party knew that her mother took pills to relieve leg cramps, so she got one for Heather, and Heather's reaction to the pills put her in the hospital."

"What does any of that have to do with quinine?"

"Quinine pills were used pretty extensively in the past as a cure for leg cramps."

"So what you have is a suspicion, not an actual fact."

"Yes," I said, "but I believe you can confirm it. When Heather sent over the recipe to me for the punch I made her for the party, she was very specific that I should follow the ingredients exactly as written. Which I did. Later, Gilley found the same recipe for the punch I made online, but that online recipe called for tonic water—not Sprite, as Heather had written it for me to make.

"I also had a conversation with . . . *someone* who told me that Heather had told her that she was allergic to tonic water. It's my theory that someone else at that party knew of or had discovered Heather's severe reaction to quinine and spiked the punch."

Shepherd stared at me with a doubtful expression, but then his brow rose, and he retrieved his cell phone. After tapping at the screen, he put it to his ear and said, "McDaniel, it's Shepherd. Listen, I need someone in your lab to read me the ingredients we retrieved from the liquid in the punch bowl. Yeah, I'll wait."

I ate my crèpes while Shepherd waited for McDaniel to come back on the line. "These are delicious," I said to him.

He rolled his eyes. A minute later, he said, "Yeah, I'm here. Uh huh, . . . uh huh, . . . yeah, okay, got it. Now I need you to do me another favor. I need you to dig around into Heather Holland's medical records. Search for any indication that she was allergic to quinine. And pass that info on to Beauperthy and ask if the way in which she died is consistent with quinine poisoning. Thanks."

After hanging up, Shepherd dug into his omelet again.

"Well?" I asked him when he didn't offer up any information.

After wiping his mouth with his napkin, he said, "Quinine was present in the punch. A fair amount of it too, actually."

"I knew it!" I said.

"What else do you know?" he pressed.

I shrugged lightly and focused on my crèpes. "I don't think I can comment further, even though I do know something very interesting. I mean, if you truly want me to butt out, then even when I have information, I don't see how I can share it with you without being accused of overstepping."

Shepherd pulled my plate away. "Hey," he said to get my attention. I looked up. "This is me asking you to butt in, okay?"

I dipped my chin in assent. "Good. Because I would've hated to have withheld this next bit. It seems there was an encounter over Heather's body not long after she passed away."

"Encounter? Explain, please."

"Carmen got up close and personal with the Angel of Death, which is one of the reasons why the assassin is after Carmen. She saw her up close."

"So did you," Shepherd said.

"Yes, which is why I'm being extra cautious these days. Anyway, Carmen heard a loud crash and came running to find the assassin standing over Heather, with shards of the punch bowl lying all around her. Carmen assumed the assassin had just killed her, and, in turn, the assassin assumed it was *Carmen* who'd killed Heather. Which is the second reason the Angel of Death is after the housekeeper."

Shepherd opened his mouth to comment, but I held up my hand.

"Wait," I said. "Just let me finish. The Angel of Death took a shot at Carmen. You'll find the bullet in the bookcase next to the door. Carmen managed to flee unharmed to Father Stephan's church, where she hid in the basement and called her sister. As it happens, Sasha worked for someone, as Carmen put it, *important* to a certain crime family. Sasha was able to glean that a mark had been placed on Heather's head—just like we suspected—and the Angel of Death was trying to collect when she was foiled by someone else. Word got back to the crime family, and they refused to pay the Angel, suggesting that the money should go to Carmen, who they think murdered Heather. The Angel, in turn, tracked Carmen down to the church and killed Father Stephan— probably because she was convinced he knew where she was and was hiding her. Carmen escaped into her sister's car in the nick of time.

"The assassin then did her homework, discovered where

Sasha lived, tracked her down, and killed her. Maybe she thought she was Carmen, maybe she wanted to kill Sasha as a way to punish Carmen out of revenge—I don't really know. Carmen witnessed the murder but managed to escape again; out of options, she fled to Heather's, hoping to hide out for a few days. Heather's house is where we discovered her and decided to help."

"How'd you get into Heather's house?" he asked.

"I'm afraid to answer that on the grounds that it could incriminate me."

Shepherd sighed. "How about this one time I pinkie-swear not to file a B and E against you?"

"That'd be swell."

"So how'd you get into Heather's?"

"When Gilley and I were directed to the back of Heather's house to bring in the punch, Gilley remembered tripping over a rock, and when he bent down to toss it out of the way, he realized it was one of those fake rocks you hide a key in. All we had to do was go back and find the rock." I was lying, of course, but the truth would've incriminated Gilley and me of more than a B and E.

"How'd you get past the alarm? We had the alarm company set it remotely after we were done gathering our evidence."

"Gilley guessed that it would be something simple, like our zip code or area code. He tried the area code digits and it worked," I said, thinking fast.

"Huh," Shepherd said. "That's a pretty lucky guess."

"Gilley is quite a lucky man."

Shepherd nodded, and I was grateful that he bought the explanation. "So where is Carmen now?"

"I can't tell you that, and I won't tell you that. But she is somewhere safe, and yes, I realize you could haul me off to jail for harboring a fugitive, but Carmen didn't hurt anyone. She worked for Heather for seventeen years, and she looked out for her."

"How do you know that?"

"Well, the second I arrived with the punch, Carmen insisted

on taste-testing it so that she knew it was free of tonic water. No way would she have cared *what* I put in it if she intended to poison Heather."

"So who killed Heather?" Shepherd said.

"That I don't know. Yet. But I think there might be a way to find out."

"Do tell."

"I need to see the invitation list that Heather sent out."

"I have that. I can print you out a copy."

"And I'll also need another word with your sister."

"What does Sunny have to do with it?"

I smiled. "She's our star witness, Detective."

An hour later, I was in Shepherd's car, pulling up to Sunny's house. We'd already heard back from the medical examiner. Heather's primary-care physician confirmed that she had a severe allergy to quinine. She'd experienced two close calls with it in her life; once when she was a young girl at a sleepover, and another time when she was traveling in Europe as a college student and had been given a drink at a party mixed with tonic water.

That incident had nearly killed her.

Heather's doctor also confirmed that she had been very reluctant to share the news of her allergy with anyone. Not even her husband.

Sunny answered her brother's knock looking tired and pale. "Hey, Stevie," she said when she saw him.

"Bun-bun?" he said, reaching for her arm. "Are you okay?"

She smiled weakly. "Yeah. The baby kept me up all night kicking up a storm. I swear he's destined to be a soccer champion." Noticing me for the first time, she said, "Oh! Hi, Catherine. I didn't see you there. Come on in, you two."

Sunny turned, and Shepherd held the door open for me. As I passed him, I whispered, "Bun-bun?"

His complexion turned a shade of pink, and he quickly explained, "My mom's pet name for her was Bunny, like Sunny-bunny. That morphed into Bun-bun."

"Uh huh," I said, smiling wickedly. "It's very cute. Especially when you say it."

"Cut me a break, okay? She's my twin. We're close."

I chuckled and headed toward Sunny's bright white kitchen. She was already at the stove, putting the kettle on and reaching for a set of mugs. "The UPS man just delivered some lavender tea. I've been dying to try this blend. It smells heavenly," she said, opening a purple tin and holding it out for me to smell.

I took a whiff. "Oh, my," I said, closing my eyes to savor the scent. "That's heaven."

"I'm hoping it'll settle both me and the baby down," she said. Then she nodded toward her brother and added, "And judging by those dark circles under *your* eyes, I'm going to send you home with some of this to help you sleep tonight, Steve."

"Don't worry about me," he said. "I can take a few sleepless nights."

Sunny ignored her brother and put a few spoonfuls of the loose-leaf tea into a baggie. She handed it to him with a stern look, and he took it with a grateful smile.

"So, what brings the two of you by?" she asked, back at the cupboard to get the honey.

"We're here to ask you more about that sleepover," I said.

Sunny's brow furrowed. "Sleepover?"

"Yes, you remember. The one where you said Heather was given some pills for her leg cramps?"

"Ahh, yes," she said. "God, that was thirty years ago!"

"Do you remember everyone who was there?" I asked.

"Do I . . . ? What do you mean?"

"Well, the thing of it is, Sunny, almost no one knew that Heather had a dangerous allergy to quinine, which was very likely the active ingredient in the pills she was given."

Shepherd jumped in with, "Quinine can kill a person if that person has a sensitivity to it. The M.E. has confirmed that quinine was present in the liquid found in Heather's stomach. We think she ingested it through the punch that Catherine brought to the party."

Sunny's eyes bugged wide. "So you inadvertently killed Heather?"

I shook my head vigorously. "No. Not me. I used Sprite, just like the directions called for, and Carmen, Heather's housekeeper, even taste-tested the punch before allowing it to be served at the party. Someone else spiked the punch, and since Heather had told almost no one about her allergy, we think that someone at that party knew about it by some other means—like from a slumber party she attended when she was a young girl."

Sunny gave a startled laugh. "That's diabolical!"

"Quite," I agreed.

The kettle began to whistle, and Sunny turned away to tend to it for a moment. Shepherd and I waited patiently, because it was obvious that Sunny was also trying to think back to that slumber party and remember who was there.

"The sleepover was fairly small, from what I remember. Only about six of us in attendance, so that leaves me, and Heather, and Sara Goodwright—she lives in D.C. now and wasn't at the luncheon. Then there was . . ." Sunny tapped her lip thoughtfully as she poured the hot water over the infuser. "Um . . . Carol Teegan, I heard she's now living in California, and then there was Pamela Hartnet—she's in New York, and . . . oh, who am I forgetting?"

Sunny stared at us blankly, and both Shepherd and I shrugged.

Sunny tisked. "I can't remember the last girl there," she said. "Drat!"

"It's okay," I said.

"No," she said, fiddling with the mugs. "It's not. It's this stupid pregnancy brain. I can't seem to remember things or concentrate on things." Looking at her brother, she said, "Tell me again why I fought so hard for so long to get pregnant?"

"Because in spite of how often that idiot you married takes off to parts unknown, you refuse to leave him, and you're hoping that having a baby will finally make him settle down."

I sucked in a breath, and Sunny winced. "Ouch!" I said angrily. "I know she's your sister, Detective, but could you be a little less of a jerk?"

"It's all right, Catherine. He's absolutely right. I am hoping that having a baby will keep Darius home more. It's a gamble, but I'm hopeful. And, of course, now that I *am* finally pregnant, I kinda can't wait to meet the new man in my life."

"I still think you should name him Steve," Shepherd said.

Sunny rolled her eyes. "I would never give him the namesake of someone so annoying."

Shepherd laughed, and I did too.

A little later, as we were leaving, I had a thought and turned to Sunny to ask, "What about the girl who hosted the party?"

"I'm sorry?" she said, obviously confused.

"You said that you couldn't remember the sixth girl at the slumber party, but did you name the girl who gave Heather the pills?"

"Oh!" Sunny said. "Yes, of course! How silly of me, and I think the reason I drew a blank is because Cora died in her teens."

"That's so sad," I said.

Sunny nodded. "She went swimming one summer morning and drowned. A rip current got her and took her way out to sea. It was a terrible tragedy."

On that very sad note, we left and spent much of the next ten minutes in silence. I broke that silence only when I noticed Shepherd had passed Heather's house and was on the way to mine. "I thought we were going to hunt for that bullet that the Angel shot at Carmen?"

"I got a text from my commander. He wants a status update, so

I have to head back to the station for a while. We can go later, say around five?"

"Six would be better," I said. I missed the boys and owed them a call. Five o'clock was that sweet time between homework and mealtime when we could usually catch up.

"Six it is," he said.

Something was still bothering me about Shepherd's interaction with his sister, however. I didn't like how mean he'd been to her during a time when I knew she was vulnerable and lonely. As I was getting out, I said, "You know, you were a bit hard on your sister back there."

He seemed taken aback. "You mean the bit about how she was hoping to keep her husband around more by bringing a baby into the mix?"

"Yes. I mean, I know it's none of my business, but I remember how close to the surface my emotions were when I was pregnant."

He shrugged. "Yeah, you're right. But at least Sunny knows that I'm only hard on her because I love her."

"So what you're telling me is that you're hard on all the people you love?"

He offered me a crooked smile. "No. Sometimes I'm hard on the people I like too."

In that instant, there was a sort of crackling of chemistry between us, and it was my turn to be taken aback. "Are we having a moment?" I asked softly.

"Maybe a little," he admitted, adding a wink.

"Well, then," I said, gathering up my purse, "I best be off before we have ourselves a full-blown flirtation."

"Yeah, probably a good idea."

Still, I sat there.

And he sat there too.

And we had ourselves something a tad more than a little moment . . .

302   Victoria Laurie

Until my phone beeped with an incoming text. I jumped at
the sound and wiggled my phone. "I'll see you at six."

"Six," he agreed.

I got out of the car and struggled not to look back as I heard his
car backing up behind me. And I made it all the way to the door
of Chez Kitty before I peeked over my shoulder and caught him
staring back at me. Another moment passed between us, until I
waved and went inside.

Chapter 16

"**W**here have you *been?!*" Gilley shouted at me the second I came through the door.

"Hello," I said nonchalantly. "Nice to see you too, Gil."

"Cat," he snapped, crossing his arms and taking up the angry stance of a mother hen. "You don't answer texts, which is totally *uncool* given that we've got a serial killer in our midst!"

"Assassin," I corrected.

"Tomato, tomassin!" he shouted. "What's the damn difference?"

I sighed. "I guess not much. I'm sorry I didn't answer your texts. I was busy."

"With your new boyfriend?" he sneered, obviously still miffed at being ignored.

"Gil," I said gently. "Truly. I'm sorry. Now can we please sit down and talk? I have lots to share."

Gilley shook his head slightly, his arms still crossed in front of him. I knew he'd eventually give in and forgive me, and it was almost comical how he was trying sooooo hard to stay mad. I waited him out and merely stood there until he appeared calmer.

"We can have a snack," I suggested. "News is always better with a tasty snack."

"What kind of a snack?"

I walked to the pantry. "I could make brownies."

"But I'm on a diet," he said. I thought his protest sounded a bit weak.

"I won't tell if you won't," I said, adding a wicked smile.

Gilley's eyes gleamed with eager anticipation. "Without nuts but with chocolate chips?" he said.

I pulled out the box and wiggled it at him. "Duh."

"Good. And I want all the corner pieces."

As the kitchen filled with the mouthwatering scent of baking brownies, I filled Gilley in on all that'd transpired since hanging up with him that morning.

Then he filled me in about Carmen and Erma. "Erma's been sending me an update every hour on the hour."

"What do the messages say?"

Gilley lifted his phone to read the screen. "Four p.m. All okay."

"Riveting."

"Yeah, I have this image of her standing to the side of her curtains peering through a set of binoculars at the traffic outside."

"I'll bet you're not far off the mark. I hope Carmen doesn't have a problem staying with Erma."

"Are you kidding? She also texted me that she loves Erma's place. It's much bigger and cozier than she expected, and Erma has been doting on her like a concerned nanny. Last I checked, Carmen was hanging out on the couch, watching Netflix and enjoying a turkey sandwich with a milkshake chaser."

"Oh, my. That must be a welcome change for her."

"Right? But we can't impose on Erma forever. We gotta solve this case, Cat."

"I know, I know. But I'm out of ideas, Gilley. I thought I'd finally nailed down a good lead with the fact that only the girls that attended that slumber party would've had any inkling about Heather's allergy. But Sunny said that all the girls from the slumber party now live in other states and weren't at the luncheon.

Well, except for one. A girl named Cora. She was the one who gave Heather the pill for her leg cramps, and I thought she could be our number-one suspect, but it turns out that she drowned twenty years ago."

Gilley pulled his tablet close. "The rip currents around here are treacherous. You're going to have to watch the boys when they come home and you guys head to the beach."

The timer on the brownies pinged, and I got up to check them. Over my shoulder, I said, "I'll definitely keep an eye out. I can't even imagine losing a child so young. The girl's parents must have been devastated. I mean, how do you ever get over something like that?"

Gilley made a noise like he agreed, but I could detect that his focus was elsewhere. After taking the brownies out and setting them on a wire rack to cool for a few minutes, I turned back toward the table, where Gilley had his nose close to his tablet and was obviously reading something. "What're you looking at?" I asked.

"I'm not sure . . . ," he told me, "but it's weird. I feel like I know someone whose daughter passed away the same way."

"You do?" I asked.

"Yeah," Gil said, tapping his finger on the face of his tablet. "There's something about that story that's familiar."

"Connected to Heather?"

"I'm not sure, but I want to say yes."

I turned back to the brownies and began slicing them. I didn't want to distract Gilley from his efforts to remember the connection, but there was something that he'd said—about the story sounding familiar—that also rang a bell with me.

The silence in the room stretched out as I cut each brownie and placed it on a plate, arranging them in a small pyramid, and allowing my thoughts to simply float around the idea that I knew that story, or something about it without really looking too closely at it, lest I push the memory too far away.

It was as I was setting the very last brownie on the plate that it finally came to me.

The gasp behind me let me know that Gilley had figured it out at the exact same moment.

I turned around to look at him, and our eyes met. We both said, "Joyce!"

I hurried over to Gilley's side as he began to tap earnestly at his tablet. At last, he had her Facebook page pulled up, and among the photos of pretty flowers and idyllic nature settings was a small plaque set in a garden that read, "In memory of our beloved Cora, who was pulled out to sea and took our hearts with her."

"It was subtle," I said, staring at the plaque. "I remember seeing it and thinking she'd lost a pet or something."

"Exactly," Gilley said, switching over to his search engine. "Let me see what I can find out . . ."

While Gilley searched, I got up again and headed back to the brownies. Bringing him two corner pieces, I set them down next to him with a glass of milk and waited for his eyes to stop darting back and forth across the screen. "Here's the article from the *East Hampton Chronicle* on July seventeenth, nineteen ninety-five," Gilley said, and then he began to read. " 'Cora Burke, age sixteen, was caught in a rip current this past Tuesday and drowned. According to her parents, Cora often got in an early-morning swim before her job as a lifeguard at the East Hampton beach. On Tuesday morning, when Cora didn't show up for work, and her parents hadn't seen her all morning, the police and beach patrol were alerted and a search effort mounted. Cora's body was discovered some four hours later, approximately three miles down the coast.' "

"That's so, so sad," I said.

Gilley's eyes continued to dart back and forth. "It is. She was their only child."

"But what could Heather have had to do with it?" I said. "Assuming, of course, that Joyce was the one who slipped the quinine into the punch?"

"I think that's an answer only Joyce can give us," Gilley said.

"Yes. First, though, we should talk to Sunny again. She never mentioned that Joyce was there, and surely she would've remembered that, wouldn't she?"

"Call her," Gilley said. "I'm going to do some more digging."

While Gilley worked his computer magic, I texted Shepherd that I needed his sister's phone number.

Why? he texted back.

I could've told him why, but it would've taken too long, and I was impatient to talk to Sunny, so I simply said that I wanted to ask her out to lunch, and he immediately sent the number over.

She picked up on the second ring. "Hello?" she said tentatively.

"Sunny? It's Catherine Cooper. Listen, I've just discovered something that might be a huge clue in this case. Do you by chance remember Cora's mother being at the luncheon?"

"Cora's mother?" she said.

"Yes. Joyce McQueen."

"Wow. I never knew her first name was Joyce. Truthfully, Catherine, I probably wouldn't have recognized her even if I'd bumped into her. After that incident at the slumber party, word got around that Cora was free with her mother's medication, and none of our mothers would let us hang out at her house again. Cora was transferred to a private school the following fall, and we never really hung out with her again. And I only have the vaguest of memories of her mother. Also, Cora's last name wasn't McQueen. It was Burke."

"She could've remarried," I suggested.

"True," she agreed. "Most women around here are on their second or third marriage anyway."

"So you don't remember her at the luncheon," I said, wanting to make absolutely sure.

"No. I'm really sorry. But I didn't really take note of everyone there. If Joyce had attended, and I didn't recognize her outright, I'm pretty sure I wouldn't remember her being there."

"What if you saw a photo of her, would that help?"

"It might," she said.

"Are you near your computer? Can you look her up on Facebook?" I motioned to Gilley to get his attention, then I mouthed, *Pull up Joyce on Facebook.*

He nodded and tapped at his tablet in earnest.

Placing my phone on the table, I hit the SPEAKER button so that Gilley could hear Sunny.

"Okay, I've pulled up her profile," Sunny said after a few moments. "But her account is private."

I looked at Gilley; he shrugged. "Try sending her a friend request," I suggested. "Maybe she'll approve it and you can search her photos."

"You think that'll work?"

Gilley rolled his eyes and nodded vigorously.

"It couldn't hurt," I said to Sunny, keeping my fingers crossed that she'd send the request.

"That's true," she said. There was a slight pause while we waited, and then Gilley's tablet gave a soft ping to announce Sunny's friend request. He approved it immediately.

"Oh, well, would you look at that!" Sunny said. "Joyce and I are now Facebook friends."

"Wow," Gilley said, with a secret roll of his eyes to me. "So cool that she was online and accepted it!"

I tapped the MUTE button on my phone, and said, "Can you not oversell this?"

"Sorry."

"Guys?" Sunny asked. "You there?"

I tapped the MUTE button again. "We're here. Did you find something?"

"Well, I'm in her photos and looking at her face, and it's no wonder I don't recognize her. She's gotten so old!"

"Her profile told us that she's in her early eighties," I said, just to speed things along.

"Wow," Sunny said. "I guess I never realized how much older Cora's mom was than my own mom. But then, Cora was an only child, and I've tried for years to have a baby and only recently got pregnant, so it probably makes more sense to me now. Still, looking at her photos here, I don't remember seeing her at the party, but I know of a way that I may be able to verify that she was there."

"How's that?" I asked.

"Letty Ergen—one of Heather's only good friends—was at the party, and she took tons of photos. She uploaded them about two hours before we all heard that Heather had died. Let me hop over to her page and take a closer look at the photos."

"Great! We'll wait."

I hit the MUTE button again and said, "Can you get to Letty's account? Is she friends with Joyce?"

Gilley tapped at the screen. "She's not friends with her, *but* the photos in question were made public, so we might be in luck."

I leaned over his shoulder as he scrolled through the photos of women at the luncheon, standing around with their drinks in hand, dressed in their jewel tones, appearing to all be having a marvelous time.

"Oh!" Sunny suddenly said.

I untapped the MUTE button and said, "What is it? Did you find something?"

"Yes, I think I did!"

"Sunny, we're on Letty's page. She made the photos public. Which image are you looking at?"

"It's the one with the four women gathered around Heather. The one where she's obviously telling a joke and they're all throwing their heads back and laughing. Do you see it?"

Gilley found the photo, and I couldn't help but feel a small tinge of anger as the thought crept into my mind that Heather was probably talking about me, and they were all laughing at my expense.

Shaking off the feeling I said, "We found the photo, but I don't see Joyce."

"If you look over Rachel Tepper's shoulder—she's the one in the bright yellow dress—you'll see a woman in a silver-blue jacket and matching skirt, right?"

I squinted at the screen. "She's out of focus. I can't tell who it is."

"True, but if you go back to Joyce's photos, you'll see that same jacket and skirt combo in the photo of her at the Art in the Park community event."

Gilley switched windows and quickly scrolled through Joyce's photos, landing on the photo in question on the third swipe. "Bingo," I whispered.

Gilley switched photos again and used his fingers to enlarge the photo of Joyce at the luncheon. "Ohmigod, Cat! Look!"

"The punch bowl!" I said. "Gilley, she's *right next to it!*"

"Yes!" he said. "We've got her! We've got her!"

"Um, guys?" Sunny said.

Gilley and I were exchanging high fives when I said, "Yeah?"

"What exactly do you have?"

"What do you mean?"

"Well, I'm no defense attorney, but my brother is a cop, so I know a little bit about when there's evidence and when there's not, and all you have with this photo is proof that someone wearing the same jacket and skirt combo as Joyce attended the luncheon. I'm sure someone will remember seeing her there, but even though in the photo she's close to the punch bowl, there's no evidence that she dumped anything into it."

I sat down heavily in the chair. "Ohmigod, you're right," I said.

"And I've reached the end of Letty's photos, and there isn't a single one of Joyce in focus. If I had to guess, I would say that she probably worked pretty hard to avoid the camera lens—assuming she did, in fact, have something to do with the quinine found in the punch."

"She did it," I said adamantly. "I can *feel* it."

"But why?" Sunny asked next. "Why would Joyce want to kill Heather?"

"Could it be over the death of her daughter?" Gilley asked. "Maybe Heather was there that day and lured Cora into the water or something."

"I would say that's plausible, except that Heather was afraid of deep water. Something about seeing *Jaws* at an impressionable age. She would *never* have gone swimming with Cora in the ocean. She didn't even like the deep end of the swimming pool."

"Well, there has to be some reason," I insisted. "Joyce would've been one of the only other people to know about Heather's severe allergy to quinine."

"True, but short of a confession, I don't know how you're going to prove it," Sunny said.

I sighed. "You're right. Dammit. And I really thought we had something to take to your brother."

Sunny chuckled softly. "Hey, don't beat yourself up, Catherine. This was some solid detective work, and my brother should be impressed. Do take it to him. Who knows, maybe he's got some thoughts about trying to provoke a confession out of her. Maybe he can tell her that he's got photographic evidence of her dumping some quinine into the punch bowl. She wouldn't know that he doesn't have it, after all."

Gilley's eyes lit up. "Thanks, Sunny. That's a great idea," he said.

I hung up with Sunny and turned to Gil. "What?" I asked.

He scrolled to the photo of Joyce at the Art Gala. "I don't know if you know this, but I'm a whiz with Photoshop."

"Why is that relevant?"

"Give me half an hour," he said.

I waited on the couch, my foot tapping, while I watched Gilley work. At last he said, "Got it," and I jumped up and rushed over to him. He showed me his finished work, and I marveled at it.

"Whoa," I said. "She's caught red-handed!"

"Yes. I went with the prescription bottle over the tonic water. I figured that dropping a few pills into the punch bowl was probably going to be less conspicuous than hauling out a bottle of tonic water and dumping it into the punch."

"That's a gamble," I said, looking at the completely doctored image of Joyce, tapping out a few pills into the punch bowl at Heather's luncheon.

"It is. If she used tonic water, she'll know it's a forgery."

"What do we say to Shepherd?"

"We pretend to have discovered this photo online. He probably won't check, and he'll use it to get a confession out of Joyce."

I tapped my lip. "Gil, I don't think we can set him up like that. He'll have to be told that the photo is a fake; otherwise, we could jeopardize the confession—assuming he could get one. Plus, if he's going to probe her about the murder, he'll have to read Joyce her rights, which will alert her to clam up and call her attorney. I think that even with the photo, we risk not getting much of anything out of her if Shepherd takes the lead on this."

"Then what do you propose we do?"

"I think we should have a talk with Joyce someplace public and invite Shepherd. If he's there, then he's not exactly questioning her, he's just overhearing a conversation about a photo we discovered online, and if that conversation happens to be a confession, then he doesn't have to read Joyce her rights before we start probing."

Gilley brightened. "Oooo, I love that idea!"

I sighed with relief. If Gilley was on board, then my logic might be sound. "Let me call Shepherd and bring him up to speed."

Five minutes into our conversation, however, the detective

was putting up all sorts of roadblocks. "We're riding a hairy edge here, you two," he said through my phone's speaker. "If I'm involved at all in any part of this, then I'll have to identify myself and read Joyce her rights; otherwise, her attorney's going to cry entrapment and get the judge to toss out her confession—assuming, of course, she tells you anything."

"But what if you simply overheard the conversation?" Gilley asked. "I mean, if we can coax Joyce to meet us at . . . I don't know . . . the local coffee shop, somewhere public so she doesn't suspect too much, and you overheard her confess to Cat, would that be okay?"

"I'd have to be sitting pretty close to overhear her," Shepherd said.

"What if I wore a wire?"

Shepherd chuckled. "I know you guys think all police detectives have access to sophisticated surveillance equipment, but stuff like that is only relegated to certain precincts in the city."

Gilley got up and moved over to the kitchen counter, where he'd set his drone. Picking it up, he said, "What if we came equipped with some sophisticated surveillance equipment of our own?"

"I don't follow," Shepherd said.

"Gilley's holding up his drone," I said to him, directing my next comment to Gilley. "But, Gil, we can't very well hover that thing above her head."

"We don't have to hover it," Gilley said. "Your mention about the coffee shop gave me an idea. If we meet Joyce at Sarah's Coffee Hut, we could hide the drone on one of the bookshelves. That table across from the front window is right next to a stack of shelves with all kinds of clutter on it. If you and Joyce sat there in front of it, I could hide the drone right above you and point the camera and the microphone directly down and capture the entire conversation."

"Hey," Shepherd said, "that's actually not a bad idea."

"The detective and I wouldn't even have to be in the coffee

shop for us to observe you," Gilley continued. "We could be in the sub shop next door and hear everything going on. That way, Joyce wouldn't be spooked if she looked around the shop and saw an East Hampton detective sitting nearby."

"That's perfect!" I said. "And, Detective, you wouldn't have to meet Gilley in any official capacity; that way, you're steering clear of the Miranda warning and simply observing a conversation Gilley happens to be capturing on his iPad."

There was a protracted silence on Shepherd's end of the line. Finally, he said, "Let's do it."

And we were off to the races.

The first problem we ran into, of course, was how to contact Joyce and get her to agree to meet with us. We had no way of directly contacting her. We had had control of her Facebook page for several days, and she either didn't check it very often or hadn't reported that it'd been hacked. So the first thing we did was to switch it back to her password, and then, instead of sending her an e-mail through social media (which would've immediately identified us), Gilley made a suggestion that I wasn't exactly thrilled with. "Her address is listed online," he said. "Why don't we just go to her house and leave a note on her doormat asking her to meet you at Sarah's?"

"Why don't we just knock and ask her?" I said.

Gilley shook his head. "She'd want to know why you want to talk to her, and that would lead to a discussion, which would end in accusations and no ability to record the conversation. No, I think a nice cryptic note will do the trick. Especially if she's guilty."

Intrigued, I said, "What should the note say?"

Gil tapped his lip. "It should say . . . I know what you did. Meet me at Sarah's tomorrow at noon or I'll tell everyone."

"I know what you did?" I repeated. "That's it?"

"I said it'd be cryptic."

"Do you think that's enough?"

"If she's guilty? Absolutely."

"Hmm," I said, trying to put myself in Joyce's shoes. "Yeah. I think that if I'd poisoned Heather and I got a note like that on my doormat, I'd show up at the designated coffee shop. Okay. Let's go with that."

Gilley beamed. "We'll deliver the note tonight at midnight."

"Midnight? Why so late?"

"To make sure she's asleep."

"*I'll* be asleep at midnight," I said wearily. It'd been a long day already. "Also, why do we need to wait until she's asleep? Why can't we just leave it on her doorstep and ring her doorbell to make sure she sees the note. I mean, she could miss the note for days if she uses the garage."

"Good point," Gilley said. "Fine. We'll go together after dinner and give her the old ding-dong ditch."

Later that night, Gilley and I arrived back at Chez Kitty giggly with excitement. Gilley had been the brave soul to creep up to Joyce's house—a picturesque cottage on a gorgeous bluff overlooking the ocean—and leave the note. He then rang the doorbell and scurried back toward the car, which I'd parked down the street next to a row of evergreens. He'd scrambled inside just as Joyce opened her front door. Through the cover of the trees, we watched the elderly woman bend low to retrieve the envelope on her front mat. She stood there, leaning on her cane for a long moment, staring at the note inside before lifting her chin to look around suspiciously. Her gaze never settled on us, however, which proved that the cover of the trees and the darkness of the evening were enough to hide us from view.

I waited an extra ten minutes after she finally closed the door to start the engine and back down the road a bit, before making a U-turn and heading home.

"Do you think she'll take the bait?" I asked Gilley, who'd been silent since getting in the car.

"I do," he said. "She's guilty, Cat."

"I hope you're right, Gil. Otherwise, we've got no leads and no one new to accuse."

The next day at a few minutes before ten, I walked into Sarah's and was immediately dismayed. A woman with flaming red hair was seated in the spot right below Gilley's drone. (He'd placed it there during the morning rush, the better to inconspicuously hide it.)

Looking around to see if another table might do, I quickly dismissed the idea. The table across from the window was the best seat in the house for our plan.

I approached the woman—who was engrossed in a book—with what I hoped was a pleasant, conciliatory expression and a somewhat elaborate but I hoped also believable excuse. "Pardon me," I said, smiling when she looked up, "I'm so sorry to trouble you, but I have a nervous condition that makes me extremely anxious in public spaces. I'm meeting my aunt here today for coffee, and this is the only table I've ever felt calm sitting in. Would it be a terrible inconvenience to ask if I might have your table? I wouldn't ask, except that I'm already feeling a bit anxious, and I'm trying very hard to avoid a panic attack."

The woman smiled pleasantly. "Of course," she said gently. "I suffer from anxiety too."

"Oh, thank you!" I beamed.

She smiled as she gathered her things and stood. Pointing to the table in front of the one I needed to sit at, she said, "All right if I sit there? I like to be against the wall. It helps me feel safe too."

Inwardly I groaned. I didn't want her to overhear my conversation with Joyce, but I couldn't really say no. Noting that she had been engrossed in her book, I said, "Of course. And thank you again."

"It's no trouble," she assured me, and I was so relieved when, after settling at the next table, she donned a set of earbuds and got back to her book.

Arranging my coat on the chair, I headed to the bar for a cappuccino, then nervously took up my seat at the table, tapping my foot while I waited to see if Joyce would show up.

I jumped when my phone pinged with an incoming text. *You look nervous*, read Gilley's text.

Duh, I wrote back.

Well, stop. She's on her way in.

Sure enough, the door opened, and in walked Joyce.

She was an elegant woman, with fine features, long, silver hair that waved with the breeze from the door, and she wore a rose-colored cashmere sweater and gray tweed slacks. Coming through the door, I noticed she limped a little with the cane.

Once inside, she eyed the café with the same suspicious eye she'd used the night before.

I almost hated that the gaze would very quickly land on me.

Gathering my courage, I stood and waved to her. She looked at me quizzically for a moment, and then realization dawned, and she appeared almost resigned. She nodded and pointed to the counter. I understood that she was telling me she wanted to get a beverage before coming to sit down, and I nodded, marveling a little at her bravery. If I'd done what she'd done and was about to confront an accuser, I doubted I'd even bother with coffee.

I watched while Joyce ordered a frothy coffee drink and a chocolate-chip cookie. She brought both over to the table and said not a word as she set them down, hooked her cane on the back of her chair, and sat down to look at me expectantly.

"Joyce," I began.

"Catherine," she replied. Snapping off a piece of the cookie, she asked almost casually, "How did you know?"

"That you murdered Heather?" I said, hoping that it might be that easy to get her to confess.

Joyce popped the bit of cookie in her mouth and chewed it while she considered me, neither acknowledging nor admitting to my accusation.

As the silence between us lengthened, I tried to move things along by reaching into my purse and pulling out the doctored photograph of her from the luncheon.

Joyce paused chewing on the cookie to study the photo. "Who took the picture?" she asked.

"One of the guests," I said, relieved that she hadn't rejected the image outright because we'd had to guess that she'd used quinine pills and not tonic water.

"So everyone knows?" she asked.

"No," I said. "A friend of mine enhanced the image to reveal you dumping the pills into the punch."

Joyce puffed out some air. "Technology," she scoffed. "You can't get away with anything these days."

I didn't know if that would constitute a confession or not, so I decided to keep pushing the topic. "Why, Joyce? Why kill Heather?"

She shrugged nonchalantly, as if I'd just asked her why she'd chosen a chocolate-chip cookie over a brownie. "It seemed . . . fair," she said. "Eye for an eye."

My brow furrowed. "But what did Heather do to you?"

"She murdered my daughter," Joyce said, and there was such venom in her eyes, such outrageous anger that it caught me off guard.

"I thought your daughter drowned," I said.

Joyce's gaze dropped to the table, a terrible look of pain washing over her expression. When she glanced up again, her eyes were misty. "She did."

"But wasn't it an accident?" I said. "Didn't she go for a swim and get caught in a riptide?"

"Yes," Joyce said, nodding. "Indeed. All of that is true."

"Then how could Heather have had anything to do with it? It's my understanding that Heather didn't like deep water."

"True," Joyce said. "She didn't. But that didn't make her any less of a shark."

I shook my head. I wasn't following the logic. "Did she tell Cora to go for a swim that day or something?"

Joyce's mouth compressed into a thin, flat line. "Yes," she said. "In so many words, she did."

"I'm afraid I don't understand," I confessed. I was surprised by how much I wanted to understand this woman's motivations. Something about her was incredibly compelling.

Joyce inhaled deeply, staring down at her lap as if carefully considering what to say next. At last, she lifted her chin and said, "My daughter, my precious girl—my *only* child—didn't simply go for a swim that day. She committed suicide."

I heard a sharp intake of breath and realized it was mine.

Joyce continued, as if I hadn't reacted. "We found the note days later. It was in her diary. She'd been writing in great detail about the daily abuse she took from Heather. She never let Cora forget that she'd sent Heather to the hospital. They were children. How could my daughter have known those pills would make Heather so sick?"

I shook my head. I didn't know.

"We had no idea that Heather was bullying Cora. She never mentioned Heather, never talked about her other than shortly after Heather came home from the hospital when Cora had tried repeatedly to reach out and apologize, but Heather and her parents wouldn't hear of it. That's why we sent Cora to private school, to give her some distance from the event.

"And I never gave Heather much thought beyond that. I'd felt terrible about having those pills so close at hand, but it was an accident. Something Cora had done to try to help Heather. My husband and I had apologized repeatedly, and we'd paid all the medical expenses, of course, but it seemed that wasn't enough for Heather. She'd held a grudge from that day forward, and the summer of Cora's junior year, she'd taken out her revenge.

"Heather's house was just down from the beach, so of course she discovered early on that Cora was working there as a lifeguard. Heather quickly made it a daily habit to taunt and bully her. When she discovered that Cora had a crush on one of the other lifeguards, Heather started going out with him, and they'd

make out on the beach in front of Cora, just to rub it in. And
when another boy asked Cora out, Heather dumped the first boy
and invited the other over to her hot tub on the night of his date
with Cora. He stood up my daughter, and Heather delighted in
telling everyone what'd happened."

"That's incredibly cruel," I said. My heart hurt for poor Cora.

"It was psychotic," Joyce said. "And still, the bullying continued. She would taunt and tease Cora every day like it was her
mission to destroy her. And so . . . she did."

Joyce paused for a long moment, her eyes flickering back and
forth as if she were actually reading her daughter's diary. At last,
she continued. "She convinced Cora that she was worthless.
That she was a nothing. That she shouldn't even be alive. She
told her that if she really wanted to do the world a favor, she
should go drown herself in the ocean. The next day, that's exactly what my daughter did."

I put a hand to my mouth. As a mother, I was fiercely protective of my sons, but even they had each other for those times
when the occasional bully came along. Cora had had no one.
She'd borne the brunt of Heather's cruel bullying without a soul
coming to her rescue. And I had no doubt that Joyce hadn't been
aware of her daughter's daily struggles. That's just how some
kids are. They take it all in and internalize it.

"All this was in her diary?" I asked.

"Yes," Joyce said. "Pages and pages of the cruelty she'd en-
dured. And it explained so much about the slow withdrawal of
our daughter over those months. Her sullen mood—keeping to
herself and her desire for long stretches of exercise. I believe she
was chasing endorphins, anything to pull her out of the depres-
sion slowly sucking the life out of her. If Heather hadn't planted
the suggestion of killing herself when my daughter was at her
most vulnerable, her most exhausted, her most depressed, maybe
Cora would still be here, but Heather always had a sense for
when to initiate the perfect strike to take down her enemies."

"Why didn't you take the diary to the police?" I asked.

Joyce scoffed at me. "And say what, exactly? Catherine, you have to remember that back then, there was no anti-bullying legislation. Things like that were simply what kids did to each other, and parents were left to blame themselves, and blame myself I did for years and years. And then, when the spotlight began to shine on the weaponization of social media, and how a number of children were being targeted and bullied through it, I began to rethink my daughter's diary and my role in her death. I realized that it hadn't been me or my husband who were to blame. It'd all been Heather.

"So I waited until my husband died, and I moved back here and retook my maiden name. I looked up Heather and discovered her still here, still evil, still conniving and cruel.

"I went to a local women's group gathering where she was a speaker, and much to my relief, I discovered that she didn't recognize me. It was so easy to become her acquaintance. I simply told her how clever she was. How cunning. She lapped it up like a hungry dog.

"And then I waited for my chance. I've had that bottle of quinine pills in my purse for almost two years, you know. While everyone was distracted over talk of you, I slipped a few into the punch and waited. But Heather didn't have any punch at the party, and I thought my opportunity had been lost. But then I woke up to read the paper and discovered that someone else had done the deed!" Joyce laughed and clapped her hands together. Smiling in near delight, she said, "That was one of the happiest days of my life. It was made only happier when I read that you were no longer a suspect because the evidence at the scene suggested that Heather had been poisoned, not bludgeoned to death."

Joyce closed her eyes, sat back in her chair, and sighed happily. "Revenge," she said. "Sweet, delicious, citrus-infused . . . it was the very best punch I ever sipped, Catherine. Thank you for making it."

My eyes widened. "I had no idea you'd use it to murder her, Joyce."

"Of course, dear. I know. Still, I'm grateful."

I opened my mouth to protest further—I didn't want anyone to think I had anything to do with Heather's murder, but at that moment a shadow appeared next to our table.

I looked up and saw the woman with the flaming red hair standing there, but she was turned toward Joyce, who was also looking curiously up at her. The woman reached over our table and pulled out a small round disc from the sugar container. I had no idea what it was, but she palmed it before reaching up to pull on the cord connecting her earbuds, and they fell away from her ears, clicking against something in her other hand.

It was then that I noticed the gun pointed directly at Joyce. "You stole my paycheck," she said to her and fired two rounds into Joyce.

I sat there frozen as the elderly woman toppled backward onto the floor, a deep red stain spreading out from her limp form as pandemonium erupted in the café. Screams filled the air, along with the sound of furniture scraping and tumbling across the bare floor as people scrambled in all directions to flee the place.

As the chaos around me unfolded, however, I remained still as a statue, stunned into a frozen posture, unable to move, to duck, to flee. It was like everything was happening slowly and distantly. I was looking at Joyce, trying to process what'd happened to her while trying to also process that the Angel of Death had come to stand next to our table and take out an old woman, and was now pointing that same gun right at my face.

"Say goodnight, Catherine," she said to me.

The words rose above the panicked screams and cries of those fleeing the scene, and they should have terrified me, but I couldn't seem to make the connection between what was happening and what'd already happened. "You killed her," I whispered, moving my gaze from the gun to the woman's face. And in that moment, that brief second or two, I saw her. I really *saw* her through the façade of her wig, and the glasses, and heavily applied makeup. I took in all of her features and imprinted them into my memory like a brand.

Her eyes widened ever so slightly, as if surprised that I was making direct eye contact, and then a cruel smile appeared on her lips, and I knew that she was about to kill me too.

I blinked, slowly, dully, almost drunkenly, and in the time it took to blink, I felt a puff of air and heard a high-pitched buzzing sound.

The next sound I heard was a gunshot, and then something hit me with tremendous force, and I went flying backward.

Chapter 17

My back connected with the chair and table behind me, which I guess broke my fall and prevented my head from slamming against the concrete floor.

Still, it hurt like a son of a bitch.

Sprawled out on the ground, I tried to move, but something heavy lay on top of me. As I feebly tried to move, I felt a wetness begin to seep through my blouse. I managed to get a hand free and felt around on my chest, which was wet and sticky. Pulling my hand up, I saw it covered in blood and felt my stomach muscles clench.

And then Gilley was there, hovering above me, his tablet clutched in his hands. "Cat!" he cried. "Are you hurt?"

I nodded, tears misting my vision. "I . . . I think I've been shot!" I gasped.

Gilley sank to his knees and put his hand on the heavy object lying on me. "Shepherd!" he said urgently. "Detective!"

It was then that I realized that Shepherd was the thing pinning me to the floor.

"What?" he said weakly.

"Get off Catherine!" Gilley cried. "She's been shot!"

Shepherd grunted and rolled to the side, sliding down off me to the floor. "She's fine," he growled.

Gilley jumped over the detective to my other side and crouched down. "Ohmigod!" he wailed. "She's not fine, you ass! She's covered in blood!"

My breathing was coming in short, raspy pants. I'd been shot. I'd been *shot!* "Call my sister!" I said, taking Gilley's hand. "Tell her I love her!"

"Oh, Cat!" Gilley wailed, tears forming in his eyes and dribbling down his cheeks. "Honey, stay with me! Stay with me!"

I closed my eyes and squeezed Gilley's hand. "Call the boys," I said next. "Tell them I love them more than they'll ever know, and if I don't make it, Gilley, . . . you tell them . . . tell them . . ."

"Oh, for Christ's sake!" Shepherd moaned.

Gilley and I both looked over at the detective. I was so angry that he was ruining my good-bye speech. I was obviously mortally wounded, and he wasn't even helping to staunch the flow of blood!

But then I saw Shepherd use one arm to painfully prop himself up, and as he did so, several drips of blood fell from just under the shoulder area of his other arm. "She's not wounded," Shepherd insisted. "I am."

The sound of sirens in the distance drew closer, but otherwise an eerie silence filled the café. Just to make sure, I began to pat myself down and quickly discovered that I was in fact completely sound . . . well, save for a bruised back, of course. Gilley helped me to sit up, and I crawled over to Shepherd, who'd managed to wiggle himself against the wall. Sitting there awkwardly, he tried to apply pressure to his wound, but the angle made it difficult. "Gilley," I said. "Take off your shirt."

"Why?"

"We need something to apply pressure with to stop the bleeding," I snapped. I had no time for explanations.

"But this is a new—"

"*I'll buy you another one!*" I roared. "Just give it to me!"

Gilley quickly pulled off his dress shirt and handed it to me. "Sorry. Of course. Sorry!"

I wadded up the shirt and pushed it against the terrible hole in

Shepherd's shoulder. Looking at his face, I could see the color draining away. He was losing too much blood. "Stay with me, Detective!" I commanded.

"Sure," he said, patting my arm with his good hand. The move was sluggish.

"Gilley," I said next. "Check on Joyce."

Glancing over his shoulder, Gilley said, "She's gone, Cat."

I swallowed hard as a wave of emotions washed over me. Fear and anger and adrenaline all fueled an instinct in me that I'd never felt before. "What happened to the assassin?"

"She got away," Gil said. "The second she shot Joyce, Shepherd ran out of the sub shop to try and get to you. It took me a minute or two to think about dive-bombing her with the drone. I'm really sorry. I should've thought of it sooner."

I shook my head, fighting tears as I pushed hard against Shepherd's shoulder while the blood continued to seep out of the wound and soak Gilley's shirt. "What's taking them so long?!" I growled.

"They'll wait until all units have responded," Shepherd said. "Set up a perimeter around the café and try to make contact with us before coming inside."

"Why?"

"Cuz they don't want to get shot themselves," he said, his words thick and slurred.

Gilley squatted down next to us. "Should I go out there and tell them to come in?"

"No," Shepherd said. "They might shoot you." Patting his pocket, Shepherd added, "Hey. Help me get my phone out. I'll call them."

Gilley worked with the detective to retrieve his phone and held it for him while Shepherd tapped at the screen with a shaky finger. After a few taps, Gil held the phone up to Shepherd's ear, and the detective said, "Hey, it's me. No shooter inside the café. You guys can come in. And let the paramedics in too. There's an officer down."

With that, Shepherd collapsed into my arms, losing consciousness.

Hours later, Gilley and I were with Sunny in the ER waiting room. We sat on either side of her, each holding tightly to her hand while we silently waited. And prayed. And waited some more.

"It's bad when it takes this long, isn't it?" she asked softly.

"Not necessarily," I was quick to reply. "It simply could mean they want to do a thorough job of repairing the wound."

"He can't die," she said wetly. "I'm naming the baby after him. He can't die before they meet, I mean, he can't. Right?"

Gilley squeezed her hand. "Hey," he said. "Sunny, Steve is going to be okay. He will be. He *will*."

Sunny stared at Gilley as if she needed to hear those words, put exactly that way. She nodded even though more tears slid down her cheeks, and I had a hard time holding my own in check.

After all, the man had dived right in front of me to block a bullet meant to end my life, and in doing that, he'd been willing to sacrifice his own life. I knew exactly how Sunny felt. Shepherd couldn't die. He just couldn't leave me with the guilt of knowing he'd done that.

I shut my eyes and began to pray again when I heard Gil say, "Here comes the surgeon."

We all stood up as Dr. Najib approached. She wore scrubs and a blank expression, but when she came to a stop in front of us, she smiled widely, and I felt such a rush of relief because no surgeon with bad news could ever beam such a beautiful smile. "He did very well," she said. "The bullet pierced his axillary vein, which is the reason he lost so much blood so quickly, but we were able to repair it and transfuse enough blood to keep him stable enough to then reinflate his lung, which had collapsed as a result of the internal ricochet of the bullet. Two ribs were also broken, but we'll just have to allow those to heal on their own."

"Oh my goodness!" I gasped. "The bullet did all that?"

She nodded solemnly. "It was a high-caliber bullet shot at nearly point-blank range. I think he's very, very lucky it didn't do even more damage."

I felt my face drain of color. The poor man had suffered all of that and very nearly lost his life—just to save me. The weight of the debt I owed him settled on my shoulders like a boulder.

"Can I see him?" Sunny asked.

"He's still coming out of the anesthesia," Dr. Najib said. "He'll be in recovery for another hour or so. When he gets moved to the critical-care unit, I'll alert a nurse to take you to him, but it will have to be a brief visit. He really does need to rest and allow his body to heal."

Sunny nodded, and she squeezed our hands. Both the relief and the continuing worry for her twin were evident in her expression.

Dr. Najib left us, and we returned to sit vigil with Sunny. "Are you hungry, Sunny?" I asked after a little while.

She sighed tiredly and rubbed her belly. "I do need to eat," she said. "The baby needs his nutrition."

I stood and eyed the clock, somewhat shocked to realize that it was nearly nine o'clock. "The cafeteria is probably closed by now, but Mitchell's is just down the street. I'll head there and bring you back something, okay?"

She smiled gratefully at me. "That would be lovely, Catherine. Thank you."

I nodded to Gilley. "You stay with Sunny. I'll bring you back something too."

He grinned as well. "Thanks, Cat. You're the best."

I left the pair and headed out to the parking lot, shivering in the cold air of the evening. I'd traded my bloodstained clothes for a pair of hospital scrubs, and the kindly hospital staff had allowed me to use the faculty shower to clean off the blood that'd soaked through. I could've gone home to shower and change, of course, but I hadn't wanted to leave the hospital until I was sure of Shephard's condition.

After making the quick drive to Mitchell's, I parked and scooted inside, hurrying to the bar, where it was warm and I could order a carryout. After settling into a barstool and being handed a menu, I was surveying the dinner entrées when I heard a familiar voice say, "Catherine?"

I stiffened. Peering over my shoulder, I pushed a giant happy smile onto my face and said, "Hello, Maks. What a sur—" I gasped before I could finish the sentence.

It was clear that Maks, who was wearing a coat and scarf, had spotted me as he was leaving, but that wasn't what took me aback. No, it was the woman beside him, strolling for the door with a quickening pace.

The Angel of Death was also leaving the building.

"Catherine?" Maks said, his gaze shifting between me and the woman leaving. And then he quickly came to me, but I slid off the chair and backed up against the bar, terrified.

"Catherine?" he said again, putting a hand out to touch me, but I jerked away.

I stared into his eyes and saw genuine confusion there. Meanwhile, the Angel of Death was waltzing through the double doors of the restaurant like she didn't have a care in the world.

And then I began to wonder if I'd really seen what I'd seen. *Had* she been the assassin I'd made eye contact with only hours before?

I pointed to her retreating form, still only just visible through the doors as they were closing. "That woman . . . ," I said breathlessly.

Maks glanced over his shoulder. "Oh!" he said, his expression blossoming with understanding. "She and I were discussing business. I assure you, there was nothing romantic in our dinner meeting."

I blinked at him and shook my head. "So you *do* know her."

"Greta? Yes, we're old colleagues. I've known her for years."

My breathing was coming in short quick pants, and I was conscious that a cold sweat had broken out across my brow. I slid sideways along the bar away from Maks. I had no idea what was going on, or why he had a colleague who was an assassin, but I didn't really want to stick around and find out.

Confusion returned to his expression. "Catherine?" he said again. "What is it? And why are you wearing scrubs?"

He stepped closer to me, and I held the menu out in front of me like a shield. "Don't!" I said loudly.

He stopped in his tracks as several patrons glanced our way.

"Ma'am?" the bartender asked me. "Are you all right?"

I shook my head, my gaze focused on Maks, waiting for him to do something that would cause me bodily harm. "No," I said. "I'm not. Call the police."

Maks's eyes widened, and there was something in his eyes . . . something like hurt. "Catherine," he said softly, "what is it that's frightening you so much?"

"Call. The. Police!" I yelled.

The bartender moved to the end of the bar and picked up the phone. A manager appeared at my side as the entire restaurant fell silent, everyone staring at me and Maks. "What seems to be the trouble here?" the manager asked.

"There's a woman in the parking lot," I told him, lowering my voice so as not to alarm anyone else. "She's armed and extremely dangerous. She shot a detective this afternoon, and she's a trained assassin. She came with him. We can't let him leave."

Maks's hand went to his heart, as if he were stunned by my accusation. But then his gaze moved to the door, and his eyes narrowed. "She drove here herself," he said softly. "I can describe her car."

I was trembling as I stood next to the manager. The bartender called out to me, "I have the police on the phone," he said. "What should I say?"

"What is she driving?" I asked Maks.

"A white Jag. I don't know the license plate."

Focusing on the bartender, I said, "Tell them that the woman who shot Detective Shepherd is leaving Mitchell's at this very moment driving a white Jag. Tell them she's a trained assassin, responsible for murdering several other people here in East Hampton, including Joyce McQueen."

The bartender's eyes widened, and he relayed the message to the dispatcher. He then said, "Can you describe her?"

"White, mid-thirties, gray eyes, brown hair, about five feet seven inches tall, wearing a tan leather jacket and matching slacks."

The bartender spoke into the phone, and Maks sat down in one of the chairs. Meanwhile a low murmur had started up among the patrons, and the manager continued to stand by my side protectively.

"It makes sense," Maks said to me. "But you must believe me, Catherine, I had no idea she was an assassin."

"Then who did you think she was?" I demanded.

"An accountant," he said simply.

"I don't believe you," I snapped at him as a hot volt of anger surged up inside me. The betrayal was almost more than I could stand. I'd had romantic feelings for this man!

"I'm sure you don't," he said to me. "And if I were you, I wouldn't believe me either. But if I may, to prove to you that I am not your enemy, please ask your sister about me."

My brow furrowed. "What?" I asked, unsure if I'd heard him correctly.

"Ask Abigail."

My eyes narrowed as my suspicions returned. "She doesn't go by Abigail, and if you knew her, you'd know that!"

He smiled almost amusedly. "Fine, then ask her husband, Dutch. Agent Rivers might confide to you about who I am and whether I'm a good guy or not."

I found myself blinking furiously as my mind tried to catch up with the words coming out of Maks's mouth. "How do you know my sister and her husband?" I demanded.

"It's a long story," Maks said. "One you should ask them about."

Distantly, I heard the sound of sirens approaching and felt both relieved and nervous about having the police show up at the restaurant.

But I also had to know, so I pulled out my phone and, keeping my eyes on Maks, I called my sister. "Cat!" Abby said warmly as she answered the call. "You have so been on my mind lately. And I've been meaning to call, but I've been working a case that's had me really busy. How are you? Are you okay?"

"Abby," I said, my tone serious. "You need to tell me about Maks Grinkov."

Total silence spoke loudly on my sister's end of the call. When she spoke again, her tone was careful . . . clipped even. "How do you know Maks Grinkov?"

"How do *you* know Maks Grinkov?" I replied. "Abby, I'm not playing a game here. You need to tell me about him."

Another long silence from my sister ensued before she finally said, "I'll need to call you back."

With that, the little brat hung up on me, and I lifted the phone away from my ear to verbally swear at it.

Just then Maks's phone rang, and he reached into his coat pocket to retrieve it. Looking at the caller ID, he smiled gamely at me before he answered the call with a cheery, "Hello, Abigail. Lovely to hear from you."

My jaw dropped. Leaving the protective side of the manager, whose attention was moving to the door and the approaching police sirens, I went to Maks and glared at him. He ignored me in favor of speaking to my sister. "I can assure you I did no such thing," he was saying. "I was looking for rental space, and she had some available. I took it without realizing she was your sister."

My sister must've asked another question because Maks's

eyes went to me, and he grimaced ever so slightly. "I don't know," he said, staring straight into my eyes. "Possibly. I'm still trying to figure that out, but if she is, I'll use everything at my disposal to protect her."

"Give me the phone," I said angrily.

Maks handed it over without hesitation.

"Abby," I said, my voice low and even, "you need to tell me about Maks."

"I can't do that, Cat," she replied. "I'm sorry, but I can't."

"Why the hell not?"

"Because it's classified."

I barked out a mirthless laugh. "This is not the time to be joking around!"

"I'm not joking. I swear. I can't talk to you about him."

It was my turn to say nothing for a long moment. At last, I said, "Is he trustworthy?"

She let out a breath that sounded relieved. "He's the most trustworthy person you're ever likely to meet, Cat. I don't know what's going on, or what you've gotten yourself involved in, but if Maks says he'll protect you and keep you safe, then he will. Even if it costs him everything."

"That's a little cryptic," I said, but I was now looking at Maks a bit differently.

"I guess I can tell you this," she said. "It once cost him almost everything to protect me and Dutch. And by everything, I mean, *everything*."

"Everything," I repeated. "You mean like his life?" I asked.

"Yes. And more."

"All right," I said, with an eye to the door as the first officer showed up on scene. "I have to go. But I'll want to talk to you later."

"Definitely," my sister said.

As I handed Maks his phone back, he said to me, "I'll be limited in what I can share with the police about Greta."

I studied his face, looking for any hint of deception, but what I found there instead was an earnestness that couldn't be denied. "Will you talk to me about her?"

"Yes."

"Fine," I said. "When?"

"Soon," he promised.

"Okay," I relented, turning to greet the officer approaching me.

The next day, I woke early after a restless night and headed over to Chez Kitty to find Gilley sipping coffee and looking rather glum. "Morning," I said, moving to get a cup of the good stuff.

"I can't believe she got away. Again!" he moaned.

"I know," I said, pouring the coffee into one of the largest mugs I could find. Bringing it to the table, I sat down and added, "Maks believes she's left the Hamptons, and likely she's left New York. He said that now that she knows that I've told him who she is, she won't want to be anywhere near him."

"But who is *Maks?*" Gilley asked.

I shook my head. "I'm not sure yet. My sister knows him, and she says that I can trust him, but who he is in all this, I have no idea."

"It's a mystery wrapped in a mystery," Gilley said.

"Yes," I agreed. "But with any luck, we're out of it. I mean, if Greta has left the area, then we shouldn't need to worry."

Gilley scowled. "Why do I have the feeling this isn't the end of it, though?"

I frowned too. Gilley had just given voice to the nagging feeling in the pit of my own stomach. "Maks is heading out of town again," I said.

"But I thought he just got back?"

"He did, but with this whole Angel of Death thing going down, he says he needs to tie up some loose ends up north."

"Where up north?"

I shrugged. "Maybe Canada?"

"So much secrecy," Gilley mused.

"On the plus side, I think I've found Erma a job."

"You have?" Gilley said. "Where?"

"A colleague of Marcus's," I said.

"Oh, God. Do you really want to risk your good relationship with that wonderfully beautiful attorney?"

"Erma had a job interview yesterday," I said. "She sent me a text while we were at the hospital, and she said it went really well. She said she and the attorney understood each other, and she thinks it'll be a great fit."

"They understood each other?" Gilley asked.

I shrugged. "Marcus told me that his colleague is a bit . . . off."

"Ahh," Gil said. "Well, that's some wonderful news then."

"It is," I said, wrapping both hands around the mug of hot brew. It was an especially chilly morning, and I was struggling to feel warm.

"What's going to happen to Carmen after all this?" Gilley asked next.

I shook my head. "I'm not sure exactly. She's going to come in and speak to Shepherd's lieutenant later this morning, and her witness statement should help fill in a few of the gaps in Heather's murder file, which, now that you've recorded Joyce's confession, can probably be closed. And Erma mentioned something to me about Carmen looking for work in Florida, which reminds me, I think I have a few contacts in the Fort Lauderdale area. Maybe someone will need some personal assistant help and I can find Carmen a job."

"That would be nice of you," Gilley said.

"I just want everyone to come out of this with a little peace," I said. "I think I still feel really bad that Joyce never found peace after her daughter died. She found revenge, but that's hardly a satisfactory ending for a long life lived."

"So true," Gil mused.

We sat in companionable silence for a bit before I said, "Any word on Shepherd?"

"Not yet. It's too early to text Sunny, but I'm anxious to know if he's improved."

"I still can't believe he dove in front of that bullet for me."

"Thank God he did, though, Cat," Gil said, reaching out to squeeze my hand.

"Yes," I said. "Indeed. And I owe him for that. We should go to the hospital later and check in on him."

"We can do that."

And we did do that. For the next three weeks, in fact, Gilley and I made the daily pilgrimage to the hospital to check in on Shepherd, who slowly but surely got better and regained his strength.

Finally, just a few days before Thanksgiving, as I was putting fresh sheets on my sons' beds, preparing to have them home for the holiday, my phone rang, and caller ID indicated it was the East Hampton P.D. "Hello?" I said, tentatively.

"Catherine," Shepherd said.

"Oh! Detective, did you get sprung from the hospital?"

"I did," he said. "And I'm just leaving the station."

"You're back at work already? Is that wise?"

"No, but I'm a stubborn son of a gun, so what're you gonna do?"

I shook my head and laughed. "I suppose just get out of your way until you come to your senses."

"I'm taking it easy," he said. "Just putting in a few hours at a time."

"I think you should be resting, but I'll table that opinion as it's not likely to dissuade you."

"Speaking of tables," Shepherd said. "You hungry?"

I glanced at my watch. It was quarter to six. "I could eat."

"Great. I'll pick you up in twenty."

Shepherd arrived looking very dapper, in gray slacks and a black sweater. He'd lost at least ten pounds, which gave him a leaner, fitter look, and one that made him even more appealing.

"You look good," I said, as I answered the door.

He smiled and offered me his arm. "Thank you. As do you."

I wondered at his chivalry and good mood. "What's up with you?" I asked, when we got in the car.

"What do you mean what's up with me?"

"Well, forgive me, Detective, but for as long as I've known you, you've never been this . . . how shall I put this . . . um . . . playful?"

Shepherd laughed. "I have my moments. And, Catherine, can you and I make a deal?"

"What kind of deal?"

"Can you call me Steve? Or even Shepherd. The whole 'Detective' thing is a little too formal for me."

I smiled. "I can do that, Steve. And if you'd prefer to call me Cat, I wouldn't mind that either."

Shepherd turned onto the road and said, "Actually, I like Catherine. It's regal, and it suits you."

I felt myself blush and found again those same complicated feelings I'd had for Shepherd when he'd taken me out to dinner before. "Okay," I said simply.

We chatted for a bit in the car about the Angel of Death case. Maks was still in Canada, and he'd flat-out refused to discuss Greta with me on the phone. I was beginning to wonder if he was ever coming back, but he kept assuring me that he would definitely fill me in very soon.

And I hadn't shared with Shepherd that Maks knew Greta. Maks had informed Shepherd's lieutenant—who'd responded to the restaurant personally—that he'd been seated alone and that Greta had approached him, told him she was dining alone too, and would he mind if they shared a table and some company? Simply to be polite, he'd accepted her invitation, and they'd had a pleasant dinner together, talking about nothing more serious than the weather.

The story sounded plausible, especially when Maks told it,

but it bothered me that he knew much more about her than he was willing to share with the police.

At some point, I wanted to try to convince him to talk to Shepherd about it, but for now, I was keeping his secret.

In short order, we arrived at our destination, and my mood went from curious and happy to upset and angry in the scope of about two seconds. "No. Uh, uh. *No!*" I snapped.

"Hey," Shepherd said, pointing to Pierre's. "Trust me, okay?"

"I cannot *believe* you brought me here!"

"Catherine," he said gently, holding out his hand to me. "Please. Trust me."

I rolled my eyes, and after a moment I took his hand. He squeezed it, then hopped out of the car and came around to my side, opening the door for me as I got out.

I followed him inside, bracing myself for all the judgmental stares that I was sure would follow my entrance into the eatery, but after I entered and we approached the maître d', I saw all the waitstaff gather in front of us to greet us warmly with smiles and gentle pats to the arm.

After we were shown to a table, I glanced around the room and realized everyone was looking at the two of us and smiling kindly. Pierre himself then arrived at our table and said, "Ms. Cooper, Detective Shepherd, you honor us tonight with your presence."

"We do?" I said, a bit confused.

"Yes," Pierre said. "You're heroes, aren't you?"

"We are?" I said, turning to Shepherd. This was news to me.

"You saved each other's lives," Pierre said. "I read the article today in the paper. What an incredible act of bravery from each of you."

Shepherd grinned at Pierre and wrapped an arm around my shoulders. "I wouldn't be here if she hadn't immediately stopped the flow of blood," he said. "And she managed to coax a confession out of a murderer all in the same afternoon."

"Extraordinary," Pierre said, bouncing on the balls of his feet.

"Tonight your meal is on the house," he said. "And I'll have my chef prepare something special just for the two of you."

With that, Pierre bounced off, and I turned to Shepherd. "You know," I said slyly, "if I didn't know better, I'd say that this is your way of apologizing to me for having arrested me so publicly."

Shepherd focused on the wine menu. "Maybe you know better then," he said. And then he lifted his gaze to look me in the eye and say, "And maybe this is also my way of having another meal out with you, Catherine. Something I could get used to."

Oh boy, I thought. *Oooooh, boy* . . .